ERA OF THE ECLIPSE

This is a work of fiction. All of the characters, organizations, and events portrayed in this novel are either products of the author's imagination or are used fictitiously.

ERA OF THE ECLIPSE – A STARFINDER NOVEL

Cover illustration by Mirco Paganessi.

Published by Paizo Inc.
15902 Woodinville-Redmond Rd NE, Suite B
Woodinville, WA 98072-4572
www.paizo.com

ISBN 978-1-64078-696-7 (print edition)
ISBN 978-1-64078-697-4 (e-book edition)
ISBN 978-1-64078-698-1 (audiobook edition)

The Library of Congress Cataloging-in-Publication Data is available upon request.

For information about special discounts available for bulk purchases, sales promotions, fund-raising, and educational needs, contact Paizo Sales at sales@paizo.com.

First Edition: August 2025

STARFINDER®

ERA OF THE ECLIPSE

Tim Pratt

paizo®

For James Sutter,

who set me on the path

1

WELCOME TO THE LORESPIRE COMPLEX

(Chk Chk and Dae)

Dae went cartwheeling down the curving hall deep within the Lorespire Complex, and Chk Chk plodded along after. The shirren mystic made a chittering, clacking sound of disgust, then spoke to his agile companion telepathically, "*Why are you doing flips?*"

"I'm not! *This* is a flip." The glimmering, glamorous pahtra converted their latest cartwheel into a handspring, bounced several feet off the ground, did a twist, and landed in a crouch right in front of Chk Chk, with both feet and one hand planted on the floor, the other hand flung outward in a dramatic gesture, and their tail curling off the other way—for compositional balance, Chk Chk supposed. But all he sent was "*Your tail is showing.*"

Dae stood up and grinned, showing off pointed teeth, and waggled their whiskers. "I know. I had this outfit made special so I could show it off." Dae was wearing a formfitting jumpsuit that sparkled all over with a thousand spectrum-shifting lights, giving them total freedom of movement *and* irresistibly drawing the eye, even if one didn't find mammalian anatomy especially attractive.

The light from the ever-present mote of hovering solarian energy beside Dae made the glitter on their cheeks shimmer. As a rule, the catlike pahtra were agile and acrobatic... but they weren't all as endlessly exuberant as Dae. Some people thought that bubbling, effervescent attitude was just Dae's stage persona, a character they created as a professional dancer and rising pop superstar. But Chk Chk had known Dae a long time, and that bouncy optimism was just *them*. Dae's people weren't known for their cheerfulness; the pahtra of Pulonis had waged a grim guerilla war of independence against the Veskarium for a long time, after all. But they'd triumphed, and their planet was finally independent and the newest member of the Pact Worlds, so maybe they'd *all* be smiling a bit more going forward.

Chk Chk kept plodding, and Dae fell into step beside him, though they gave the impression that they might leap off in some new direction at any moment. "*This is a momentous... moment,*" the shirren said. "*We should be attentive and absorb the experience fully.*"

He sometimes wondered what they looked like walking together (and they were constantly walking together, down the endless corridors of Absalom Station, backstage at countless clubs and theaters and vidcast studios throughout the Pact Worlds, across the floors of bars and cruise ships—Dae didn't do "sitting still"): the charming pahtra solarian in garments of lights and the reserved shirren mystic in dark robes that shimmered with prismatic flashes, like rainbows in a storm. "The cat and the bug," he'd overheard a producer call them once and had made a quiet note to ensure Dae never did another show for *him*. The pair probably seemed mismatched, but they weren't; instead, they completed one another.

"*Stop bouncing for a minute,*" he sent in frustration. "*You are my best friend, but you are also a* lot."

"Come on, Chk Chk, this is it, we're here, we did it, we're *Starfinders* now!" They spun, their solarian mote orbiting them like a jaunty moon.

"*Junior probationary Starfinders, really,*" Chk Chk said but then relented. "*That's my point. We're here in the heart of the Lorespire, where only members of the Society are permitted. Look around you! Take in the history!*"

The curving hallway was lined with niches holding artifacts collected from across the galaxy, everything from broken helmets and statues of shiny black stone to infamous weapons and strange relics. The ceiling was hung with tattered, ancient banners from scores of worlds. Framed maps lined the walls too, with old and wildly inaccurate depictions of the galaxy, different solar systems, and assorted worlds.

Chk Chk paused to look at one map, which depicted the Pact Worlds (minus Pulonis, the only member outside the Golarion system). There was Aballon, the jungle world of Castrovel, Akiton, Verces, and the encircling asteroid belt of the Diaspora. That smudge off to one side might have been Aucturn. This was an *old* map, without Absalom Station marked out in its place third from the sun. Instead, there was a burnt spot, a hole in the map with ragged edges where the vanished planet Golarion had been.

Dae spared the map barely a glance before grabbing Chk Chk's robe and tugging him forward. "Come on, we're going to get our *first assignment*, why are you looking at old drawings?"

"*I think this map dates from before the Gap,*" Chk Chk said. "*Without the Gap, we wouldn't even have the Starfinder Society, you know. Before the Society became explorers and cartographers and trailblazers, they were just trying to understand the cause of the Gap and how long it lasted and to find out the fate of the lost world of Golarion.*"

"Uh-huh. And how did that work out for them?" Dae said. "Five hundred years later and Golarion is just as mysteriously disappeared as ever, and nobody is even supposed to study the Gap anymore because of all the *horrible disasters* that happened, whatever those were."

"*Three hundred years.*" Chk Chk corrected them pointlessly. "*But it's true: First Seeker Lanrah, who led the Society from 160 to 162 AG, attempted to solve the mystery of the Gap, with terrible—*"

Dae just went on. "Who cares about the Gap anymore, anyway? So what if everybody lost their memories way back in pre-Drift times? Pretty much all the people who got magical amnesia are dead now, and the ones who aren't have five hundred years of new memories to keep them occupied."

"*Three hundred. Or thereabouts. The exact edges are a bit... fuzzy.*"

"I'm all about living in the here and now, Chickie, and Golarion is gone, but there are a billion trillion smillion *other* worlds out there waiting to be discovered, and *we're* going to be the ones to discover them! Doesn't *that* make your mandibles quiver?" This was accompanied by more spinning.

Chk Chk gave in and chittered in mild excitement. He *did* love to travel and explore, possibly as a consequence of his early life as an adventurer... of sorts. Chk Chk had gestated in a larval container that his father Keskodai had carried on his belt during his journeys across scores of worlds, and those formative years as an observer of action had left a mark on the shirren's psyche. Chk Chk had witnessed many things and learned much of the nature of suffering and joy, but all at a remove; he needed more experiences of his own. How else could he hope to process and understand his emotions, good and bad, into art?

Proximity to Dae's burgeoning fame as a dancer had afforded many opportunities to travel, and being Starfinder agents would afford even more. Members of the Starfinder Society were generally autonomous, free to pursue their own interests, but as new agents, they'd been asked to help a more senior member, and of course, they'd leaped at the opportunity. And there they were, in the heart of the Lorespire, and—

"Dae and Chk Chk?" A harassed-looking human with her hair in a messy bun, wearing glasses with purple lenses, emerged from one of the unmarked doors along the corridor. "I saw you on the cameras. Come in, come in." She turned away.

Dae cocked their head. "Hi, who are you?"

She huffed and said, "I'm Seraphina, an archivist. I'm who you're supposed to come *see*."

"*We were told we'd be assisting Starfinder Chronis?*" Chk Chk said in a questioning manner.

"Yes, you *are*. Chronis is the one who found this trove, come on." She hurried through the door with a last beckoning gesture.

Dae and Chk Chk exchanged one of their glances—they could be "telepathic" without even bothering to use telepathy sometimes—and shrugged simultaneously before following her. They entered a room crammed and crowded with shelves that held ancient dusty drives, data disks, and weird burnt-out crystals, among the more familiar shapes of spell gems, spell chips, and spell ampoules, as well as less identifiable items. The shelves formed passageways that twisted into a labyrinth, and the duo barely kept Seraphina in sight as they wound their way deeper into the maze. There were lights overhead, but they were dim, scarcely brighter than Dae's mote.

"Everything's gone all black and white," Dae grumbled. They could see in the dark, much better than Chk Chk, but they preferred the full-color-spectrum world to the gloomy monochromes of darkvision.

"Some of the materials react poorly to excess illumination!" Seraphina called over her shoulder. "Come on, we're nearly there."

"*Is this... the Archives?*" Chk Chk sent. He'd heard tales of the Archives, where countless rare wonders collected by the Society over the centuries were stored, and the Archive's Cortex, where a wealth of digital information was housed. He'd expected something... grander. And less jumbled.

"What? Gods, no." Seraphina came to a stop in a little clearing, like a plaza in the center of an ornamental maze. She stood next to a battered metal table that held... a box—not even an impressive box—a dusty box, and smallish, or anyway, not even big enough for Dae to sit in. "The Archives are elsewhere in the Lorespire Complex, under the tender care of Celita, head of the Dataphiles. I *love* the Archives. The Archives are amazing. I guess it's halfway possible *some* of this stuff will end up there eventually, but, no. This is just one of our sorting rooms." She patted the box. "And this is what you'll be sorting."

"*Sorting?*" Chk Chk looked around in dismay. "*We were under the impression we would be field agents, not... file clerks.*"

"You wanted to join Chronis on his next long-range expedition, right?"

"Yesssss?" Dae said, in a tone that sounded more like *Maybe?*

Seraphina shrugged. "This is what he's asked you to do to prove your usefulness. You can say no, but I doubt he'll set aside berths for a couple of junior agents who won't even do him a tiny little favor."

Chk Chk exchanged another glance with Dae. He suspected he'd be the one doing most of the sorting, while they would be bored and make sorting difficult. Well, they both had their talents. "*Very well. What does this process involve?*"

Seraphina finally smiled. "Chronis found this box hidden inside a sealed bulkhead in the Lorespire while he was renovating his quarters. The materials inside are pretty old, maybe even from the time of the Gap—it's physical media, not digital, actually written down. A lot of people kept records that way right after the Gap, because everything digital was garbled, and they didn't trust computers or the infosphere anymore. Your job is to read it all and see if there's anything of interest."

"That's all?" Dae said. "We're supposed to sit here and... read?"

"And take notes as you go, authenticate any details you can by cross-referencing with our existing historical databases, and finally, create a précis of the most relevant information for Chronis. You get to read three hundred pages so Chronis can read three."

"*How is this related to the expedition?*" Chk Chk asked. Chronis was taking a long-range exploration vessel into an unexplored sector of the galaxy, and they were eager to join in. They were hoping to make a reality show about their experiences—well, Dae's, mainly. Chk Chk preferred to be behind the camera.

"It's not related at all," Seraphina said. "It's probably a waste of time, old love letters or business ledgers or something. But Chronis is something of a romantic, and he likes the idea of discovering some historical treasure trove behind a wall in his bedroom. Except *he* doesn't have time to read it all. That's junior agent probationary work." She nudged the box a few inches in Dae's direction. "Have fun! Take a break to eat in a few hours if you want. Don't bring food or drinks in here, though." She waved and hurried away.

Dae flopped themselves dramatically down on a chair. "I cannot *believe* I am being subjected to this."

Chk Chk took the lid off the box, and dust puffed up from inside. There were papers heaped in there, messy and disorganized, but pretty well preserved; they didn't look like they'd crumble if he touched them. "*It's written in Common, at least, so we can both read it.*"

"Oh good." Dae climbed on top of the table and then stood on their head, moving their legs through slow, elaborate toe-pointing poses.

The documents in the box were handwritten, but it was a very neat and orderly hand, each letter formed exactly the same way every time it appeared, the spacing perfectly regular. "*Hmm. This script looks almost mechanical—makes me think of SROs, or anacites, even... but it's more fluid than that. I wonder if an android wrote this.*"

Dae lifted their hands and balanced just on the top of their head but made no further contribution to the discussion.

Chk Chk sorted through the pages, which were a bit jumbled and mostly upside-down. Most of it was written on regular sheets of blank paper, but there were parts scribbled on bits of scrap paper, and the very first page, way down at the bottom, was written on the back of a bar menu. He read that one. Then he read it again. Then he looked up.

"*Dae,*" he said. "*I think... this might be important.*"

Dae spun toward him too fast and fell off the table, but of course, they landed on their feet. "What's it say?"

Chk Chk began to read it out.

2

MIND THE GAP

(Tyrcell)

This is the story of how the world ended, and what my friends and I are going to do about it.

The day everything changed for the worst, I woke up on a sticky floor underneath a table in a bar. As I rolled over and groaned, I thought about how unfair it was that androids like me can get drunk just like all the squishy ordinary biologicals do. If we can live so much longer than they do, can't we also do something about the hangovers? In truth, long life didn't strike me as a great deal right then. I was more in a craving-the-sweet-release-of-death sort of place.

I couldn't remember what kind of enjoyable trouble I'd gotten into the night before, but it must have been epic. Actually, I couldn't remember anything about the night before. *Actually* actually... I couldn't remember anything about any of the nights before that either. I tried to remember when I'd felt worse and didn't come up with anything; I couldn't even remember any time I'd felt better. My memories were all fog and uncharted space.

Now, my brain is more robust than most of the squishies, but even we noble androids can get glitches, so I crawled out from under the table and sat in a chair and stared at my surroundings and waited for my memory to come back. I knew my name: Tyrcell. I knew where I was: a bar. And I knew I was the manager of that bar, on a temporary basis, taking care of things for a friend named Bric who was traveling to Castrovel. But... I couldn't remember anything *about* my friendship with Bric. I couldn't picture his face or remember how we met, good times we'd had, or fights. It was just information, dry and factual, like a sign flashing in my brain "Bric is your friend, and this is his bar," with no other context.

I rose and walked around, taking in the space, groping for something familiar. The bar was just one big room, with metal floors and gently curved walls. The floor was crowded with tables (still dirty, with glasses and spills on them; probably should have cleaned up before passing out). There was a little stage in one corner with a microphone stand on it, and a vidscreen was mounted on the wall above, displaying nothing at the moment. The walls were covered in framed pictures of different sizes, but when I got close to them, the photos were all blurred out. That didn't seem right. There were large doors that I thought led to the corridors outside, and a small door that led to a little office, furnished with a desk and a few chairs. Boring.

I went to the bar instead, dropped onto a stool, and looked at a menu. It listed a lot of cocktails with stupid names: The Diaspora Daiquiri, The Shanavan Spritz, The... I squinted. The... something... Gimlet. The second word was garbled, not even letters, just squiggly shapes. I knew a lot of languages (I don't know how I knew that I knew, but I did), and those weren't letters in any of them. Was it some kind of misprint? Then I noticed there were more jumbled words at the top of the menu, where the name of this humble establishment was written: Bric's [incomprehensible gibberish] Bar.

I went under the bar and pulled out a pile of menus, and they all had the same weird errors. My mind had weird errors too. I banged the heel of my hand against my head as if that would shake something loose, but it didn't do any good. I was starting to get a little freaked out. Had I drunk something so potent it had done permanent damage to my memory?

I went to the main doors, which were closed and locked, and punched in the keypad code to make them slide apart. I remembered the code, but I couldn't remember what I'd done the day before? Or any day? There was a barred metal gate across the open doorway, and beyond, an empty stretch of curving corridor.

I poked at my mind. I knew I was in an artificial habitat called Absalom Station. Absalom Station was as populous as a large city; I knew that too. Absalom Station orbited... wait. Did it orbit anything? Trying to think was like walking through a house with great big gaping holes scattered randomly in the floor.

Someone was shouting down the corridor to the left, or shrieking, really: "You aren't my partner! What have you done with her?"

Two figures came into view—both human women, one with short spiky black hair who was walking backward with her hands in the air, the other taller and blond with great stomping boots, waving a large kitchen knife; the one with the knife was the one shrieking. "If you were really her, I would *feel* something when I looked at you!" she shouted and jabbed the knife at the smaller woman, though it seemed more like a dramatic gesture than an actual intent to wound.

"Excuse me," I called, and they both paused to look at me. "What seems to be the problem?"

The blond woman waved her knife, more in my direction, and I was glad to have the bars of the security gate between us. "I woke up with this *impostor* in my bed, and I thought, 'That's my wife,' but I can't remember marrying her, or anything else about her, so she's got to be some kind of monster, messing with my mind! I don't believe I was ever married at all!"

"I can't remember you either!" the one with spiky hair said. "But you don't see *me* trying to stab you about it!"

"I bet you don't even bleed red; you're some kind of shape-shifter, so let's find out!" The irate woman advanced on her not-wife, and I reached instinctively for the pistol on my right hip, the one with all the nonlethal options, except it wasn't on my hip, and why should I have any weapons at all? Wasn't I some kind of underemployed part-time bar manager? I'd seen a stun baton behind that counter, but that was no good except at close range, and I didn't want to experience close range with a knife-wielding woman who was having some kind of psychotic break. Maybe I could throw a glass at her as a distraction and give the black-haired woman time to turn and run. Or... maybe she *was* an evil shape-shifter? She didn't seem evil, but that's just how someone evil would try to seem, probably. Maybe I could decide it was none of my business and just shut the door again. But... no. That didn't feel right. I sighed. It seemed I was one of nature's meddlers.

Then a new player appeared on the stage of the corridor, sauntering in from the left. He was ratfolk, or—What was the term?—ysoki. He was shorter than the black-haired woman but much stockier, wearing black overalls with silver seams, like he was some kind of technician but wanted to show a little style. He was trailed by a dark blot in the air about as big as my closed fist, so he was a solarian, but not one of the bright and shiny photonic ones you saw most often. This was a solarian of the black-hole persuasion—what were they called again? (I couldn't remember. I also couldn't remember any specific time I'd seen *any* flavor of solarian before, but somehow I knew what they were. It was like my mind had been replaced by one of those primers human children use when they're learning to read, with a picture of a ball and the word *ball* written above it: no context, just labels.)

The blond woman apparently saw the newcomer as further evidence of a plot against her and lunged at her not-wife, screaming, knife raised, but the ysoki gestured casually in her direction, and her lunge stopped. Well, it didn't stop completely, but it slowed drastically, as if she were moving through thick syrup instead of air, and her scream faded into a low-frequency sound like a distant percussion track.

The ysoki walked up to the other woman and said, "Are you all right?"

"I—yes." She clutched at his furry arm and beamed at him in gratitude. "Thank you!"

He nodded, patted her hand, removed it from his arm, stepped past her, and then plucked the knife from her attacker's hand. He looked at it for a moment, then walked a few steps over to me and said, "Could you put this away somewhere it won't get stuck inside anybody?"

I nodded and took the knife, then said, "That's a neat trick. It's a gravity thing, I guess?" He nodded and turned to look at the woman who was still lunging in slow motion. "You should work in a bar," I said. "You'd be a great bouncer."

He stuck his littlest finger inside one of his rounded ears, wiggled it around for a moment, twitched his rodent nose, and then shrugged. "Maybe I am a bouncer. I don't really remember what I do. I woke up with my hands inside a starship engine, so maybe I'm a mechanic, but it could be that's just a hobby, or who knows, maybe I was stealing parts. My memory isn't working too good."

"Wait"—(You have to forgive me. This was all new to me at the time, and I was a little slow, though not as slow as the blond woman)—"You lost your memory? Me too. Or parts of it, anyway. And it sounds like they did too."

The black-haired woman joined us, hugging herself and shivering a little. "Her name is Valentine," she said. "She's my wife. And I'm Starla. I... don't remember much besides our names and the fact of our relationship."

"I remember my name too," the ysoki said. "It's Carn. But the rest..." He shrugged, then walked over to the blond woman. "Your hearing isn't slowed down, Valentine. You're getting this? We're *all* having the same kind of trouble you are. If I let you loose, will you settle down? Blink twice for yes."

She blinked, ponderously, and then again, also ponderously.

"I'll trust you about halfway," Carn decided. He reached for the blot of darkness beside him and began to pull out a long black pole, or maybe the blot *became* a long pole, but when he was finished pulling, he was holding what looked like a charcoal drawing of a blocky hammer, rendered in three dimensions. "This hammer will cover the *other* half." He gestured with the hand that wasn't casually holding a huge hammer, and Valentine finished her lunge, stumbling into nothing.

She turned, scowled, blew some loose strands of hair out of her face, and said, "OK. You're probably not *all* mind-controlling shape-shifters. And if you are, I'm too outnumbered to do anything about it."

"I think we're all just as confused as you are," I offered. "Does anyone have any idea what's going on?"

Carn grunted. "Terrorist attack, innit? Some wizard or something cast a spell to cause mass amnesia, who knows, maybe on the whole station."

"Terrorists?" Starla hugged herself again. "Like who? Who's out to terrorize us?"

The ysoki wiggled a finger in his ear again. "I can't really remember. But it just stands to reason somebody must hate us and our whole way of life. Somebody hates everybody for something."

"I don't know who I am or who you people are, but I could use a drink while I figure it out." Valentine looked at me pointedly and then past me, more pointedly, at the bar behind me.

"Well," I began, not sure where the sentence I was starting was going to end up, but then I didn't have to finish it at all, because howling alarms shattered the air around us, and red emergency lights started to flash on and off up and down the corridor.

3

ENTER THE HELLKNIGHTS

(Tyrcell)

Elsewhere on Absalom Station, other things were happening, and most of them weren't good. I learned about all of this later, some of it pieced together from the stories of others, some of it from direct observation, and the rest of it from my friend (well, usually my friend) Melezheun. She has a special insight into people's minds, which is to say she can read them.

Using magic or psychic powers to detect thoughts always struck me as cheating. Where's the challenge in *that*? Of course, I have an agile android brain that lets me analyze the fleeting microexpressions of assorted species with ease, along with the added bonus that people tend to think androids aren't savvy about emotions (or even in possession of any), so they aren't as guarded around us. To be fair, most androids *aren't* great at parsing the emotions of biologicals—I suspect mostly because we don't care—but I must have made a study of the subject at some point, and maybe even upgraded my perception apparatus somehow. That aptitude definitely makes me better at playing cards, which may well have been the impetus for my upgrades in the first place. Maybe that's cheating too. But cheating bothers me a lot less, as a rule, when I'm the one doing it.

Anyway, in order for the later parts of this story to make sense, I should fill you in on a couple of the key players, so when the grenades and plasma torpedoes start flying, you won't wonder, *Who are these guys, and why are they trying to kill this charming android?*

First, let's meet Astrachios, who sucks.

—

Astrachios sat with his back against a bulkhead, skull ringing like a temple bell. Someone had fetched him a mighty blow, and he was trying to take off his helmet, his fingers stupid and fumbling as he loosened the straps. He finally wrestled it loose and stared into the blank iron faceplate with its straight line for a mouth and empty holes for eyes. He *felt* as blank as that metal visage.

His hands were encased in gauntlets embossed with decorative winding chains, and with his mailed fingers, he caressed a dent in the side of his helm. No wonder his head was thudding. Without the helm, he would have had a crater in his skull. Instead, he merely had a crater in his memory. His name was Astrachios; he was on Absalom Station... everything else was void.

There were red-and-black things on the floor and a terrible stench in his nostrils, but he left his eyes unfocused and the scent unexamined. *Sometimes it's better not to know.* That thought floated through his mind, complete and unattached, but struck him with the force of divine revelation.

He tried to stand, but his ankles were wrapped in dark chains. He bent forward as best he could in his mail shirt, fumbled at the chains, then discarded his gauntlets, exchanging defense for nimbleness. Once the chains were loose and puddled on the floor, he stood up, swaying.

Those red-and-black things on the floor were two bodies in pools of damp blood. They were both apparently human—though it was hard to tell for sure, since they were wearing armor and gauntlets—and they wore iron helms just like the one Astrachios had taken off, though theirs were... a lot more dented.

He could read the battle in the positions of their bodies and their wounds, as though he was seeing it play out before him. They had entered this austere chamber where Astrachios lived. They sought to subdue him and used magical, or perhaps technologically enhanced, chains to bind him. But Astrachios had reached for a weapon... He scanned the area, and there was an electroflail on the floor nearby, a two-foot-long metal haft and a seemingly unconnected metal sphere. The flail could deliver powerful electric shocks along with bludgeoning damage, electricity arcing between multiple opponents to stun them, and this particular weapon had aftermarket inertial generators that increased the strength of its impacts. (Why could he remember the details of his weapon's specifications but nothing about his own history? He had a brain injury, obviously, but what a peculiar way it manifested!) Before the chains could bind his arms, he had grabbed the flail, stunned his enemies, and then...

Bashed their heads in, it looked like. Thoroughly and with vigor. Blood and other things oozed out of the bottoms of their dented helms, sluicing down their necks and chests and all over the floor. There was a baton by the hand of the corpse on the right, a long collapsible metal tube with a ball at the end, doubtless equipped with inertial generators of its own. That must be what put the dent in his helmet.

"Self-defense," he murmured. "It must have been."

But they hadn't been trying to kill him. From the chains, it was clear they'd been trying to capture him. *Why?* Was he a criminal? Revulsion bubbled up within him at the thought. But they were dressed the same way he was, and they were clearly members of the same order, whatever that was. Was he a traitor, then, or some kind of apostate? If anything, that idea revolted him even more than the prospect of being a criminal.

He stood amid the carnage, indecisive. Should he run? Or submit himself to justice? The latter, certainly... if he could remember what the justice was *for*. If he couldn't remember his crimes or his treachery, how was he culpable for them? What purpose would accepting punishment serve, when he didn't know what he'd done to incur the penalty?

His original crimes were a mystery anyway. There would doubtless be additional consequences for the two murders he'd obviously committed. He stepped over the bodies, moving toward his door, a darker metal panel in the wall. Was he in a cell *already*, and these his guards? No, a prisoner wouldn't wear a helmet, gauntlets, and mail or have access to a personal weapon. The room was just a bit cell-*like*, with its narrow bunk and small shelves. He pressed a button to open the door and stuck his head into a long hallway lined with similar doors, most standing open. Was this some kind of barracks? Was he a soldier?

He cocked his head, listening to distant thumps and shouts and wails and bellows. Something was going on, some commotion, some *disorder*. (That revulsion rose in him again. He liked order, that much was clear, but he must have liked freedom more, or he wouldn't have killed his would-be captors.) Were those sounds of chaos related to his situation? There didn't seem to be anyone in the immediate vicinity. Better to get away from the scene of the crime, wasn't it? Or even...

He stepped into the room across the hall from his and found that it mirrored his own quarters, with no personal effects in view and only a rumpled blanket on the bunk to indicate anyone used it at all. He hurriedly returned to his room, put his gauntlets back on, and grabbed the larger corpse (*do the hardest job first,* his brain whispered), dragging it into the empty room. He returned for the other corpse and dragged it in too, heaping one on top of the other. Moving their bodies was easy enough. He was strong, at least. He took the fallen knight's baton, rolled it around in the blood to make it look like an obvious murder weapon, and then tucked it away in the blankets in the other room as if hastily and badly hidden.

Then he returned to his own quarters and used his blanket to sop up the fresh blood on the floor. He couldn't clean up every trace of the crime, not without tools or solvents, but the floor was dark, textured metal, and once he finished, the mess wasn't apparent. Bashing in heads didn't make as much mess as disemboweling someone. *How do I know that?*

He took the bloody blankets into the other room too, smeared a few blots onto his absent neighbor's floor to make it look like the cleanup had happened *there*, and then shoved the mass of cloth under the bunk.

Astrachios stepped back and considered the scene. If no one investigated too deeply, it might serve. If nothing else, his actions would muddle matters. Sometimes, one knew a suspect was guilty but lacked the evidence to prove it, and so it was necessary to manufacture that evidence in order to achieve the necessary results—

He frowned. Was he some sort of security officer or investigator?

Astrachios returned to his chambers, shut the door, sat on his bunk, and then said, "I am an idiot." His mind was clearing, at least, though his memories weren't returning. He sat and put his head in his hands and laughed to himself. *At* himself.

He'd cleaned the crime scene almost on autopilot, doing so instinctively, to hide his guilt, but what was the point? He was clearly part of some organization, and *other* members of that organization had come to take him into custody. It was unlikely the dead men were the only ones who knew about Astrachios and his crimes! When those dead men didn't return with him in chains, *other* soldiers—or knights or whatever they were—would come, and when they found bodies *across the hall*, would they be fooled? Of course not. He'd just wasted time he could have used for escaping. If he wasn't going to turn himself in, he had to get out of there.

Astrachios rose and opened a cabinet on the wall. There was a spare helm inside, and that was good—it would hide his features. He donned the mask, put his electroflail on his belt, and started to leave, but something pricked at his attention. He turned in a circle, scanning the room, and then saw, under his own bunk, a small rectangular case with a handle on top. He knelt, pulled it out, and opened the clasps.

There were components of darkly burnished metal nestled inside, some kind of disassembled machinery of cylinders and curves—

The disparate elements resolved themselves, and he saw how they would fit together. "An injection sniper rifle," he said. Specifically, a Wraith-Sting Hornet, designed to fire darts loaded with injectables, be they lethal, nonlethal, or psychotropic; there was an array of darts stored in the case's lid. This was the weapon of an assassin... or a hunter. He looked at the chains on his wrist and nodded. He was some kind of bounty hunter, then, from an order of the same? He closed the case. Yes, he'd be keeping this. It belonged to him.

There was something else under the bed: a book. He slid it out, frowning. Paper books weren't common, unless they had some sentimental or... religious value. "Am I religious?" he muttered. The thick tome was bound in black, with golden letters etched on the front which read *The Measure*. He flipped the volume open, trying to ascertain what kind of book it was. Not an engineering manual, despite the title.

The text was small, crowded, and dense, but at the front, there was an introduction by someone named Lictor Hamal, explaining that this was the sacred text of the Order of the Chain—the division of Hellknights devoted to hunting down fugitives, anarchists, and lawbreakers and making sure everyone kept their proper place in society. And Hellknights were... a group of sects devoted to spreading and upholding the law. Facts sprang into being in his mind, lining up neatly. The organization of the Hellknights was modeled on the strict hierarchies of the mighty armies of Hell itself, and their orders made alliances with those devils with whom they shared common cause. The Hellknights were a lone force of strength and resolve in the wilderness of the galaxy, out to impose order on the unbearable chaos of the universe. *Yes!* That mission *sang* in his mind, it was what Astrachios was *for*, he was—

A lawbreaker. He must have been, or else why would two of his brothers have come to take him away in chains? And what a monstrous crime it must have been, for him to murder them rather than submit to justice! What had he done, and why?

Sometimes it's better not to know.

He would leave this place and wait for his memory to return, seeking medical care if needed. Once he knew the nature of his crime... he could surrender then if he felt doing so was appropriate. Astrachios secured his weapons and set off purposefully down the hall.

Not all the open doors led to empty rooms. In one, a Hellknight was kneeling, facing away from the door, lashing his bare own back with an old-fashioned whip of many tails while he sobbed. *A reckoning. That is the way of the Measure and the Chain,* Astrachios thought approvingly, and then he frowned at the intrusion of knowledge. Knights of the Chain mortified the flesh to better themselves, he *knew* that... he just hadn't known that he knew it. He shook his head and continued down the hall until he found a crossroads, the wall marked with a holographic signpost. An exit was to the right, and the chapel was to the left.

He hesitated for a moment and then turned left.

The chapel had vaulted ceilings held up by pillars wrapped in chains. Long ranks of backless benches filled the space, and there were a few signifers and armigers—knights and their squires, essentially—there, some muttering to themselves, some staring upward, some just staring into space. None took any notice of him beyond a brief glance. One of them was... crying? That was wrong. That bubble of revulsion welled up again. Hellknights were cold, emotionless forces of order. Even with a head injury, confronted by the reality of a monstrous crime, Astrachios hadn't *cried*.

He went to the front of the chapel and sat on one end of a bench. An older human knight in elaborately decorated black armor sat at the other end, bareheaded, staring at the icon on the altar: a five-times-life-sized gauntleted fist, wrapped in chains. A symbol of the order, Astrachios knew.

He glanced around. No one else was wearing their helm. He was more distinctive with it than he would be without it. Up front, with his back to the room, no one was likely to see his face anyway, so he took off the helm, then bowed his head. Why had he come here? *For comfort,* his mind answered. *For guidance.*

"Astrachios, isn't it?" the knight on the far end of the bench said.

Astrachios moved his hands closer to the flail at his belt. He'd already killed once to avoid capture. The punishment for that would be horrific, he was sure. He wouldn't be able to defeat everyone in this room and escape... but would he try? He thought he might try.

"I know your name," the knight said, his tone mild. "I also know my own name, Mikiel. I know the names of most of the people in this room. I think I must have been in a position of some authority? But I can't remember a blessed detail about any of you *besides* your names and ranks. How has the cleansing affected *you*?"

Astrachios risked a glance. "The... cleansing?"

Mikiel chuckled. He had a dark beard, streaked in the center with white, and hard lines around his mouth. He wasn't normally someone who laughed, that was for sure. "That's just what I'm calling it." He waved his hand. "Our memories have all been scoured clean, by what means I do not yet know."

"You mean... none of *you* can remember either?" Astrachios could not conceal the joy in his voice.

Mikiel cocked his head. "No, of course not. You thought you were the only one?"

"I... only just woke up," Astrachios said. "I thought I was going mad."

"You're a bit of a slugabed, hmm?" the man said with a touch of asperity. "If you are mad, so are we all. Everyone here woke up today, rather earlier than you, to find our memories gone. This affliction struck some of us worse than others—a number of these people barely remember their *own* names, let alone those of their compatriots, but even the least affected can't remember much beyond a few bare facts. Some of us sealed the doors to our complex in case this mass amnesia is a precursor to some kind of attack, but... we don't even know who would be trying to attack us. We're Hellknights, it seems. Are there... Heavenknights?"

"I don't know," Astrachios said honestly. His heart was singing songs of praise to... whatever Hellknights worshipped. *They don't know what I did,* he thought. *No one knows what I did! I'll get away with it!*

"I came here to meditate," Mikiel said. "To clear my mind—but the problem is, my mind is almost *entirely* clear. I suppose soon I'll have to stand up and try to figure out what in the nine layers of Hell is going on and see if we can get our memories back. Wait. Are there nine layers of Hell, or is it ten?"

"I... can't recall, sir." Astrachios kept his voice calm even as he clenched his mailed fists. They must *not* recover their memories. If the others got their memories back, they'd know what he'd done. And worse, *Astrachios* would know what he'd done—what atrocity he'd committed that made murdering his fellow knights seem like a better choice than meek surrender, and he didn't want to know that. *Ever.* "I think I remember you," Astrachios said slowly, frowning as if recovering a dim memory. "I think... I served at your side, as your lieutenant and right hand?"

"Really?" Mikiel brightened. "That's good. I can use all the hands I can get."

—

All right, back to me, your android interlocutor. I admit I had to improvise a bit of the dialogue, but that's the gist. Writing all that down almost made me feel sorry for Astrachios. Did it make *you* feel sorry for him too, o reader of the future?

If so, don't worry. It'll pass.

4

BRING THE HAMMER

(Tyrcell)

Back in Bric's "Blank" Bar, we were blissfully unaware of the cankerous, black-hearted Hellknight threat growing elsewhere on Absalom Station. Well, maybe not "blissfully." Nobody was feeling much bliss—shrieking sirens and red strobes are powerful obstacles to serenity. When the lights and noise started, I opened the gate for the others, and we all retreated into the bar. I button-slammed the outer gate shut and then the door, which cut down on the shrieking but didn't eliminate it.

"Are we going to die?" Starla shouted as we huddled around the bar.

"Eventually," Carn the ysoki said, rather too placidly.

"We're under attack!" Valentine said. "That must be it—they wiped our memories, and now they're assaulting the station, conquering us while we're confused!"

The ysoki shook his head. "Invasion is a different alarm. This is the alarm for a public health emergency. Like a pandemic or solvent leak or chemical spill."

"How do you know that?" I asked.

Carn shrugged. "How do I know anything? But I think the sirens are meant to get our attention, and then there should be an announcement—"

The noise abruptly stopped, and the blank vidscreen on the wall flickered to life. A narrow-faced humanoid in some kind of blue uniform gazed uncertainly out at us, cleared his throat, and said, "Hello? I think I should be... addressing Absalom Station now?" He coughed into his fist, winced, and said, "Sorry about all that noise, I didn't know pressing the button would be so dramatic. I'm just doing what it says in this emergency procedures manual I found on the desk. My desk?" He held up a tablet with words wavering on the screen. "So now I'm supposed to, ah, give you all an update on the, er, public health emergency. So. As you may have noticed... we all, apparently, have some sort of amnesia. If you *don't* have amnesia, please do get in touch with us. The exact effect of the... malady... varies from person to person—possibly species to species, we don't know yet—with some individuals forgetting all personal information, while others recall key facts, like their names and occupations and the identities of their family members and associates. But even those who remember some salient details don't seem to remember anything specific. For instance, I know my name is Gerome, and I know I am an android and a safety and public information officer, but that's all."

We all watched, rapt, as Gerome sighed and slumped. "I wish I had more to tell you. We don't know if this is an attack launched by domestic terrorists or outside forces, or if it's some kind of accident, or if the cause is mystical, technological, or both. We don't know if the effect is limited to Absalom Station, or if our troubles extend to other worlds and habitats—our local infosphere is severely damaged and currently offline, as you may have noticed, and our communications systems are only intermittently functional. I am assured that scientists and wizards and clerics are taking measurements, studying lore, and attempting to contact any sympathetic deities. We are working to resolve the problem to the best of our abilities. In the meantime, we urge everyone to stay calm, remain in your homes, don't engage in looting, and await further details. We will update you as soon as possible."

"Good of him to mention looting," Carn said, dry as asteroid dust. "The idea might not have occurred to some people yet."

Gerome glanced down at his tablet and then back up at the camera. He appeared shaken. "That is the end of my prepared statement. But since I'm here..." He rose, and the perspective of the camera shifted, swinging around the room, which was some kind of circular control center surrounded by windows, or curved screens that mimicked windows.

The android officer pointed the camera at one of the windows, then zoomed in until the sides of the frame vanished. The view was just empty space, with distant stars pinpricked here and there. "Does anyone else think something is wrong with this view?" he demanded. "There's supposed to be something *there*, right? Some kind of... something? This view, it's just... it *horrifies* me. Something is missing, something big, something essential, it's on the tip of my tongue, it's on the edge of my *brain*, it's driving me *crazy!* Go... Go... oh, go away, get away from me!" His voice rose steadily, and by the end he was shouting. Then the perspective skewed again as he hurled the camera at the window, the view spinning as it bounced and landed on the floor, pointed upward at an angle to show two other people in blue uniforms struggling to drag the ranting Gerome through a door. The vidscreen went black.

We all stared at the screen, and then we all stared at each other, and then Carn said, "Seems like we're in good hands, eh?" and that made all of us laugh, the way you laugh when the alternative is weeping or drinking yourself into oblivion or both.

Not that we dismissed those alternatives, especially the latter. Shortly after the vidcast ended, I was sitting at a table with Starla, Valentine, and Carn, and we were all drinking. It turned out I knew how to make drinks, including all the drinks on the menu, *except* the Gimlet with the garbled name, which seemed like an odd gap in my knowledge, though my knowledge was mostly odd gaps, so I didn't think much of it.

After several minutes of brooding silence, Carn said, "I can't stomach on an empty drink," as he shoved himself back from the table. He frowned. "No, wait. You know what I mean. Is there food here?"

"Little salty snacky things," I said. "Nothing substantial."

Carn grunted, opened the door, and went out into the hall. I drifted over and stood in the doorway just in case any looters decided our booze was worth the trouble. Carn sauntered down the hall, not far, and rattled some kind of gate, then sauntered back. "There's a restaurant next door," he said. "Closed, nobody inside. I can see through the little window." He came back into the bar, and I sealed us in. Carn walked over to the wall that divided Bric's "Blank" Bar from the restaurant he'd just perused and started thumping the metal.

"What are you doing?"

"Looking for the right spot." Carn removed a bulkhead panel, stepped into the gap, and said, "See? This is the restaurant's wall, right through here."

"I probably could have guessed that," I said.

"I think I'm gonna put a hole in the wall," the ysoki said from inside the crawl space.

Starla and Valentine walked over to see what the excitement was all about. "You're going to break in there?" Starla said, sounding scandalized. "And steal food? But that's, like... isn't that looting?"

"Not necessarily," Carn said. "Maybe I *own* that restaurant. Or maybe you do. I don't remember, do you?"

"I think the odds are probably pretty low." Valentine had her arms crossed over her chest and was frowning.

"Then we'll pay for what we take, eh?" Carn said. "I've got some credsticks on my belt, and Tyrcell probably has some in the safe behind the bar."

"Are we going to pay for the damage to the wall too?" I asked, more amused than bothered.

"We can just say the hole was there when we got here," Carn said, ducking back out of the space between the walls to shrug at us. "Who's to say otherwise?"

Starla seemed worried, but Valentine said, "Works for me. We gotta eat. This is special circumstances."

"We could go back to our rooms," Starla countered. "We had a little kitchen. Maybe there's food there?"

Valentine shook her head. "I can't stop you from going, and you should do what you think is best, but I feel safer in a group right now."

"It would be nice if we could stick together," I said. "But we can all go to your quarters if you want. That might be a nicer place to wait out the emergency than the bar."

"There isn't room there for all of us," Valentine said. "There was barely room for the *two* of us." She looked at Starla and frowned. "I'd assume one of us lived there alone, but there were clothes in both our sizes. We must have been willing to get really cozy. I wish I could remember"—she shook her head—"no, this is better, there's more space here. But we can go and get some clothes, supplies, bedding, stuff like that, and bring it all here?"

"Works for me." I liked having a little tribe, however ad hoc and impermanent; I had no idea then what our foursome would grow into. Everything was terrible, but it was better to endure terrible things in a group.

"Let's go after we eat." Carn reached into his black mote and drew out the big hammer again, and we all moved back to give him room. He stepped halfway into the crawl space and let loose. A series of reverberating clangs, one squeaky ysoki curse, and a laugh of triumph later, Carn had bashed a panel loose that was big enough to pass through if we ducked. Within moments, we were on the other side. The restaurant was small and fancier than Bric's bar, with more polish on the tables and less grit on the floor. There were big leafy plants in stone pots here and there, and loops of white cloth hung down from the ceiling, creating an outdoor-dining feeling even though we were in a windowless section of a space station.

Carn went around the counter and through a swinging door into the back, and we drifted along after. There we found a compact but well-equipped kitchen, an extremely well-stocked pantry, and a walk-in freezer that puffed out cool vapor when Carn looked inside. "They must've just stocked up for the week," the ysoki said. "We've got enough in here to last us for ages." He grinned at us, whiskers twitching, and said, "Everyone hungry?"

We all chorused our agreement.

He rubbed his nimble hands together. "I'll do the cooking. Maybe I'm a worlds-famous chef, huh?"

The evidence suggested he was not, in fact, a worlds-famous chef, but he managed a sort of eggs-and-vegetable hash that was edible, especially when I fetched more drinks from the bar next door to wash down the clumps. We ate companionably at a large round table near the rear of the restaurant and sat back in contentment for a bit. Then Starla said, "I'll wash up. Looters wouldn't do *that*."

We all murmured our thanks as she gathered our dishes, and Valentine stared at her as she walked away. "She's *cute*, isn't she?" Valentine said. "I mean, she is, right?"

"I don't think I'm attracted to humans," Carn said. "You're all weird and hairless."

"She's not my type either." I wasn't sure I *had* a type, come to think of it. I was fairly sure I didn't have a gender either, as far as that went. "But I can see how she might appeal to someone who found that sort of thing appealing."

"I can imagine that I *would* have been interested in her," Valentine said. "But it's *just* imagining, you know?" She rapped the side of her head with her knuckles. "I hope the science clerics, or whoever, figure this mess out soon. Maybe there are some photos or something back in our room, to show me what we were like together, or videos... Should we all go over, get some pillows and cushions and stuff?"

"Sure, but somebody should stay here," I said. "To keep watch and let us back in. *We* aren't looting, not exactly, not in spirit, but that doesn't mean nobody else will be, and I'd rather not come back to broken glass and a stolen safe."

"I don't really want to leave Starla alone," Valentine said. "Carn, can you keep her company, and me and Tyrcell will go hunt for supplies?"

The ysoki belched and then nodded amiably. Valentine went to the kitchen to make sure her partner was amenable to the plan, and Carn beckoned me close. I leaned in.

"What if this mess doesn't even get cleaned up?" he whispered. "What if this is just how it is from now on, and nobody ever remembers anything again?"

I thought about that. "Then I think things on this station are likely to get very strange and probably very ugly."

Carn nodded, nose twitching. "It's good we have a home base, huh? Businesses have better locks and stronger doors than private residences." He looked around. "This is a whole little commercial corridor along here. I wonder what kinds of places we've got on the other sides of the *other* walls? Might be worth taking a look." He cocked his head. "That is... if you don't mind me sticking around and doing a little constructive demolition?"

I knew, the way I knew my own name (and not much else), that I would be fine on my own, more than capable of handling my business, but I liked having people around me, both because they brought resources I could use and also just because... they were people. "You stopped Valentine from murdering her spouse, and you got me something to eat, Carn. I should be asking if you're OK with *me* sticking around."

"I'm gonna let you in on a secret," Carn said. "I'm just a guy with a hammer who doesn't know what in the eight or ten layers of Hell, is going on. I just need somebody to keep giving me problems to solve because if I don't keep busy, I think my brain is going to eat itself out of worry."

"I think I can come up with an unlimited series of problems for you," I promised him.

Valentine returned. "Starla says it's all good. I thought she might want to go herself, pick out some clothes or whatever, but she says she doesn't even know what we've got, so I should just grab whatever looks good." She shrugged. "Ready to go, Tyrcell?"

"Almost." I'd reached for a nonexistent holster earlier, and that meant I had guns, and I didn't strike myself as the kind of person who would have gone to even a part-time job without my weapons, so I went back to the bar to look for them.

There were no guns hanging anyplace obvious, so then I tried the safe under the bar, which, fortunately, opened in response to my biometrics. Bric must have trusted me. There were a bunch of credsticks inside, some data cores, and... a gun belt with two pistols. I strapped it on, patting the hilts. I knew the one on the left was an arc pistol that packed a nasty shocking punch, and the one on the right was a needler, currently loaded with nonlethal options. I practiced drawing them a few times and was pleased to discover that my *muscle* memory, at least, was intact.

"Don't guess I can get one of those?" Valentine said, and I turned to find her watching me from the other side of the bar.

"I hate to break up the set," I said.

She chuckled. "That's fine. I still have my one true love." She drew the kitchen knife from her belt. "You handle trouble at a distance, and I'll handle close range."

"Do you expect trouble?" I asked.

She shrugged. "I was pretty focused on driving the evil shape-shifter out of my house before and wasn't really paying attention to anything else, but no, there weren't any roving gangs of looters or anything in our hall. But everybody was probably still pretty confused then. I don't know what to expect, now that people have had time to get all worked up." She grinned, and I noticed a gap between her two front teeth, which she must have chosen not to have corrected because she found it aesthetically pleasing. "But none of us know what to expect about anything at this point, right?"

"Right." I came around the bar, called through the wall opening to Carn to tell him we'd be back soon, and then set the bar's door to seal itself after us.

Honestly, we did pretty well. We made it almost a thousand yards before anyone tried to rob and murder us.

5

FAST TALK
(Tyrcell)

Valentine and I stepped around a corner and encountered a dwarf wearing most of a pressure suit, except for the helmet, and holding a plasma rifle in visibly shaking hands. "Your money or your life!" he shouted.

"Why in the world do you want our money?" I asked, drifting a little to the right. Valentine got the idea and drifted a little to the left. Two targets were better than one.

He moved the end of the gun back and forth, pointing at each of us in turn. "Stop moving or I'll put a hole in you!" His voice was more panicked than menacing.

"If you do that, you'll also put a hole in the wall," I pointed out, still moving, though more slowly. "Or should I say, *hull*? Because we're right on the edge of the station here, don't you realize?" We weren't, but he seemed confused, and confusion in an enemy is a wonderful thing. "That's a blue star plasma rifle—quite nice—but if you pull the trigger, you'll fire a beam a hundred feet long, and rather less than a hundred feet past me, there's a whole lot of hard vacuum, and none of us want *that* in here with us."

"I'll shoot her, then." He pointed the rifle at Valentine.

"Look at me!" I said. "I've got guns too. If you shoot her, then I'll shoot you, and then she'll be dead, and you'll be dead, and I'll be sad, and who does that outcome serve?" My voice was a soothing balm.

The dwarf was not particularly soothed. He jabbed the barrel of his gun toward Valentine and said, "Just give me your money!"

I considered going for my pistols, but then Valentine might die, so I held up placating hands instead, palms out. "We don't have any money, but again... What do you want money for? None of the shops are exactly open for business. Most of them are abandoned. I'm guessing you want to steal our money so you can buy things, but why not cut out the middleman and just steal the *things*? That's what we've been doing."

"I don't..." The point of his rifle dipped. "I wanted to leave, to get away from the station, but the... the people in the thing, the hangar? They wouldn't release my ship; they said I had to pay undocking fees first, but I don't have money, or maybe I do, but I don't know where it *is*."

"Those people are trying to rob you," I said, projecting total certainty. "There's no such thing as *undocking fees*. They just got their hands on the hangar controls and decided to extort you. In fact, you should go point your plasma rifle at *them*."

"They have a lot more guns than I do." His rifle dipped farther, drooping to match his outlook.

"Where would you even go if you got back on your ship?" Valentine said gently.

He shrugged. "There's a—What do you call it?—shipping manifest back in my cargo hold. It says I'm supposed to make a delivery to Castrovel. Maybe things are better there. Maybe *they'll* remember who I am."

"Maybe," I said. "I can see why you'd want to find out. I'm sorry we can't help you. We don't even remember where we keep our credsticks."

The dwarf sighed. "Right. Of course. I'm... sorry for all that. I'm just feeling a bit desperate."

"Aren't we all?" I said. "Listen, if I were you, I'd skip the whole armed robbery thing. When other people get involved in a crime, it's too messy, there's too much potential for disaster, and somebody might get hurt. What you want to focus on instead is *burglary*—that's when you go into a place, ideally when nobody's around, and steal whatever you want. That's a lot less trouble all around than robbery, and there's no risk of somebody shooting back, you know?"

He scrubbed a hand through his bristly hair. "That makes sense, yeah."

I put a hand on his shoulder and turned him toward a branching corridor. "There are really rich pickings down that way." I didn't know if that was true, but I was pointing him away from both our destination *and* Bric's "Blank" Bar, so it worked for me.

"Much appreciated," he mumbled and walked on, disappearing around a bend.

When I turned back, Valentine was smiling at me. "Well. Couldn't you just charm the ears off an elf?"

I was faintly embarrassed and faintly pleased. "Oh, I don't know. I just figured it was worth a try. Talk is cheaper than pistol cartridges anyway. I figure most people we encounter are going to be more scared and confused than actually, properly *villainous*."

Valentine took the lead again, and I followed, this time with my nonlethal pistol in my hand but held down against my thigh so I wouldn't startle any strangers we encountered. We went down a side corridor and on into a residential section of the station, with an arched ceiling dotted with screens that mimicked skylights, letting ersatz sunlight shine down. There were two levels of apartments on either side of the space, the upper ones with tiny balconies, the lower ones with tiny patios, all holding small tables and chairs, all unoccupied. The windows on both sides of us were opaque. People were heeding Gerome's call to stay inside their homes, it seemed.

Mostly. There were two people standing in a small plaza in the center of the space, next to an overturned metal bench. They were hulking figures, one a dragonkin, the other an orc or an unusually hefty dromaar (sometimes called a half-orc), both dressed in dark blue coveralls and chunky boots. The dragonkin swung his foot, kicking someone or something I couldn't see, and he snarled, "Fix us, you grass-faced filth!"

"My apartment is over here," Valentine whispered, tugging at my elbow, pointing at one of the ground-floor apartments. "Come on, we can get in and out before they notice us."

I hesitated, then sighed. "They're hurting someone. I should see who and whether or not they have a good reason."

"It's not our *problem*," she said.

"You weren't my problem either, until I made you my problem."

Valentine groaned. "It was nice of you to help us, but you can't help everybody."

"I can help the people who need help who are directly in front of me, though. You can go into the apartment. I'll be OK."

"They're enormous, Tyrcell. They could break you in half!"

"They have big muscles, but I have small arms." I drew my other pistol and gave her a decisive nod. She shook her head and hurried off to her rooms, and I walked just close enough to the duo to get them within range of my nonlethal weapons.

"What's the trouble?" I called.

They turned, scowling. Yes, the bigger one was definitely dragonkin, and the other was an orc woman. Dragonkin were inherently dangerous, with scary breath weapons, and they often formed intense psychic pair bonds with other intelligent creatures. I knew they most often bonded with ryphorians, but it wasn't unheard of for them to team up with another species, so maybe the orc was their partner. I wondered if the amnesia affected their bond—or even broke it—or if the connection somehow survived our mystery amnesia. (I also wondered why my mind was still capable of serving up information about other species and cultures when I couldn't remember ever even seeing a dragonkin before, but mostly, I was grateful.)

"Did you lose your memory?" the orc asked me.

"Yes, it seems like everyone did. Didn't you see the vidcast?"

The orc grunted. "Didn't see nothin'. We saw the one who *made* us lose our minds, though. Hey, stop it, you!" She reached down and lifted a struggling figure off the ground.

Their victim—or the architect of all our troubles; who knew, maybe the duo was right—was a lashunta woman, one of the tall skinny ones, greenish in complexion, with short antennae on her forehead and colorful swirling ridges on her face. Her garments were clinging, shiny, and deep purple, matching the highlights on her facial whorls. She had the eerily perfect symmetry of features common to her species, but her captors didn't seem especially charmed by her aesthetic pleasantness.

"*Help me!*" she cried out to me telepathically, and I replied, "*I am,*" hoping my thoughts would only transmit to her.

"So she's the one who erased all our memories?" I asked. "How did you find her?"

The dragonkin and orc exchanged glances. "She was sittin' on this bench here," the orc said. "Just sittin' and... and gloatin' over all the trouble she caused."

I nodded briskly. "How do you know she's the perpetrator?"

"She's one of those lashuntas!" the orc cried. "They got *mind* powers; everybody knows that."

I nodded, stroking my chin. "You make a good point. Even if she's not the one who did this to us, she might be involved in the conspiracy. I'd better take her in."

She projected her thoughts at me: "*What are you doing?*"

"*Avoiding bloodshed,*" I thought as firmly as I could.

"Take her in where?" the orc asked. The dragonkin cocked his long serpentine head at me thoughtfully, or as close to thoughtfully as he could manage.

"I'm an agent working for station security, part of an emergency task force created to find out who's behind this amnesia attack. We don't know if the lashuntas are the masterminds or not, but it's an avenue we're exploring."

"We were going to kick her until she fixes us," the orc said, and she shook the lashunta by one arm, making her wince and even vocalize her distress.

"Unlikely to succeed," I said. "We think this was a coordinated effort by a large group, and it will take more than one of them to reverse the effects. You two have done a great service to the station by capturing this suspect, but I'll take it from here." I moved a little closer and pitched my voice low. "If you see more lashuntas, it's imperative that you do *not* approach them or engage them at all—observe from a distance only. If they are involved in this attack, and they realize we're onto them, the whole group of conspirators might flee, and we could be stuck like this forever." I holstered my weapon, walked straight up to the orc, clasped her hand, and shook it firmly while making direct eye contact. "With the help of citizens like you, we'll get through this. Be well and be careful. Thank you again."

"I, ah..." The orc looked down at our clasped hands, then let go and released the lashunta. I took the hapless victim by the arm, rather less firmly than the orc had, though I scowled a lot. "Right. You're welcome."

I saluted and stood at stiff attention until the orc and the dragonkin departed, the latter's tail lashing back and forth in agitation. "We'd better get into cover before they decide nothing I said made any sense," I said and hurried toward Valentine's rooms.

The door was ajar, and when we ducked into a small, neat apartment, we found Valentine shoving clothes into a pillowcase. She nodded to the lashunta, warily, but even though I barely knew her, I knew Valentine was always wary. "Who's the new stray?" she asked.

"*I am Melezheun,*" the lashunta sent, with great dignity. She turned to me. "*Thank you for helping me.*"

"I'm Tyrcell." I pointed. "That's Valentine. We've got a safe place not far from here if you want to join us?"

"*I... would appreciate a place to catch my breath and calm myself,*" Melezheun replied. "*It has been a very trying day.*"

"For all of us—" I began to reply, but then the vidscreen on Valentine's wall flickered to life. A leering face appeared, like a skull with gray leather stretched over it. This was clearly a corpse, but a lively one, with glowing, antic eyes. When he spoke, his voice wasn't the dry withering thing I expected from... what, a necrovite? Instead, it was resonant and rich, a voice to stir the blood of an audience, even the bored ushers lurking at the back of the theater who'd seen the show twenty times before. "Greetings, citizens of Absalom Station! I am vidcasting today from my mobile studio, the good ship *Moghoul*, currently floating just off your Fardock!"

"Undead!" Valentine shouted. "Look, we *are* under attack!"

"Do attackers usually say 'Greetings'?" I asked. "Maybe I just don't remember."

The undead man didn't look exactly like a human corpse, but he was certainly humanoid, and when he stepped back, he revealed a gleaming starship bridge. He was wearing a suit of shimmering prismatic cloth that caught light and reflected rainbows, and he held a microphone in one bony hand. "You might ask yourselves, 'Who is this person, and why are we lucky enough to see him on our screens?' I'll tell you: My name is Zo!" He flung himself down into a levitating egg chair, which spun around a few times before Zo! (you could hear the exclamation point, somehow) stopped and faced the camera again. He sat with his legs crossed and a somehow more serious expression, even though his perpetual exposed-tooth grin was unchanging and unchangeable. "Yes, indeed, my name is Zo! I bet most of you over there in Absalom Station know *your* names too. But do you know anything else?" He shook his head solemnly. "Probably not, based on the many *meaningful conversations* I've had with your citizens this morning. It seems we've all got a touch of the old amnesia."

He leaned forward, put his bony elbow on his knee, and propped his chin on a gnarled fist. "Everyone is asking me, they're saying, 'Zo! You're undead! You must have lived for *ages*! How long is the gap in *your* memory?'" The undead turned his radiant rictus grin to the cameras. "It's hard to say, my friends. I can remember things that happened, oh, thousands of years ago, I think, but then there's a *crater* in my memories, just a great big blasted hole, and how big is that crater? How many years did it swallow? I couldn't tell you. But it's big enough, I think, to swallow up the lifespans of just about everyone listening to this—and maybe the histories of their homelands too. This gap in our memories stretches back, back, back!" He spun again. "The other question on everyone's addled and emptied-out mind is: *What caused this?* I've got a few callers on the line who want to share their theories."

The image abruptly shifted into a split screen, with Zo!'s face on one side and that of a tired-looking human woman wearing scrubs on the other. "Welcome, Dr. Bellapheron!" Zo! boomed. "What is your professional opinion?"

"I think this mass amnesia is most likely some sort of unknown contagious degenerative disease, spreading rapidly, almost certainly airborne—"

"*Bzzzt!*" Zo! cried, imitating a buzzer noise. I almost laughed. "I'm not sharing your air, so that doesn't explain why *I* can't remember, or the other people in the vicinity, all safely tucked away in their own respective vessels, does it?"

"Maybe... a coordinated act of sabotage, some kind of bioweapon," she said, frowning.

"I'm *undead*, Doctor! I don't *get* diseases! No, no prize for you, so... *next*!" The doctor's face vanished as she opened her mouth to answer, and a grizzled ysoki with whiskers singed off one side of his face appeared. He was squinting with his right eye; the left eye was covered by an intricate ruby lens. "What do you think, Mr. Fen?" Zo! asked.

"Mind control," the ysoki grunted. "Probably all those lashuntas running around here, being telepathic at us all the time. They wiped out our memories so they can, ah, rob us blind."

"I grow weary of this," Melezheun muttered. I patted her arm, and she looked at me, surprised, and then gave me a hesitant smile.

"Say more," Zo! encouraged.

The ysoki frowned. "Well, if you don't remember what's yours, what belongs to you... I mean to say, let's say you own a golden crown all covered with jewels, but you don't remember you own it, see? Then if somebody steals it, you won't even know it was stolen, and then you won't report it, right? So. The perfect crime."

"A bold hypothesis!" Zo! cried. "But in addition to my resistance to disease, I'm also immune to every known form of mental manipulation, at least at the level a lashunta could manage. But perhaps... it was divine intervention?" The ysoki vanished, replaced by a blond human woman with her hair in elaborate braids. "We have here a cleric of Iomedae, the god of justice and... ah, humans, isn't it?"

"Well," she began, but Zo! interrupted her.

"What does your god have to say about all this?"

The cleric frowned. "We have, many of us have, in the spiritual, ah, community, attempted to reach our, ah, the gods, and, well, they say... they say nothing."

Zo! reared back dramatically. "The gods *themselves* have abandoned us?"

"No!" she said. "No, no, they still grant us their magical boons, and they will respond to other entreaties, but on the subject of this memory loss, they... have no answer. They don't even acknowledge the questions."

"Troubling!" Zo! said, but not as if he actually found it troubling.

"Iomedae did say... or I'm told she said... only that 'Golarion is safe. Fret not.'"

"Golarion," Zo! said. "Hmm, that name rings a bell. It's a planet, isn't it? Somewhere hereabouts?"

"I don't know," the cleric said. "Some of the people I've spoken to think it was a planet, others believe it was a city, and others believe it is a person or a god... Our sacred texts recount the ascension of Iomedae from mortal to godhood, but in every copy of those texts, there are now sections that have been smudged or blacked out or redacted, including the name of the world where she lived, all the places she traveled, and the people she knew... perhaps she came from this Golarion, if it is a place?"

"Perhaps!" Zo! said. The image flickered. "Oh, dear, it appears the station communications team is trying to block my signal, but don't worry, the *Moghoul* is indomitable, and I will be—"

The screen fuzzed to black.

"Golarion," Melezheun said. "Perhaps we can look into that. It is a place to start."

I cocked my head at her. "'To start...' what?"

She turned her dark eyes on me, her antennae twitching. "To start figuring out what caused this... gap, of course. What could be more important?"

The chatter of ballistic small-arms fire somewhere nearby made us all flinch. "Not getting killed, for one," I said, hand on the butt of my lethal pistol. "But sure, we can add figuring out this 'gap' to our list of action items."

6

CALLING ZO!
(Chk Chk and Dae)

Dae was finally driven to read by boredom, picking up the pages after Chk Chk finished with them, and when Dae reached the part about Zo!, they gasped. "Chickie! Did you see this? Zo! was there! It looks like he's the one who *named* the Gap 'the Gap,' even!"

Shirrens supposedly had unreadable facial expressions, but Dae had known Chk Chk since he was a larva and recognized the amusement in the set of his mandibles. "*Indeed. We know that Zo! Media was founded immediately after the Gap. If this account is genuine, it discusses his very first vidcast. Though that program sounds rather less... elaborate than the shows he produces today.*"

"True," Dae agreed. "Nobody he interviewed even got exploded or eaten by a monster."

Zo! was famous *and* infamous *and* legendary. He was an elebrian necrovite (probably) who operated out of the Halls of the Living on the undead world of Eox (supposedly), but his true origins were shrouded in mystery... for obvious reasons, if he was older than the Gap. Zo! was a media mogul, producer, performer, journalist, and actor—his show *The Necromancer* had run for two centuries, and only ended when Zo! decided to move on to other projects, not because viewership ever significantly dipped. He was best known in Dae's time for the game shows he created and hosted, where the stakes for the contestants were often death (or worse), as well as his reality shows, which often involved sending mindless undead camera crews into worlds and habitats full of natural hazards and hostile organisms to record the consequent mayhem.

"He was super nice when I met him on *So You Want to Dance Among the Stars*," Dae said. They'd won first place in that interstellar dance competition a few years earlier, one of their various launchpads to pop stardom.

"*You didn't actually meet him,*" Chk Chk said. "*The judges were there at the studio station in person, but Zo! hosted the show via holographic transmission.*"

Dae rolled their eyes. "You are so *analog*. It still counts as meeting someone if you have a conversation virtually."

"*So you've 'met' the millions of fans who've sent you comments on your vidcasts, then?*"

"The ones I've commented *back* to... I mean, sort of... Listen, Zo! gave me a *personal* comms code, OK? He said call him anytime... if I wanted to discuss this idea for a show he wants to do with me."

Chk Chk's mouthparts wriggled. "*You didn't tell me he offered you your own show!*"

Dae winced. "It's, ah... well, the premise was, I'd perform a choreographed acrobatic dance while avoiding various traps and hazards... and each week the routine would get harder and more dangerous... and then for the series finale the audience members would be allowed to bring weapons so they could shoot at me."

"*That... sounds like something Zo! would host, yes. I can see why you turned it down.*"

"I didn't say *no*," Dae admitted. "I said I'd think about it, because otherwise what if he never offered me another role?"

"*Very diplomatic,*" Chk Chk said. "*You know... Zo! could help us with this assignment. If you actually could reach him.*"

Dae nodded. "That's what I was *getting* to. The archive lady—"

"*Seraphina.*"

"Right, she wanted to know if this document was authentic, right? So we can call Zo! and ask him if this account of his first vidcast is true, or if it's just, like, Gap fan fiction. Though even if it's fiction, I guess the writer could have looked up the details of the show..."

Chk Chk gestured in the negative. "*While you were reading, I was searching the infosphere.*" He tapped his sleek gauntlet, which held an array of useful technology in a stylish guise. "*Zo!'s earliest vidcasts weren't usually recorded, and for the few that were, the data was lost in the chaos during the first years after the Gap.*" Chk Chk paused. "*I found that out from a transcript of the commentary track from* The Essential Zo! *commemorative bicentennial boxed set.*"

"That's great!" Dae said. "Or that's a tragedy for the history of the performing arts and everything, but it's great for us! He'll be able to tell us if this heap of words is real or not. I'll call him right now." They fiddled with one of the bangles on their arm, opening a holographic interface, and entered the complex code Zo! had given them.

The "direct" number didn't actually go directly to Zo!, of course; Dae had to talk their way past two of his assistants, one coldly efficient, the next cautiously warm. When they were finally on hold for Zo! himself, Dae caught Chk Chk's amused look and made a face. "I only had to talk to two assistants! And I didn't have to get past an automated system at all! That's as 'direct' as it gets for someone like Zo!"

"*I did not say anything,*" Chk Chk said.

"Not with your *mind*, but with your squiggly *face* you did."

"*'Squiggly?' I am considered quite attractive by shirren standards.*"

"By their *squiggly* standards—hello, oh my gods, Zo!"

The familiar-to-everyone-who-owned-a-vidscreen face, with the skeleton grin and glowing eyes, appeared in the holographic display hovering over Dae's arm. "Oh happy day, it's Dae! And your serious friend there, that must be Night?"

"I am Chk Chk," the shirren said aloud. "I believe you met my father, Keskodai?"

"Ah, the mystic with the most-ic!" Zo! said. "I know him by reputation, at least, as so many know *me*. You're out of the larval tube and all grown up, I see. Now, Dae, I'm *so* pleased, and I admit surprised, that you've reconsidered my offer—"

Dae cleared their throat. "No, Zo!, sorry, I don't... well, my schedule doesn't really allow for that kind of commitment. You see, Chk Chk and I are agents of the Starfinder Society now, and—"

"Could be a reality program there," Zo! mused. "I only have three minutes to spare, but hit me with your pitch."

"Um, wow, yes, actually, we were thinking of recording our mission, but, no, the reason I called is, we're going through some recently discovered files here in the Lorespire Complex, and we've uncovered what *seems* to be an account of the very first day of the Gap, written by someone who was there on Absalom Station at the time, and...

you're in it? We were wondering if we could send over some text for you to review, and maybe you can tell us if the account is genuine?"

Zo! was somehow able to change expressions despite having a face very like a skull, and he suddenly looked intrigued. "The first *day*? People weren't writing much then. They were mostly running around shooting each other, looting, trying to seize control of territory, and so forth. And then the data banks on the station were purged by the Order of the Eclipse—well, it wasn't *called* that yet, of course—and most of the few accounts there were ended up lost."

Dae held up a sheaf of paper. "This one is written down, like, old style. I think the archivists sprayed the pages with some kind of preservatives to stop it from crumbling into dust. We can send a scan, or—"

Zo! waved an impatient hand. "Read me the relevant bits. Two minutes."

Dae hurried to find the right spot and read the account of Zo!'s vidcast, making a point to perform it well; Dae wanted him to keep in mind they were a great performer in case he ever needed a cohost or contest judge or some other role that *didn't* involve the audience trying to kill them.

When they were done reading, Zo! stroked his bony chin, then nodded. "Yes, that's accurate. I remember it like it was just three hundred years ago. Which it was! Oh, that was quite a day. I woke up on the *Moghoul*—what a fine ship that was, for its time—with no idea where I was or what I was doing there. My earliest available memories did *not* involve space travel, I can assure you of that. They were much more along the lines of burning ziggurats and a field of skulls on spikes stretching to the horizon... But I had vidcast equipment all around me, and I was wearing a very sharp suit, and even then, I yearned to make a genuine connection with as many people at once as possible. So I turned on the cameras, hacked into Absalom Station's public-address system, and just went on from there. The rest is recent history. Hmm." Zo! tapped his cadaverous chin. "I think I know who wrote that account you read from... and I think I might know who they eventually *became* too."

"Who?" Chk Chk asked.

"Are you asking me for *spoilers*?" Zo! said, mock aghast. "Perish the thought. I really do have to go, darlings, but call me back when you get to the part about the Arcanamirium, hmm? I might be able to provide a little context for you then." The projection winked off.

Dae looked at Chk Chk. "There's a part in there about the Arcanamirium?" That was Absalom Station's premiere college of magic, certainly the finest institution devoted to technomancy in the Pact Worlds, where spellcasters went to teach and learn and experiment. It was famed for its trove of mystical alien artifacts as well as the caliber of its faculty. Dae had often admired the university's spires while idling in the parks of the Eye, near Swordlight Cathedral and the Hamisfore Theatorium. Dae had spent a *very* satisfying monthlong residency at the latter recently and had noticed some of the younger mages in the audience occasionally taking a break from their dusty old studies to feed their need for beauty (or maybe just to leer at the hot pahtra dancer; Dae knew their appeal was a broad one).

Chk Chk shuffled through the papers. "*I haven't seen anything here about the Arcanamirium yet, but many pages remain.*"

"Then keep reading!" Dae found this all much more exciting knowing it was actually factually *true*... plus, if Zo! found it interesting, it must empirically be so. "Seraphina is going to be impressed, and then *Chronis* is going to be impressed, and then probably the *First Seeker* will be impressed!"

"*Also, we'll gain valuable insights into the earliest days of reliably recorded history,*" Chk Chk said.

"Oh, sure, that too." Dae stretched out on top of the long table and gazed up at the dark ceiling. "Wouldn't it be amazing if Zo! produced our show about being Starfinder agents? I thought we were going to have to fund it independently!"

"*We haven't even asked Chronis if he'd permit us to record for broadcast on the journey,*" Chk Chk said. "*He hasn't even actually* invited *us on the journey. Though if this manuscript is as significant as it seems, I suspect he will.*"

"Would you like to start recording now, just in case?"

Chk Chk looked around the cramped, dim, overstuffed storage room. "*The dramatic possibilities of the setting are positively overwhelming.*"

"You joke, but this could totally be the 'humble beginnings' part of our story. The rags the riches rise from! Besides, we won't be in this room forever. There's a great big world out there, and we're going to *light. It. Up.*" They leaped off the table, landed nimbly on their feet, and began to dance, drawing their solar ribbon out of their mote, dialing down the heat and dialing up the brightness, and whipping the line of light around them in an intricate series of loops and swirls as they moved.

"*I take it back,*" Chk Chk said. "*You're plenty dramatic all on your own. And as you know, I am recording everything, constantly, to gather material for my video installation series* Dark Souls of the Night."

"Oh right." Dae had heard a lot about that project over the years: Chk Chk had been documenting for as long as they'd known him, with the intention of creating a show in several decades. It was essentially a montage of all his lowest, most humbling, most despair-filled moments, starting with footage of disasters his father had experienced while Chk Chk was still in the larval tube, interspersed with imagery of burning spaceships and forests and stars going nova and collapsing into black holes. It was all a big metaphor about rebirth, renewal, and resilience, but Dae couldn't imagine working on such a time scale. They were a dancer, alive to the energy of the present. Dae lived in the moment, but Chk Chk somehow managed to live in *all* the moments: past, present, and yet to come.

"*Now, please, sit down,*" Chk Chk said. "*This will go faster if we split up the manuscript. You can read the later chapters—*"

"I'll sit," Dae said, and did, letting their ribbon return to the floating mote. "But give me the pages as you finish them. I'm not going to read the story out of order. Don't you have any respect for narrative?"

Chk Chk only sighed and bowed his head and shuffled to the next page.

7

CRIME AND CONTEMPLATION

(Tyrcell)

After we looted—sorry, no, packed up; it was Valentine's rightful property, even if she couldn't remember owning it—as many useful things as we could find in the apartment, we tried to return the way we'd come, but there was the small matter of a gang war in the corridor. How had people already had time to form *gangs*? Though I had a lashunta mystic and a knife-wielding human at my side and a ysoki solarian and diminutive chef back at our (what else could you call it) lair. So, yes, we'd already found each other, but we weren't a *gang*. We were just a... gathering of like-minded individuals.

Melezheun was the one who kept us from walking right into a crossfire. She grabbed my shoulder as we approached a corner, turned me toward her, and stared at me wide-eyed as she sent, "*There is danger near. Let me link our minds.*"

I didn't know what *that* meant, but Valentine and I gasped at the same moment as the sensation of cold water washed over my brain. Then I could sense them: an angry cluster of sapients, milling around just ahead, in a clump... no, *two* clumps, on opposite ends of the corridor we'd almost stepped into. I gave Melezheun a considering look. This was some kind of mental battlefield link, to let all of us share her early-warning system; that could definitely come in handy.

Gunfire interrupted my speculations—the chatter of ballistic small arms, but much louder and closer this time. Then those milling clusters of minds surged toward each other. I chose to expeditiously back down the hallway, with Valentine and Melezheun in tow. Once we'd put some distance between ourselves and the immediate danger, we paused in a little alcove next to a generator room, and they both looked at me like *I* was supposed to know what to do next. "We need a map," I said. "So we can find an alternate route back to the bar."

Melezheun cocked her head at me, then pushed on the generator room door, which was marked with a lightning bolt symbol and the words Authorized Personnel Only in several languages. We went inside and found rows of tall humming pylons doing electricity things. It smelled of ozone and body odor and oil. There was a screen on the wall, smudged with fingerprints and dark gray smears, and when Melezheun touched it, she somehow expressed distaste at the sensation without actually showing any expression at all. Our minds weren't linked anymore—I was just learning to read her. (It's a shame I didn't learn to read her *better*, before it was too late.)

A brutally basic home screen appeared, filled with the sort of data that station repair people would find useful and necessary: duty rosters, schematics, and, yes, maps. She poked at the screen some more, then sent a wave of frustration at us. "Everything requires passwords."

Knowledge bubbled up from the mysterious reservoir of unknown-knowns in the depths of my mind: something about how underpaid and undervalued maintenance workers didn't tend to expend a lot of extra effort for their lousy jobs, and something else about how a lot of different people probably needed to use this workstation. The last thing anybody wanted was to waste time trying to remember a million passcodes for a million different systems and terminals... so there was a certain tendency to default to the default, and never change the manufacturer settings. And, huh, upon reflection, it seemed like I knew a *lot* of those default settings.

"Let me take a stab at it." I winced at my choice of words, and glanced at my knife-wielding friend, Valentine, but she didn't seem to notice. Maybe she didn't think of herself as a stabber.

A few delicate finger taps later, and the system thought I was one of the authorized workers, and I pulled up a station map. Wow, Absalom Station was *big*. I'd known that, intellectually, but looking at the whole thing laid out on the screen really drove it home (like a pneumatic bolt to the skull). The station, viewed from above, was a circle with several irregular spikes protruding around the rim, like a broken star. Some of the spikes were connected by curving sections of habitat, forming the segments of incomplete rings. The center of the star was a vast dome, the Eye, filled with gardens and the best residential addresses in the station and important fancy centers of learning and culture like the Arcanamirium and the cathedral. The rest of the station was arranged around the Eye, miles (and levels) of corridors and hangars and shops and apartments and factories and hydroponic farms and aquaculture tanks and embassies and barracks and server rooms and who knew what else.

I traced a finger over the map. If we arbitrarily called that spike "north," then we were down in the southeastern quadrant. Which meant we weren't too terribly far from Fardock, where that strange fellow Zo! was floating; it was just to the southwest, past some residential and business sectors that might be passable if the good citizens were staying holed up like Gerome told them to. Though the surly dwarf with the plasma rifle had come from that way. If we could make our way over there, deal with whatever gang was running the docks, and get our hands on a ship, maybe we could escape this zone of amnesia and reach a world where people knew what was actually going on. It occurred to me that maybe this amnesia was even caused by a *field* of some kind, like a communications jammer, but for our minds: If we could put some distance between ourselves and the station, maybe our memories would come back?

It was the glimmer of a plan, and I found even the idea of a plan was a great comfort. But that was a long-term thing, since we weren't about to abandon Carn and Starla. That meant the *immediate* plan was to get back to base, so I found the necessary settings to pull up a local map. Bric's bar was on the edge of the Lorespire neighborhood, Drifter's End, and, yes, there was something called the Lorespire marked near there, a tower in a vast hangar surrounded by gardens and smaller outbuildings. It looked like there was a museum over there, and some kind of archive, maybe about the history of Absalom Station or even the whole system?

I actually thought, *That might be worth checking out, to see if we can fill in some of the holes in our understanding*, but of course, by the time we actually made it that way, days later, our friend Astrachios and his friends had already... well. There's no reason to get so far ahead of myself. The Lorespire itself was outside what I was already thinking of as "our space," and we had no reason to go there yet. In fact, if we went to that ladder there, into those maintenance tunnels, then... wow. "Look, we can come up right inside Bric's bar if we go that way. There's a maintenance hatch in the office; I didn't even notice it."

"So let's go that way," Valentine said, with the blunt pragmatism I was starting to get used to from her.

"Well, yes," I said. "And then we should make sure nobody *else* can come up that way and surprise us." I memorized the relevant bits of the map as well as I could, wishing I had an external data core handy so I could just download all the info. People think androids are "walking computers," but we're not—we're biomechanical, powered by nanites so incredibly sophisticated that I can't control them any more than a human can control the flora in their gut biome. Androids and organics are more similar than the latter realize and the former like to admit.

"Let's head out." I gathered my crew (it really did feel right, having a crew, even a tiny one), and we slipped back out of the generator room, and made our way down a series of grimy corridors, clearly mostly used by maintenance people, until we found the access hatch leading to the lower levels.

The problem was, between us and the hatch, there was something horrible on the ground, and we all stopped to stare at it: a gray mass, globular, veined, and bloody.

"Did somebody rip out someone else's *brain*?" Valentine asked. "And then... kick it?"

"A giant's brain," I said. "A *giant* giant's brain."

Melezheun brushed past us and knelt by the mess. Her hand hovered over the mass, not quite touching it. "This is a contemplative."

I sidled around the mess, and, yes, there was the body that gave the big brain the necessary context: It was a tiny thing, like a doll dangling from the bottom of the brain. I didn't exactly remember, of course, but I knew that contemplatives were one of the more uncommon species on the station. They're essentially big floating brains, with nearly vestigial four-armed humanoid bodies dangling underneath, and they're mostly scientists, doctors, researchers, and the like, at least on the station. Their species comes from Akiton, I think, and they're famously harmless and abstracted, mostly interested in living the life of the mind. "Why would someone kill one of them?"

"They probably thought the contemplative had something to do with the amnesia," Valentine said. "The same way those thugs blamed our lashunta friend here. You see a big floating brain, and something is wrong with *your* brain, so if you're a fool, you might see a connection."

"They are not dead," Melezheun said. "They are hurt, perhaps grievously, but still alive. We should take them with us."

I considered the situation. My inclination was to help, but in this case, helping would slow us down a lot, and it was probably a doomed effort anyway. What would we do if we got the injured contemplative back to the bar? Slash some high-proof liquor on their wounds and hope for the best? I didn't think our first aid kit was up to the job. "I don't know if that's the best idea."

"If you were the one here on the floor," Melezheun said, "you would feel differently."

"Yes, and it's not like I'm heartless—I *did* help you. But you were capable of moving on your own power, and you were overall in... much better shape."

"If you do not wish to help, I will manage on my own," Melezheun replied stiffly.

I sighed and looked at Valentine, who just raised an eyebrow at me. She hadn't even wanted to help Melezheun. "I didn't say I wouldn't help. I was just weighing the options. But yeah. If we can, we should, and right now, we can. Are you in, Val?"

She shrugged. "It'll be easier with six hands than four." That was as close to enthusiasm as I figured I could expect.

We managed to array ourselves around the contemplative and lift them up by their limbs, letting their big brain dangle but not quite drag on the floor. That position couldn't be good for their scrawny little neck, but we were doing the best we could. Fortunately, the access hatch was nearby and amenable to opening after I dredged up the right default codes from my memory. Even more fortunately, the hatch opened onto an elevator instead of a ladder. I didn't think we could have manhandled (or androidhandled, humanhandled, and lashuntahandled) that big brain down a set of rungs, however devoted Melezheun was to rescuing strays.

The elevator hummed as it took us down, then opened onto a long curving tunnel full of exposed struts, with infrequent light bulbs protected by metal cages on the walls. The neighborhoods upstairs weren't especially fancy, but this tunnel was brutally utilitarian and reeked of burnt rubber and old solder. We walked a few hundred yards, awkwardly carrying our comatose load, and then I whooped when I spotted a little hovercart. It was just a two-seater, with a small cargo bed in the back for transporting light equipment, but it was loads better than walking. The cart didn't want a passcode at all but just hummed to life at my touch. We carefully arranged the contemplative in the back, and Melezheun sat with them, while Valentine and I took the front seats.

The journey was a lot faster and more pleasant after that, and we didn't encounter roving gangs of subterranean cannibals or skin-eating mutants or anything. We *did* pass a lot of access hatches leading to other places in the Lorespire neighborhood, though, and I took note of those for future reference. If we could change the access codes to keep outsiders from getting in, these tunnels could be our own personal shortcuts throughout the area.

After a couple of wrong turns, we finally found the hatch that led up into Bric's bar, but unfortunately, that one *did* have a ladder.

"I'll go up first and see if we can get some help. Maybe there's an antigravity harness laying around somewhere." I ascended, convinced the trapdoor to open for me, and climbed out into a grimy little utility room full of pipes and conduit. It was at the back of Bric's office, in what I'd assumed was a closet. That door was unlocked, so I stepped through into the dusty, uncluttered space. I paused to open the bottom drawer of Bric's desk, removing a bottle of very fine brown liquid I'd somehow known would be there and taking a restorative swig. "Good old Bric," I said, with as much genuine fondness as I could muster for someone I didn't actually remember at all. He clearly kept the best stuff for himself. Then I put the bottle back where it would be safe and pushed on into the main bar, hoping Carn had returned from his wall-smashing adventures.

He had. And he'd brought what looked like the whole neighborhood with him. There must have been a dozen people in there, sitting around the tables beyond the bar, humans and ysoki and even another android, all talking and laughing and drinking. Seeing all those strangers together made me a little unsettled, probably because of the miniature gang war I'd almost blundered into. I walked toward them and cleared my throat. "Who's all this, then?"

"Hey, Tyrcell!" Carn jumped up. "Everybody, look, it's the person I told you about, it was their idea to make this our home base."

They all raised their glasses and cheered for me, and, I admit, I liked *that* part. "Welcome, everyone," I said, because there's no point being ungracious when you're so greatly outnumbered. "Carn, can I talk to you for a minute?"

Carn slapped some shoulders and patted some backs as he made his way over to me, and we returned to the office. "What's up, boss?" he said when I shut the door, and, yeah, I kind of liked that part too.

"Who are all these people, and why are they in my bar?"

"I can introduce you around." Carn was twiddling his finger in his ear again, which it seemed he did when he was nervous or contemplative, or maybe just when it itched. "But they were holed up in the other shops on this side of the hall, you know? I was knocking down walls, building connections, and everywhere I went, I met people, and they were scared, listening to all the gunfire and whatnot out in the corridors. They all agreed we should band together, for strength in numbers and cooperation and all that. I found some real useful stuff too. There's an electronics repair shop, and a junk-store pawn shop with a lot of weapons and other things, and there was one of those emergency care medical clinics with an android doctor hiding inside—"

"A doctor! Good, we need one of those." I'd been distracted by the crowd in the bar and nearly forgotten. If Carn was bringing in *useful* people, I had no grounds for complaints.

Carn looked at me in alarm. "Are you hurt?"

"No, not me. Come on, there's a hole in the bottom of the closet in the office—"

Carn nodded sagely as he followed. "Oh, like a maintenance access hatch. I wondered how you got back in here without me noticing.

I thought maybe you'd remembered you knew how to teleport or something. That would be useful."

"Right, no, I wish. But, like you, I picked up a couple of strays too. There's a lashunta named Melezheun—she's OK—but there's also an injured contemplative, unconscious, and we need to find a way to get their giant brain up this ladder." I looked around the office. "I was hoping to find an antigravity harness, like maybe Bric used one to lug the kegs around, or maybe we could find some rope—"

Carn looked at me with a sly grin, reached out one hand, and wiggled his nose. The desk chair rose about three feet in the air, spun around gently once, and then settled back down in its original position. "Gravity is sort of my thing," Carn said, with the modesty of any accomplished master.

8

COMMUNITY BUILDING

(Tyrcell)

Carn levitated the injured contemplative up through the hatch without banging their oversized brain around too much, though beads of sweat dotted the fur on his forehead by the time he finished. Three of us grabbed a limb each, while Melezheun supported the gray veiny head, and we carried the contemplative through the office and into the bar. The android doctor, Bindi, who had a shock of black hair sticking straight up as if she'd been electrocuted, ran over and took in the state of the victim at a glance. "Let's get them to my clinic."

The newcomers had been busy improving our lair, and the hole leading from Bric's bar into the bistro next door had been widened enough to accommodate our passage with only a little ducking and squeezing. Beyond the bistro was a repair shop, where a gnome wearing a set of complex lenses soldered something at a workbench and completely ignored us as we tromped by. Then we passed through a gym with one of those antigravity swimming pools that's like a giant sphere of water floating in the air, where a human in a tiny bathing suit was doing circular laps. Then we went through the extremely overstuffed pawn shop Carn had mentioned, with assorted musical instruments and guns hanging on the wall all chained up, and *then* we reached the clinic, all gleaming white walls lit by white lights; I felt healthier just standing in it. There was a hole in the wall there too, leading onward, but I didn't know what lay beyond. We were developing quite the little warren, though, with free movement safe from the public spaces of the hallways beyond.

Bindi beckoned us back to one of the exam rooms, and we set the contemplative down on a hovering exam table surrounded by gray equipment studded with blinking lights. Then we all stood around looking at the brain oozing sticky blood onto the table until Bindi said, "Unless any of you have medical training, you can clear out, all right?"

"If I'm a brain surgeon, I don't remember many of the details," Carn said, so we all cleared out. Valentine patted me on the arm, nodded to Melezheun, and then said she was going to find Starla. Carn said, "I'll come with. I wanted to run some logistics stuff by you."

Being a big-picture person, I didn't want to talk about management, so I just waved and stayed behind, congratulating myself on my skill at delegating. Then I looked at Melezheun and said, "Do you want to explore farther? None of this was open when I left this morning." (Well, I say "morning." There's no real "night" or "day" on the station, but for the ease of social interaction, there were broadly agreed-upon schedules.)

Melezheun gave me a gracious nod, and we sauntered to the nearest hole in the wall. The space beyond that was empty, just wires dangling from the walls and scuffed-up carpet: Some concern had gone out of business and been torn out right down to the fixtures. The next hole led to a space absolutely *crammed* with furniture, with chairs stacked to the distant ceiling, couches standing on end, and ranks of mattresses lining the walls.

"This must be some kind of storage space for a home furnishing shop. Lucky for us. We can move some of this stuff around and turn that empty shop into sleeping quarters. Once we've opened up some more space in here, it'll be a good place for people to bed down too."

"You are... creating a shelter?" Melezheun asked. "For people who do not know where their homes are?"

"I hadn't really thought of it that way," I admitted. "I just woke up in this bar, then met Carn and Valentine and Starla; we ran into you, and Carn ran into these *other* people, and... nobody knows what's going on, but things are already getting bad out there. You saw it. You *lived* it. I guess I just... want to make a place where nobody is shooting at anybody else? I'll welcome anyone who pitches in and doesn't make trouble. But I think, given the choice, most people would rather cooperate than attack each other. Those people out there, rampaging around, maybe one percent of them are actual predators—the rest of them are just scared and confused and lashing out."

"Even the ones who seized me?" She sounded more curious than outraged at the idea.

"They were *extremely* confused," I said. "And I was, luckily, able to make them even more confused, but this time in our favor."

"That was rather deftly done," she said. "I almost believed you were going to take me in for suspicion of conspiracy myself. I am grateful for your aid. I'm not sure I ever said so. I may have been a bit... confused myself."

I waved that away. "You kept me from walking right into the middle of two gangs trying to kill each other. I wasn't keeping score anyway, but if I were, I'd say we're even."

We continued through the next hole in the wall, ducking low, and I wondered how far Carn had gone with that hammer of his.

Not much farther, it turned out. After another restaurant (the kind with the little stoves at each table so you can cook your own tidbits, which seemed—to me—to negate the whole point of a restaurant) and some kind of chemical supply company (that was much more useful), we crawled on and reached the end of the line. The last shop wasn't a shop at all, but a section security office filled with tactical screens and locked weapons cabinets and communication equipment. There was nobody holed up in there with guns, which probably meant the personnel had taken off, either to deal with the violence breaking out or to flee from it, and they hadn't returned... yet.

I decided it might be a good idea to change the access codes, since I knew (without knowing how I knew) security personnel weren't very good team players if you were outside their chain of command. I didn't want somebody in my new community who believed the person with the most guns was automatically right, and too many so-called peace officers leaned that way.

The security office controls didn't use the default passwords, to their credit. But their passwords *were* written down on a piece of paper stuck to the underside of a desk drawer, so give them a few demerits and call it net zero. I rekeyed the codes on the external door and disabled all remote access, and—ta-da—we had our very own command-and-control center.

Melezheun had been looking at the screens while I dealt with all that necessary housekeeping, and she called me over. She pointed to one screen. "Is this us?"

"That's right outside, yeah, our stretch of corridor. I guess we own it all, from this end to that bulkhead. We'll want to reinforce all the doors in our complex, to keep people from barging in from outside, and I had this idea about using the maintenance tunnels to get around if we can lock them down well enough to ensure the safety of our people."

"What's this area here?" she asked, pointing to another screen.

"I think that's the Lorespire." The screen showed a beautiful, tapering tower, much more elegant than its icon on the map I'd consulted, surrounded by graceful low buildings and ornamental gardens. "It's not far from here—obviously, if this security office covers that area too. I don't know what the Lorespire is, exactly, but according to the map we found, there's a museum over there, and archives, so maybe it's the headquarters of some historical society, or a school, or just a really pretty file room?"

"We should go there," Melezheun said. "The station infosphere is still down, but if there is an archive, we might be able to find out why all this is happening—or at least learn who we were before we forgot everything."

"I agree it could be useful, but we've got more immediate concerns, don't we?" Despite myself, I *was* thinking of logistics—how long we could feed that many people, where they'd all sleep, and how we could scale things up if and when we needed to.

Melezheun sent a wave of frustration at me again. "I am a historian—I *know* that, just as you know you were managing that bar—but I do not know any *history*! Not my own or anyone else's. For all I know, I *worked* in the Lorespire. You found me not far from there. Do you have any idea how maddening it is to find the very core of my essential self missing?"

"I have some idea," I said. "I think almost everyone on the station does."

Melezheun slumped in the chair behind the console. "I... suppose so. My malady is universal. But it bites at me, so keenly, because at the very center of me, there is a desire to understand, and to know the truth." She caressed the screen showing the Lorespire. "Will you take me there, please?"

I yawned, then winced. "That wasn't a yawn as commentary. I'm just very tired. Yes, we can go to the Lorespire. It's probably a good idea to meet the neighbors anyway. Maybe they'll want to join forces." I thought a tower that big, with all those outbuildings, doubtless had a lot of places to sleep, and maybe a good stock of supplies too. "But it's been a long day. I need to talk over some security stuff with Carn, to make sure our little slice of the station is safe, and then everyone will need to get some rest, so... tomorrow morning, we can put together a small team and go over there."

Melezheun bowed her head, and though she wasn't sending her thoughts, I could tell she was thinking of just going by herself at that moment. But then some people ran across the screen showing the Lorespire grounds, furtive and hunched, and I couldn't quite tell if they were running *from* something or just sneaking around. I leaned forward, accessed the controls, and swapped through other cameras to get a better view of the area.

It soon became apparent that the various doors connecting the complex around the Lorespire to the rest of the station had been barricaded with a tangle of unidentifiable metal objects, and there were figures darting here and there, shoring those up and adding to the defenses. "We aren't the only ones thinking about security."

"Do you think they will let us in?" she asked. "If we make it clear we come in peace?"

"'We come in peace' sounds like something a marauder would say. I sure wouldn't open the door to someone who talked like that. So maybe not. But maybe they didn't lock down their maintenance tunnels, or they think the current passcodes are good enough to keep them secure. If that's the case... we can probably get in, and with luck, they won't attack us on sight. If they're all historians, they probably won't be heavily armed... right?"

"I am not armed at all," Melezheun said, a touch bitterly, and then pointed at one of the gun cabinets. "Can you open that up, so I can remedy the situation?"

—

After that came hours of talking, planning, organizing, glad-handing, reassuring, active listening, and pretend listening, but eventually we got our little cohort—at this point about twenty individuals strong—into some semblance of order.

Valentine helped me reprogram and seal off the maintenance tunnels in the region, and Carn used his capacity for heavy lifting to help some of the others reinforce the exterior doors in our interconnected warren. Many of them we simply welded shut; since we had makeshift connecting interior doors, we didn't all need individual access to the corridors beyond. We left the security office door fully accessible because it was heavily armored anyway, along with the bar door because it was at the other end of our complex and because it was also surprisingly tough—Bric must have been a little paranoid. At that point, our whole side of the hallway was a single defensible complex, with multiple maintenance hatches allowing access to tunnels that could secretly carry us beyond the safety of our borders. We began to make plans to send out scouts to adjacent neighborhoods to see if we could expand our mutual-aid-and-defense network, starting with our morning journey to the Lorespire.

I was about to bed down on a mattress I'd dragged into the bar's office—having decided leadership deserved the perk of a private bedroom—when Dr. Bindi came in. "The contemplative is stable, though not yet conscious. I have treated numerous other minor wounds in the community, but nothing else was nearly that serious."

"We really appreciate the help, doc. You've got a place to bed down?"

"I have a cot in the clinic. Judging by the presence of toiletries and the like, I often spent nights there anyway, in the... times before." She looked troubled.

I said, "You look troubled."

She laughed, a bit harshly, and said, "Why shouldn't I? We've all been afflicted with some horrible amnesia! It's affecting the whole station. If it's medical, I can't figure out how it was caused or how it was spread, which means it's probably magical, and magic *that* powerful, unleashed on us all, is a profoundly troubling thing to contemplate."

Carn sauntered over from the bar and leaned in the open doorway. "Maybe we asked for it." We both turned and stared at him, and he shrugged. "Maybe, y'know, something really horrible happened, we all agreed it was better to forget about it so we could start fresh, and some of the priestly types got the gods to agree." He shrugged again. "Maybe it's better if we *don't* know the truth."

"Not a philosophy I can embrace," Bindi said. "The truth is always better. I would never have agreed to give up everything I knew about myself and my loved ones." She frowned. "At least, I don't think so. I must have *had* loved ones? There are photos in the clinic, but the faces are all blurred."

"Figuring out what happened to us, and why, is right near the top of our to-do list," I reassured her. "I'm not smart enough to work something like that out—I know that—but I seem to be good at putting people together in the service of a common cause, so I'll *find* the people smart enough. OK?"

"I don't have any ideas of my own, so I suppose it will have to be." She slouched off, muttering to herself.

See, that's why I'm a leader. I just have that knack for *inspiring* people.

"Good night, Carn," I said, when he kept leaning in the doorway. "You're the real reason all this is happening, you know. If Valentine had actually managed to stab Starla, I probably would have just shut the door and hidden in my bar for a month or two."

"Nah," the ysoki said. "I haven't known you all that long, Ty, but I already know you well enough to say you would have helped. You've been helping people all day. You went out to get pillows and spare clothes and came back with *two new people*. You doubled your party!"

I laughed. "Maybe I'm just watching out for myself. There's strength in numbers."

Carn waved a hand. "Those people out there running around with guns, those little gangs that are forming, they're gonna turn on each other, is the thing. Once you start solving all your problems with gunfire, gunfire is all you get. You didn't shoot Valentine when she was waving that knife around, even though you could've run for your pistols. And after she calmed down, you invited her into your home. You invited all of us, and even though we're making sure the doors are locked and guarded, you aren't going to shoot anyone who comes looking for sanctuary. You're working out how to *expand*."

I thought Carn was being a little overly lavish with the praise—I was only trying not to make the worst day of everyone's life any *more* difficult. "I'm just doing what anyone would do."

"But you're not, boss." Carn shook his head. "We've all heard how other people are doing it. Bang-bang, zap-zap. You've seen it: the violence, the fear, the lashing out. No... you're trying to do things a different way. You're probably not the only one on the whole *station* trying to do things that kind of way, but you're the only one in the immediate vicinity." He yawned. "I'm just glad I ran into you first and not some of those other people. Anyway, I'm gonna get some sleep and then see about putting together a team in the morning to go make nice with the people in the next hall."

"Good idea. I might want you to come with me and Melezheun, though, to check out the Lorespire."

"That would be a good get. That complex is the heart of this whole district. They've got parks in there too, trees and grass and artificial sunlight. I can take or leave that stuff, but I know a lot of the people in here like it." Carn saluted, badly—he hadn't been a drill sergeant in his past life—and shut the door behind him when he went.

I bedded down and dreamed my android dreams. They weren't prophetic dreams, as they were completely devoid of smoke and blood and screaming.

9

MAKING THE LAW
(Tyrcell)

What I didn't know, because how could I have, was that my future least favorite person, Astrachios, had been just as busy that first day as I was. Picture him, in his stupid armor probably, deep in conversation with Mikiel, whom everyone looked to as the leader of their confused order. And that's the operative word: *order*.

"We can turn this disaster into an opportunity," Astrachios said, sitting on the edge of a metal chair in Mikiel's room, which was bigger than his own but not any more lavish. "We've lost a lot, but we haven't lost our essential purpose. We're meant to bring order and law to the chaos around us. There's plenty of chaos. We should get to work."

"We don't even know what the law *is*, though," Mikiel replied.

That's when Astrachios got that gleam in his eye. "But neither does anyone else. That means we can *make* the law." He leaned forward and started jabbing at the tabletop. "I've been looking over the station maps, at least those portions that aren't corrupted by data loss, and we're close to something called the Lorespire—some sort of archive, with a museum of the history of Absalom Station. If we seize the Lorespire and keep its secrets from everyone else, we would become the ultimate arbiters of truth on this habitat, because there wouldn't be any documentation to dispute us."

"Go on." Mikiel made a rolling gesture with his hand and nodded with a look of interest.

"Then we could not just uphold the laws, but craft the laws in the first place. We just need to find someone with the right kind of legal mind to draw up papers that say, oh... that the entire station becomes a protectorate of the Hellknights in times of crisis and chaos and that we're supposed to institute martial law until things settle down." He paused. "Who knows? Maybe that's the law *anyway*. The point is, it should be. We know it's just and proper for us to take charge. Why shouldn't we create laws to reflect that justice?"

Mikiel sighed. "I don't like the idea of rooting our authority in an act of dishonesty, but these are extraordinary circumstances. I have to trust that the ends will justify the means. If we can gain control of the station and stem the tide of chaos, then it will all be worthwhile. Nothing matters more than restoring order."

"I couldn't agree more," Astrachios said.

—

It took me longer to get out of the bar and into the world than I'd planned because I wasn't used to being the president, or whatever, of a very tiny nation-state. Maybe we could call our settlement the Tyrcellium. Hmm. No. That sounded like an antifungal medication. It also drew too much attention to me; I didn't want to be the first person anyone who got mad at our community thought about assassinating.

As soon as I emerged from my bedroom/office, I was beset from all sides. Did we have any more oatmeal? (I didn't know we'd had any in the first place); Why were the blankets so scratchy?; Why hadn't I gotten everyone's memory fixed yet?; Did I have anything that could treat a hangover?—and on and on and on.

I dealt with all of that as best I could, but when people continued to cluster around me in the bar area (they all woke up earlier than me, apparently), I grabbed hold of Starla's elbow and said, "Everyone! I'm sure you know Starla. She is our new head of supply and logistics! Let Starla know what you need, and she'll organize it. Starla, as one of the original founders of this autonomous zone, I duly authorize you to form foraging parties to go out and scrounge or trade for more supplies."

Starla looked at me, startled, and then sighed, accepting her lot. That's what happens when you get in on the ground floor of a grand new endeavor: You're expected to help hold up the roof.

"That's fine, but what are you going to do about *him*?" some human said, pointing at a glaring dwarf. "He's half my size, but he gets the same amount of food! How's that fair?"

I looked around and caught sight of Valentine sitting at the bar in front of a cup of something steaming. I gave her a nod. She raised one eyebrow, then picked up her knife, climbed on top of the bar to stand so she towered over everyone even more than usual, and said, "Hey! I'm Valentine! I'm also one of the founders of this community, and I'm the one in charge of conflict resolution and dispute mediation." She twirled the knife, which was impressive, given how large it was. "If you've got problems with each other you can't resolve by being decent and talking things over, you just come to me, and I'll solve them for you *real* quick." She grinned, and that was sufficient to break up the clump of complainers.

I whispered, "Thank you" to Starla, who just sighed again and said, "I guess I'd better get started on inventorying my supplies." Which was such a good idea I was surprised I hadn't thought of asking her to do it myself.

I found Carn eating breakfast in the bistro—oatmeal, naturally. "I'm giving everybody jobs," I said, sitting down across from him. "Or rather, I'm giving a few people jobs, so *they* can give other people jobs, and your job is security."

"I noticed that." Nothing much seemed to ruffle Carn.

"I figure one of the best ways to make us more secure is to expand our borders so we can acquire more resources and just generally promote our way of life: peaceful, cooperative, not shooting-each-other-based—all that stuff you were talking about last night."

"So we're back to the Lorespire again," Carn said. "Probably lots of resources in there. And since it's some kind of library or whatnot, the people inside most likely don't have that many guns."

I nodded. "Melezheun, the lashunta we picked up yesterday, thinks there could be information inside to explain what happened to our memories... or at least find out about some of the things we've forgotten." I paused. "Does the word *Golarion* mean anything to you?"

Carn's brow wrinkled, and yes, there went the finger in the ear. "That undead fella on the vidscreen, the cleric he interviewed, she said something about that, yeah? 'Golarion is safe'? Good for him. I wish the rest of us were. Who's coming with us to the Lorespire?"

"It's busy around here, so I want to keep it small. You, me, and Melezheun should be enough to get a sense of what's going on over there. We can talk to whoever's in charge and see if they want to join forces or at least open communication and trade. I've got cases of liquor in the back. Scholars like those."

"Maybe I used to be a scholar, then," Carn said.

I grinned. "Want to meet me in the security office in, oh, fifteen minutes?"

"Yup."

I slapped the table, nodded, and went in search of Melezheun. She was in the clinic with Bindi and the contemplative, who was conscious and floating. None of them were saying anything, but they were making various facial expressions, so I realized they were in three-way telepathic communication, and I wasn't party to the call.

Then a cool, soothing, somehow pale blue voice spoke in my mind, and the contemplative swiveled in the air, orienting their frontal lobes toward me. "*We understand you saved our life. We are profoundly grateful. Our name is Soubrette's Last Elegant Algorithm. Many prefer to call us Sue.*"

I considered shaking one of their four tiny hands but opted for a smile and a nod instead. "I'm Tyrcell. We're all glad you pulled through, Sue. Melezheun was the one who saved you, though, really. I just helped with the carrying. In fact, I could use her help again, so if you don't mind..."

"*Wait, Tyrcell.*" The blue voice took on a darker shade. "*We wonder... We hate to ask when you have done so much for us already, but... would it be possible for you, or some of your friends, to accompany us to the Arcanamirium? We remember very little of our past, as we gather is the norm, but we know the school of magic is our home—we belong there, and we wish to join our peers. We are sure they are studying the situation. If anyone on this station can unlock the secret of what happened, and even reverse it, it will be the people there, in the greatest center of magical learning.*"

I whistled, considering. "The Arcanamirium is way over in the Eye, Sue. Normally it would be a nice little jaunt, but with all the disorder and unrest out there, a trip that long is a much bigger undertaking. Can you give me a day or two? We've got people out talking to the neighbors, so I hope to get a better sense of where the safest routes might be, as well as which parts of the station we should avoid."

"Sue should not travel yet anyway," Bindi said. "As I *told* them. They still have healing to do. Maybe in two or three days, they could *consider* such a trip."

"That's perfect, then." I was discovering that I had vast reserves of only slightly false bonhomie. It helped that I liked all these people. "We'll reopen the subject once you're feeling better." Then it was the handshake problem again. I felt like a shoulder pat or something would be appropriate there, but I couldn't pat those tiny shoulders without hitting their brain in the process, so that time I settled for a little wave, caught Melezheun's eye, and headed out.

Melezheun followed me. "Are we going to the Lorespire now?"

I noted the neutriad pistol at her belt, the one she'd liberated from the security office, and wondered if she'd slept with it under her pillow. It was a nasty little piece of work, an energy weapon that fired blasts of force—basically a gun that approximated a fast-moving tram car hitting you in the face.

"That's the plan. We'll see if we can make contact with whoever's running the complex. But, since it's better to be safe..." We reached the security office, and I opened up cabinets and found a few adjustable vests that were definitely stabproof and somewhat laserproof and probably not at all plasmaproof. "I was thinking we should armor up a little."

She sniffed. "I am wearing mindmail." She held up her hands, and links of iridescent chainmail flowed up out of her sleeves and over her hands. Wasn't *she* fancy—she had a whole suit of high-tech armor hidden beneath her flowing clothes. "That's why I wasn't hurt more badly when those thugs kicked me yesterday. The force fields absorbed the impacts."

"And here I thought you were just tough. Wow. I wish you had a spare set." I pulled on a ballistic vest and adjusted the buckles.

Carn walked in, managing to look like he'd just wandered this way by accident, trailed by his dark mote of solar energy. "Armor, huh?" He nodded. "Good idea. Nobody can really hit me when I'm paying attention, but I can't look everywhere at once." He strapped on a vest like he'd worn them a thousand times before, and I wondered if he *had* worked security in his prior life. Carn squinted at Melezheun. "Is that lashunta mindmail? Very nice. If people start shooting at us, you should lead the way, being the most bulletproof and all. You're sorta small to hide behind, but maybe I can turn sideways." He grinned.

"I am happy to be your shield if you will be my hammer. I have heard of your prowess." More shimmering mail flowed up out of her collar and around her head, until the armor covered everything but her face and her antennae.

"I am good at hitting stuff," Carn said. "You can't solve *all* your problems that way, but the ones you can, I'm the one to solve them."

The two of them seemed to be getting along—good. I'd had some concern since they were so different, but sometimes really different people complement each other.

I checked the cameras to make sure the area just outside was clear, then opened up the inner door of the security office. That led to a tiny alcove in front of the outer door to the hallway: It was basically an airlock, but without all the pressurization and alarm lights. Probably designed that way so bad guys would have a hard time storming the office.

"I like this door. We can leave, and there's no chance of anyone barging their way in past us." We squeezed into the alcove, shut the inner door, and then opened the outer one. The corridor was still empty. We hadn't seen much foot traffic since we locked things down. People were either hunkering down in their own safe spaces or out looking for easier pickings than us to rob and burglarize.

Off to the right was "our" hall, with the doors to the shops and restaurants we'd combined into our lair, the corridor curving out of sight to join the maze of passageways that led to various living quarters and deeper into the station. There were blast doors recessed into the ceiling at regular intervals—to seal off discrete areas in case of sudden holes appearing in the station's outer walls—and we'd managed to gain control of those from the security office, strategically lowering a few. As a result, we had a pretty-well-defended chunk of the station under our control, with the capacity to expand.

We didn't control *all* the entrances and exits, though. Directly to our left, there was a heavy metal blast door that blocked our entry to the Lorespire Complex. We hadn't lowered *that* door, and it was unresponsive to the security office overrides and all my passcodes, which meant somewhere on the other side there was a better hacker than me. Even if we could have opened that door, we knew from the camera feeds on the other side that the locals had barricaded all the entry points with piles of furniture and scrap metal and who knew what else. Those were formidable enough to slow us down so snipers in the spire could take us out. Or the defenders could just shove them back into our hallway with long pointy sticks, if they wanted to go more analog.

So we weren't even trying to get in that way. We were going to take the low road instead.

We crossed the hall, and I pried off an access panel and unlocked a maintenance hatch. Once I had that open, I waved my compatriots in, and they descended the rungs of the short ladder to the tunnel below. I had added a little gauntlet to my wrist, with enough memory to hold maps of the sector downloaded from the security office systems. When we got down there, the cramped, narrow passages matched the schematics, and I chose our path with the confidence that came from external validation.

"I like how you come up with these plans to do stuff," Carn said, bringing up the rear. "As long as I'm doing things, I don't have much extra time to think about how terrifying and confusing everything is or worry about what we're going to do in a week, or a month, or a year if we don't get our memories back. Having plans, giving people jobs, it helps everybody. If our people have projects, like expanding our territory and foraging supplies, they focus on that instead of the giant scary void. It's like... distraction through action, right? Pretty smart."

I chuckled. "I wish I could say it was an intentional strategy, but I'm just doing what comes naturally. I tried to sit and brood when I first woke up yesterday, but I was no good at it. I'd rather be moving forward."

"I am perfectly capable of moving forward *and* brooding," Melezheun said. "In fact, I am doing both right now."

"Well, you're talented," Carn said.

We were under the Lorespire Complex by then, and the ceiling above us suddenly rumbled, as if a herd of beasts were stampeding through the campus overhead. "What is *that*?"

"It does not sound good," the lashunta said. I got that cold tingle in my brain again, and Carn swore.

"I am sorry, I should have warned you," Melezheun said. "We call it a battlemind link. A psychic connection among us that allows us to share our senses to some extent—it will make us harder to surprise. It also allows us to coordinate our actions, almost automatically, should we need to fight."

"I never felt lonely inside my own head before," Carn said. "I think I will, after this." He held up one hand in front of his face, and I blinked as my vision tripled and showed his hand from multiple angles. Then my brain figured out the trick to sharing senses, and it stopped disorienting me.

"Is this our exit?" Carn gestured at a recess in the wall on the right that held a hovering antigravity platform.

I checked the schematics and nodded. "If I'm reading this right, we should come out in a section of the Lorespire where there aren't any doors leading elsewhere in the station. I figure there's less chance of motion-sensing autocannons mowing us down instantly if we come out there."

We crowded onto the little platform and sent it upward. The elevator stopped in a low-ceilinged, squared-off little shed, where dim lights came on automatically, revealing dusty shelves and discarded tools.

I was just reaching for the door controls when I heard voices—harsh laughter and garbled shouts, mainly. They weren't close by, but they might *come* close by, so I hesitated.

It was good that I did, because a moment later, a shuddering boom made the whole shack tremble, followed by a chorus of screams.

10

INVASION OF THE LORESPIRE

(Tyrcell)

"Raiders," I whispered as I found the off switch for the lights. The hints of illumination through the cracks in the shed walls probably wouldn't be visible from the outside, but I hadn't survived this long—which was to say, a day, basically—by being careless.

There were more voices, shouting, and then the thunder of boots running, and all of it was getting louder. We were jammed so close together in the shed that Carn's elbow was jabbed into my stomach and Melezheun kept stepping on my foot.

"But how could marauders get through those barricades?"

"This could be a civil-war-type thing," Carn responded. "The archivists turning on... I don't know... the groundskeepers? Or I guess the other way is more likely. Either way, we might be looking at factions and such."

"Or they might have crept in like we did. There are maintenance tunnels on the other side of the complex, no doubt—"

"If you will both be quiet for a few moments, I will see what I can learn from their minds." Melezheun sounded only a little exasperated, and we quieted down. A moment later, she murmured, "There are people out there... lots of them, mmm, at least twenty..."

I wanted to say, "Who are they and what are they doing and what do they want and what should we do," but opted to stay quiet. Melezheun had proven herself calm and decisive in a crisis, so I should let her calmly decide things.

"*I can hear their thoughts,*" she sent (telepathic communication suddenly seemed sensible in our circumstances). "*It's a bit of a jumble and hard to pick out individual threads against the noise of the whole. But it seems they are a company of Hellknights, and they crashed through the barricades and seized the Lorespire by force.*"

"*That must have been the thundering-herd noises from earlier,*" Carn sent.

I groaned. "*Hellknights?*" I thought at them. "*They're fanatics obsessed with upholding laws, no matter how big or small.*" What a baffling worldview. Sure, laws were useful things to have around in some circumstances, but you couldn't go around letting them dictate how you lived your life. "*What laws could a bunch of archivists have possibly broken?*"

"*So they're like cops?*" Carn said.

"*No,*" Melezheun said. "*They are aligned with devils. They seek to emulate the hierarchy of Hell. To make this plane a Hell. They are dangerous as individuals, and more so as an organization.*"

"*Still sounds like cops,*" Carn muttered.

"*They might be even more dangerous now,*" I said. "*They lost their memories too. Imagine if you've lived your whole life under a strict order, and then order breaks down. Not just the order around you, but the order inside your own* head. *What would you want to do?*"

"*Try to impose order again,*" Melezheun sent.

I nodded. "*By any means necessary. I bet they'll try to take over the whole station. And our own community is in the nearest corridor. What if these zealots target us next?*"

"*That is a problem for later,*" Melezheun said. "*For now, the problem is getting into the Lorespire without being discovered and before they lock this whole area down.*"

That surprised me. "*Melezheun, I think our mission of peace and community-building is finished before it began. We can't stand up against a company of Hellknights. Half a company, sure, we're formidable, but there are just too many of them.*"

"*I did not come here to expand the borders of your new principality, Tyrcell,*" she sent. "*I came to find information about what has* happened *to us and about this Golarion, whatever that is. You do not have to accompany me if our goals no longer align.*"

I sighed. "*These Hellknights are supposed to be the fanatics, Mel. They whip* themselves *with scourges—What do you think they do to people* outside *the order?*"

She stiffened—startled by the nickname, I think—and then shook her head, but she smiled a little when she did it, at least. "*I understand that your guiding principle is to protect your people... and that you consider me one of them. I am grateful for that. I am also sure my determination to carry on must seem strange to you. But please understand... to me, all this fighting, the chaos, it is just noise. It is temporary. Eventually, things will settle down into a new equilibrium, and when they do, the question of what happened to our memories, and why, will be the most important question in the world, the galaxy, and all the planes. I choose to focus on it now. We are both of us, in our own ways, looking to the future.*"

"*'Eventually' is all well and good, but we have to live long enough to get to the future,*" I countered. "*If you try to get into the Lorespire, I don't like your odds.*"

"*The Hellknights closest to us have moved on,*" she said. "*I can sense the presence of thinking creatures, Tyrcell. That will keep me from blundering into our enemies. I believe I can make my way into the spire and see what information might be gleaned. I understand if you want to go back. Perhaps you could wait for me—*"

That wasn't going to happen. Mel was right: She was part of my group, my tribe, my family, whatever I was building. "*No, I'll go with you. I can do the covert thing. I think I might have a knack for sneaking around. Carn, though, you don't have to come if you don't want to. I know this isn't what you signed up for.*"

Carn sniffed. "*Wouldn't be much of a head of security if I let the leader of our community walk into enemy territory alone. Besides, following your lead has worked out for me so far, boss.*"

I stifled a chuckle. "*We met yesterday, Carn. That isn't objectively very far.*"

"*You gotta start somewhere,*" he said agreeably. "*Anyhow, I agree with Mellie. This hole in my memories isn't going to stop bothering me. Let's sort it out.*"

"*Thank you both,*" she murmured in our minds.

I gave Mel a nod, and she opened the door, a thin sheet of metal that slid sideways into the shed's frame—no motors, pure analog, and it needed oiling. We all winced at the squeal. I peered out and didn't see an invading army or even any piles of corpses, so that was a good start, though we heard distant shouting, and there was smoke rising in various directions. Setting things on fire seemed like a bad idea in a space station, but who was I to question the tactics of the proud and (presumably) ancient order of Hellknights?

Gods, the Lorespire Complex was lovely, or it would have been, in the absence of violent chaos. It was a vast open space, the ceiling shimmering blue like open sky—screens, or projectors, of course, but they were convincing. Bright full-spectrum light shone down from a sunlight disk, and there was grass beneath our feet. Stands of trees dotted the space, mingling with the various small and large structures all around, creating the impression of a small and prosperous university village.

The Lorespire itself was the nearest structure, an elegantly tapered silver tower dotted here and there with windows and small balconies. We were around the back, where they kept the compost bins and gardening tools. The tower was beautiful from all sides, though. There was writing inscribed on the walls, spiraling from the base to the distant top, with words in a few languages I could read and scores of others I couldn't, all glowing faintly through magic or technological luminescence. The bits I could read said things like "Knowledge is power" and "Diversity in knowledge, unity in purpose" and "Explore, report, cooperate." Inspirational thoughts for the archivists and scholars, I supposed, though they were currently learning that, actually, a company of heavily armed Hellknights was power too—and of a rather more obvious sort than knowledge.

A quick scan of the surroundings didn't do much to reassure me about our chances of slipping through unnoticed. Off to the left, about thirty yards away, two Hellknights in ridiculously overcomplicated and bulky armor stood with their backs to us beside a building with arched windows on the sides and fluted columns up front: That was the museum, according to my maps, though a museum of what, I couldn't say. The knights were trying to pry the doors open with a long stick or polearm, and I didn't think they were planning to respectfully appreciate the cultural artifacts once they got inside.

Meanwhile, off on our right, a group of three people in fluttering robes raced past, looking over their shoulders in a way that suggested pursuit was imminent. There was a whir and a blur as something came whipping through the air in a flash and wrapped around the legs of the one at the back, sending him sprawling face-first onto the ground. The others ran on without even a look back; well, who could blame them? The captured archivist rolled over and tried to untangle his legs, which were bound by some kind of bola. Which meant the person who'd *thrown* the bola was going to be along soon. Luckily for us, a cloud of smoke drifted in our direction, obscuring the victim from sight... and obscuring us from any hostile eyes in that area too. The Hellknights by the museum hooted with glee, and something crashed; they'd broken their way in, which meant their attention was occupied. We weren't going to get a better chance.

I gestured to Mel and Carn, and then we hurried out of the shed, fast and low, toward the base of the Lorespire. There was a low, rounded door there, not the grand entry on the far side I'd seen on the surveillance cameras but something more modest and workaday. I could hack my way into the control panel, and then—

There was no control panel. The door was shut with a *mechanical* lock, like, the kind with a keyhole and tumblers and cylinders inside.

"*Oh, those pretentious retro jerks,*" I muttered. "*Do they write on wax tablets in there too?*"

"*I can smash it in,*" Carn offered, but I shook my head. Big hammers made big noise.

"*Anyone in there?*" I asked Mel silently, and after a moment's concentration, she shook her head.

I knew how to pick locks, even old-fashioned historical curiosities like this lock, but I didn't have any tools, did I? I reached out to touch the keyhole... and my index finger flowered, the tip opening on an invisible hinge to reveal half a dozen delicate jointed and curving metal probes. I grinned. I had *augmentations*. I tried to move the probes, and they obediently wiggled, so I put my picks in the keyhole and let muscle memory take over. It hadn't let me down yet; I should trust it more.

A moment later, the door unlocked with a soft click, and I eased it open. Empty, as promised. Mel and Carn followed me inside, and I relocked the door behind me. We were in a spacious storage room, with high ceilings and dusty floors, surrounded by shelves filled with all kinds of stuff: toilet paper, data drives, extra desk chairs, disposable cups.

"*I don't sense anyone nearby,*" Mel said. We crept to the inner door, and I pressed my ear to the metal. No minds, maybe, but what if there were drones? Who knew what kind of armaments the Hellknights traveled with? I didn't hear any beeps or clatters, so I decided it was safe enough.

That door was locked too, though at least it was electronic this time. The security office system had supplied me with assorted emergency overrides, and this was an emergency, right? The door accepted my credentials, which claimed I was chief of sector security. I felt I'd earned the promotion. After easing open the door and confirming there weren't any autocannons trained on us, I led the way into the corridor, locking the door after.

We were in some unlovely administrative section of the building, with worn carpets, doors made to look like dark wood, and smudged windows offering views into small rooms crowded with old desks and shelves. "*These are the offices for junior archivists,*" I said, using my keen observational senses to read the sign D. Calhoun—Junior Archivist painted on the nearest door. "*Where are we headed, Mel? This is a pretty big place, and I didn't find a map of the interior.*"

"*One of these offices could work,*" Mel said. "*I just want to access the Lorespire's private database. We—wait. Someone is coming!*"

I quickly circumvented the lock on D. Calhoun's inner sanctum, and we all went in, hunched over, because the windows were half the height of the wall, and we didn't want whoever was coming to get a glimpse of us. I eased the door shut without so much as a click, and we all crouched in the dim office, waiting and listening.

"*Two Hellknights are approaching,*" Mel sent. "*It's easier to sense their thoughts when there isn't a crowd of them... I caught a name just now—Astrachios. His mind is... gods, what a stew of fury and guilt and anger!*"

(We didn't know what he was guilty about then; I found out about the whole murdering-his-own-people stuff much later.)

At this point, I could hear the actual voices of the approaching Hellknights and the thud of their boots down the hall. They certainly weren't equipped for stealth.

"You're saying it's *good* that so much of the information here is already corrupted?" a lilting voice said.

"It's perfect, Rakhiel," a masculine (but slightly reedy) voice said. That must be Astrachios. "Now we can say we found anything we want, and there's nothing to contradict us. We can claim Absalom Station is a Hellknight outpost and we're its rightful defenders, and that we have all the documentation to prove it here in the Lorespire. We've got plenty of those scholars rounded up now, so we can have them help us fabricate whatever records we need. Once we purge..."

They moved on, out of earshot, and I sighed in frustration. "*I wish we could hear them better. It would be good to get some sense of what they're up to here, besides breaking things.*"

"*I found a doohickey in the security office,*" Carn said. "*Surveillance device, supposedly it can turn on microphones remotely and let us intercept the audio, at least over short distances. If they've got comms in their armor...*" He reached into one of the pouches on his vest and drew out a flat, black palm-sized device. After a moment, he grinned and handed each of us an earbud and slipped in one of his own.

I put the bud in, and Rakhiel was speaking. "—far as that goes, I can draw up any documents you want. I found all sorts of supplies in my rooms; I think misinformation was my specialty. Still, your plan seems a bit dishonest for a member of the Order of the Chain. Aren't you lot supposed to hate liars?"

"I'm allowed to lie to criminals and miscreants to further the goals of my order. It says so right in the Measure. All these people refusing to submit to our authority when this is an obvious time of crisis that requires our leadership? They *are* criminals and miscreants."

"It's not just your order anymore, though," Rakhiel pointed out. "I was a member of the Order of the Gate, judging by all the swirling-vortexes-and-eyeballs decorations on the armor in my room, not that I'm going to wear all that."

"I took note of your... unconventional sartorial choices," Astrachios said.

"Just because I'm a member of a rigidly stratified hierarchical organization doesn't mean I have to give up all my personal style. Besides, I'm not a brawny brute like you, I can't stand all that plate. I like to stay agile. Ah, here we are. Just let me access the server here... uploading the worm... All right. My point is, the Hellknights are *one* order now. Mikiel recruited the Order of the Gate, the Order of the Nail, and the Order of the Scourge, and we're all working together to keep chaos from consuming the station. We need to band together for numerical force, I get that, but... I have my doubts that all those different worldviews will mesh for long. It helps that no one can remember anything, but eventually stress fractures are going to show."

"I've been thinking about our different orders," Astrachios said. "We're in a new world, in a new situation, with new challenges. Maybe it's time for a new order. One created to face the particular challenges of the moment. What do you think?"

"I think the Order of the Pyre might call that heresy and decide you need to burn," Rakhiel said, amused. "What are you thinking, an order that specializes in seizing the ports and gaining control of the station's life support systems? The Order of the Infrastructure?"

"No, no." Impatience thundered from his every word. "Those are tactical concerns, Rakhiel. I'm sick of tactics. Are—are you listening to me? What are you looking at?"

"Not looking. Smelling. I thought I picked up an... emotional emanation."

"You can sense emotions?"

"I have all sorts of skills, Astrachios. I got a whiff of something... but this place is full of people hiding out and quivering in fear. There's a lot of emotional background noise. Anyway. What were you saying? Tactics?"

"Tactics and strategy. We have too much of the former and not enough of the latter."

Rakhiel snorted. "You weren't sick of tactics when Mikiel sent you up into the tower and let you pick off fleeing scholars with your sniper rifle. You were in your element."

"I appreciated the target practice, yes," Astrachios allowed. "But that's all little-picture stuff. I'm talking about strategic concerns—

higher-level problems. The main thing we need to do is take control of *information*. That's the most precious resource there is now, don't you see? Because no one knows what's going on or what their place is in the world. The people on this station are desperate to be told who they are and what they're supposed to do. Someone needs to decide what the truth is, tell the people that truth, and make sure no one else tells them *differently*. That's why we're here. Whether the Lorespire contains the truth or not, people will believe it does, and we're the ones who get to *tell* them. Whatever truth we want them to hear."

"Hmm. You may have something there. Do you know what kind of devil I am, Astrachios?"

I closed my eyes and pressed my face to the wood. A devil. Great.

"I can't say I do, no," Astrachios said.

"We all look the same to you, hmm?"

Astrachios barked a laugh. "I wouldn't say that. Most of the devils I've seen don't have long trunks that ooze black slime."

"You noted my noble proboscis? It's one of my best features, I've always thought. I'm a sigveir, Astrachios. Some call us propaganda devils." There was a bit of a sneer in her voice. "We're trained to spread rumors and innuendo and misinformation, to turn people toward our cause, whatever that cause might be. I think I might be a good fit for your new order, don't you?"

"Then you think it's a good idea?" Astrachios was pleased, one thing I already never wanted him to be.

"I think it's... an idea worth exploring. We'll have to proceed carefully, though. Remember what I said about factions developing. We don't need anyone deciding we're a faction that needs quashing."

Astrachios said, "This could be the beginning of a beautiful strategic partnership. I think the first thing we should do is... *fzzz... bzzzt...*" Their words faded into static and then silence.

"*Out of range,*" Carn said. "*Handy little gadget, though. I think I'll keep it.*"

"*Are we all clear now, Mel?*" I asked. "*No more foot patrols wandering through?*"

"*I sense no one else.*"

"*It's a shame,*" Carn said. "*I was hoping I'd get to hit someone with a hammer. Hitting walls is fun, but hitting a Hellknight, that just seems more* right, *somehow. Maybe hitting Hellknights with a hammer was my job in the old days.*"

"You might yet get your chance," I muttered quietly. "*There's a terminal in here, Melezheun. Will that work for you?*"

"*We can try, though from what the knights said... if the information is already corrupted...*"

"*I doubt they're data scientists,*" I pointed out. "*You said you're a historian. You might see something they don't.*" If that bit about loading a program into a server didn't mean we were too late, but we were there, so we might as well try.

We got the terminal activated, and with a little hacking, I managed to secure administrative credentials so Mel could pillage the Lorespire's local infosphere at will. She sat at the desk and deftly maneuvered through menus and submenus. "*I know how to do this!*" There was something like awe in Melezheun's thoughts. "*This feels as natural to me as walking across a room.*"

"*Just walk fast,*" I said.

"*I will need to concentrate, which means I cannot listen for approaching minds,*" she said. "*You will have to keep watch for me.*"

"*Good. We like to stay occupied.*" Carn and I crouched near the door, keeping lookout through the window. Melezheun hummed quietly to herself as she worked, and Carn wiggled a finger in his ear, and I waited perfectly still with no distracting nervous tics, because I keep all my nervous tics on the inside, where they belong.

"*Hmm, yes, most of the data is corrupted, at least to some extent,*" Mel sent after a while. "*It is as if whatever destroyed our memories also corroded the archives here. I should not be surprised, since even photographs and written texts were affected. Whole swaths of the archives are simply unreadable, overwritten with lines of nonsense, while other sections seem mostly intact, but then turn out to be truncated or redacted or encrypted. I am running a search on that word,* Golarion, *and there is* nothing. *The system has scanned hundreds of thousands of files so far, and yet—*" Then came the mental equivalent of a gasp. "*Search complete. And there is a file that contains that word.* One *file.*"

"*What does it say?*" I asked.

11

OUT OF STORAGE
(Chk Chk and Dae)

"Well? What does it *say*?" Dae made grabby hands, and Chk Chk swiveled away, hugging the pages to his chest.

"*I am* trying *to* read. *When I am done, then* you *may read.*"

Dae sighed and flung their body across the table dramatically. "To think, Tyrcell and Carn and Mel were right here—well, not right *here* here, but probably nearby, down some hallway, back before the Lorespire Complex belonged to the Starfinder Society, back before there even *was* the Starfinder Society. We're walking in the same place where they walked! Sort of, anyway. Once we actually walk somewhere again."

"*Mmm.*" Chk Chk was also burningly curious about what Tyrcell and the others had found in the old Lorespire's garbled infosphere, but it was hard to concentrate when Dae was chattering, even for someone who'd had as much practice doing so as Chk Chk.

Dae grabbed at the stack of unread pages on the table and started rapidly flipping through them. "Port, ship, hmm, oh, here's some fighting, there's that floating brain person again, ooh, here, they go to the Arcanamirium, that's what Zo! mentioned!"

Chk Chk took the pages back and squared them neatly. "*Didn't you say something about respecting the narrative?*"

"I know, I know, I wasn't really reading, I was just *peeking*. They're just all so clueless! I was looking to see if they *ever* got a clue. They don't even know what Golarion even is, you know?"

"*It's hundreds of years later, and we barely know what Golarion is,*" Chk Chk pointed out.

"Of course we do! It was a whole *planet*, it orbited the sun... you know, right around here, where the station is. People lived there for a long time, and the Starstone used to be there too, right? And then the planet... went... somewhere. Somehow. For some reason. And nearly all the records about it vanished along with everyone's memories in the Gap." Dae frowned, apparently unhappy with the actual depth of their knowledge.

In this case, though, Dae wasn't particularly uninformed. They knew as much as anyone. "*Yes,*" Chk Chk said. "*We can see those from the distant past were painfully ignorant when their feeble wisdom is compared to the vastness of our own understanding.*" He tapped the pages stacked in front of him. "*Do you realize we're reading about the founding of the Order of the Eclipse in here?*"

Dae growled. "I hate those guys. First of all, they're best buddies with the Veskarium, and I know there's a truce and all that, but still, you can tell the quality of somebody by the company they keep. Second of all, their stupid Paralictor Prahama has jammed broadcasts I was on at least *three times*! Like why? I wasn't inciting anybody to riot! I was dancing! But the order just threw communications blackouts over whole planets until the locals finally chased them off. They're close-minded little censor jerks, flying around in Citadel Zirval and just *looming* over people. When you see that giant space fortress slide into orbit, it's got a definite chilling effect on self-expression."

"*The Order of the Eclipse sees itself as the ultimate arbiters of acceptable information,*" Chk Chk said. "*They know rebellious propaganda when they see it... and they see it everywhere. I think this Astrachios was the founder of that order, and now we know his motivation was rooted in personal shame, not some high-minded nonsense about maintaining order at all costs. This information will be invaluable to scholars—and I suspect the Order of the Eclipse will fight hard to suppress the dissemination of their origin story at all costs.*"

"I'm going to turn into a scholar myself if we don't get out of here," Dae declared. "I'm wasted in an archive, Chickie. Look, I skipped ahead a little, we know they go to the Arcanamirium, Zo! said so too, so why don't *we* go there? You know, we can retrace their steps, do a sort of living history kind of thing?"

"*I don't know,*" Chk Chk said, but in truth, he was feeling a bit cooped up too. "*I don't think we should take these files out of the storage area. Even with the preservatives, these papers are delicate and one of a kind—*"

"We've been scanning the pages to make a digital record as we read anyway, so how about I just scan the rest of the pages now?" Dae said. "I'll take care of it; you just keep reading, and pretty soon we'll have a digital version you can read while we walk."

"*I will bump into things if I read while I walk.*"

"I'll steer you around the obstacles, or wait, better yet, we can convert voice to text, and we can both *listen* while we walk. Ooh, what kind of voice should Tyrcell have? I'm thinking they're a charming bad-boy type—"

"*Tyrcell is clearly agender,*" Chk Chk said.

"You can be a bad-boy type of any gender," Dae argued. "Sometimes I'm a bad-boy type! And you, Chickie, you may be a he/him, but you're *never* a bad boy."

"*I can be bad,*" Chk Chk objected. "*Haven't you seen me brood? You know my art. I revere Zon-Shelyn, the Embrace of Beauty and Pain.*" Chk Chk made sculptures and sometimes paintings and occasionally holographic installations and of course wrote poetry, but all his art had one thing in common. He sought to turn the overwhelming, often incomprehensible experience of being alive in this strange universe into experiences that could be shared communally. Joy shared was joy doubled, and misery shared was misery halved. "*And you know I've always embraced the* pain *side the most, Dae. I don't think all art is pain... but pain makes the best art for me.*"

"I never said you weren't a *sad* boy. And my art is only if I get lazy and don't do my warm-up stretches first." Dae began to methodically scan the remaining pages with their wrist gauntlet, moving swiftly but efficiently. They did almost everything well when they could be bothered. "A true bad boy wouldn't be afraid to take a walk with me."

"*Fine,*" Chk Chk said. "*I suppose it wouldn't do any harm for us to stretch our legs a little. Once you get the rest of the pages scanned, we can take a walk to the Arcanamirium. It would be... interesting... to follow Tyrcell's path.*"

Dae worked faster, and once they had all the pages scanned and uploaded, and the originals were neatly stored away in their box, they crept out of the storage area. They didn't encounter Seraphina or any other authority.

"*What do you think they'll do if they catch us sneaking off with Starfinder Society material in our possession?*" Chk Chk mused.

"They will probably congratulate us on our courage and boldness," Dae said. "Courage and boldness are what the Society is all *about.*"

"*Mmm. I don't know about that. This might, technically, count as investigating the Gap, and there is a strong prohibition* against *investigating the Gap, because of the aforementioned horrible things—*"

"Who's investigating anything?" Dae said as they emerged into the corridors of the Lorespire. "We're just reading and taking a walk." Dae set off, with Chk Chk hurrying to follow.

The shirren mystic caught sight of a figure in the hall behind them, half hidden by a carved pillar—a humanoid, wearing a dark green hooded cloak. Was the stranger watching them? "*Dae, I think...*" The figure stepped away from the pillar and hurried around a corner, vanishing from sight.

"What?" Dae bounced with impatience.

"*Hmm. Nothing, really.*" That part of the Lorespire wasn't open to the public, so whoever it was must have permission to be there. So what if they were a bit mysterious? Starfinder agents often cultivated such an air.

"'Nothing'?" Dae said. "That's boring. Let's go do *something* instead."

12

YARAESA'S MESSAGE

(Tyrcell)

"*It's just a fragment of a text file.*" Melezheun gazed at the screen, expression intent. "*It says... 'In the time of lost time, Yaraesa became, and in her shrine, the truth remains. The other gods have all forsaken you, but by her grace, she may awaken you. In the center of great learning, you may yet appease your yearning. If you can form a syzygy, then her truth may set you free.*'"

"*What's a Yaraesa?*" Carn asked. "*And what did it become?*"

Yaraesa I knew, vaguely; I was more curious about what a *syzygy* was.

Melezheun turned in the chair, head cocked to one side. "*Yaraesa is a goddess. She was a mortal lashunta, once.*"

"*A goddess of what?*" Carn asked. "*Memory? That would be handy.*"

"*In a way. She is the Lady of Wisdom—goddess of knowledge and learning and science. The stories say she was a scholar who attained total understanding of all disciplines of learning over the course of her lifetime and then ascended to divinity. This loss of collective knowledge, of all our memories... it must* pain *her. Those who follow Yaraesa strive toward mental and spiritual self-perfection, always seeking to expand the borders of the known. I think...*" Melezheun pressed her hand to her chest. "*I think* I *followed her, or at least admired her teachings.*"

"*If any of the gods might be willing to tell us what happened to our memories, I guess it would be her,*" I said. "*I don't know much about getting in touch with gods, though. Do we light candles and chant or something?*"

"*I am not a cleric,*" Melezheun said. "*I have no idea how to draw the attention of a god, apart from flagrant blasphemy, which isn't the sort of attention we want. But Yaraesa is worshipped by scholars, and... if we can find this shrine mentioned in the text file, then someone there might know a way to reach her, yes?*" Melezheun stared at the screen, and I saw her mouth, *all forsaken you.*

"*How many shrines to Yaraesa are there on this station, though? It could be anywhere.*" If the shrine was on this station at all, I thought, but I didn't want to be *too* pessimistic; the text file didn't say either way, though.

"*No, not anywhere.*" Melezheun swiveled back and forth in the chair, pondering. "*I wouldn't expect to find a shrine to Yaraesa in Downlow, Botscrap, or Pipetown.*" Those were a few of the more rough-and-tumble districts on the station, and I agreed, they probably worshipped more practical deities, or at least used their names in curses. "*We're most likely to find a shrine where a large number of her worshippers would congregate, and her followers are scientists, scholars... and technomancers. Yaraesa melded the disciplines of magic and science in her work. There are a great many technomancers on Absalom Station, but they have only one center of great learning I can think of.*" Melezheun spread her hands and beamed.

I nodded. "*The Arcanamirium. I agree that's our best bet.*" Sue had even offered to give us a guided tour of the place, but getting there safely was the problem, though hardly our most pressing one. Still, Melezheun was happy, and like Carn said, it was good to have something to focus on besides "Everything is falling apart around us." No reason to throw sand in her gears. At least, not until it was absolutely necessary. So I put on a smile in return and said, "*It looks like we've got a clue. We should hide that file, though, so Astrachios and Rakhiel don't find it. If we figured this out, someone else might, and we don't want a company of Hellknights storming the Arcanamirium.*"

"*A bunch of techno-mages could put up a better fight than the scholars here did,*" Carn said. "*The Hellknights might hesitate to invade that place. But... you never can tell with zealots.*"

"*I'll delete—oh, no.*" Melezheun stared at the screen. "*They're purging the files!*" Her fingers flew across the keyboard, and her antennae twitched furiously. "*They've released a worm... it's eating through the whole Lorespire infosphere, replicating itself and destroying everything as it goes. The Hellknights have people who are good at technology as well as breaking things and killing people.*"

"*It's a total loss, then?*" I asked.

"*I'm sure there are local copies of some materials downloaded onto individual stations and tablets, and perhaps even air-gapped terminals, but the knights are certainly capable of smashing* those—"

"*Wait,*" I said. "*They're in the system. Does that mean they can see that...* you're *in the system? That someone is logged in, I mean? And where they're logged in* from?"

Melezheun's eyes widened, and she stood up so fast the chair rolled away from her and bumped into the wall. "*We should go.*"

We hurried back into the hallway, heading for our back door and our maintenance-tunnel getaway. "*Can you sense anyone ahead with your fancy mind powers?*" I asked.

"*Let me pause for a moment so I can concentrate.*" She closed her eyes, leaning against the wall—all this mind work was wearing her out, I could tell—and then groaned. "*Yes, there are Hellknights between us and the way out.*"

"*Then we need another way out.*" Unfortunately, I didn't have schematics of the Lorespire's interior, and any data I could access from these terminals was probably getting chewed up by the Hellknight deletion program.

"*This place is big,*" Carn said. "*Already it's like a maze, and there are Hellknights stomping around all over, inside and out. I really don't like being lost in a maze. I wonder if it's some kind of generational trauma? I'm not sure how I rate our chances of finding another exit. Can you tell how many Hellknights are between us and the back door, Melezheun?*"

Her eyes glazed a bit. "*Just two,*" Melezheun said after a moment. "*I think they travel in pairs so they can watch one another for... heretical thoughts or improper actions.*"

"*Is it the ones we heard before, Astrachios and Rakhiel?*" I asked.

"*No, no. The flavor of these minds is different. Simpler. But no less brutal.*"

"*So there's two of them,*" Carn said. "*And we've got three of us. That's the best odds we're going to get, Tyrcell.*"

"Agreed. You'd better get your hammer ready. Mel's mindmail aside, I think you should take point, Carn, since Mel and I have ranged weapons. We can fire past you. And Mel, since you can't scan for minds while we're moving, can you watch our rear, make sure nobody sneaks up on us?"

Melezheun nodded and loosened her force pistol in its holster. Carn grinned, reached into his mote, and drew out his hammer, the blocky head swirling with shadows. "*I wonder if maybe I worked in demolition in my past life? Because swinging this thing feels real good and natural.*"

"*Let's find you something to swing at, then.*"

We eased down the corridor, stealthy as we could be. I had my pistols ready, lethal and nonlethal both. Carn peeked around the corner, then pulled back. "*They're in the hall here,*" he sent. "*Definitely Hellknights. They aren't hurrying, but they'll be here in a few seconds.*"

I buzzed with fear, but fear feels pretty similar to excitement, so I tried to convince myself I was experiencing that instead. "*Let's rise to meet them.*"

Carn rushed around the corner, and I followed, with Mel at my back. There they were, a couple of bulky armored humans filling the whole space between us and our exit. One of them wore a chest plate decorated with a star of red-tipped whips and had a heavy electroflail at his belt. The other's armor was decorated with a spiky wheel, and he wore a wickedly toothed grindblade at his hip. My pistols were meant to pacify and disable or, if necessary, kill; these two were carrying weapons that were designed to *hurt*.

The expressions I glimpsed through the open faceplates of their helms said they were surprised to see us, and I was tempted to try to bluff and banter my way past them... but these were zealots, and you can't charm a zealot. The best thing to do with a fanatic who wants you dead is to hit them as hard as you can as often as you can until they learn to look for other targets.

They reached for their weapons, both grinning savagely. "What have we here?" one said. "A rodent, a robot, and a... a... grasshopper."

I didn't have a chance to critique their insults, because Carn had his hammer up, and he suddenly roared and ran at them.

The knights squared up, weapons drawn—and then slowed down, looks of comical outrage on their faces as the air seemed to thicken around them. Carn was messing with their gravity, slowing them down, and I *would* have shot them in their faces with needles full of knockout juice, except the ysoki was in the way.

They weren't totally frozen, and they were moving faster than Valentine had when Carn froze *her*—either slowing down two people was harder than doing just one, or they were stronger and better at fighting the effects, or maybe it was just harder for Carn to concentrate on messing with gravity when he was also in the midst of a full-throated charge.

His efforts were sufficient, though. The knights weren't anywhere near fast enough to block the hammer blow Carn aimed at Spiky Wheel's chest. The knight skidded backward a couple of feet, but didn't go down, his armor absorbing the blow—that chest plate was probably more than just metal. The Hellknights looked low-tech, but they probably had all sorts of built-in systems for redistributing the force of impacts. The knight slowly lifted his grindblade, his face streaming with sweat from the effort, and then turned the weapon on, making the nasty spines and spikes start to churn and whir. That blade would chew through anything it touched.

Carn smashed the hammer down on the knight's gauntleted arm, knocking the sword to the floor, where it buzzed and gnawed at the carpet, bouncing around. Carn stepped back, away from the chattering sword, and his concentration must have lapsed, because the other knight leaped into motion and crashed into him, pinning Carn against the wall and trapping his hammer between them, where it couldn't do him any good.

I pointed my nonlethal pistol, adjusted a dial, and fired. A guided flechette looped around and struck the knight pinning Carn, right in his snarling face. He reeled backward, swatting at himself, then dropped to his knees, shaking his head. He *should* have been facedown and snoring instantly—they grow their zealots tough around these parts.

The other knight bent to retrieve his grindblade and brandished it with a snarl, heading for the ysoki. Carn increased the force of gravity on the knight again, grunting with the effort this time. The knight took a slow step forward, like he was walking into a stiff wind uphill through syrup, but the chattering tip of his blade got closer and closer to Carn's face.

Melezheun *flowed* around me to get between Carn and the knight, reached out with her hand, and pushed the blade of the grindblade aside. I gasped, expecting to see severed fingers go flying in all directions, but then I remembered her mindmail, which covered everything but her face, and a grindblade against that wouldn't do anything more than make her hand tingle.

Then she calmly drew her neutriad pistol and pressed it against the Hellknight's chest. That's when I knew she'd never used a weapon like that before. "Wait!" I shouted, but she pulled the trigger before I could stop her.

A neutriad pistol fires a pulse of pure, bludgeoning force. That pulse will hit a target up to fifty or sixty feet away and punch them straight backward, possibly right through any inconveniently placed walls. Force weapons are very good for clearing a crowd or knocking somebody down when you really don't want them to get up again anytime soon. The pistol has built-in inertial dampeners to reduce the recoil, of course... but when you put the muzzle right up against a few hundred pounds of overmuscled thug in armor and trigger it, point blank, those dampeners can only stifle the equal and opposite reaction so much.

Melezheun weighed about a third as much as the knight, so while he went flying back and hit the floor so hard he bounced, the recoil flung Mel straight backward at the same time.

Fortunately, she landed on something pretty soft. Unfortunately, that something soft was me. We lay there groaning on the ground for a moment, and then there was a loud thump as Carn made sure the knight didn't get up. Carn walked over to us, looked down, and said, "They're both out. This is probably a good time for us to go."

Melezheun's weight left me—Carn helped her stand up—and then I rolled over and got to my feet too, aching all over. "I am so sorry," Melezheun said, wincing and rubbing her neck. The mail had protected her, but it could only do so much. "I didn't know it would do that."

"My fault," I said. "I should have... given you... a small-arms... tutorial." I didn't think any of my essential body parts were broken, and my assorted contusions wouldn't kill me. "Let's get... out of..." I didn't finish, tired of hearing myself gasp, but instead just flapped a hand in the direction of *away*.

We made it out through the storage room and onto the grounds. There were Hellknights tromping in and out of the museum, carrying artifacts and heaping them on the ground, and one knight with his own big hammer was methodically smashing everything to bits.

"*Horrible,*" Melezheun sent, and I didn't disagree, but we'd done enough knight-fighting for one day. They were occupied in their acts of cultural destruction, so we crept along, and once we got to the shed and took the elevator down to the maintenance level, I locked the hatch, and then the system, so no one could follow us. At least not without smashing a hole in the floor and climbing down, but with luck, we hadn't left any trail for the knights to follow.

A slow, trudging, limping time later, we were back in the security office, dropping into chairs with a chorus of groans. "It's good to be home safe," Carn said, stowing his hammer back in his hovering mote.

I couldn't stop myself from loosing a derisive snort. "'Safe'? There are Hellknights next door. How long do you think it'll be until they decide to annex our corridor into their glorious empire?"

"We can hold out for a while, I think," Carn said. "And I say that as your head of security. Especially since we know they're coming. If we have to retreat behind our blast doors, we'll lose some real estate, but they aren't getting through those with any kind of ordnance that won't blow a hole right in the hull of the station. Eventually they'll find another way in—the maintenance tunnels maybe—but we can make sure they encounter some nasty surprises. It won't be quick, and they'll fight for every inch."

I nodded. "You're right, but they'll get through eventually; zealots don't quit until they run out of zealots. We need a *reason* to hold out. There's no point in buying time if you aren't going to do anything with that time." I took a deep breath, and then let it out. I didn't think Melezheun was going to like this. "We need to get a ship, take our people off Absalom Station, and find a place where everyone *doesn't* have magical amnesia. Because if things have broken down this much in two days, how much worse is it going to get here?"

"But... what about the Arcanamirium?" Melezheun said. "The shrine to Yaraesa? There might be something there, some key to the secret of Golarion and our collective amnesia."

I shrugged. "The truth won't do us any good if we're dead. We have to prioritize."

That gave her pause, and she nodded. I'd expected her to argue more and fight harder to investigate our clue. I wish I'd paid attention to how quickly she acceded, and that I had wondered more about why. Things might have turned out differently if I'd asked her more questions.

But I was focused on other things. We left the security office and went deeper into the complex, where our people were shifting furniture and playing dice and having conversations and quietly arguing, doing all the things normal people do even in a very abnormal situation, which was heartening, in a way. Back in Bric's bar, we found Dr. Bindi deep in consultation with Valentine and Starla. They all looked up at us alertly when we arrived, and Valentine said, "How did it go? Did you establish diplomatic ties or whatever?"

I pulled up a chair and joined them, Melezheun and Carn following suit. "Not exactly. You can't forge diplomatic agreements with Hellknights. A whole company of them took over the Lorespire Complex by force. I don't know if they're planning to set up a permanent presence there or if they'll leave once they finish wrecking everything. We overheard a couple of the knights talking, and they want to seize control of all the information on the station so they can make up a story about how they're the ones in charge here. Since they're supposed to uphold the law, ostensibly, it would be inconvenient for them to leave records disputing their version of reality lying around. They purged the data banks in the Lorespire, and I'm sure that's just the beginning."

"Do you think we're in danger here?" Valentine asked, twisting a bottle around and around in her hands.

"We are absolutely, one trillion percent in danger," I said. "How *much* danger, I don't know. I can't imagine our little suite of rooms has any kind of strategic value for the Hellknights, but also, I think they smash and subjugate anything they encounter, just on general principle." I steepled my fingers and put on my most convincing face. These three were influential in our tiny society, and if I got them on my side, others would follow. "Our immediate goal is to make ourselves seem too insignificant, or failing that, too much trouble, for the Hellknights to bother with. Our secondary goal is... I think we need to get out of here. Not out of the bar—off the station. If we can get a ship, we can take our people elsewhere. Maybe this amnesia is a local effect, and if so, we can get out of it and maybe even get our memories back. Wouldn't that be nice? If not, maybe we can find people who haven't been affected and get them to help us."

"That sounds pretty vague, as far as plans go," Bindi said. "It depends on a lot of uncertain things coming to pass."

"Uncertainty is the order of the day," I pointed out. "You want a certainty? I'm certain the station is descending into lawlessness, and while I like a little lawlessness as much as anyone, a *lot* of it is detrimental to the health and well-being of people like us." I decided it was time for a little unpleasant honesty. "We now have Hellknights for neighbors... and we had to hit a couple of them quite hard on our way back home, so they might be looking for us. I probably should have mentioned that earlier."

Starla groaned and covered her face, but Valentine just looked thoughtful. "A ship is a useful thing to have, you're right about that. Access to space travel gives us all kinds of options. We recently—"

I held up a hand. "Just a second, I want to run my ideas past you. We know a gang has seized the nearest port, but we might be able to trade with them—we have a lot of useful stuff here, especially with the clinic, since your chemprinter can synthesize drugs, doc."

"Until I run out of reagents," Bindi objected. "I've got a decent supply of universal polymer bases I can convert into various sorts of matter, so we should be fine when it comes to the basics, but rarer chems and medications require special ingredients, and those are in short supply."

That wasn't necessarily a problem, as I pointed out. "The port has the cargo ships, and some of *those* will have reagents in their holds, so there's a basis for trade already—those raw materials don't do the port gang any good, but we can turn them into useful items in exchange for things *we* need."

"What if they're more the hit-you-over-the-head-and-rob-you than the trade-with-you types?" Bindi asked.

That was a possibility I'd considered as well. "We've always got the maintenance tunnels. We own those in this sector, we rekeyed all the codes to our liking, and we locked everyone else out, unless they take a welding torch to the hatches. If need be, we can use the tunnels to infiltrate and try to steal a ship. That's dangerous, and we'd have to secure an unused dock or hangar to stash the ship, but—"

"Or we could just introduce you to the house sitter," Valentine said.

"The who?" I asked.

She rolled her eyes. "I was trying to tell you about it, but you wanted us to hear your plans first. They're great plans. Really top-notch. It just turns out they're totally unnecessary. Because my darling wife here"—she put her arm around Starla—"already had plans of her *own*."

13

THE HOUSE SITTER
(Tyrcell)

Starla had taken her made-up-on-the-spur-of-the-moment job seriously, and that very morning she'd created a "community outreach program." Basically, it was a squad of our more competent and imposing citizens, who expanded the reach of our society by... going out and knocking on doors and asking people if they wanted to join up.

At one end of our hallway was the entry to the Lorespire Complex, but the *other* end led to more residential and business areas, and Starla's emissaries had been visiting them, one corridor at a time. As a result, they got a few guns pointed at them, but the promise of food and medicine and the chance to join the safety of a group got plenty of positive responses too. The people who chose to go it alone were politely left to their own devices and told we'd do our best to keep marauding murder gangs from getting into the area, and, no, we didn't want anything from them in return, just please don't shoot at us, thanks.

Starla walked me through the new corridors of our domain, the blast doors open to encompass the newly integrated areas. They were mostly halls full of small apartments like Starla's own, but there was a neighborhood grocery depot and a hardware store too, and *those* were welcome additions. Most of the residents had their doors open, and everyone was talking to their neighbors—there was a sort of block-party atmosphere as people got to know one another... and to know themselves.

"How many people do we have in our, uh, sphere of influence now?" I asked.

Starla smiled and waved and called someone by name as she went by. I realized I'd made a good choice by impulsively putting her in charge of this program, and wasn't that just a testament to my natural leadership skills? "I haven't done a census yet," she said, "but at least a hundred, I'd guess."

I wondered how many Hellknights there were on this station and then realized numerical superiority didn't matter much, since most of my available troops weren't troops at all, just regular and confused people, while the knights were armed and armored and also took joy in murder. "You're doing great work here, Starla."

"You started it all," she said. "We're just continuing the precedent you set: Everyone is welcome, and everyone contributes whatever they can. So far we haven't encountered anyone who's actively hostile—a few people are afraid and hiding out and shouting at anyone who gets too close, but they'll come around. We're offering people a sense of stability, and that's what they want most. We even told them our leader was trying to figure out what happened to us and was off searching the Lorespire for clues."

"That is... broadly true," I said.

She took my arm and grinned at me. "Everyone thinks you're very brave and daring and busy and important. It weirdly helps that you haven't been around much, actually; it builds your mystique, you know?" She paused. "Plus, we can blame unpopular stuff on you."

"That's what a leader is good for," I said. "But you've really impressed me here. I'm *able* to run around being brave and daring because you and Valentine and the doc are looking after things so well."

We moved from apartment blocks into a narrow park, with artificial full-spectrum lights above and blue-tinged grass and shrubs on both sides of a meandering paved walkway. The space was dotted with benches configured for the comfort of various species. A contemplative, not Sue but another, was floating off to one side, watering some flowers, and Starla waved and greeted them. A couple of humans were kissing on a blanket on the grass next to a tiny mirror-smooth pond, completely oblivious to our presence. "People feel safe enough to make out in public?" I said. "We must be doing a good job."

"That's a sign of a healthy society, right there," Starla agreed.

We transitioned into a neighborhood where the apartments were larger and more widely spaced apart, and presumably more lavish, with lots of plants in large pots out front and ornamental flowering vines creeping up the walls. "We're getting closer to the outer hull," Starla said. "Some of these places have *actual* windows inside, not just vidscreens." There weren't as many wide-open doors there, but there were a few, and those people who were out and about waved as we passed.

Starla led me around a corner to an ornamental stone arch with force-field generators embedded inside it, currently turned off. "The security office had override codes, or we would have never gotten past this," Starla said. "Come meet the house sitter."

We walked under the arch and down an illuminated path lined with shrubs, which took several sharp turns. There were more force-field generators there, subtly embedded in the walls and floor. I had a knack for spotting them, it seemed. "Somebody around here likes their privacy. They must have been very important. Or widely despised."

"Maybe both," Starla said. "We may never know." We finally passed beneath another arch, this one made of twisted metal in a harshly angular design, to stand before a set of twelve-foot-high doors, intricately carved with thorns and vines. The walls on either side were blank gray metal, apart from a couple of softly glowing sconces illuminating the front steps.

"Is this real wood?" I caressed the doors, looking closely at the dark grain.

"I'm not a materials scientist, but I think so. Fancy, huh?"

"Very." I didn't think there was any actual wood anywhere in our whole complex—everything was metal or plastic or glass or some other artificial substance, occasionally made to look like something more organic. "So this is the house, huh?"

"A private residence for someone big and important, we figure. Two coming in," she said, and the door swung open, revealing an anteroom of muted tile and dark walls, with a crystal chandelier overhead. "I added us to the house security system," she said. "Otherwise, walking through these doors is a dangerous proposition. The mansion is full of nasty surprises and almost totally unhackable—our security office override codes don't work on the systems inside. I'm surprised they worked on the outer force fields, but I imagine station security insisted on that much for public-safety reasons."

"If the Hellknights do come, we could all fall back here," I mused. "It's like a castle keep—the people who live outside the walls can come inside when the invading army gets too close."

"That's a cheerful thought," she said. "But Valentine said exactly the same thing, so it's probably a good idea." She walked across the threshold. "Helio! Are you here?"

An aiuvarin (what some would call a half-elf) wearing a pale yellow silky robe slouched into the foyer, barefoot and sheepish. He was barely taller than me, but the pointed ears and slight frame revealed his ancestry. He looked young—it's hard to tell age with people who possess elvish heritage, but something about his expression and his eyes suggested he wasn't actually centuries old, but barely decades. "Hey, Starla, what's happening? Who's your friend?"

"Helio, this is Tyrcell, Tyrcell, this is Helio, the house sitter."

Helio's eyes widened. "Whoa, you're, like, them, right? The big boss person?"

"Not so big, and not so bossy. I'm just helping out where I can."

"Come on in and get a drink or whatever." Helio turned and padded out, and we followed him into the biggest open space I'd seen outside the Lorespire Complex. The mansion was a baffling combination of indoor and outdoor space. The ceiling must have been sixty feet above, arched and rounded and lit by shining spots, and there were half a dozen actual trees growing in the room. A stream flowed under a section of transparent flooring, and there were couches and chairs and tables set up at whimsical intervals alongside mossy boulders and shelves and plinths holding assorted objects of art. A spiral staircase led up to a floating platform suspended a mere thirty feet above us, which presumably allowed access to even more of the house.

Helio went to a bar that seemed to be made of a rough-hewn tree, except the surface was glossy and lacquered, and started mixing drinks. Starla and I sat down on hovering antigravity barstools—come on, that was just showing off—and exchanged a glance. "Nice place you have here, Helio," I said.

"I'm just the house sitter, like she said." He put a glass of some murky green liquid in front of me. "I admit, when I woke up, I was like, 'Whoa, I don't know who I am, but who I am is rich,' but then I found the binder."

I raised an eyebrow.

Helio reached under the bar and lifted out a slim black tablet with the words *The Binder* illuminated on the front. He tapped the screen, and a fan of holographic pages appeared, spreading across the length of the bar. "House rules," read one, above a numbered list that seemed to run to hundreds of entries, and others said, "Plant feeding and watering schedule," and "Bathroom cleaning procedure," and "Waste management protocols," and occasionally there were videos (muted, fortunately) of a stern-looking white-haired elf glaring and mouthing what I assumed were more instructions.

"See rule one?" He gestured. "'Helio will remember this is not his house; he is only the house sitter.' So that's me. I don't know who owns the place or where they went, but..."—he shrugged—"they probably don't know either, so I doubt they'll be coming back anytime soon to kick me out."

"We're doing more of a communal ownership thing anyway, just lately." I swiveled on my stool and looked around. We could fit a hundred people in just this one room, if it came to that, and even Hellknights would have trouble getting through all those force fields outside, let alone past the "nasty surprises" Starla had mentioned. We might even be able to set up an illusion or a hologram to hide the entry arch entirely. This was nice. "I assume you're OK with... joining our collective?"

Helio shrugged. "Starla said I could keep my room. It's just a little one behind the kitchen anyhow. The rest of it, it's not mine anyway, you know? I get lonely too; I can tell that about myself. I wouldn't mind some company."

I was tempted to claim the inevitably lavish master suite for myself, but it was better to stay in Bric's bar, where people could find me when I was around, anyway—I guess I wasn't the kind of leader who likes to live as far as possible from the people he's supposed to lead. "This place will really help us, Helio."

"It gets better," Starla said. "Helio, do you mind if I show Tyrcell the rest?"

"I'd say my house is your house, but it's not even my house, so go for it." He gestured with his glass, then wandered over to a chair set before the largest vidscreen I'd ever seen.

Starla took a taste of her drink, made a face, and pushed the glass aside. I sniffed mine, and it smelled bitter and astringent, so I decided not to bother with a taste. Helio doubtless had many talents, but it seemed tending bar wasn't one of them.

I figured we'd go up the stairs, but instead, Starla took me around the bar to a textured gray wall that shimmered open as we approached—some kind of holographic camouflage. *Ooh.* I was interested in anything rich people wanted to hide. We went down a wide hallway lined with paintings in frames—planetscapes, mostly, with a portrait or two of severe-looking elves, maybe just for variety—and then to a small elevator paneled in wood with brass railings. Once we got inside, Starla pushed a button marked with an *H*, and we descended.

"H," I said. "For... hot springs? Health spa? Or just heaven?"

"Hangar," she said as the doors opened and revealed just that—an immense private hangar that contained not one, not two, but three ships. There was a small needle-nosed pleasure craft that could fit maybe three people, all done up in gold and white; a medium-sized cruiser in burnished brass tones, like an oversized bumblebee; and a bulky, boxy, matte-black thing that filled about half the available space, but nevertheless seemed to deflect the eye—some kind of cargo ship or freighter with a stealthy vibe, which made me wonder exactly what kind of business had made our absent elves so rich. "Import/export" was probably what they *told* people. There were immense hangar doors, and also semipermeable force-field projectors, so the doors could open and let the ships in and out without venting any air in the process. This was a sweet setup, much faster and easier to use than the usual complexes of airlocks and docking tunnels.

"So now we have a castle, and a back door," Starla said. "Plus transport. I figure we can fit all of us in the cargo hold of that freighter, if all else fails, and the cruiser will hold overflow if our society grows. And if you want to do an exploratory trip, to look for help, that little three-person ship would do the job well, don't you think?"

I impulsively seized her and kissed the top of her head. "Starla. This is *amazing*. I wonder if I know how to pilot these things..."

I walked down the last steps to the floor of the hangar and circled around the smallest craft. "That's the *Harrowdown*," Starla said, "according to the service records I found, anyway. The medium cruiser is called the *Black Swan*."

"And the big one?"

"There are no service records for that one at all," Starla said. "I think they might have used it for smuggling."

"Then we can name it whatever we want. How about we call it *Starla*, in honor of the one who found her?"

"That could be confusing," Starla said, "since I'll probably be on board at some point. How about we call it the *Last Resort*, since that's what it is?"

"The naming rights are yours, so consider it done. Hmm. We should set up the communications and make sure we can talk to each other, and then Melezheun and I can take this ship out and try to get beyond the local amnesia field, if that's even what we're dealing with—"

Helio appeared in the doorway. "Hey, uh, that guy is on the vidscreen. The skeleton guy. He's saying some stuff." The house sitter shuffled off again, having imparted little in the way of actual information, but if it was important enough to rouse Helio into action, it was important enough for us to go take a look. Starla and I joined him back in the main room, where Zo! was indeed gazing out of the screen and speaking. Images of starships and planetary bodies and moons and space stations flickered across the graphic background behind him.

"My merry little relay drones have been swooping through space in every direction, making contact with any communications systems they can find," Zo! said. "Nearly every ship they've encountered has been happy to open their comms to us, letting us boost the signal even farther, and now we've got a broadcast net that extends from the robotic outposts of Aballon to the mining camps of the Diaspora, and the outer worlds will be along soon enough. But with this new reach comes grim news: this Gap in our memories extends at least system-wide. So far *everyone* your humble correspondent has contacted has suffered the same sort of memory loss, dashing our hopes that this was an isolated incident limited to Absalom Station and its environs."

The screen behind Zo! zoomed out to show a map of the solar system, planetary bodies pulsing. "For those of you who've set off on ships in search of sanity, sense, and safety, be advised... those are all in short supply. Whatever caused this mental breakdown, it's bigger than any of us, and even the gods must surely tremble in the face of such power... unless they're the ones who did it to us, of course. For now, this is Zo!, and before I sign off..." His face loomed closer to the camera, filling the screen, his eyes going from glowing to blazing. "I'd like to ask whoever down there on Absalom Station is trying, very amateurishly, to jam my transmissions? Please stop. Otherwise I'll be forced to triangulate your position and send some of my *other* drones to teach you a lesson about the importance of a free press." He stepped back and said, in a brighter tone, "More updates coming soon, including interviews with the denizens of assorted worlds and habitats, as part of our new series, *Minding the Gap*!"

The screen winked off.

"Well, Hell," I said. "So much for getting help from outside."

"That's always the way, dude," Helio said. "You've got to, like, help yourself." He heaved himself up out of a deeply cushioned armchair. "Speaking of, I'm gonna help myself to another drink."

14

THE GODS ARE AGAINST US

(Tyrcell)

I admit it—I was depressed by Zo!'s news, and I got a little drunk. I sat on the floor in my office, my back against the wall, and Melezheun sat beside me. We'd found intoxicants that suited our respective physiologies behind the bar, and we'd shut the door for a "high-level strategy conference," and we'd actually *both* gotten a little drunk.

OK, medium drunk.

"The thing is," I said, "what it is... the thing, I mean, what the thing is... is... there is no safe place. What's happening here is happening everywhere. Now, some of those other places have air just, floating around, and a lot more open space." I gestured vaguely. "Planets and moons and things, you know? Maybe those are saf*er*, but even those places, a lot of them have cities, and what Absalom Station is, is a city, and all the *cities* are going to be a mess. Yes?"

Melezheun just raised her glass in affirmation.

"So that means... what that means is, if nowhere is safe, we have to *make* a safe place. You see what I'm saying? This." I thumped the floor, which hurt my hand a little. "This place has to be our safe place. I thought we could flee to safety, run away, but we have to build our safety instead."

"What I've been thinking about," Melezheun said, "is gods."

I squinted at her; she was a little blurry for some reason. "Gods. What good have they ever done anybody?"

"I was more thinking, how many gods are there... do you think?"

"Uh, you've got your Iomedae, Sarenrae, that Yaraesa you like, Desna, Weydan, Abadar, of course, uh, Ibra, right, Pharasma... I don't know. I could come up with the names of twenty or thirty, if I included some of the scary ones that eat people or whatever. Why?"

"I think there are a lot more gods than that." Melezheun stared at the ceiling as if there might be stray gods lurking there. "Every species and culture and planet has its own gods, so there must be scores of them, maybe more. Maybe hundreds."

"So many? We'd be tripping over them, you'd think."

"Look." She gestured with her drink hand and spilled a little. "There are gods of cowardice and bad accidents and data and vengeance and the stars *and* the empty spaces between the stars. Gods just sort of... coalesce, don't they, like mist? Or they bloom like mold. Whenever there's an idea powerful enough to attract the right... energy... belief. Whatever. And new ones pop up every so often, like Yaraesa did, going from mortal to divine... but the gods don't die very often, and they don't usually retire, so there's just... more and more of them, as time goes on."

"Makes sense to me," I said. "But, well... most of the gods don't really impact anyone's lives. They barely even talk to their clerics. They keep to themselves, doing... goddish things."

She nodded, antennae bobbing. "Yes. But they are all, every one of them, more powerful than any mortal, and... if they ever worked together... think of the things they could accomplish. Amazing things. Terrible things." She slugged back her drink, which she'd named the Golarion Grasshopper, presumably because it was green and because Golarion was on her mind and maybe in small vengeance against what that Hellknight had called her.

I grunted. "It's a good thing the gods tend to feud and scheme and backstab each other instead of working together, then, isn't it? Maybe that's, like, a defense system the universe put in place, to keep the gods from causing too much mischief among us mortals. Or maybe it's just the fact that anyone who becomes a god must have an ego like a supermassive black hole."

"This thing that happened to us, though," Melezheun said. "This Gap. It was one thing when we thought it was just Absalom Station and the ships nearby. But if this hole in our memories, the alteration of records, the corruption of data, happened all at the same time, across the *whole system*... Who else could have done that *but* the gods?"

I frowned at the floor and at my drink and at her. "Yaraesa. Said that thing. About how all the other gods had forsaken us. Like. You think the gods worked *together*? To do this to us? And Yaraesa... objected? Or abstained?"

"Even if the gods didn't cause the Gap, they made some agreement not to *talk* about it," Melezheun said, spill-gesturing some more. "Because Zo! did that interview, and the cleric said the gods won't explain it. Either they *did* this to us, or they're colluding to cover it up because they can't *undo* it, and isn't that a terrifying idea?"

I thunked my head back against the wall. "Ugh. Thanks for that. But I can't worry about gods. I gotta focus, though, on the, you know. The immediate. Keeping these people safe. Keeping *us* safe. And that means continuing to expand and defend our borders and making alliances with powerful people. Absalom Station is a bunch of gangs and fiefdoms now, and we need to unite them where we can. Sue asked me again if we could go to the Arcanamirium, and I think we should." I put a hand on her shoulder. "You want to go, right? You can look for that shrine and see if Yaraesa wants to share whatever the other gods are hiding, maybe get some answers?"

"I am afraid of the answers," she said. "But... I suppose we must look."

I should have asked her more questions. I should have inquired more about the nature of her fears. If I had, then what happened in the Arcanamirium wouldn't have taken me so viciously and brutally by surprise.

But, in my defense, I was really very drunk.

—

I checked in with Valentine the following morning, once I was conscious and mostly rehydrated. She'd set up a rotation of trusted people to watch the monitors in the security office in case the Hellknights came pouring out of the Lorespire Complex in a horde, so we could drop our barriers and strategically retreat. She was in the swivel chair before the bank of screens herself when I arrived and asked for an update.

She shrugged. "It looks like the Order of Blissful Ignorance has moved on, after smashing things up and looting supplies and artifacts. The fire-suppression systems kept any of their burning from getting too out of hand. We've seen some survivors crawl out of hiding and start to reinforce their barricades. Maybe they even learned something from how their defenses failed last time. Starla is going to send a delegation to them later today, and assuming the archivists don't try to kill them on sight, we think they'll be pretty receptive to joining our cohort." Valentine sighed. "Not that they have much to contribute apart from hungry mouths at this point, with the Hellknights carrying off everything of value and smashing the rest."

"They've got space," I pointed out. "The complex is big, with lots of places for people to sleep and work and maybe even get a minute of silence to themselves. I bet they've also got an industrial-grade kitchen, so we can feed everyone without working out of three different restaurants." The house sitter's pantry had enough food in it for a small army to withstand a siege, and I made a mental note to ask Starla to inventory all of that, even though she was probably already doing it.

"True," Valentine said. "Every solution brings more problems, though. Carn is interviewing potential lieutenants—we've got more territory than he can oversee security for personally, especially since you keep dragging him away for your little side projects and field trips."

"Is that a hint of reproach I hear? Would you rather have me wandering around here all the time, making suggestions, butting in, second-guessing your judgments—you *are* the judicial system here at the moment, you realize—and making a nuisance of myself?"

She snorted. "If one of us has to get into gunfights with Hellknights, I'm glad it's you. This Melezheun of yours is really focused on getting answers to the big question, isn't she? Most of the people on this station are wondering where their next meal is coming from and if their neighbors are going to kill them, and you two are off trying to sort out the metaphysics of the situation."

"We figure either the gods did this to us, or they know something about whatever *did*. The gods could help us—they could intercede and smooth things over and ease our transition. But they aren't. Did you ever think maybe the chaos serves their interests? If we're all scrabbling around, focused on basic survival, we won't have time to ask big, uncomfortable questions. Well, me and Mel, we're *going* to ask those questions. Which reminds me, have you seen Soubrette's Last Elegant Algorithm? I'm organizing another field trip, this time to the Arcanamirium, and they wanted to go. I could use a native guide, anyway, even a mostly amnesiac one."

"Why do you want to go to the Arcanamirium?" Valentine asked.

I decided not to go into the whole "there might be a clue there hidden by a goddess," and instead just said, "You don't see the advantage in recruiting a bunch of technomancers to our cause?"

"Sure, but they're way the Hell over in the Eye, and that's *far* outside our territory. We've done pretty well the past couple of days with incremental expansion, and now you want to, what, establish a colony deep in what we can only assume is extremely hostile territory?"

"Not a colony," I said. "Consider us an envoy to another nation. We can create a strategic partnership with the technomancers, share knowledge, set up defensible trade corridors, stuff like that."

"You're probably going to get murdered just getting there," Valentine said.

I pressed a hand to my chest. "You don't have faith in your fearless leader?"

"Fearless is fine," she replied. "I'm more concerned about you being senseless."

"Trust me," I said, and she rolled her eyes, but she didn't actually laugh, which I took as a win. "Now, where can I find Sue?"

—

Sue was with Dr. Bindi in the clinic. She was reluctantly giving the contemplative a clean bill of health. "You've healed remarkably quickly," she said grudgingly.

"*Mind over matter,*" Sue said. "*We have more conscious control of our bodily systems than most biological organisms do.*" They swiveled toward me, body rotating beneath the huge head. Like a jellyfish swimming through a sea of air, I thought, and then wondered when I'd ever seen a jellyfish. Was there an aquarium someplace on this station? Probably.

"*Tyrcell,*" Sue said. "*We were going to come looking for you. We must reiterate—*"

"Your desire to get to the Arcanamirium? No need. I was coming to tell you I'm organizing an expedition, and I'd love to have you on board. It's probably going to be dangerous, though. It might be tricky to find a helmet that would fit you, but we should try..."

"*We have already made inquiries,*" Sue said. "*The... miscellany shop... had a small and broken force-field generator that we have repaired and adapted for our own use, as we do not wish to be clubbed over the head again.*" Sue rotated, showing off a small cylindrical pack strapped to their back. A moment later, a shimmering field enveloped their bulbous head and doll-sized body, just a haze in the air, and then it vanished. "*May we ask why you've decided to go to the Arcanamirium now?*"

I glanced at Bindi. I trusted her, but I wasn't sure I wanted word to get around about the message from Yaraesa. Fortunately, she brushed past me to go do something busy and important, giving me and Sue a moment alone. "We're hoping to open diplomatic relations with the technomancers—they'd be good allies to have—but also... we found something interesting in the Lorespire Complex. We think it's a message from the goddess Yaraesa."

"*The Lady of Wisdom?*" Sue said. "*Fascinating. What was the significance of this message?*"

"If we're interpreting it correctly, there's a shrine somewhere in the Arcanamirium, and within that shrine... some kind of clue about the cause of the Gap."

Sue bobbed in the air, drumming their small fingers against their thighs, and then said, "*Hmm. If anyone knows anything of substance about the subject, it is likely to be the gods. The implications of one god breaking from the others to share information with mortals... that's interesting. We assume you wish for our involvement to help you secure entry to the Arcanamirium?*"

"Also you're good company," I said.

Sue didn't laugh; not much of a laugher, that one. "*Would you be willing to let us join the greater mission as well? We feel we may have useful skills to offer in your quest for the truth.*"

"Sue, I would be *delighted* to have you on board." I meant it. Courage, resilience, and a great big brain were all major assets.

"*We are pleased.*" I got the sense that, from Sue, that was the equivalent of ecstatic enthusiasm. "*When will we depart?*"

"Give me an hour to get things together," I said, and Sue hovered out of the clinic. I went into the outer office and found Bindi inventorying the contents of a cabinet, a vicious scowl on her face. "Could you put together a little first aid kit for me?" I asked. "Medpacks, medkits, sprayflesh, stimulants, anything that can keep us going in the field, in case we encounter trouble?"

"I can do that. I can also task one of these to accompany you." She gestured—she was wearing some kind of fancy high-tech glove with glowing fingertips—and a hand-sized, buzzing drone, opalescent and gleaming, emerged from a cabinet and bobbed over toward me. "It's got a medical subroutine and even a surgical suite, but we're talking stitches and emergency amputations here, nothing advanced."

"That's fantastic! How many of these do you have?"

"A handful," she said. "But I've got a couple of engineers retrofitting general-purpose drones for medical purposes. Do you know, with all the expansions, we still haven't found a single other medical professional? A ratio of one doctor to two hundred patients isn't ideal, especially when my patients are so many different species, but these drones can help with less serious cases."

"We've got two hundred people now?" I was stunned. "That's, like, double what I thought."

Bindi nodded. "Starla just finished a census. We found an emergency shelter late last night—early this morning, really—that had about fifty people hiding out inside, most of them children." She sighed. "I don't even *do* pediatrics. My specialty is neurosurgery! Which was useful for helping Sue, but otherwise, I'm refreshing my memory out of medical textbooks, half of which have random swaths of data corruption." She put her hand on my shoulder and looked me in the eye, android to android. "Tyrcell, while you're out gallivanting around the station, try to find me some more doctors, would you?"

"I'll add it to the list. Thanks, doc." I went to look for Carn, the medical drone hovering at my shoulder. "Uh, do you... talk?" I asked it.

"I have a basic conversational suite suitable for voice-activated commands, but I am not sapient, or even sentient," the drone said.

"I can also activate Bedside Manner mode if you wish to be told everything will be all right, even when things will obviously not be all right."

"Sure, do that," I said. "There's nothing wrong with keeping up morale."

I found Carn in the bar—sitting at a table, to my horror, with the enormous dragonkin and dromaar who had beaten up Melezheun. I unclipped my pistols and sidled over, trying to get a clear line of fire that wouldn't risk injuring Carn.

The dragonkin saw me and groaned and buried his head in his hands. The dromaar looked at me and winced. "OK!" she said. "We're supposed to say we're really sorry and we won't ever do it again and we were just confused and *please* let us join you!"

Carn turned in his chair and gestured to me. "These two came in and asked for a security job. Melezheun saw them, turned on her armor, ran over, and started punching them, which, fortunately, didn't do too much damage. She seemed to forget she had a big gun strapped to her belt, so that was lucky. Anyway, I got the three of them all settled down, and we had what you'd call a conflict-resolution seminar. These two expressed their regrets for their bad behavior, and Mel read their minds and said they were actually sincere and then said 'fine' and stomped off. So..." Carn shrugged and turned back to our new recruits. "I dunno, though, I mean, you two like to beat people up, but that's not what the security job *is*, mostly; it's more keeping the peace."

I took my hands off my guns. "How about we start you off in the kitchens," I said. "There's always lots of work to be done in those. If that goes smoothly, we'll see about transferring you into something more... fighty... later on."

The dragonkin didn't look up, just nodded, and the dromaar patted him on the shoulder. "We just... we woke up, and our minds were all messed up, so we thought somebody must have *done* it to us, but now we know it's happening everywhere, so it probably wasn't anyone here. It must have been the gods or something."

"Can we punch the gods?" the dragonkin said, voice muffled from inside his hands.

"If the gods disrupt the operations of the kitchens, you have my permission," I said. "Why don't you go look for a woman called Starla and tell her you're going to help out, and she'll tell you where to go and get you settled and—"

"Actually, go see Skettlehelm," Carn said, and then he proceeded to describe someone I'd never heard of in a place I didn't know about. The de-escalated duo went off to follow his instructions, and I took one of their seats.

"What's a Skettlehelm?"

"Starla's new second-in-command. He's handling the job assignments since she's more focused on the community outreach. We've got too many people to run everything ourselves anymore. We gotta *delegate*."

"I could have sworn I was the leader here," I said. "I didn't ask for the job, but I took it, and I don't know when it... got away from me." I didn't think I sounded annoyed. I don't think I *was* annoyed. I was mostly bemused.

"You delegated to *us*," Carn pointed out. "Which is good leadership. So are we going to the Arcanamirium?"

"If you can be spared from your duties here."

He shrugged. "I'm good at delegating too, it turns out. Maybe I used to be a middle manager. Probably not, from all the grease under my fingernails, but you never know. Anyway, I've got some good people watching the doors and all. When do we leave?"

"Soon," I said. "Let me go talk to Mel."

—

"I'm proud of you for forgiving those two idiots," I said when I found her sitting behind the counter in the junk shop, soldering something to something else.

"I was so furious I forgot I had a gun, or I would have killed them," she said, not looking up from her work.

I leaned on the counter. "Well. Nevertheless." I paused, but that seemed to be the end of that topic. "So. Are you ready to go to the Arcanamirium and decipher the mysteries of the universe?"

She put down the soldering iron carefully and nodded, still not meeting my eyes. "I suppose someone must."

"Better us than the Hellknights," I said. I know I didn't *actually* jinx us merely by mentioning the Hellknights, but later, in the midst of all the violence, I must admit, I wondered if I had.

15

THE CONDUCTORS
(Tyrcell)

"We have to hit the Arcanamirium next," Astrachios said, slamming a mailed fist down on the scarred metal table. Mikiel regarded him calmly from the other side.

(Tyrcell here. I should confess I'm making up some of the details for this part, but it's all pretty plausible, and I can attest to the outcomes.)

"Storming the Lorespire by force was one thing," Mikiel said. "We did not expect particularly strong resistance there, nor did we encounter any—apart from the ambush in the administrative offices, and both those men will recover."

"The cowards," Astrachios fumed, and at Mikiel's frown said, "I mean the ambushers, not the knights, of course. I was right there in that same corridor, just a little bit earlier. I must have walked right past wherever those vermin were hiding."

Mikiel stroked his mustache thoughtfully. "Cowards? Vermin? Whoever they were, they defeated two members of our order, which suggests they are rather formidable, even considering the element of surprise." He consulted a tablet on the desk. "A ysoki, a lashunta, and an android. I have descriptions here, and we'll definitely be making inquiries. Still, having two of our people out of commission while they heal is a higher cost than I wanted to pay for the mission."

"We achieved our goal to control the information there," Astrachios countered. "And we also seized valuable supplies. I still think we should have left a force in the Lorespire to keep the archivists in check. They could have been valuable puppets, lending the weight of their authority as historians to any pronouncements we chose to make—"

"The citadel of the Order of the Nail was breached and looted by raiders while you were off on your little mission," Mikiel said. "It took the remainder of our forces to drive them back. We can't spare personnel for babysitting duty." He reached across the table and put one gauntleted hand atop Astrachios's. "You succeeded: There's nothing in the Lorespire archives to dispute our claim as rightful rulers of Absalom Station. Be content with that. Your devil friend Rakhiel has drafted protocols that say the Hellknights may be petitioned by any concerned citizen to assume command of Absalom Station for the duration of any emergency. She is inserting the new articles into the corrupted station infosphere, and soon we'll arrange for some third party to discover them and petition us for help. Once we have a binding agreement in place with a representative of the citizens of the station..." Mikiel smiled. "We *love* binding agreements. Your idea was sound. You did well."

Astrachios nodded, pleased despite himself at the praise, but then his relentless mind returned to its earlier track. "That Arcanamirium is a major threat to our agenda, sir. You *know* the technomancers are trying to find a way to reverse this amnesia."

"I don't doubt it," Mikiel said. "I'm not averse to getting my memory back, personally. I'll grant you, the current chaos offers us many opportunities to seize and consolidate power, but I still mourn what I have lost and hope to regain my past."

Astrachios couldn't very well argue with that, not without confessing the reason why he didn't want *anyone* to remember the past. "Then let me take control of the Arcanamirium and the scholars there, and we'll have them restore *our* memories, and no one else's. That will leave the remaining population of the station in a more... suggestible state. Plus, there may be records in the academy that dispute the narrative we're creating. Wizards are great ones for writing everything down."

Mikiel smoothed his mustache again; it was a nervous habit, but at this rate, he'd rub it right off his face. "There is some sense in what you say. The wizards and technomancers in the Arcanamirium could make trouble for us if we give them time to organize. They're egotists, as a rule, focused on their personal projects, which means they're likely still in disarray, thus vulnerable." He came to a conclusion. "Very well. Once Rakhiel is finished drafting her articles, you may take her and two other knights with you—any men of your choice."

"Only four of us? Sir, we can't possibly take over the Arcanamirium with such a small force!"

"I'm not sure we could conquer that organization with any force we could muster, Astrachios, at least not without unacceptable losses. Take your squad to the Arcanamirium and claim authority over the Eye. Tell them you've come to return stability to the region. They won't accept your authority or your protection, but you can probably manage to meet their leaders, and while you're there, you can gather *information*. Take note of their resources and defenses to help us plan a more decisive strike at a later date. But step carefully. Technomancers are an arrogant and intractable sort—they bristle under the yoke of control and resent lawful authorities like ours." He sighed. "I wish I could remember ever actually *meeting* one of them, but I know what I say is true."

"I won't let you down, sir." Astrachios rose. A force of four Hellknights against the might of the Arcanamirium? He didn't relish their chances in a fight, but they could probably do some damage along the way.

—

"A force of four people against an unknown number of highly skilled technomancers and wizards, on their own home territory?" Carn said. "I don't really like our chances in a fight."

"It's a good thing we aren't fighting," I answered. We were walking through a maintenance tunnel, occasionally ducking underneath dangling loops of conduit and squeezing past protuberant pipes, making our way around the perimeter of the Eye. The Arcanamirium was, naturally, way on the other side of the great domed space, and the idea was we'd circle around in the maintenance tunnels until we got close. If everything went well, we'd be able to make it all the way to the Arcanamirium before doing any traveling on the surface, where the roving gangs were roving around. (Spoiler: Everything didn't go well.) "'We're ambassadors hoping to form a strategic partnership,' and 'Oh, hey, our lashunta friend really wants to do some praying. Is there by chance a shrine to Yaraesa around here?' It should all go smoothly."

"That's what you said about the Lorespire," Melezheun pointed out.

"Be fair, Mel. Who could have predicted Hellknights?"

"*It is likewise difficult to predict what our fellow technomancers will do,*" Sue mused, hovering along, shimmering in force armor. I was wearing ballistic plate under my clothes, Mel had her mindmail, and Carn was pretty much a walking tank in plates of black carbon-fiber stuff with powered leg armor, his black mote hammer resting on his shoulder. It turned out that junk shop had all kinds of treasures hidden in the back room; we suspected the unassuming owner had supplied local criminals, though he denied all knowledge. (Not that he'd remember his criminal behavior anyway.) I had to admit, Carn in particular didn't *look* like a peaceful envoy, but the rest of us were more subtle, and ambassadors were allowed to have bodyguards, right?

Sue went on. "*We hope the inhabitants of the Arcanamirium will be willing to talk to us, at least, before taking any aggressive action to repel us. Scholars enjoy talking, and because our storehouse of spells is often limited, we prefer to hold them in reserve until we absolutely must use them.*"

"See?" I said. "No fight, all talk. It's going to be great."

(Spoiler: It wasn't great.)

We reached a sealed door with an access panel beside it, and I blithely entered my security override... It didn't work, just buzzed at me and flashed red. "Uh," I said, with my customary eloquence in the face of obstacles.

"I think we've moved beyond our section of the security grid," Carn said. "The maps in the office were corrupted, but from what I could tell, we just had codes for the Lorespire Complex, and the surrounding residential area. We must be in a different sector, with different security measures."

"No problem. Maintenance guys are predictable." Trying the default passcodes had worked before, right? I tried all the administrative codes, then all the easy-to-remember common codes, and then the panel flashed red twice and locked me out of further attempts for an unknown period. "Well. They're usually predictable." I pressed my head against the metal hatch blocking our progress, then turned to Carn. "Can you smash this down?"

He stuck a finger in his ear, then shook his head. "This isn't like the walls between the shops. Those were cheap and thin, built to partition up a larger space into smaller properties. This is more like our blast doors. Solid, airtight, strong, meant to seal off sectors in case of emergency—floods of solvents, poisonous gases, that sort of thing. I could maybe put a dent in it, but I can't put a hole in it, not on any kind of timescale that's useful to us anyhow."

"Then we route around the damage," I declared. "We'll backtrack to the last ladder we saw—it's not far—and then go to the surface until we find *another* maintenance hatch we can open or smash and drop back down into the tunnels. Right?"

Everybody shrugged, even Sue. They did not seem inspired by my plan. In fairness, neither was I. But it was *a* plan.

We returned to the nearest ladder and clustered at the base while I pulled up a map on the gauntlet on my wrist. My schematics were downloaded from the security office, and bits of them were pixelated, and other bits were blurred, but they were better than nothing.

"I think we're here." I pointed. "The closest major landmark is Bluerise Tower. That's... headquarters for various corporations, right?" The information was hazy in my mind, either because of the amnesia or because whatever kind of life I'd lived before didn't have much connection to corporate matters. The whole waking-up-hungover-underneath-a-table-in-a-bar thing pointed toward the latter.

"*Yes,*" Sue said. "*It is still quite some distance from the Arcanamirium, however.*"

"We knew it was going to be a long walk. Let's go topside. It's a corporate district, and corporate types shouldn't be a problem, right? They wear nice clothes and look at spreadsheets and make calls all day. Way more harmless than technomancers."

More shrugs. Nobody applauded my insight. A lesser android might have found the lack of enthusiasm in his troops demoralizing, but fortunately, I'm immune to things like insecurity and self-doubt. I went up the ladder, opened the hatch (my codes still worked on those), and poked my head out, ready for trouble.

Trouble was not apparent. I'd emerged into a wide corridor with a high, curved glass ceiling, half the panels showing pretty blue skies with drifting white clouds, the other half showing... Zo!, who was running down some hallway, camera drones bouncing and making the image jump around. He was gesturing and saying something, but there was no audio on the screens, and it's hard to read the lips of someone who doesn't have any lips. He'd clearly left his ship and entered the station, though. I wondered why.

The screens showing Zo! glitched and then started displaying blue and white too, but those panels weren't synced up with the rest, so instead of a seamless illusion of sky, the clouds drifted and then fragmented or disappeared and reappeared elsewhere, like they'd been in a teleportation accident. The overall effect was disconcerting, but then, what wasn't lately? The corridor was tiled, clean, gleaming, lined with potted plants, and was clearly a conduit meant to funnel large numbers of people from one place to another. Those large numbers of people weren't in evidence, so I called "All clear" down the hatch, and the others joined me.

I took the lead, with Carn covering our rear, Melezheun and Sue between us. The corridor curved gently around... and dead-ended at a heavily barred metal gate, with a bunch of people in power armor holding plasma weapons on the other side. The armor was blazoned with logos that presumably indicated their corporate affiliations, but none of them meant much to me.

"Stop right there!" an amplified, distorted voice called as several of the corporate goons stepped forward and poked the muzzles of their weapons through the gate. The fact that there weren't scorch marks on the walls or corpses piled on the tile gave me hope that we could talk our way out of this situation. We all stopped, as ordered, and Carn moved to the front, shielding Sue and Mel with his armored body.

"Hello!" I called. "We're a delegation from Lorespire district, hoping to make connection with other communities for purposes of mutual—"

"Get out of here, freeloading scum," the amplified voice called. "We don't need *takers* in here. Everyone in the Bluerise district pulls their own weight."

"Ah. No, we're not freeloading scum, as you say, but a duly

authorized ambassadorial delegation from another community, interested in mutual—"

"Did you say you're from the Lorespire?" another voice, somehow even harsher and more distorted, said. "What, you mean like... books?" The distortion didn't hide the contempt.

"Lore in all its... various forms... but it's the whole district. We've got restaurants, residential areas..." I trailed off before I said "a doctor" and "spaceships" and other things that heavily armed corporate security forces might wish to take for themselves.

"Oh, they've got *restaurants*," the leader said, and I got to hear how a lot of hulks in power armor sound when they all laugh at once through their voice changers. They probably altered their voices and wore full-face helmets because they were jerks all the time, and if people knew who they were under their armor, they'd get drinks thrown in their faces whenever they were off duty. "We've got the whole *Bluerise Complex*, you losers. We've got restaurants too and world-class chefs and an *armory* and..." Someone whispered, and the leader trailed off, presumably having been reminded about the importance of operational security. He then concluded with: "We've got loads better stuff than you've got, and we're better able to protect it, and we're not big on sharing around here. Now beat it, before we put a bunch of holes in you." He paused. "Praise Abadar."

None of that seemed like the opening of a negotiation, nor did it appear to require a response, so we just backed away down the corridor until the curve hid us from their sight and firing lines. "Now what?" I asked.

"Perhaps we should go back home and reconsider our approach?" Melezheun said. "We can try to find something we can use to bribe the guards. They're capitalists, after all. Or we can attempt to find more complete schematics that will reveal an alternate approach."

"*That may not be necessary,*" Sue said. "*May we see the map?*" I obliged, and Sue pointed. "*We think, logically, this must be the location of a transit hub. People come to work in the Bluerise district, and they must come from other residential areas. Surely there is a maglev or a tram or* something *to facilitate their commutes.*" They gestured at the tiled floor and elegant glass ceiling. "*This certainly looks like the transit corridor for a high-end district, don't you think?*"

"That makes so much sense, Sue! Thank you." I considered the map. "So if we just backtrack and then keep going..."

We backtracked and then kept going, following the tiled corridor in the other direction, and eventually found an elegant sign that said Bluerise Station in a variety of languages. There was a metal gate across that archway too, but instead of a horde of armed guards, there was one ysoki man sitting on a stool, wearing grease-streaked coveralls and puffing on a vaporizer that curled out sweet smoke. A bloody bandage was wrapped around most of his head. He held a nasty-looking gun that bristled with exposed gears, but he didn't so much point it at us as gesture vaguely in our direction to make sure we saw it.

"Harya," he said.

"We're doing well," I said carefully. "We're trying to get to the Arcanamirium."

"Yuh." He took a long puff, then said, "We go there." Then he puffed again and stared at us. I wondered if he was smoking something psychoactive, or if his head injury had addled him, or if he was just... like this.

"Can... we... go there?" I asked.

"What have you got to trade." His voice was flat, no inflection of inquiry, just like he said the same phrase a thousand times a day, though the station hardly seemed to be bustling.

"Oh, we've got credsticks—"

"Don't need credsticks. Don't need transit passes either, or stamps or coupons or lottery tickets or passes to see a magic show. None of that means anything anymore anyhow. What have you got to *trade*? Food. Ammunition. Medicine. Tech."

"It looks like you got a nasty bump on the head," I said.

He nodded. "Somebody got in through a maintenance tunnel, tried to hop a tram without paying. We all got into a scrap." The ysoki smirked. "Now he's biomass in the reclamation vats."

That was ominous, especially delivered so matter-of-factly. "Well, we've got a medical drone. We could use that to fix you up."

He perked up. "Let us have the drone, and we'll give you an all-month pass: free movement anywhere our lines run, which is most places, and more to come."

I shook my head. "That's tempting, but we might need it. We'll treat your injury in exchange for a trip to the Arcanamirium and back, though?"

"Nah." He was pouting. "For that, you can buy a one-way trip."

I was still learning about myself, but I knew I was the type to worry about the *immediate* problem and trust that I'd be able to find a solution for future problems when the time came. "It's a deal."

He nodded, not very graciously. "You can keep your weapons, but keep 'em holstered." He eyed Carn's big hammer until Carn turned it back into a floating mote. "You're under surveillance, so don't try nothin' funny when you're in here."

The ysoki guard had some compatriots lurking back in the station, it turned out, and they came forward to keep an eye on us while the medical drone extended tiny arms to unwrap the ysoki's bandage, then did things with needles and sprays to treat the nasty gash across his forehead. Once the people on the other side of the gate were satisfied that we'd done as promised, they opened a small door and ushered us inside. I noted some nasty countermeasures embedded in the wall around the gate and was glad we hadn't tried to force our way in.

The ysoki returned to his stool, not much more cheerful despite having his wound treated, and a middle-aged human in greasy coveralls gestured for us to join her.

"Where you from?" she asked as she led us through the dimly lit station, a white-tiled space full of echoes and shadows. About two-thirds of the lights were out. Power failure? Or conservation? Or was it just easier to hide their security people that way?

"The Lorespire neighborhood," I said.

She grunted. "We haven't expanded our lines to Lorespire Station yet—there's a mess on the tracks from a collision when the automated systems went down. We're working on clearing it, though. Give us a few days. What are you doing way over here in Bluerise?"

"We're trying to make contact with other groups. Like your people." This seemed like a good bunch to know.

"We're the conductors," she said. "Transit workers, we think, and passengers who were on the trams and pods when this Gap thing happened. That was in the wee hours for most people, though, so nearly all workers. Enough of us remembered how to run things that we were able to lock down the platforms and take control of the vehicles and the tunnels. It turns out most of the stations are meant to be used as shelters in case of emergency or an attack on the station, so they're easy to defend. We don't have much in the way of supplies, though, just a couple of dining cars and a few food stalls, but it's real easy for us to trade. We offer safe passage to fully two-thirds of Absalom Station." She paused. "Of course, once you reach your destination and leave the concourse, the whole 'safe' part goes out the window, and you're on your own."

"What have you heard about the Arcanamirium?" I asked. "Safety-wise?"

"It's a shit show," she said shortly. "The Eye, it's all open space, you know? Beautiful, I hear, that great big dome, Jatembe Park, gorgeous architecture, sculptures, all that. It's impossible to compartmentalize, though; it's too sprawling, so it's almost impossible to defend. The major structures are all sealed up. You know: the Swordlight Cathedral, the Arcanamirium, the Hamisfore Theatorium, the Bastion. So your religious types, your wizard types, your theater types, and your station-security types, they're all holed up, worried one of the other groups is going to make a play. The Bastion actually *did* try to take over the whole Eye yesterday, but the clerics and wizards scorched their butts and sent them scuttling back into their fortress. Guns are only so good against people who can turn you inside out by praying about it real hard, you know?"

"So we're likely to get turned inside out as soon as we leave the station?" I asked.

She chuckled, though I didn't think my question was that funny. "Not from what I've heard, no. Like I said, the main structures are sealed up. The park itself is sort of a neutral zone, though. People wander around in there. I'm not saying nobody gets attacked, but they don't get attacked in an *organized* way. It's muggers, not soldiers. Delegations from the four groups—well, three, nobody wants to talk to the Bastion people anymore after their attempted hostile takeover—hold meetings at this big gazebo and talk about forming a central government, but... I mean... it's only three days since the world ended, so I don't expect things to get rebuilt real soon."

"You seem very well informed," Melezheun said.

Our conductor grinned, showing off a gap where she'd lost a tooth, probably recently. "One of the things we accept in trade is information. That is, if they don't have food, ammunition, medicine, or tech to offer. We'd rather have that stuff, but if you've got juicy gossip, we'll let you ride a stop or two, sure. You're lucky I'm giving away all this information for free, but I can't help it, I'm a talker."

"Perhaps we could talk longer?" Mel said. "I don't know about the rest of you, but I could use a rest."

I was surprised Mel wanted to wait. She'd had such zeal for discovering Yaraesa's secret before. What had changed? Before I could ask, the conductor shook her head.

"We don't like to have outsiders cluttering up the concourse," she said. "No offense, but we like to see you all move along promptly."

We descended an escalator (which wasn't running, so just stairs) and reached a platform next to a silver lozenge of a tram car. Our conductor thumped the side of the vehicle, and a door opened, revealing a couple of armed guards who greeted us in a relatively friendly way. We all tromped inside, settled into seats, and waved goodbye.

The door slid shut, and a smoothly mellifluous voice spoke from an overhead speaker. "Next stop: Arcanamirium Station."

We settled back to enjoy the ride. It was the last thing we enjoyed for a while.

16

LINES OF CONVERGENCE

(Tyrcell)

"We have to do something about this undead meddler." Astrachios glared at a vidscreen on the wall of the shop they'd just broken into. The shopkeeper had refused to recognize their authority, so they'd beaten him up until he handed over the food and water they'd demanded. Mere threats might have been enough to make him comply, Astrachios thought, but the knights he'd brought with him, Wilhum and Storg, needed to beat someone up a few times a day, or they got restless. The shopkeeper's failure to *immediately* do as he was told provided a useful excuse to let them off the leash a bit. He'd selected them because they were reliable blunt instruments... and because they weren't curious or smart enough to ever figure out his secret.

"Oh?" Rakhiel was spinning a rack of sunglasses, occasionally plucking off a pair to try on. None of them really suited her, mostly because she didn't have a proper nose. As a sigveir devil, she was roughly humanoid, tall and lean, her skin a dark greenish gray, but her face was dominated by four curved tusks surrounding a long, elephantine snout that trailed halfway down her chest, oozing dribbles of dark slime. In lieu of bulky armor, she wore a black, slick-looking jacket reinforced with hidden armor plates; at least that served to hide the bony spikes on her back.

"Listen to this!" He found the volume control on the screen and pumped it up.

Zo! was jogging down a corridor, trailed by hovering cameras. "—just had a run-in with a pair of Hellknights who claimed they were the defenders of the station, and when I asked on whose authority, they said, 'The law,' and when I said, 'Which law, exactly,' they said they were taking me into custody, but we can't have *that*! There's nothing more crucial to the health of a society than the free press, so my drones tased them, and I ran away—"

Astrachios turned the volume back down. "You see? He flouts our authority, assaults our brethren—"

"And sistren, and neitherren," Rakhiel murmured.

He ignored her. "Plus, he's... he's out there *telling* people things, with no regard for how people will react to the information! He has technology that allows him to hijack broadcasts all over the station, to infiltrate the infosphere... it's unacceptable. He needs to be stopped."

"So we'll stop him. I've got an arrest warrant drawn up, and a writ of summary execution too, whichever seems more useful." She patted her jacket, then turned toward him, wearing a pair of bulbous mirrored sunglasses that reflected Astrachios's own hard, frowning face back at him. "I think we should keep the necrovite in custody, personally, instead of killing him. And not just because killing his kind is a daunting proposition. Zo! has already developed a reputation on the station as someone who tells the truth, no matter the consequences... so wouldn't it be nice if we could coerce him into telling *our* version of the truth?"

"That's a good idea," Astrachios admitted. "You're good at this."

"Why, thank you." She pressed a hand modestly to her narrow chest. "You know, I've been thinking about a name for our would-be, could-be new order. How about"—She paused dramatically—"The Order of the Penumbra."

He frowned. "What in Hell is a penumbra?"

Rakhiel sighed. "That's the problem. It's like a shadow... a special kind of shadow... in astronomy... it's the perfect name, really, for an order that suppresses information, but if nobody knows what the word means, it's not too effective."

"It's no scourge or nail or pyre or chain," Astrachios agreed. "And Order of the Shadow sounds like a group of amateur assassins. But you might be on the right track. Something astronomical. Hmm. We'll keep thinking about it."

Storg and Wilhum emerged from the back, where they'd dragged the shopkeeper for his formal reprimand. They were both a little bloody, but blood looked good on Hellknight armor. Storg's left eye, which had been lost at some point and replaced by a multifaceted glowing red lens, pulsed steadily, like a heartbeat.

"Go now?" Storg asked with his customary eloquence.

"Go now," Astrachios agreed.

They set off toward the Eye, stalking two by two down trash-strewn corridors through a business district where the shops were alternately looted or barricaded. There'd been some kind of riot there, clearly—there was a corpse lying face-down to the side of the corridor and scorch marks on the walls—but the violence had moved on or burned itself out. The mess made Astrachios sick for reasons it took him a moment to understand. When he did, he grimly suppressed the thought, but it was still there: This reminded him of the blood and signs of violence on his awakening. That disorder lived in his *mind*, and he must root it out. If he could create order on the station, would it help him impose order on himself too?

The comms in his helmet buzzed, and Mikiel's voice said, "Astrachios. We received an... interesting communication at the citadel earlier today. It claims a small group of citizens have discovered a clue to the cause of this mass amnesia, left by the goddess Yaraesa, and they are en route to the Arcanamirium to track down further information. I think it would be in our interests to find this god-given secret first, don't you?"

"Yes, of course," Astrachios said. The pulse of his thudding heart was beating in his ears. One of the *gods* was meddling in his affairs too? He would find her secret and destroy it.

"Find it, and secure it," Mikiel said, in a twisted echo of his own thoughts. "I know we benefit from keeping the population of the station in ignorance, but I don't much like ignorance myself, so I'm curious to find out what it says."

"What's the source of this information?" Astrachios asked.

"The sender was anonymous. We're trying to track down the provenance, but so far all we know is the tip came from one of the station security offices—they have a distinctive encryption signature—but we haven't narrowed it down any further. We may have allies among the station's law enforcement personnel. Wouldn't that be nice? I don't know how reliable the information is, but since you're going to the Arcanamirium anyway, you should check it out. Be on the lookout for an agender android, a male ysoki, a female lashunta, and one of those bulbous-brained contemplatives. The information they seek is hidden in a shrine to Yaraesa, somewhere in the Arcanamirium."

"An android, a ysoki, and a lashunta?" Astrachios said. "That sounds like the group that assaulted our brothers in the Lorespire Complex." The contemplative was new. Maybe the ambushed knights hadn't seen that one floating in the background.

"Yes, thank you, I did notice that," Mikiel said. "If you find them, it's worth bringing them in for questioning too, don't you think? Particularly sharp questioning, I fancy. Oh, and Rakhiel, I wanted to let you know that our plan is going smoothly. We've already been petitioned by several terrified citizens, all begging us to impose martial law and restore order, as outlined in the documents you uploaded to the infosphere. We'll create some official documents proclaiming our authority and begin to expand our territory. Be sure to tell the technomancers they're under our care now. They won't agree, but it's important to lay the groundwork for prosecuting them for noncompliance later."

After Mikiel signed off, Rakhiel chuckled. "Because I have tremendous foresight, I already created a few documents along those lines." She reached into her jacket and fanned out a handful of laminated pages. "These give us full authority under the Emergency Stabilization Act to seize what we need and require cooperation from the citizens."

"Let me see those." Rakhiel handed one of the documents over, and Astrachios admired her handiwork. The writ included holographic details, official seals bristling with spines, and lots of elegant cursive. The document positively *radiated* authority.

So did a morningstar with blood dripping from the head, of course, but intimidating people with documents was so much faster and less messy. "Let's go claim some new jurisdiction, shall we?" Astrachios said.

—

I didn't realize how swiftly the ovoid pod of the tram car was moving until it began to rapidly decelerate, and we all swayed, except

Sue, who just hovered. Mel and I were seated, but Carn stood holding on to an overhead strap and chatting with the guards. Maybe I should have made him head of community outreach. He was comfortable talking to anyone, maybe because he treated everyone as an equal who probably had something interesting to say.

"Arcanamirium Station," the overhead voice trilled as we slowed to a stop, and the doors slid open.

"Thanks for the ride." I rose, and the conductor guards nodded at me as we disembarked.

Bluerise Station had been gleaming and austere, but Arcanamirium Station was far more elaborate—the platform was like a subterranean grotto, with fake stonework that looked like cave walls and fountains that mimicked waterfalls and still pools. There were benches that blended into the rock, and the lights overhead weren't glaring bars of white light but a thousand dots of softly winking imitation stars.

"Pretty," Carn said.

"Show-offs," I said.

A local conductor, this one a human dressed in pale yellow robes and bearing a staff, rose from one of the benches and smiled at us. "Welcome to Arcanamirium Station, offering easy access to the gardens and all the other wonders of the Eye."

"You don't look like a transit worker," Melezheun observed.

"I suspect I was just a passenger," the conductor said. "I remember that my name is Scarsifal the Wise, so I was probably a member of the Arcanamirium in my past life, but the conductors are the ones who fed me and protected me, and so I am pleased to join their ranks."

"We're headed to the Arcanamirium ourselves," I said. "I don't suppose you remember anything about the place that might be useful?"

"See the tall building between the cathedral and the theater?" Scarsifal said. "Probably full of technomancers and wizards. That's the sum total of my recollection. The amnesia hit me rather hard. I like to think it's because I had so much wisdom to forget." He frowned. "Unless 'the Wise' was an ironic name? There's an enormous orc down here named Tiny, after all. I hope it wasn't something like that. I'd love to think I at least possess the capacity for wisdom.

Well, come along. I'll take you to the exit." Scarsifal led the way, metal-shod staff banging on the faux-stone floor with every step. We climbed up another dead escalator to the station concourse, which was less ostentatiously decorated than the platform, and our conductor led us past more friendly-enough guards to another heavy metal gate.

Scarsifal peered through the bars at the low tunnel beyond, then unlocked a small door and ushered us through. "Go straight ahead and up the stairs, and you'll emerge right across a path from the Arcanamirium. Watch out for... socially maladjusted types roaming the gardens. We thank you for your patronage and hope you'll keep us in mind for all your transportation needs." He clanged the door shut, gave us a last wave, and went away.

We got back into our ready-to-be-ambushed formation and proceeded along the dim tunnel. Half the lights were off, with broken glass scattered on the floor from their shattering. The peace and stability of the conductors didn't appear to extend out from the concourse. We tried to avoid walking on the glass and making noise as we sidled along, up a short set of stairs, through an exit covered by a curving shade structure of opaque glass, and then...

We were in the Eye. I just stood and stared, stunned and awestruck. I *must* have been to this place before—I was a resident of Absalom Station, and surely *everyone* went there at some point. But I couldn't remember, and the experience of standing beneath that dome struck me with the force of a revelation.

How had the engineers even constructed a dome so vast? It stretched overhead, so high there were clouds forming up there. This part of the station had its own weather. Light poured down from illuminated bars on the dome's struts and mimicked true sunshine, and the gardens thrived beneath that glow. There must have been acres of them. From where I stood, I could see ornamental hedges and stands of fruit trees and riotous blossoms of flowers, with neatly tended paths winding through them all. Here and there I spied hints of sculptures, gleaming metal shapes tucked away amid the foliage, and ornamental structures: gazebos, pergolas, and arching footbridges over burbling streams. There were shining spires off to the right, gold-capped minarets and bell towers, which must belong to the Swordlight Cathedral, but blended perfectly with the natural majesty. The garden of the Eye was an oasis of peace and life, and I found myself hunching my shoulders in anticipation of that peace being shattered by small-arms fire or explosions or screams.

But I only heard birdsong. There were *birds*. Or maybe a sound system, but I chose to believe the former.

"This is real nice," Carn said in one of his habitual understatements, gazing around with his hammer once again resting on his shoulder. Melezheun stood with her eyes closed and her face tilted up to the light, absorbing its warmth.

Sue, though, only had eyes for the Arcanamirium, just across a wide boulevard from the station exit. The contemplative floated, gazing at the structure, murmuring something I couldn't quite catch, but it was enough to get our attention and make *all* of us look.

The finest university of magic on Absalom Station—and in the whole solar system, for all I knew—was an imposing sight. It wasn't just one building, which I should have anticipated—the campus was behind a set of ornamental metal fences and took up several blocks. The whole was surrounded by an imposing fence of some oily-looking black metal that shimmered with a nacreous rainbow where the light reflected just right. There were numerous buildings arrayed beyond, with paths twisting among them, and hints of more parks and gardens. There was a central structure, though—the "tall building" that Scarsifal had mentioned. The tower rose to a height that must have rivaled Bluerise Tower, but this wasn't practical corporate architecture. This structure was a work of art, festooned with decorative arches, twinkling stained-glass windows, flying buttresses (How did I know what *those* were?), and spires that spiraled like animal horns. The overall impression was that of a wedding cake for a marriage of the gods of death.

"That's a big gate," Carn noted. The black shimmering fence did have a set of main gates, closed at this time, and as we approached, glowing red lines appeared on the metal in swooping circles and lines that made my eyes water.

"*Agh*, what is that?" I averted my gaze.

"*Mmm, a magical glyph that wards and protects,*" Sue said. "*It is meant to deny entry to those who don't belong.*"

"That's bad luck for us, then," I murmured. "I've been to a lot of places since I woke up on the floor of the bar, and I've never seen one where I more obviously did not belong."

"What would happen if I smashed the gates down with my hammer?" Carn asked.

"*Hmm,*" Sue said. "*These particular wards... they would disintegrate you before you struck the first blow.*"

"Like... turn me to dust?" The ysoki blinked rapidly.

"*There might be a little dust left,*" Sue allowed. "*But it would probably be more of a... greasy ash.*"

"There's probably a service entrance or something we can try instead," Carn said.

"That would be all sealed up," I said.

"Maybe there are more tunnels?" Melezheun said. "We've had good luck with those."

"We're a delegation," I complained. "We just need to *talk* to someone. Shouldn't there at least be a bell we can ring?"

"I'm sure they know we're here," Melezheun said. "They're wizards. Perhaps you could just shout?"

"Shouting would attract muggers," Carn pointed out.

While we were discussing our options, Sue drifted closer to the gate. "Be careful there," I called. "We don't want *you* turned into greasy ash!"

"*We have... we wonder...*" The contemplative lifted one of their small hands, and something glittered there. I zoomed in my vision—realizing for the first time that I *could* zoom in my vision; at least one of my eyes was more mechanical than bio—and saw a miniature signet ring on their tiny finger.

"What have you got there, Sue?" I unzoomed my vision and moved closer but kept one eye on the gate in case it should—I don't know what. Lunge at me? Who knows what technomancers can get their gates to do?

"*We have this ring, and it is etched with a glyph as well, but we were unsure what its purpose was—we could sense it possessed magic, but we could not determine its nature or purpose. Now we think...*" Sue shifted forward, lifted the ring, and pressed it against the gate.

I winced and half turned away, prepared for a flash and sizzle and the aforementioned greasy ash... but instead, the gate split in the middle, and the two halves swung inward ponderously. "*Come close to us,*" Sue said, and we crowded around, almost jostling that great brain. They floated, and we walked, like a single four-headed creature. I could feel the magic of the gate doors on either side of me, like an electrical field making my teeth buzz. Once we were clear, the gates swung shut with a sharp and sudden clang behind us.

And then, we were in. Or at least partway in. The steps leading up to the main building were gray stone smoothed by the passage of who knows how many wizardly feet over who knows how many years. I wondered how old Absalom Station was—decades, centuries, millennia? Looking at this building, I could imagine it was the last.

We moved cautiously, still as one, toward the immense front doors. They were carved with an image of a figure in robes, holding a staff, whom I assumed was some god or another, in the midst of vanquishing a hideous tentacled abomination.

A small door off to one side of that epic portal opened, and a figure in a black robe hurried out: a lashunta, shorter and even more slight than Melezheun, looking around like a rodent on the watch for swooping birds of prey. "More prodigals returning?" the lashunta said. "What, *all* of you are residents here? What are your names?"

"*We are the only member of the academy present,*" Sue said. "*Our name is Soubrette's Last Elegant Algorithm.*"

The lashunta gestured, and a shimmering blue oval appeared in the air before her. She flicked her fingers, and white letters appeared on the blue, scrolling past. "Yes, here you are... a lecturer in the evocative arts. And... the glyph of entry recorded by the gate matches your identity, and you look like your picture, more or less." She smiled briefly, there and gone. "Good enough. Many of our records were mysteriously corrupted by the Gap, but we found a course catalog for the current quarter, so we have *some* idea who's supposed to be here." The lashunta narrowed her eyes. "Who are your... friends?" The shimmering oval vanished, and she put her hands inside her sleeves. I wondered what kind of weapons she had in there and if *they* would turn us all into greasy ash. Or all of us except Sue, anyway.

The contemplative drifted forward, between us and the lashunta. "*They are our companions and protectors. Tyrcell is the leader of a community near the Lorespire Complex, and these are their close associates, Melezheun and Carn. They escorted us, to ensure our safety, and hope to make a diplomatic association with the Arcanamirium. We agreed to lend the weight of our voice to their entreaty.*"

"In exchange for their protection?" she demanded.

"*Not at all. Our recommendation is sincere.*"

"Hmm. You're sure you aren't here under duress or otherwise coerced?"

Sue bobbed gently in the air. "*We are not. These people saved our life when doing so gained them nothing. They have earned our gratitude and our trust.*"

The lashunta reached into her robe and lifted out an amulet that pulsed a gentle white light. "You're telling the truth, and no one else has control of your mind. Very well."

The carving of a god on the door suddenly bulged outward and twisted, and then it wasn't a carving anymore, but a real bearded human wizard holding an equally real staff. "Welcome to the Arcanamirium!" he boomed jovially. "I am Hathor, the warden of the door, and this is Belezeth, our lorekeeper."

"Not that I have much lore to keep these days," Belezeth muttered, tucking her lie-detecting amulet back in her sleeve. I was glad Sue hadn't told any untruths about our mission; they'd just selectively left out certain elements of the truth, namely our interest in the shrine of Yaraesa. If the wizards found out about the secret hidden there, they might decide they were the only ones qualified to find it.

"Should I take them to the headmistress?" Belezeth asked Hathor.

He yawned and stretched and shook his head. "She's off having another meeting with the head cleric of the cathedral and the impresario of the theater about forming a unified autonomous zone. But when she comes back, I'm sure she'd be interested. We haven't had any diplomatic delegations from beyond the Eye yet! We assumed it was all lawless chaos out there, honestly. That fellow Zo! had a devil of a time making it here from the dock. He seemed to be fleeing one gang or another every five minutes the whole way."

Zo! was in the Arcanamirium? "We're doing our best to give people a place of safety," I said. "An alliance with your community would definitely help with that."

"Well, of course," Hathor said cheerfully. "We're wise and powerful. It's hard to see what use we'd get out of the arrangement, but then, I'm not a diplomat, am I? I'd better step back into my illusion. Belezeth will remind you where your rooms are, Lecturer Algorithm. You can await the summons of the headmistress there. I don't imagine it will take more than a few hours."

As we approached the door, Carn paused and pointed at the carving of a tentacled, many-eyed monster. "Is that art, or a real thing, just hidden like you were?"

Hathor winked. "We wouldn't be very good wizards if we went around telling all our secrets, would we?" He stepped toward the door and seemed to meld into the wood, becoming a carving with his staff upraised again.

Belezeth gestured us through the smaller door. As we followed her, Melezheun spoke up in my mind. "*Should I ask if they have a shrine to Yaraesa on the premises?*"

"*Might as well,*" I thought back. "*Just keep it subtle, and don't tell her why we're curious.*" We stepped into an anteroom with a vaulted ceiling that seemed nearly as high as the dome of the Eye, with glowing orbs of illumination bobbing at random intervals above, reflecting off a polished white floor etched with black glyphs of the non-flesh-annihilating variety. (Or maybe they could annihilate flesh, and just weren't doing so at the moment.)

"Lorekeeper," Melezheun said. "I wonder, is there a shrine to Yaraesa somewhere on the premises? I wish to give thanks for our safe arrival."

Belezeth glanced back at us. "I doubt Yaraesa had much to do with your survival, sister. The gods are never much use to us at the best of times, and these are the worst of times. But yes, I think there's a shrine in the Zernebeth Memorial Technic Library on sublevel delta. I'll task a servitor drone to escort you later if you like. Be sure the lecturer joins you, though—we can't have outsiders wandering the grounds unattended. Not in these dire times."

"*Can it be so easy?*" Melezheun sent to me.

I thought a groan at her. "*Why did you have to say that?*"

17

THE ARCANAMIRIUM
(Tyrcell)

"Nothing's ever easy," Astrachios complained as Rakhiel rifled through the dead wizard's clothes and snuffled at his corpse with her trunk. "He must have a ring or an amulet or something on him!"

"He's got half a dozen rings and amulets, it's just that none of them are the one we're looking for." The devil opened the wizard's mouth and peered inside it like he might have had an amulet hidden there. They knew the Arcanamirium was shut tight and only opening the gates to accredited students and staff at this time, all of whom possessed a magical passkey, though the *shape* of that key could vary, from jewelry to a book to, even, a literal key.

"He doesn't—ha." She tore open his robe, her fingernails sharp as knives, and tapped his scrawny chest. "He's got the entry glyph tattooed on his body, right over his heart!"

Astrachios looked down and wrinkled his nose. Lines and spirals were etched in red on the dead man's pale skin. "Well, peel it off, I guess. We're not lugging his whole corpse around with us." He turned and stalked off to see how the other knights were doing.

The wizard, who'd claimed his name was Scarsifal the Wise, had tried to cast some spell on them after the Hellknights had arrived and tossed the corpses of the guards off the tram car. Astrachios had been ready with his rifle, though, and putting a beam of energy through the man's eye at a mere hundred yards was effortless. The fight had gone out of the other conductors at that point, but Wilhum and Storg were being extra menacing to make sure they stayed compliant.

Wilhum was explaining to the surviving conductors that they were under the protection of the Consolidated Order of the Brotherhoods of Absalom Station (which was Mikiel's unwieldy name for their efforts to bring stability to the habitat).

"You have no *authority* here!" one of them bellowed.

"I have guns," Wilhum said. "Guns are authority."

Astrachios stepped in. "Please forgive my associate's bluntness. It's been a trying journey." He reached into his breastplate and drew out a much-folded laminated document. "As you can see here, we are duly appointed agents of the provisional authority, here to impose martial law, requisition necessary supplies, and compel cooperation in our efforts to restore order. Absalom Station is in terrible shape, as I'm sure you've noticed. We're going to make everything calm and clean and nice again."

"Who put you in charge?" the same pugnacious conductor demanded. "Just because you have some document doesn't mean anything!"

"We were petitioned by a coalition of concerned citizens stationwide," Astrachios said. It was true too. Several groups had formally requested the assistance of the Hellknights after Rakhiel's documents were disseminated into the infosphere. Some of them had even requested help *without* a Hellknight putting a boot on their necks first. "Chaos is a temporary aberration. Order *will* be restored, and we're going to see to it."

The conductor opened his mouth again, but Astrachios held up a hand. That was about as much patience as he could force himself to exhibit. "If you have further objections, you can address them to the barrel of Brother Wilhum's gun, all right?" That quieted them down.

Astrachios nudged a fallen ysoki conductor with his boot, and the woman groaned. Still alive. Good. "Don't kill any more of them, if you can help it," he said to his knights. "We don't know how to run this station, and control of the transportation network will be a great help to the Consolidated Order."

"Ha," the ysoki at his feet said, turning over and spitting out blood. "We triggered the alarm when you arrived, you idiots. This station is sealed off, and the other conductors will just route traffic around us. You haven't seized control of anything. You just killed a node in the network. What a waste. We were doing *good*."

The temerity! "You aren't doing *me* any good," Astrachios replied. He considered letting Storg loose on them, but they weren't there for wanton killing. Only necessary killing, or ideally, *strategic* killing.

"But you are citizens under the protection of my order, and we'll take care of you anyway. Storg, find a storage room or something to lock them in."

He stalked off, fuming, to rejoin Rakhiel.

—

(Poor Scarsifal. We heard about what happened to him from one of the conductors who survived the Hellknight assault by hiding out in the tunnels; he even showed me the security footage, so that last bit is one of my rare depictions of Astrachios that didn't require any guesswork from me, though I am making assumptions about his pissed off and impatient emotional state. I never knew Astrachios *not* to be pissed off and impatient, though, so it's a safe bet. He was a bit more eloquent, at moments, than I usually give him credit for. You can see how he ended up running his own order, sort of. But we'll get to that.)

We were halfway down a corridor that seemed to stretch for miles when Belezeth got a call on her communications device or telepathic diadem or whatever she had and sighed. "I have to leave you, but hold on, I'll summon a servitor." She reached into her robes and twiddled around, and then something came scuttling down a wall from a vent I hadn't noticed before—a silver orb about the size of a human head, scurrying along on a dozen multijointed limbs and waving a few more that were tipped with what looked like shards of crystal. A single lens set in the upper hemisphere of the orb pulsed a gentle green. Belezeth said, "This is Unit MRDBL9781601256607, a voice-activated semiautonomous servitor drone. It will take you to your rooms and any other authorized areas in the Arcanamirium campus. Fare you well." Belezeth rushed off back the way we'd come.

I looked at the silver orb, and it looked back, still clinging to the wall, between two animated portraits of stern and scowling headmasters. "M-R-D-, what?"

"Murderball," Carn said.

"I don't like *that*," Melezheun said. "Let's call it Mr. Double instead."

"Informal designation Mr. Double applied," the orb said in a fluting alto voice. "How may I be of service?"

"*Please show us to our rooms,*" Sue said.

"Right away, Lecturer." Mr. Double scuttled down the wall to the floor and set off, leading us down the corridor, through a door on the right, down another rather more narrow passageway, up a spiral staircase, and finally into a drafty set of unadorned halls lined with more doors. Some of them were open, revealing wizards reading or staring into space or sobbing into their cupped hands. I wondered what was happening behind the *closed* doors.

Mr. Double directed us to a suite at the end of the hall, and Sue drifted inside. The rooms there were not very impressive, though I lived in the back office of a bar, so who was I to judge? There was no bed, no desk, and no chairs, but that made sense, as contemplatives mostly just floated around. There were screens on the walls, though, and input devices, and a cabinet full of doll-sized clothes. "Let me know if I can assist you further," Mr. Double said and then crawled up the wall, onto the ceiling, and pulled in its many limbs, its green lens going dark. It looked like a security camera or a broken light fixture.

"This is cozy," I said, "but should we go see if we can find the shrine?"

"Of course," Melezheun said. "But didn't Hathor say something about Zo! being here in the Arcanamirium?"

I nodded. "Were you hoping to get his autograph or something?"

Melezheun sighed. "No, but he seems to have a great deal of information, and I wonder why he came. Do you think he's following clues, like we are, to find out the cause of the Gap? Maybe that file about Yaraesa wasn't the only clue pointing to the Arcanamirium? If we can talk to Zo!, perhaps he'll be able to add some greater context?"

"Maybe he's broadcasting," Carn said, activating one of the vidscreens on the wall.

After a bit of scrolling, he located a broadcast channel that showed Zo! sitting at a large wooden table across from a technomancer. I thought the wizard was an elf, but it was hard to tell, because his head and most of his face was covered by a complex metal helmet decorated with spinning gears and sparking antennae. "—is my Mental Acuity Enhancement Device for Arcane Explication," the maybe-elf said.

"How *interesting*," Zo!'s voice dripped sincerity, and his eyes were ablaze with pale fire. A few camera drones hovered around in the background, ready to provide different angles. The interview was taking place in some kind of study, the walls lined with shelves stuffed with books and crystals. "Tell me, Professor Angleterre, how does your new invention work?"

"Magic," the professor said, or rather sneered. "Melded with technology, of course."

"Elegant in its simplicity," Zo! declared. "Tell me, what is the purpose of your creation?"

"It's right there in the *name*, necrovite! The helmet stimulates the electrochemical processes of the brain, allowing for intuitive leaps, rapid cogitation, and precise memory retrieval! Once I activate this device, it will correct whatever damage has been done to me by the Gap, as you call it, and restore my mind to its former glory."

"It's not active now? The little wheels are spinning—" Zo! made a twirling motion with his finger.

"It's warming up," Angleterre snapped. "Now. Prepare to witness the restoration of a great age—" He reached up and flipped a toggle.

I looked away from the screen, wincing, at the result, and I wasn't the only one. Carn managed to turn the volume down, which made the screaming less distressing. When I peeked back at the screen, Zo! was wrenching the half-melted, sparking wreckage of the helmet from the professor's head and holding it up to a camera, while a drone zipped in and sprayed fire suppressant foam on Angleterre's burning hair.

Carn bumped the volume back up. Zo! said, "—will continue my investigation here in the Arcanamirium, where the finest minds of the system are working *diligently* on the problem. Next up, we'll visit a shrine of Yaraesa and entreat her aid. Maybe the Lady of Wisdom is feeling more talkative than the *other* gods lately."

Melezheun stared. "He's going to the shrine?"

"We may as well meet him there, then," I said. "It'll give you a chance to talk to him, maybe, Mel."

I looked at Sue, who said, "*Mr. Double? Would you please escort us to the shrine of Yaraesa?*"

The murderball on the ceiling pulsed green and said, "Right away, Lecturer."

—

Astrachios and company emerged from the same station in the Eye that we had, but they were a lot better armed. They tromped right up to the Arcanamirium gate, and Rakhiel brandished the tattooed square of skin they'd flayed off Scarsifal.

The glyphs glowed, and the gates swung open. Astrachios laughed. "The most powerful magic users on the station, and it's this easy to get through their wards?"

"I wouldn't count on this being their only line of defense," Rakhiel said. "But it's a good start." She folded the skin swatch up and stuffed it inside her jacket, then drew a pistol.

"Storg, you take point," Astrachios said, and the hulking knight walked through the gate, head swiveling. Wilhum followed him, then Astrachios, with Rakhiel taking up the rear. They paused at the bottom of an imposing set of steps that led to an elaborately carved set of doors. (I'm not going to describe all that again; we were just there.)

"There's something funny about that door," Storg rumbled. He wasn't much of a talker, so Astrachios listened when he did.

"Funny how?" he asked.

Storg tapped his temple beside his left eye. "This eye of mine, it does this and that. Detects magic. There's magic all over this place, a-course, but there's an illusion on that door. It's hiding something. Can't see what. Good illusion."

"Remind me, Rakhiel," Astrachios said. "Are illusions generally grenade-proof?"

"My memory has been giving me trouble," Rakhiel said. "But not that I recall, no."

"Perhaps you should cast a counterspell, then, Wilhum."

The big man—the other big man—looked at him blankly, then scratched at his beard. "What?"

Astrachios tried not to sigh. Not everyone was built for banter. Wilhum was made for other things. "I want you to blow a great big hole in that door," Astrachios said.

Wilhum brightened at that and swung the heavy grenade launcher off his shoulder into the ready position. Astrachios didn't favor that sort of weapon, preferring the precision of his own sniper rifle, something even the most elegant and sophisticated grenades couldn't match, but there were times when you simply needed to make an impact. Wilhum muttered to himself and fiddled with dials; his launcher apparently sported a variety of munitions. "Concussion, no. Cryo, nah. Screamer, ha! Barbed shrapnel, best not..."

"Are you members of the academy?" a voice called down from the stairs, and Astrachios looked up to see a lashunta woman in robes peering down at them from the top step.

Rakhiel put her hand on Wilhum's arm and gave Astrachios a significant look. "Hold, there," he said, taking a step forward. "Whom am I addressing?" he called.

"I'm the lorekeeper here," the lashunta said. "Are you on the faculty? You don't *look* like you're on the faculty."

"We're representatives of the Consolidated Order of the Brotherhoods of Absalom Station," Astrachios said. "We have been charged with bringing order to our habitat in the wake of the... recent unpleasantness."

"Charged? By whom?"

"By the masses yearning for peace and stability," Astrachios said. "We've come to help secure the Arcanamirium—"

The lashunta mage consulted a glowing oval. "The gates say you're... Scarsifal the Wise, our minister of logistics, but you aren't. How did you get his glyph of entry?"

"We borrowed it," Rakhiel said. "He fully supports our mission."

"I'm going to have to ask you to leave," the lorekeeper said firmly. "The Arcanamirium is fully independent and autonomous."

"If we could speak to someone with a bit more authority?" Astrachios said. "If you'll just look over our documents—"

"I don't care about your *documents*. You zealots aren't welcome here! Depart immediately or you will be removed!" She reached into her sleeves.

"Ah, the limits of diplomacy," Astrachios murmured, and then gestured to Wilhum.

The knight grunted and raised his grenade launcher, and the lorekeeper shrieked and turned to run. The immense wooden doors shimmered, and a staff-wielding figure started to step out of the wood—but it was too late for all that.

Wilhum's grenade launcher coughed and lobbed three orbs through the air in quick succession. The grenades followed slightly different trajectories, and each one hit their target with a splat and adhered—sticky bombs of some sort, then. One of them stuck to the chest of the man who'd emerged from the illusory door, and he shouted and scrabbled at himself, trying to peel the projectile off...

But not for long. The grenades detonated, sending wreckage flying, with bits of wood and wetter things scattered halfway down the steps.

Wilhum looked at Astrachios and raised one hairy eyebrow. "Well done," Astrachios said. "Secure the entryway."

Storg and Wilhum rushed up the steps, kicking bits of dead wizard and broken door out of the way, and Astrachios and Rakhiel followed. "Reconnaissance, wasn't it?" the propaganda devil said. "Go in, meet with the leaders here, and take stock of the situation? I'm sure that was in the briefing somewhere."

"Reconnaissance is the *priority*," Astrachios corrected. "But how are we supposed to reconnoiter anything if we can't even get inside? I made a command decision in the moment. Besides, they refused to recognize our authority, and that's treason."

"I might have charmed us in," the devil pointed out. "I can be very charming, assuming I don't have to overcome any prejudice against my people, and wizards are generally an open-minded bunch."

"We might have use for your charms later," Astrachios conceded. "But I thought it was a good idea to let Wilhum and Storg have a little fun so they don't get all bottled up and erupt into violence at an inopportune moment later when we're negotiating with an archmage or something."

"Very forward-thinking and farsighted," Rakhiel said. "I'm going to stand behind you mostly, though, while we're in here, so if some wizard decides to turn our bones to jelly, you can be my meat-shield."

"A leader is comfortable in the front," Astrachios said. They entered the foyer, which was only a little scorched. Wilhum and Storg dragged the lashunta back, dangling between them, as she gasped in pain with every step.

"She tried to do magic," Storg said. "Broke her fingers. She stopped."

Astrachios looked at the clutches of randomly jutting sticks at the ends of her hands and winced with involuntary sympathy. "I see." He reached out and touched the lashunta under the chin, making her jerk her head sideways. "You're the lorekeeper. I have a question about your lore. Where is the shrine of Yaraesa?"

She blinked at him, her agonies briefly forgotten. "Why is everyone so interested in *that* place today?"

—

The journey wasn't very long, and the destination was more pleasant than I'd anticipated. "Sublevel delta" had sounded pretty remote and, frankly, dungeony to me, but the nice thing about having wizards around is they like to keep things looking fancy so they can show off how rich and smart they are.

Mr. Double escorted us along a few airy hallways lit by floating motes of light, down a spiraling ramp that shimmered like an oil-slick rainbow, and finally deposited us before a set of open glass doors with the words Zernebeth Memorial Technic Library glowing in silver above, cycling through various languages, including—if I read the whiff right—one that was pheromone-based.

"There are over one... one... over one libraries in the Arcanamirium," Mr. Double said. "Apologies. I have encountered bit rot in my guidance system. There are libraries. This is one. The shrine to Yaraesa is behind the curtain in the rear."

We stepped through the doors (well, Sue floated). The ceiling was impressively vaulted, and the floor gleamed, made of some kind of black metal shot through with ribbons of silver, but it wasn't a very *big* library. There were three long tables set at haphazard-seeming angles, inset with terminals and surrounded by scuffed chairs. And to the sides were half a dozen small cubbies, with single chairs in front of them, for those who preferred a less communal approach to study. The numerous shelves held the things you'd expect—scrolls, books, data drives, crystals—along with several odd bits of broken machinery, all strange curves and angles, and sealed jars of fluids in nauseating colors. More junk shop than library, those last parts.

I paused beside a pedestal by the door, with a model of a metal hand displayed inside a glass cube. The appendage was humanlike, except for a second thumb; I could see how that might come in handy. (Ha! I can help myself, but I don't want to.) I wiggled my fingers. Maybe I should upgrade. I looked at the plaque and saw this wasn't a model, but the *actual* hand of a person called Zernebeth, who was once the leader of something called the Technic League. They were "an early and influential innovator in the melding of magic with technology." Good for them. I wondered if they'd lost the hand before they died or after.

"Shrine's back here," Carn said, and I nodded and headed toward the back of the library. Melezheun was lingering by the shelves, picking up the peculiar objects and turning them over before putting them down again. I was a bit surprised she wasn't racing to the shrine. I got the sense she'd cooled on the whole endeavor, but I wasn't sure why.

"It looks like we got here before Zo!" I said. "Unless he's come and gone already, but assuming that broadcast was live, I doubt it. We can hang around until he shows if you like? See if he knows anything we don't?"

Mel gave me a weak smile. I sorely wished that I could dip into *her* thoughts. "I suppose we should look at the shrine," she said.

"That is what we came for," I said.

"I'm just... afraid of what we might find, Tyrcell." She hugged herself and looked down. "The gods worked together to hide something from us—*all* the gods. What if it is something that truly needs to be hidden? Or what if... what if they do something even worse than the Gap to make sure their secret *stays* secret?"

"I don't make it a policy to go around doing whatever the gods say," I replied. "For one thing, there are so many gods saying so many different things, you can't possibly please them all anyway. And we know this *one* god, Yaraesa, values wisdom and inquiry above all other things, right? She left that message for someone to find and follow. We're the ones who found it. I'd say we probably have at least one god who is *on* our side. Besides, we started pulling this thread, and I can't see us stopping until we get to the end. It's too important. We can't let fear make all our decisions for us, or we'll never do anything at all."

She closed her eyes, then slumped and sighed. "Tyrcell, I have made a—"

"Oh, hello."

I recognized the voice and whipped around to see Zo! standing there, big as life (or big as undeath, anyway), surrounded by hovering camera drones. "You're Zo!" I said, displaying my trademark perception *and* suavity.

"I am! And who might *you* be? You don't look like studious young technomancers. That's a compliment, by the way." One of his glowing eyes briefly dimmed. Was he *winking* at me?

I'd seen the cameras, but now I really *noticed* them. Was I being vidcast? Was I showing up on thousands of screens all over the station, as we spoke? I found myself grinning. "I'm, ah, the name's, uh, Tyrcell, and this, this lovely, she's Melezheun, and our friends back there, that's Carn and Sue, I mean, Soubrette's Last Elegant Algorithm, they're a lecturer here, but we're, we're not, we're, I guess you'd say, community organizers? Not gang leaders, it's not like that—"

"Calm yourself, fellow! I'm not broadcasting live right now." Zo! turned to Melezheun, twinkling with good humor. "Being on camera takes some people that way. They start talking and can't stop, and I am *ever so happy* to take advantage of that, oh yes! But I don't broadcast myself walking down hallways unless I'm being pursued by monsters or it's a very interesting hallway." He strolled over, nodding to all of us. Being in his presence was strange, probably because he was an incalculably ancient techno-magical abomination of untold power, and he was *smiling*. All skeletons smile at you—they have to—but with Zo!, you could tell he really meant it. It wasn't exactly that he liked us, I don't think, but he was prepared to be *amused* by us.

"What brings such an interesting group of attractive and intelligent individuals to this corner of the Arcanamirium?" Zo! asked.

I didn't want to go on blithering, so I lined up my words neatly in my mind before speaking. "We're—"

Mr. Double suddenly began to blare a Klaxon wail, startling all of us (except Zo!, who just cocked his head). The shrieking siren diminished enough for us to hear the drone's calm voice. "There is a security situation in progress. Hostile forces are active on the grounds. Countermeasures are being deployed. Please shelter in place until the situation has been resolved."

And then a great big metal gate fell out of the ceiling in front of the glass doors and sealed us inside the library.

"*Now* I'm broadcasting," Zo! said, delight evident in his voice.

18

MYSTERIOUS FIGURES

(Chk Chk and Dae)

"How can you read and walk at the same time?" Dae asked, bouncing along the hallways of the Arcanamirium, led by a hovering drone that was far more modern than the scuttling thing described in Tyrcell's account.

Chk Chk glanced away from the projected screen that half filled his field of vision and said, "*I am very intelligent and talented, of course.*"

"Well, did it say what they found in the..." They glanced up at their guiding drone, then opted for something like caution. "Thing? In the place?"

"*Not yet. This Tyrcell seems to enjoy building suspense. Their account doesn't read like a factual account, but more like the transcription of a tale by a storyteller who is delighted by the sound of their own voice.*"

Dae nodded. "Yeah. Tyrcell's version of the Hellknights also seems a little... I don't know. Rakhiel is smart, and I guess Astrachios too, but they're kind of bumbling at times, and their violence is so over the top. The Hellknights are usually more grim and controlled than that. Maybe they were different right after the Gap."

"*Perhaps,*" Chk Chk mused. "*But we shouldn't assume Tyrcell is an absolutely reliable narrator, and we know they're filling in gaps with imaginings and suppositions. Tyrcell hates Astrachios and the Hellknights and wants to make sure any readers do too. That doubtless colors the account. I'm sure Storg and Wilhum must have been a bit more... nuanced, in reality, at the very least.*"

"I bet Tyrcell wrote down the quips and witty retorts they *wished* they'd said but didn't actually say in the moment too."

"*It is something I would be tempted to do in my own memoirs,*" Chk Chk said.

"You think the basics are reliable, though?" Dae asked. "The whats and whens and who's if not all the whys?"

"*I hope so,*" Chk Chk said. "*That's what we need to verify.*"

"Hmm. To think, we're walking where they might have possibly actually also walked." Dae had never been inside the Arcanamirium before, and it was certainly impressive, if in a somewhat old-fashioned way, with the arches and portraits and so forth. "And where Zo! walked too!"

"*I am beginning to think Zo! has walked almost every surface in the galaxy that can be walked upon,*" Chk Chk said. "*People say he is old, but according to this, he is* very *old.*"

"He doesn't look a day over ten thousand. Oh, this way, droney?"

They hung a left, following the drone down another hallway. They seemed to have the whole cavernous place to themselves. The technomancers must have all been off in their labs or libraries or pocket universes or whatever. Dae had seen one living person, but just briefly—a tall, lean humanoid in a dark green cloak, trailing far behind them in an endless corridor, but the next time Dae looked around, the stranger was gone. Mysterious figures on mysterious errands were probably totally routine in the Arcanamirium.

Chk Chk clicked in delight when they rounded their next corner. "*The black ramp with the shimmer! I was just reading about this. We really* are *following in their footsteps.*"

"That's what I'm *saying*," Dae said.

They'd talked their way into the Arcanamirium by claiming they were Starfinder agents researching a historical document, which was *true*, even if this particular excursion wasn't exactly authorized. It was possible their superiors in the organization wouldn't mind, but they'd opted to ask for forgiveness rather than permission. (With luck, their trip would go unnoticed, and they wouldn't even need the forgiveness part.)

The front doors of the building had been replaced, obviously, since the time of Tyrcell's account, but they hadn't been restored to their original design, lacking the elaborate carvings. Chk Chk, who always keenly sensed the transience of all life and beauty, felt a pang at that loss of a cultural artifact and a heightened hatred for the Order of the

Eclipse, who'd been causing misery since before their organization even had a proper name.

"If you want to visit a shrine to Yaraesa, this is hardly the one I'd recommend," the drone said in a smooth, resonant voice. "It is the oldest one in the complex, but also the smallest and least impressive. We have nicer ones upstairs, which include the expected meditation alcoves, but also one right in the middle of a busy activity hub, for those adherents who prefer to study in livelier environments. Besides all that, there's an actual temple to Yaraesa nearby on campus, dedicated a century ago by some of our lashunta faculty, and it is said to rival the Lady of Wisdom in elegance, though obviously not in size."

"No, this is the one we're interested in," Dae said. "Because of its historical, ah, significance."

"I am not aware that it has any particular significance," the drone said. "But please yourselves. It is just ahead, and the shrine is through the shelves toward the back. I'll wait here until you are ready to leave."

Dae and Chk Chk drew together, side by side, and slowly approached the room at the end of the hall. "Does it look like it does in the book?" Dae whispered.

"*No,*" Chk Chk said. There were no glass doors, no floating letters in a score of languages declaring it a memorial library, no long tables, no cybernetic hand on a pedestal. There was simply a holographic display that said Archival Material Overflow G, and inside, ranks of overstuffed shelves with narrow aisles between them. This place made the Starfinder Society file room where they'd started the day look sparsely filled and meticulously organized.

"In we go." Dae slipped between the shelves, turning sideways to get past jutting boxes. Chk Chk pulled his robes in close to his body and followed suit, flashing back to a memory of his father squeezing through a cramped cave system during Chk Chk's larvahood. This endeavor wasn't equal in peril, of course, but Chk Chk was still excited. He wished he knew what to expect from the shrine, but he hadn't gotten that far in Tyrcell's account yet.

"It's here!" Dae pushed aside a dark red curtain hanging in an arched doorway. "Oh, this isn't so bad! The drone made it sound awful, but there's a really pretty old statue and some nice cushions, wow, it's dusty, though, I guess no one comes down here anymore." They looked back at Chk Chk. "So. Where do we look to find the secrets of the galaxy?"

"*I'll see,*" Chk Chk said, pulling up the next part of Tyrcell's document.

19

SYZYGY
(Tyrcell)

"What's happening?" I asked Mr. Double. "What kind of security situation? What hostiles?"

"Reports are still coming in," the drone said. "A group of Hellknights somehow breached the outer gate and subsequently forced their way into the tower. They have... preliminary reports indicate that they killed Hathor, the warden of the door."

"But he had a great big staff!" Carn said. "He seemed like serious business!"

"He was prepared for many things," Mr. Double said, "but he did not foresee an assault by grenades."

I looked at Mel. "Do you think it's the same Hellknights from before? Are they *following* us?"

A shadow passed across her face, and she visibly wilted. "I don't... I didn't..."

"Dear viewers, I am *besieged*," Zo!'s voice boomed. His cameras swooped around the room, swallowing up footage. "The Arcanamirium is under attack by Hellknights! They've been attempting to seize control of various sections of the station in recent hours, claiming authority derived from documents *conveniently* discovered earlier today in the infosphere and promising to restore order. As my most loyal watchers have heard, they have even tried to jam these broadcasts, as if Zo!, the voice of the people, can ever be silenced! Now it seems we may have firsthand witnesses to their vile depredations." Zo! swung around and pointed at Melezheun and me, cameras hovering over his shoulders, lenses watching us. "Who are these invaders, then?"

I would *not* sound like an idiot on camera. "We had a run-in with a group of Hellknights in the Lorespire Complex—they stormed the place, destroyed all the records they could get their hands on, and killed innocent people. We listened in on a couple of the knights, a human and a propaganda devil—"

"Astrachios and Rakhiel," Melezheun supplied, though she kept looking down at the floor.

"Yes, them, they were talking about how they're *glad* the Gap happened, because it gives them an opportunity to seize control of the station. They said they can fabricate documents that claim the Hellknights are supposed to take over the station in times of unrest, so they can seize power. They went to the Lorespire Complex to destroy any evidence to the contrary, and I bet they're here to do the same thing—"

"Sorry, sorry," Zo! said, waving a hand to cut me off. The floating cameras were flashing various red lights. "They're jamming my broadcasts again... I don't know how much of that got out. I can frequency hop to get us back online, but it will take a few minutes. They're getting wise to my techniques, so I have to keep inventing new ones." He drew a handheld terminal from inside his jacket (How, when it was so formfitting? Maybe he had a compartment carved into the walking corpse he called a body) and began manipulating it. "That's all interesting stuff, what you were saying, though," he said absently. "It's always nice when the villains have a clear motivation, other than just being pains in the nether regions for the fun of it."

"We are unable to accurately locate the Hellknights," Mr. Double said. "They have deployed cloaking, jamming, and scrambling technology, and appear to be simultaneously in all areas of the campus at once. Our security systems have been unreliable since the event known as the Gap. We are deploying our forces to check each potential location individually. We ask that you continue to shelter in place until the situation is resolved."

"We don't have much choice when there's a big metal gate in the way," I pointed out.

"I could get through that," Carn said thoughtfully. He'd pulled his hammer out at some point and was swinging it back and forth idly.

"*Please do not destroy Arcanamirium property,*" Sue said. "*A small force of Hellknights cannot prevail against the might of the Arcanamirium. Once the intruders are located, they will be captured or killed or, at the very least, driven away. We should do as the drone says. In the meantime, perhaps we can investigate the shrine?*"

"We may as well." I glanced at Zo!, who seemed fully absorbed in his technical difficulties. That was good. I wasn't sure I wanted whatever we found to be broadcast immediately all over the station. What if it was really bad news? People were freaked out enough.

My loyal foursome drew together and headed to the back of the library, where a red curtain screened off the space beyond an arched doorway. There was an icon etched above the archway, and it took me a moment to understand what I was looking at—a model of an atom, with a brain in place of the nucleus. One of the Lady of Wisdom's holy symbols, I presumed.

I moved the curtain aside, revealing a pleasant alcove, which would have been crowded if we'd all tried to jam inside. The walls were lined with shelves holding various scientific texts, with reading lights set here and there, and there were cushions in blue and green scattered over the floor to recline on. The space was dominated, though, by a statue of Yaraesa, about three-quarters life-size, assuming the lady had been about Melezheun's height in mortal life. The statue depicted a lashunta in an elegantly draped garment, sitting cross-legged, arms extended, head tilted back. Sinuous glowing symbols curved along her arms and legs and ran down her cheeks from her whitened eyes like tear streaks. A complex orrery of slowly rotating golden rings and spheres hung suspended by magic above her head, symbolizing her understanding of the universe... or something like that, I assumed.

One of Zo!'s hovering cameras floated in, its lights still dull, and bobbed up near the ceiling. The drones weren't transmitting anymore, but maybe they were still recording—looking for anything interesting their master might make use of later on.

Carn stepped into the space and started looking over the sculpture, tapping it with his knuckles as if listening for hollow places, even lifting the whole thing with a grunt and peering underneath for a moment. "If there's a message hidden in here, I don't see where."

"What did the file fragment say exactly?" I asked Melezheun. I remembered it perfectly well myself, but she seemed so distracted and troubled, I wanted to give her something to do.

Mel blinked, twitched her antennae briefly, and then recited: "In the time of lost time, Yaraesa became, and in her shrine, the truth remains. The other gods have all forsaken you, but by her grace, she may awaken you. In the center of great learning, you may yet appease your yearning. If you can form a syzygy, then her truth will set you free.'"

"So what's a syzygy?" I asked. "That's the bit I don't get."

Sue spoke up. "*A syzygy is an astronomical conjunction—a configuration of three or more celestial bodies oriented along a straight line.*" The contemplative drifted closer to the statue and gazed at the orrery. "*This seems to be a depiction of the major bodies of our solar system, though with an extra planet, unless this orb here is meant to represent Absalom Station. Let us see if we can move them...*" The glowing golden orbs started to shift around on their floating rings, nudged by Sue's telekinesis. We all watched as the contemplative carefully moved all the orbs into a line: Aballon, Castrovel, Absalom Station, Akiton, Verces, Eox, Triaxus, Liavara, Bretheda, and Aucturn. (I remember the names of all those planets easily enough.) They weren't exactly to scale, though the bigger planets had larger orbs, and there were smaller spheres orbiting some of the larger ones, which must have been moons. Sue nudged those lesser bodies into line too, until we had a string of about fifteen planetary bodies, all in a line. They stayed in position, the whole set revolving together over the statue's head. The spinning arrangement of shapes seemed to transform from a bright line to a bright point and back again, and I found myself getting slightly mesmerized.

"*They locked into place when we aligned them,*" Sue said. "*We're not holding them in place with our abilities anymore. But we don't see—*"

Then the white eyes of the sculpture glowed, and a holographic projection filled the air above the orrery, several lines of numbers and symbols shining in stark white.

"More riddles," I muttered.

"*Of a sort.*" Sue bobbed in the air. "*These are mathematical equations, each one based around a different universal constant. We think... we must have used a great deal of mathematics in our discipline. Each equation resolves down to a simple number... here, can someone take note of these digits?"*

"Sure," I said, and Sue rattled off a string of digits, with pauses in between so I didn't get them intermingled. I punched them into my gauntlet's onboard memory, then looked at the whole list. It meant nothing to me. "So what does it mean?"

"*They are coordinates, we believe,*" Sue said. "*The first set of coordinates are astronomical, and the latter set are terrestrial, though we don't know for which planetary or lunar body. Astronomical coordinates are a bit tricky to decipher, as we're sure you know—every body in every solar system is constantly moving in relation to everything else, so in order to designate a given body with coordinates, you need to select a frame of reference, and there are many options: Is this a system centered on the observer, or the sun, or the galactic center? And then you have to account for the time of the observation, of course, as objects move in time simultaneously with space... give us a few moments to review the possibilities.*" Sue drew their small legs up and folded them together, placed their hands on their knees, and then just... floated in contemplation.

Melezheun and Carn moved closer to me. Carn was grinning, and Mel was wide-eyed with wonder. "It's a treasure map," I said. "And the treasure is... an explanation of what caused the Gap? Or maybe how to fix it?"

"We better put these little planets back where they were." Carn moved over to the orrery. "There are Hellknights wandering around, and we don't want them finding this info." He pushed on the Absalom Station orb, and it swung out of alignment, and then the others began to move on their own courses too. The statue's eyes stopped glowing, and the hologram vanished.

"Cameras, to me!" Zo! shouted from the other room, and our watchful eye near the ceiling buzzed out. I exchanged glances with my friends (except Sue, who was still in hover-thought), and then we left the alcove and went back to the main room. Zo! stood straight as a pillar, hands on his hips, gazing out through the gate.

"What's going on?" I asked.

"Don't you hear the drumbeat of distant boots?" Zo! said.

"Someone's coming. Perhaps we're about to be rescued." But then he chuckled like he didn't think that was likely at all. I didn't think so either.

—

"Our meddlers from the Lorespire Complex are here!" Astrachios led the way through the Arcanamirium with a sort of seething glee. They'd left the lorekeeper in an unconscious heap in the foyer, after extracting the information Astrachios was so happy about. "*And* that filthy necrovite Zo!, who's out there spreading information like a contagion all over the station. They're *all* going to the shrine! We can take them out in one fell swoop."

"I'm feeling quite fell myself, now that you mention it." Rakhiel kept pace with him, but her attention was focused mostly on her wrist gauntlet, which she was using to deploy an array of surveillance countermeasures: feeding false information to the Arcanamirium's cameras and drones and motion sensors, spoofing tracking devices, and generally obscuring their actual location. Propaganda devils had natural skills to sway the minds of mortals, but Rakhiel had wholeheartedly embraced the capabilities of modern technology to baffle and mislead as well.

The Hellknights turned a corner and found themselves facing two members of the Arcanamirium at the far end of the hall: a stocky dwarf and a towering (if relatively slender) nuar, one of the pale minotaur-kin; there were a few of those among the ranks of the Hellknights, though they tended to be heftier than this specimen, and none would be caught dead in that purple robe. *This* nuar was about to be caught dead in his, though.

"Someone's cow got out of the pen," Rakhiel observed, amused, and Wilhum chuckled.

"The invaders!" the dwarf shouted, and he raised his hands, doubtless to cast some unpleasant spell. Astrachios had his rifle at the ready and didn't even bother with the laser sight or scope—from this distance, he could put a needle through the dwarf's eye socket, and he did. Said needle was long enough to penetrate the dwarf's brain, and the poison it pumped out on impact was probably unnecessary. Better safe, though. The dwarf stiffened, then fell straight backward, and Astrachios switched to firing on the nuar instead. A shimmering, convex shield of bluish light appeared before the wizard, and the needles pinged off harmlessly.

The nuar roared and charged toward them, pushing the force shield—magical or technological, Astrachios couldn't tell—before him like a battering ram. Astrachios braced himself, and Storg and Wilhum stepped up on either side of him to form a line so they could meet the charging bull head-on.

Rakhiel, on the other hand, laconically drew one of her pistols, dropped to one knee, cocked her head, and squeezed off a single low shot.

The nuar howled as the projectile slipped under the bottom edge of the shield and clipped one of his feet, obliterating the limb below the ankle joint in a puff of pink mist. The nuar fell to the floor face-first, the shield vanishing, and Rakhiel calmly put another round into the top of his head, right between the curving horns.

"Wanted to punch it," Storg said sulkily.

Rakhiel patted his beefy shoulder, or the pauldron that covered it, anyway. "You'll get more chances, big man." She walked on down the hall, adjusting settings on her wrist gauntlets again. "Our dead friends didn't notify anyone that they'd found us before they died. Silly of them. We wouldn't do nearly that well against all the wizards in this place at once. It just takes one with enough time and space to cast something nasty."

Astrachios and the others joined her, with Storg and Wilhum giving the fallen a few unnecessary kicks in passing. Soon afterward, they found the downward-spiraling ramp the lorekeeper had described. They descended to find a hall blocked off by a barred wall of metal, like a portcullis. Beyond the barrier, there were glass doors, some floating letters in a language Astrachios didn't recognize, a small library with tables and nooks for studying... and a few people and drones, standing behind that gate, openly gazing at the Hellknights, as if a thin screen of metal could protect them.

The three in back were the meddlers who'd attacked his brothers in the Lorespire—the ysoki, the lashunta, and the android—but he was more interested in the one standing front and center.

Astrachios grinned and pointed. "It's that cursed necrovite Zo! We caught him!"

"I'm not cursed!" Zo! shouted, either offended or pretending to be. "You think a curse made me like this? Absurd! I did this to myself on purpose! It took *ages*, and it cost a fortune! If anything, I'm *blessed!* Not by the gods either, blessed by Zo! I'm older than some of the gods we have around these days anyway." He stepped closer to the gate. "I'd love to interview you, if you don't mind. Astrachios, is it, and Rakhiel? And you've brought along a couple of walking slabs of violence, those are always useful to have on hand, I'm sure."

"How does he know our names?" Rakhiel hissed, her habitual cool broken for once.

"We must not be controlling the flow of information as much as we should be," Astrachios replied, though it troubled him too. Were people *talking* about him? What were they saying? What did they *know*, and how did they know it?

"I have a source who claims you falsified the documents giving Hellknights authority over the station," Zo! went on.

There were *cameras*! They couldn't let him say these things! Astrachios snarled, took aim with his sniper rifle, and fired. The bars of the gate were spaced widely enough to let a needle through, and an explosive tip would take off that grinning skull of a head. Oh, it wouldn't kill him; necrovites could survive a little decapitation, after all. But it would definitely shut him *up*—

The metal gate flashed briefly blue, and the needle fell, wasting its charge with a pop that put a small crater in the floor. Astrachios growled. Of course it couldn't be a mere physical barrier, not in this place; there was some magical force field woven into the metal as well.

Force fields weren't perfect, though, and they couldn't resist a dedicated onslaught of firepower indefinitely. He stepped back and patted Wilhum on the arm. "Take down that gate, would you, brother?"

Wilhum grunted like a pig presented with a trough of fresh slops and swung the grenade launcher off his back.

20

SUE FALLS

(Tyrcell)

"Probably we should leave," Carn said after the first grenade slammed into the gate and detonated against the force field. The magical barrier muffled the sound of the explosion, so it was more a dull roar than a shattering aural Armageddon, but it still made the whole room shake, and one of the vials of gross fluid fell off a shelf and shattered, releasing a gut-churning stink of rancid oil.

"Leave? And miss out on all this fantastic footage?" Zo! gestured to send his camera drones to cover his preferred angles. "Zo!, under siege! The Hellknights, revealed as base murderers! The people will love this! Assuming I can get the transmission out; I coded a frequency-hopping algorithm, but the blackguards are doing their best to stymie me."

I ignored Zo!, since he was ignoring reality, and addressed myself to Carn. "I'd love to leave, but there's only one way out, and there's a metal gate, a magical force field, and four Hellknights in the way."

Carn put that finger in his ear and wriggled his nose. "Did you forget how we got into the shops next door?" He swung his hammer in a pendulum motion.

I looked around. "We smashed through cheap bulkheads in a, frankly, low-rent business district. This is the *Arcanamirium*. These walls look like stone, and who knows what kind of magical fortifications they have?"

"Nah. This library was originally a bigger space they subdivided later, see?" He pointed at the wall to our right, though I couldn't tell much about it, since it was covered in shelves. "I couldn't smash through one of the original walls, probably, but I can get through *that* one."

"Let's do it!" I'd been prepared for a firefight, but when your enemy has a grenade launcher, it's not much of a fight, really. Mel and I helped Carn move the shelves. (Sue was still hovering in back, maybe unaware of the whole altercation; they struck me as a deep thinker.)

We dumped precious artifacts and texts on the floor in the process. I made a point of moving the glass vials and jars carefully, since the one that had broken already made me wish I could selectively turn off my olfactory systems. Maybe that was an upgrade I could look into if we lived long enough.

As soon as we'd cleared enough shelves for Carn to start swinging, we moved out of his way, watching, rapt, as grenades continued to boom against the force field.

Carn hit the wall with his hammer, and nothing happened. Then again. And again. And again. "Carn," I said. "I don't think—"

On the next swing, the wall cracked, just a little, but I shut up. I knew Carn pretty well by then, and I had no doubt he could turn that little crack into an exit, given time.

Another dull grenade thump struck, and I wondered if we *had* time. "Will you check on Sue?" I asked Melezheun. Mostly I wanted Mel as far back in the library as possible in case the grenades broke through and the Hellknights followed. She nodded and disappeared behind the curtain.

I walked over to Zo!, who was muttering to himself and squinting around the space. He said something about *mise-en-scène*, then noticed me, and turned his glowing regard in my direction.

"Tyrcell! These are exciting times, aren't they?"

"I wouldn't mind slightly quieter times," I admitted.

"Oh, not me," Zo! said. "Time is a deep well, and the hours can be hard to fill. If we didn't have all this excitement happening naturally, I might find myself compelled to manufacture some."

That wasn't reassuring. Since we were in something of a holding pattern while Carn hammered and the force field held up, I wanted to satisfy some of my various curiosities. "I know this might not be the right time to ask questions," I began, but Zo! interrupted me.

"I've discovered that *I* quite like asking questions, and I certainly ask them anytime I please, so go ahead!" Those fiery eyes seemed to dance with mischievous delight, as if we weren't under fire at all... but then I recalled that, as a necrovite, Zo! was the next best thing to immortal.

Even if his body was shredded and torn to pieces, his mind and soul were stored somewhere else, and so long as their container was intact, he would simply regenerate. Being in a firefight might *be* delightful for him, for all I knew. It was a break from the monotony of eons.

"You said in one of your broadcasts that you've been alive a long time. So long you still have memories when the rest of us don't, right?"

"I do," Zo! said. "Though I'm not sure how long ago my memories stop. I thought I'd be able to calculate the duration of the Gap by counting forward from the last date I can remember, but it turns out, all the timekeeping devices in the system are compromised! No clock or calendar on any ship or computer can agree on what time, day, month, or year it is. Those files that survived are no help either; their time stamps are garbled or nonsensical, spanning tens of thousands of years, with files that are clearly newer showing older dates of creation... it's all just nonsense, designed to obfuscate and confuse us. A bit like what the Hellknights are trying to do. We're going to have to invent a whole new calendar, and I suppose this will come to be known as 'year one after the Gap.'"

I didn't want to talk about timekeeping methodologies. "But you remember *some* things, right? From your past?"

"Oh, so many things." His eyes pulsed brightly.

"This Golarion the gods mentioned, the thing they claimed is 'safe.' You said it's a planet?"

Zo! nodded again. "Yes! Now, I confess, I found myself a little... addled, during that early broadcast. Having a hole that's centuries or perhaps millennia wide blown into your brainpan will do that." There was another thump of grenade impact then, as if to punctuate his point. "The details escaped me—in fact, the details seemed almost to deliberately *flee* from me—but once I had time to focus and reflect, I recalled more. Golarion was a planet *right here*, third from the sun in this little solar system. I believe this station once orbited Golarion, in fact, and the population was likely mostly derived from people who lived there—or whose ancestors once had."

A whole planet had vanished. But it was safe? How? "Then... what was Golarion like?" I asked, since Zo! wouldn't be able to answer the other questions.

"Oh, it was a bit of a mess, as I recall," Zo! said. "The details are fuzzy, even for me, I assume because of the meddling of the gods. It was a world, with cities and seas, empires and jungles, palaces and temples, hovels and stables, art and history, music and war, and regional cuisines that people outside those regions found repulsive." He paused. "Most of that is conjecture, mind you, but I bet I'm right."

"Do you have any guess about what happened to Golarion?" The thumping and crunching of Carn's hammer was a steady backbeat to our conversation.

Zo! shrugged. "I have no memory of Golarion exploding or being nudged out of orbit and falling into the sun or being pulled into a black hole or anything like that. But if I were a betting man—and I *am*, I love a good wager—I would wager that this gap in our memories and the disappearance of Golarion are related. Wherever it went, and why it went there—I think *that* is the secret the gods have banded together to protect. The word *Golarion* does not appear in any documentation anywhere on this station, as far as I can tell, nor do any descriptions of its peoples, its climate, its geography... nothing. It's all been scrubbed out, cut away, smudged to illegibility, bit-rotted and redacted." He moved a step closer to me and spoke in a conspiratorial whisper. "Makes you wonder, doesn't it? How awful the secret must be for the gods to work together to protect it? And how very angry they'll be if their secret is revealed? Perhaps these Hellknights have a point, eh? Information *is* dangerous." Then he stepped back and threw his arms wide with a flourish. "But the universe is dangerous too, and I wouldn't want to live anywhere else!"

There was another explosion, louder this time, and I watched the force field shatter into a cascade of bluish shards that disappeared before they struck the floor.

Just then Melezheun popped out of the alcove, followed by the floating contemplative. "Sue figured it out!" she said. "We know where Yaraesa wants us to go!"

—

"That's enough with the grenades," Astrachios said when the force field fell. "I want to capture some of them alive."

"That'll be tricky if you want the necrovite," Rakhiel said. "We might need a time machine."

"What?" Wilhum said, confused as usual.

"Yes, very funny," Astrachios said. "I'm OK with blowing Zo!'s head off to keep him quiet—he can regenerate in a cell in our citadel, and once his mouth works again, we can force him to make a broadcast supporting our claims. The people will believe him."

"Not a bad idea," Rakhiel said. "Though it's hard to make a necrovite do anything they don't want to. The immortal are tough to threaten. He can just sit there with his mouth shut and wait for us all to die of old age, and then get on with his unlife."

"Maybe we can convince him our cause is righteous," Astrachios said. "Otherwise, well. I'm sure necrovites can feel pain, or at least discomfort. We have the resources of the combined orders of the Hellknights at our disposal. We can break him."

"It should be fun trying, anyhow," Rakhiel said. "Do you want all the meddlers alive too? It could be hard to drag them all out of here."

Astrachios considered. "Just the android. It sounds like they're the leader, so they can give us the codes to access their enclave, which will make annexing it easier. As for the rest"—he made a flicking-away gesture—"they all can die." He unholstered his sniper rifle. "For my part, I'm going to kill those cursed camera drones."

—

"Carn, how's that hole coming?" I called.

"Almost there," he grunted, and I saw he was—there was already an opening big enough for Melezheun to wriggle through, and it would be wide enough for the rest of us soon.

I knew we didn't have much time before the Hellknights breached the gates, assuming they didn't just start shooting us through the bars. I flipped one of the long tables over, dragged Melezheun behind it to conceal us from fire, and beckoned to Sue to join us.

There was a loud crack, and one of the cameras spun around, hitting a wall and dropping to the floor. "My cameras!" Zo! cried, outraged. "You monsters!"

There was another crack, and another camera fell. Several more blasts followed in quick succession, projectile and energy weapons both, and the force field around Sue's head flashed blue as it absorbed the impacts. That brain of theirs did make an obvious target, but they were nearly to the table—

Then the contemplative's refurbished force-field generator glitched, or simply reached its limit, and Sue's head exploded right in front of us, a red crater blown into their big, beautiful brain. Melezheun screamed, and I did too, I think, as organic matter spattered us and Sue's small body dropped to the floor like a puppet with its strings cut.

We only had a moment for horror, because a bullet hole appeared in the table about an inch from my head. We were hidden from sight, which made us harder to hit, but concealment wasn't the same as actual cover. We were running short of six-inch-thick steel plate, unfortunately. (My brain was a rambling mess, trying and failing to process the fact that Sue was gone, as quickly as a finger snap.) But I needed to focus. My people needed me. The people I had left.

"Mel. Melezheun!" I had to shake her to get her attention: she was staring at the tiny crumpled form of the contemplative. "I'm going to provide covering fire, and you need to get through the hole Carn made!"

"*I don't—I can't—this is my fault—*"Her telepathic projection was fragmented and confused, so I just shouted, "Go!" and then popped up, firing with both pistols through the gate, making the Hellknights scatter and duck. *They* didn't even have a table to hide behind out there, but they had armor, and none of my rounds did more than inconvenience them. They weren't as complacent as the knights we'd faced in the Lorespire: even my guided flechettes spent themselves against force fields before they could find soft spots to penetrate.

Melezheun rushed for the hole in the wall, which had grown much bigger, and clambered through. Carn stepped toward the gate, dropped his hammer, and scowled ferociously. The Hellknights charged toward us, but slowly, as if they were caught in jelly. "I can cover the retreat," Carn said, voice strained with effort.

"Remarkable!" Zo! said, for the benefit of the half a dozen floating cameras that Astrachios hadn't managed to destroy yet. "Such courage under fire, even faced with the loss of their colleague, a promising young contemplative scholar named Soubrette's Last Elegant Algorithm, murdered in cold blood by invading—" One of his cameras exploded into shards in midair, struck by a Hellknight projectile. The zealots themselves were moving slowly, but once their projectiles got outside the range of Carn's gravity manipulation, they moved plenty fast.

"Zo! Come on!" The necrovite looked at me for a moment before nodding.

"Yes, of course. My directional microphones picked up the Hellknight dialogue, and they want to take me captive, which I doubt I'd enjoy very much." He crawled through the hole, the remaining camera drones following after him. I didn't think the Hellknights could see the hole from their vantage point, but they'd figure out we'd escaped pretty soon.

"Carn, you come right after me!"

"You got it, boss." His fur was matted with sweat. Keeping all those Hellknights from barging into us was really taking it out of him.

I went to the hole and through, into a storage room, judging by the stacks of crates and boxes. Melezheun was there, hugging herself, but there was no sign of Zo! "Where did he go?" I asked.

"He said he had an interview with the first spell lord, whoever that is, and he was late already. He wished us well, and said he'd love to interview us sometime." She closed her eyes. "Sue. Sue *died*."

"I know." I put a hand on her shoulder. "We'll make sure they didn't die in vain. And we *will* make those Hellknights pay." I meant it. They'd killed one of my people.

Carn jumped through the hole headfirst, and a moment later, there came a series of brutal clangs as the Hellknights started to smash down the metal gate.

"Now we run," I said, as Mr. Double lead us to the exit.

—

Once Wilhum and Storg breached the gate, Astrachios looked through the hole in the wall and cursed. Their enemies weren't bottled up anymore—they could be anywhere in the sprawling vastness of the Arcanamirium, and they were doubtless telling every technomancer they could find exactly where the Hellknights were located. He was furious and wanted to kick over tables and smash glass, but he needed to focus and salvage what he could from the situation. "We'll need to retreat soon," he said. "But let's take a look at this shrine and see what the big secret is."

He stepped into the alcove, pushing aside the curtain, which was riddled with bullet holes and scorch marks. The interior held a bunch of texts and cushions and a statue, but a quick search didn't turn up any hidden data drives or anything else of interest. "If they found something, they must have taken it with them." *Waste, waste, this was all a waste!* He kicked the sculpture of Yaraesa, knocking a small chip off the pedestal, but it was too solid for him to smash apart.

"But look what I found." Rakhiel stepped in, holding one of Zo!'s camera drones. Its carapace was cracked, and its lens was shattered, but she'd opened a panel on the back and had plugged in a wire from her gauntlet. "The recordings Zo! made are intact, and look here. We've got footage of our meddling friends doing something to the statue, see?" Astrachios crowded close to look at the screen, watching holographic equations appear above the statue. The dead contemplative's voice, tinny in the small speakers, said something about universal constants and coordinates and then began to list off numbers.

"'Coordinates'?" he echoed. "These numbers lead to something Yaraesa has hidden away? Some secret truth."

"Either a gift from the gods or an elaborate prank," Rakhiel said. "I don't think anyone's had time to plan a complex scavenger hunt as a practical joke in the last few days, though. Everyone has been pretty busy. Do you think Mikiel would authorize us to take a ship?"

"If he doesn't, we'll take one anyway," Astrachios said. "This is *my* order now." A glance at the devil. "*Ours*. A new order, created to meet the needs of the moment. If Yaraesa hid away a secret, we need to make sure no one learns it but us. We can't risk the destabilizing effect an uncontrolled divine revelation could have."

Storg was standing in the doorway, and he said, "If a god has a secret to share, why not write it in white fire across the heavens? Let everyone know it?"

"Factions, my dear Storg," Rakhiel said. "The gods have them, just like everybody else. It's clear that most of that godly mob want to keep whatever happened to our memories a secret. Yaraesa disagrees, but if she says so too loudly, the other gods might gang up and smite *her*. So instead she leaves little clues for lowly mortals to find, so she can get her secret out without attracting too much of the wrong sort of attention."

"Seems like being a god should mean no one gets to tell you what to do," Storg rumbled. "You'd be the one telling, seems like."

"Everyone answers to someone, brother," Astrachios said. "I don't want us to answer to Mikiel anymore, though. He's focused on gaining control of the station, which is fine, but we have our eyes on the bigger picture. We need to control the flow of information." He looked at Rakhiel. "How would you feel about... a schism?"

"I read a bit about rogue orders yesterday," Rakhiel said, "when I got a glimmer of how things were going to develop. The self-proclaimed orders don't *always* fail horribly. But... I'd say let's try asking Mikiel for a ship to pursue the fugitives first. They are wanted criminals who brutally attacked two Hellknights, after all. He might go for it. We can leave the message from a god out of it. If we do have to go all schismatic, it'll be easier with a ship, eh?"

Astrachios nodded. He'd prefer not to fight his own people. *Again,* his treacherous mind whispered. *And last time, you defeated them, two against one.*

He shook off the thought and went back into the library, where Storg was breaking things. Astrachios crouched next to the contemplative's corpse behind the blasted, overturned conference table.

Astrachios stuck his fingers into the charred wood of the table, streaking them with ash, and used it to blot a rough circle onto his chest plate.

Then he dipped the fingers of his other hand into the contemplative's cratered head and swirled them around until they came out dripping red. Head wounds were always bloody, and brains were highly vascular, but he was still shocked by the quantity of crimson there. This creature was almost nothing *but* brain. Astrachios used the cooling blood to draw a ragged corona around the circle of ash.

Then he stood and faced his assembled knights, the first of his new order. "This is our holy symbol now."

Wilhum and Storg looked at him, nodded, and knelt together to make their own ash-and-blood approximations of his new symbol on their own chest plates.

Rakhiel didn't follow suit but nodded thoughtfully. "I like it. Branding is very important. Did you have any thoughts about a name? Unless you've warmed up to *penumbra*."

Astrachios hadn't come up with anything to his satisfaction, but he decided to start speaking and see if inspiration struck. "The Order... of the Shadow... That Blots Out the Sun."

Ah. No inspiration yet, then.

"Hmm," Rakhiel said. "That's pretty good. I'd say we're definitely getting there. The symbol, that's ten out of ten. The name... not quite that high. Let's keep workshopping it, yeah?" She knelt, dipped her bony fingers in the grisly paint, and made a circle-and-corona symbol on the lapel of her jacket, small and understated. "After we're done escaping this place, since every technomancer in the Arcanamirium is about to descend on us."

—

We ended up recovering from our ordeal in a dining hall on an upper floor of the Arcanamirium, where a profoundly annoyed elf technomancer demanded we tell her everything we knew about the Hellknight incursion. I gave her a blend of truths and half-truths, omitting mention of the secret message in the shrine but leaning heavily on our experience with the knights attacking the Lorespire and the fact that they'd falsified the documents that supposedly gave them authority to impose martial law. I concluded by saying, "This was a scouting mission to test your defenses, and you should expect a full-scale attack in the near future."

"We will be ready," the elf said. "Once you're prepared to go, tell your drone, and we'll see that you're escorted back to the transit station." She paused. "We could... give you rooms... for one night only. If you need them."

The offer didn't sound very sincere. "No, we'd like to get back to our people as soon as we can," I said. She looked visibly relieved, nodded, and then swept out, presumably to take part in the Hellknight hunt.

What little welcome we'd enjoyed at the Arcanamirium had been dependent on having Sue in our company, and Sue was gone. I was taking their loss pretty hard, though being an android, I probably didn't show it. Sue was one of us, someone I'd pledged to protect, and instead, I'd put them in harm's way. I had to do better.

The others weren't doing well with the loss either. Carn was slumped and sighing and picking at his fingernails. And Melezheun... she was a wreck, trembling and twitching and muttering to herself. Our medical drone hovered around us, buzzing pointlessly. It had taken care of all the scrapes and scratches and contusions we'd collected during the firefight, but it couldn't do anything about our emotional distress (well, it could have dosed us up with tranquilizers, but that was ill-advised in such a volatile situation).

"I'm going to look for some food," Carn said, never one to sit still for long. He headed for the back of the room, where there were various panels and interfaces that promised sustenance, and began to peruse his options.

I scooted closer to Mel on the bench. "I'd ask if you're OK, but that's a stupid question," I said. "But... how not-OK are you?"

"Very not-OK." She stared at the floor.

I nodded. I could relate. "We'll avenge Sue's death, Mel. We'll find Yaraesa's secret, and we'll fix everything—"

"Sue's death is my fault, Ty."

I put a hand on her arm. "Hey, don't say that. We *all* agreed to come to the Arcanamirium, to see what Yaraesa left for us. That wasn't your decision alone. And what happened... that's on the Hellknights, not you."

"No." She moved away, turning her head so I couldn't see her face. "It's *my fault*, Tyrcell." Melezheun shrank into herself, and her next words were barely a whisper in my mind. "*I sent a message to the Hellknights, telling them about the shrine.*"

21

CALLING ZO! BACK

(Chk Chk and Dae)

"She *what?*" Dae shouted when Chk Chk read Melezheun's confession. "Why would she do *that?*" They flung themselves down on a heap of old cushions, puffing up clouds of dust.

"*I haven't gotten to that point yet, but… I could hazard a guess.*"

"I thought Mel was better than that," Dae muttered, sinking deeper into the ancient pillows. "She seemed so, I don't know… *good*."

"*I'm sure she was. In part. People are complex, and it was a complicated time. As we've read, the days following the Gap didn't bring out the best in everyone.*" He drew in a deep breath, composed his thoughts, and said:

"*Is the blade sharper*
when driven into your back
by the hand of love?"

"Poetry," Dae muttered.

As usual, the first idea wasn't necessarily the best. You had to get those top-of-mind ideas out of the way to dig deeper. Chk Chk considered, then said:

"*Nothing is colder*
than the moment you step out
of the warming sun"

"Hmm," Dae said.

Still not quite right. Maybe:

"*The ice cracks beneath*
your feet, so far from the shore
freezing water waits"

Dae clapped politely. Chk Chk sighed. "*Betrayal is a potent theme. I will think on the subject more. There may be a whole poem cycle there. But for now… we should see if Tyrcell's account still holds up.*"

Chk Chk gazed at the projection that overlaid his visual field: a crude drawing Tyrcell (or someone) had made of the statue and the alignment of the spheres in the orrery. The statue before them was clearly the same object. "*The presence of this statue further verifies the validity of this document. It is not* conclusive *evidence, but... unlike cracking ice, this story is getting more solid all the time.*" Chk Chk walked to the statue, consulted the drawing, and began to gently push the floating orbs above Yaraesa's head into place. "*Oh, look, someone updated this statue, see?*"

Dae struggled upright from the cushions and squinted at the arrangement of spheres. "Did they?"

Chk Chk tapped a segment that was more teardrop-shaped than spherical. "*They added the* Idari, *between Verces and Eox. That ship didn't arrive until hundreds of years after the Gap. And Aucturn is gone... someone must have removed it from the orrery after the planet was destroyed.*"

"It's been an eventful few centuries, hasn't it?" Dae said. "You'd think solar systems would be a little more stable than that."

"*Indeed. But if we hearken back to the original configuration...*" Chk Chk tugged and twisted, lightly at first, then with more force, and the shining metal representation of the kasathan worldship *Idari* popped loose from its ring. Chk Chk set the piece aside, then said, "*Hmm. The ring where Aucturn used to be is still here... and I can see a flaw in the metal where the planet's model was removed, so perhaps if we pretend it's still there, and include that spot in the alignment...*"

"Oh!" Dae leaped to their feet. "Before you get all syzygy with it, we should call Zo! He said we should get in touch when we got to the bit about the Arcanamirium."

"*It's a good idea,*" Chk Chk said. "*Perhaps he can offer some guidance and insight.*"

Dae paced around while waiting for their call to navigate the requisite gauntlet of automated systems and sentient assistants, and then said, "Zo! It's me, Dae, and we're in the Arcanamirium, right beside the shrine to Yaraesa, and we read all about your whole... everything, with the shoot-out in the library and—oh right, sorry." Dae fiddled with their gauntlet, and a holographic image of the necrovite mogul shimmered in the air. Chk Chk paused in his careful arrangement of the orrery to see what Zo! had to say.

"Oh, Tyrcell," Zo! said, with what sounded like real fondness. "Now, *they* could have been a star. Some people think androids can't be all that charismatic, but Tyrcell had an intensity, and when they paid attention to you, you felt like the center of the universe. Of course, I usually feel like that anyway, but it's a novel sensation for the little people. Tyrcell wasn't very comfortable on camera, but that can be handled with training or, failing that, the right pharmaceuticals. Ah, you're in the little alcove at the back of the library! I didn't really go back there, though I saw footage later. Move the curtain aside, let me look at the library... oh, dear. It had a certain charm before, but now it's just storage. Ah, well, it was all shot full of holes and exploded with grenades, with a giant hole hammered in the wall, so some renovation was necessary. That fight in the library wasn't the only time someone has tried to kill or capture me, but it was one of the more memorable. Those Hellknights." Zo! couldn't really make a disgusted face, but his tone conveyed it. "They were the roots of a very ugly tree that still blocks out the sunlight today."

"The Order of the Eclipse," Chk Chk said out loud. "This document is, in part, a record of their founding, isn't it?"

"Oh, yes," Zo! said. "Their order didn't have all the branding sorted out yet, I don't think they even had that *name* at that point, but yes, the fight for control of information on Absalom Station in those early days is what spawned that clan of spacefaring censors. You know, I haven't produced much scripted material in recent centuries, enjoying the possibilities of reality programs more, but there might be a historical epic in all this, don't you think? I'm sure securing the rights to that document would be tricky, but it's just *history*, really, and nobody owns the rights to *that*..."

Chk Chk was afraid Zo! would spiral off into the commercial possibilities before providing them with any information of value, but Dae gave the necrovite a nudge. "Can you tell us... I don't know... anything?" Dae said. "About Tyrcell or Melezheun or where they were going or what happened to them after that fight?"

"Not really," Zo! said. "We parted ways after we escaped the Hellknights. I had an interview to conduct with some archmage or another. I'm afraid I never saw any of their little group again."

"Oh." Dae slumped. "That's too bad."

"I didn't say I never *heard* of them again, though," Zo! said, with his usual keen sense of drama. "In the weeks that followed, the political situation on the station became rather fraught. Essentially, Absalom Station became a collection of city-states, some allied, some at war, some studiously neutral, some expansionist, some isolationist. The Hellknights, of course, claimed they had dominion over *everything*, and produced copious documents to prove their case, but most people weren't interested in 'laws' that predated the Gap, even if they'd been legitimate. The general sense was that everything had changed, and that meant everything was up for grabs. As a journalist, I was able to visit most of the more stable communities that sprang up, and I even helped facilitate communication among the factions. There were a few unpleasant moments, of course, attempts to hold me prisoner and the like, but nobody puts Zo! in a corner. Not for long, anyway."

The necrovite tapped a long, gnarled finger on his lipless teeth, deep in thought, and then resumed. "During my little tour, not long after the affair in the library, I visited a community, one of the more organized and peaceable ones at the time, located where the Starfinder Society headquarters is now, in the Lorespire district. I asked about their founding, and they told me about an android and a ysoki who stepped in to stop a fight between two women who'd been married before the Gap and who'd turned on one another in their terror and confusion the day everyone lost their memories. From that small intervention, an act of defense and kindness, a mutual trust was born, and soon others joined them, and their community grew. I asked if I could meet these founders, realizing they were the people I'd met in the Arcanamirium. And the leaders of the group—the same two women who'd been fighting that first day!—told me, for the cameras, their leader was off on a diplomatic mission. In private, they admitted Tyrcell and Carn had left the station on a secret mission to investigate the cause of the Gap. I have no idea where they went or if they ever came back, but if you find out, let me know, would you?"

"Of course!" Dae said.

"Excellent. And I'll keep thinking about that historical epic. Maybe I'll even find a place for you in it, Dae. While it's true there weren't any pahtra on Absalom Station back then, how many people these days actually *know* that? Plus, the nitpickers and haters love shrieking about anachronisms—complaining is their favorite thing to do *anyway*, so I always try to include a few historical inaccuracies, to keep them engaged. I'll be in touch."

The floating Zo! winked out of existence, and Dae flung themselves back down onto the cushions again. "Tyrcell and Carn vanished, Chk Chk! They might have *died*! What if we get to the end of this document, and it just stops in midsentence, and there's a scrawl of ink and then a blood spatter?"

"*We scanned all the pages and did not encounter any bloodstains,*" Chk Chk said reasonably. "*As for the vanishing, Tyrcell and the others found coordinates—I suspect they went to investigate them. Assuming the account is true. Which we might be able to test now...*"

Dae bounced to their feet and stood next to Chk Chk as the shirren moved the last orbiting orb into position. The model of the Pact Worlds—made before the Pact Worlds was even a political entity—formed a perfect single line... and then the eyes of the statue began to glow, and numbers and letters appeared in the air over Yaraesa's head.

"I can't believe it still worked." Dae clutched Chk Chk's arm. "We have to figure out where these coordinates lead! Hurry, decipher them!"

"*I don't think we have to, Dae. We have Tyrcell's document, after all, and they deciphered the data already. We can just read ahead...*" Chk Chk pulled up the text and scrolled. "*Oh. Ugh.*"

"Where are we going?" Dae asked.

"*Not a place anyone would choose to take a holiday,*" Chk Chk said. "*But at least it won't take long to get there. Let's get to the ship before the Starfinders realize we've wandered off.*"

"Oh, they've been buzzing my gauntlet for an hour," Dae said. "I just sent all the calls to my voicemail. There are now... a lot of voicemails."

Chk Chk checked his own system, which had been set to the silent Focus mode while he read. "*Oh, dear. Mine too.*" His gauntlet converted the voice memos to text, and they were all from the archivist Seraphina and were all variations on "Where did you go?" and "Did you really just leave without saying anything?" and "Are you kidding me?" and "I thought you were serious about this."

"Should we tell them we're investigating?" Dae asked. "We're *supposed* to do that. We're validating the histor... ic... ness!"

"*The problem is, by investigating the manuscript, we're also investigating the Gap, and that is... not something the Starfinder Society looks kindly upon. I'll just send her a note and say that you're horribly ill, and I'm holding your hair back while you throw up everywhere.*"

"Why do *I* have to be the one throwing up?" Dae demanded.

"*I don't have any hair to hold back,*" Chk Chk said. He composed a message, then reset the orrery, making the statue shut down. He couldn't get the miniature *Idari* to go back into place, so he just balanced it on the proper ring and hoped someone else would fix it later. They left the alcove and threaded their way through the shelves and out of the storage area.

Dae said, "Huh, there's that guy again."

"*Which?*" Chk Chk looked up, but the hallway was empty.

"I don't know," the pahtra said. "Some person in a green cloak. I saw them upstairs and even thought for a second they might be following us. I just caught a flash of them going up the ramp. At least, I assume it's the same person. Maybe green cloaks are popular around here."

Chk Chk chittered in concern. "*There was a person in green loitering in a corridor at the Lorepire,*" the shirren said. "*They hurried off when I noticed them. Could it be the same person?*"

"Why would anyone be following us?" Dae said. "I mean, I'm a little bit famous, so people *do* follow me, but they usually just ask for a picture or an autograph or if I can cast them in my next vid or if I want to meet their cute single niblings. They don't usually run away. Oh no, do I have a stalker? Those are so tedious and sad."

"*An ordinary stalker would have difficulty entering the Lorespire,*" Chk Chk pointed out. "*The part we were in isn't open to the public.*

If we are being followed, don't you think it's more likely it has something to do with this story we're investigating?"

"I don't know." Dae did a handstand, which they often did while thinking, and cocked their head sideways to look up at their friend. "Who's going to stalk us because we're reading some memoir from hundreds of years ago?"

"*Someone who knows what the memoir says?*" Chk Chk offered. "*Someone who doesn't want us to follow where it leads?*"

"I think you're being paranoid," Dae said.

"*Almost certainly,*" Chk Chk said. "*But that doesn't mean I'm not also right.*"

22

OUT OF ABSALOM
(Tyrcell)

When Mel confessed, I went as cold as the vacuum of space. "Explain," I said, nothing else.

She slumped farther, still not looking at me. "I was afraid. Isn't it usually fear that makes people do stupid, terrible things?"

"Afraid of what?" I couldn't fathom what could have led her to commit such a betrayal.

"We talked about it a little... before." She snuck a glance at me, then averted her gaze again. "Whatever happened to us, whatever caused the Gap... we know the gods are either behind it or complicit with it—all of them except Yaraesa. They wiped the minds of everyone in the system, perhaps the galaxy, perhaps the *universe*, to cover up... we don't know what. Something important." She took a breath, steeled herself, and turned to face me. "If we defy the gods, Tyrcell—not just one, but all of them—what will the consequences be? Imagine that we manage to restore everyone's memories. What will the gods do *next*, to hide their secret? What comes after mass mind-erasing? Something even worse, I fear. So I... started to think the Hellknights had a point. I don't agree with their *goals*, but controlling the flow of information, keeping people from finding out the cause of the Gap... it might be the best thing, because the alternative could be so much worse."

I couldn't believe what I was hearing. "You were the one who wanted to pursue all this in the first place. You pushed us to investigate!"

"At first, yes. I was focused on everything we'd lost. I was obsessed with finding out who I was. But then..." She reached for me and clutched my hands, her eyes searching my face. I didn't pull away, but my hands were inert in her grasp, just objects attached to me, not an avenue for connection. "But then I realized the opportunity we have. It's a powerful thing, to begin again, with a clean slate. I don't know what I was doing before all this, but I know what I'm doing *now*, and it's meaningful. More meaningful than anything I can imagine I was doing before. We're building a community, creating a safe place for people. I don't know who I was, but I know who I am: the person working with you to make a better world, and with Carn and Starla and—"

"And Sue." My voice had no inflection at all. "Until you got them killed."

Melezheun released my hands and bowed her head again. "I know. That wasn't supposed to happen. I thought it would take us longer to get to the Arcanamirium and that the Hellknights would have come and gone with the secret before we ever arrived. I sent the message from the security office before we set out. I did not realize we would find a working transit system. I tried to delay us in the Arcanamirium, encouraged us to rest, to give the knights time to reach the shrine and destroy it... but the timing did not work out as expected. I also did not know they would attack us that way."

"Because they'd been so delicate before? Melezheun..." I shook my head. "This is messed up."

"Will you cast me out?" Melezheun said.

I stared at her. I hadn't even considered the possibility... but the community *was* mine, or at least, mine and Carn's and Starla's and Valentine's, and they certainly treated me like the leader—when it suited them. If I told them Melezheun had gotten one of us killed by betraying us to the Hellknights, they'd probably demand her exile. I could banish her at this moment, on my own authority. I knew she'd accept it.

The idea broke my heart. *She* broke my heart. "Is there any reason I should keep you in our community?"

"You probably shouldn't," she said. "I do not think I would forgive me, in your position. I cannot forgive myself in *mine*. I have not yet done anything to earn that forgiveness. But..." She took a deep breath. "I will. If you will allow me. I made a mistake, Tyrcell, and the consequences were horrible. Sue's death will haunt me forever. But I see now... even if the Hellknights had beaten us to the shrine, even if no one had gotten hurt, my choice was still the wrong one. I am to blame for Sue's death, yes... but so many have died on this station since the Gap, and so many of those who still live are lost and afraid and miserable, and *that* is not my fault. The gods are responsible for those losses. All the gods except Yaraesa, the one who was brave enough to dissent—brave enough to leave clues to help us find the truth. I was afraid, and that fear controlled me. I will *not* let that fear control me again. If you allow me, Ty, I will devote myself to this cause, and to our community, above all else."

All my data analytics told me she was sincere. I was good at reading people, and I believed Melezheun would be incredibly loyal, motivated by her guilt, and would go to great lengths to prove herself worthy of forgiveness. In fact, if I wasn't careful, I thought she might look for a way to sacrifice her life for the cause. I'd need to keep an eye out for that.

After a long moment of consideration, I answered her. "I don't forgive you, Melezheun. But, well... it's not like I haven't screwed up a lot of things in my life, and I can only remember a few days of that life. The fact is, we could still use your help." I looked over at Carn, who was munching on some kind of meat on a stick and heading our way.

"Will you tell Carn?" Mel asked. "What I did?"

"Not if you promise to stop sucking so bad," I said.

She almost smiled. "I promise, Ty."

The subject wasn't settled, but it was settled enough. "What are you *eating*?" I said, shifting my focus to Carn.

"Hmm," Carn said, holding the object at arm's length and examining it. "Protein?"

"We should probably get going." I looked around for Mr. Double. "Can you lead us to the transit hub?"

"Certainly," the scuttling orb said, crawling out from under a table. "Be advised: The Hellknights have fled the Arcanamirium, pursued by several of our battlemages. Their route is unlikely to intersect ours, but we cannot guarantee your safety once you leave our campus."

"You didn't guarantee our safety while we were *on* it," Carn pointed out.

"Even so," Mr. Double replied.

Our helpful drone led us out a side entrance—apparently the front way had been damaged by the Hellknights—and down an elevator to a tunnel that connected through a hidden one-way door to the transit hub. "Care to join us?" I asked the drone on the threshold. "We could always use another set of manipulator arms in our community."

"I am not even remotely tempted by your offer," Mr. Double said. "Have a pleasant continuation of your worldly existence." The door shut in our faces, blending seamlessly into the wall.

The conductors were pretty cranky (as you've now read, the Hellknights screwed things up pretty bad for them), but we told them that the knights were being chased by battlemages, and that cheered them up. That news wasn't enough to pay for passage back to the vicinity of the Lorespire, but it turned out Carn had quietly filled his pockets with cheese and nuts and crackers and dried meat from the dining hall, and *those* were welcomed by our benefactors.

"I didn't realize you had a thieving streak," I said while we sat together on a bench, waiting for the conductors to get their operations back online after the Hellknight incursion.

"We don't know that it was theft," Carn said. "Maybe I was the head of the whole Arcanamirium before the Gap, and all that stuff belongs to me anyhow."

"Hmm. Seems unlikely, buddy."

"I guess so. But I figured we needed that stuff more than they did. They can always magic up some more."

"In times of upheaval, it's good to be flexible in terms of your morals," I agreed. I almost said "Right, Mel?" just to make her feel included, then realized it might sound like a reference to her... questionable decision-making, so I shut up instead.

"So what next?" Carn said. "We got this clue... What do we do with it?"

"We follow it," Mel said. "Wherever it leads."

Carn stuck his finger in his ear and wiggled it around. "Well," he said at last, "I didn't have any other plans for the afternoon. Space travel it is."

Eventually the tram system got back online, and we continued our journey home. We even made arrangements with the conductors to get the Lorespire station connected to their system, promising to send people to help with repairing damage and clearing out debris in exchange for discounts on travel. The last leg of the trip took place walking through the maintenance tunnels, and when we emerged into the hallways of our community, they were *bustling*.

"Do you recognize any of these people?" I asked Carn.

"A couple," he replied. "But not most of them. Starla's outreach program must be going well."

We went back to Bric's bar, which was still headquarters until we came up with something better. I called the community leaders to my office and told Starla, Valentine, and Dr. Bindi the bad news about Sue. Mel didn't stick around for that part, saying she needed to get some rest, but I knew it was because she couldn't bear to listen to me describe the horror she'd caused. She didn't kill Sue, the Hellknights did that... but there are levels of culpability, and Mel owned some of that blame.

My friends were all upset about the news, especially Bindi, who was also pissed off. "I went to a lot of trouble to keep Sue alive, Tyrcell."

"We'd better make sure they didn't die for nothing, then," I said. "We found coordinates, left by Yaraesa—it's a literal message from the gods. Just about the last thing Sue did was figure out our destination."

"So you're going to investigate?" Starla asked.

"I hate to leave the community again so soon after coming back, but if we can figure out what caused the Gap, and if we can *do* something about it—"

"There's nothing more important," Starla said.

"We've got things under control here," Valentine said. "We're growing fast, which leads to various sorts of trouble, but it also means we have more resources, and so far, the useful people have outnumbered the pains in the ass. Asses. Whatever. We'll keep the lights on and everybody's bellies full while you go save the universe. If anybody asks, we'll say you're out doing diplomacy."

"Would you like to trade jobs, maybe?" I asked. "I'm getting a little sick of away missions."

"Like you'd know the first thing about supply-chain management,"

Starla said. "We've all got our strengths. You should embrace yours. You know: vision, diplomacy, intrepidness."

I snorted. "As opposed to skills that are actually useful?"

"Your words, not mine," Valentine said. "Good luck, boss."

"I'm nobody's boss."

"True, but what are we supposed to call you?" Starla said. "Glorious Leader? Your Grace? Mx. President? First Person?"

"I was leaning toward Tyrcell the Great, but you can't give yourself a nickname. Let me know if someone else suggests it, though."

—

I toyed with the idea of addressing the whole community before we left, telling them we were off on a mission to find the truth... but we weren't a dozen people banding together for safety in Bric's bar, living in each other's back pockets, anymore. Our population was in the hundreds by then and included immigrants who'd left other groups—gangs, really—because they'd heard we were more peaceful and stable. Carn said he figured there were at least a few spies in the mix, sent by those gangs to gather intel on us, and keeping our discovery to a close circle seemed a lot smarter. Officially, the story was we were off on another diplomatic mission, in an attempt to create a stable political system on Absalom Station, and we might be gone a while.

Carn, Melezheun, and I stood in the hangar, considering our starship options. Nobody had broken in and tried to steal one, which I thought spoke well of our community (or maybe Carn's security measures). In theory, nobody besides our senior people even knew the hangar was there, but Helio the house sitter knew, and he was an idiot, so word had probably gotten around.

We had three choices of possible transport: *Harrowdown* was small and fast, *Black Swan* was bigger but still pretty fast, and *Last Resort* was a flying warehouse. "I think it's got to be *Harrowdown*," I said. "It's cozier than I'd prefer, especially for a voyage this long, but it's the fastest ship here, and we should leave the larger ones in case the community needs them to escape."

"It's small, but at least it's real fancy," Carn said.

"There is that." I lowered the ship's ramp, and we walked on board.

The *Harrowdown* was a modified racer with cabin space added in the back, sacrificing acceleration speed for roomier quarters. It would have been spacious for one, comfy for two, and could just about fit three. I checked out the cockpit and was pleased to find that I recognized the controls, and when I called up the manual, it didn't tell me anything I didn't already know; it just reminded me that I knew them. "I know how to fly this thing!" I called, and Carn whooped.

"I call the bottom bunk," he said.

"You don't want the top bunk?" Melezheun said. "I think I'd feel sort of hemmed in on the bottom."

"There are probably burrows in my genetic history," Carn replied. "A ceiling right in front of my face feels like safety to me."

That little interplay meant they were giving me the biggest bed in the ship's tiny private cabin, without even thinking about it. Leadership is a burden, but it's also got perks.

"Are you excited to visit your ancestral home world and all that?" Carn said. Springs squeaked as he flung his bulk into a bunk.

"Mmm," Melezheun said. "Castrovel is just a dot on a star map to me. I don't know if I've ever even been there. And we're not even going to Castrovel, anyway—just to the moon."

Oh, yeah, our destination. We were headed to Elindrae, the only satellite of the planet Castrovel, the second world from the sun and birthplace of the lashuntas. The coordinates designated a specific landing spot on the moon, down to the square meter, or so Sue had told Melezheun.

The information we were able to find about Elindrae made it sound like the most boring place in the system, and for once, I didn't think the corrupted data and gaps in the records were hiding anything interesting. Most of the other charted worlds were home to established civilizations or at least enigmatic ruins, but Elindrae was just... a big rock, pockmarked with craters from millions of years of meteor impacts. It was barren, uninhabited, with no atmosphere at all, not even a toxic one. It wasn't an obvious place to hide away the secrets of the universe... but then, why would you put those in an obvious place?

I returned to the cabin, where Mel and Carn were lounging on their bunks, chatting. "Let's get our supplies on board, and then... we might as well head out."

"Onward to adventure!" Carn said.

"Eventually," Melezheun said. "Even in a ship this fast, with a good supply of thasteron fuel, we're looking at a journey of several days at best."

"With luck, we can beat the Hellknights there this time," Carn said.

I looked at Melezheun, who looked at me, and then we both looked at the ysoki. "What do you mean? What makes you think they're going there?" I spoke delicately; he didn't know Mel had told the Hellknights about the secret in the shrine.

Carn rolled over on the bunk and sat up, hands resting on his knees. "We should assume they found the coordinates too, after they stormed the library. Maybe they didn't, but I'm head of security, and that means planning for the worst. Why do you think I packed so much ammunition?"

"I guess I've just been thinking of the Hellknights as... an Absalom Station problem," I admitted. "They seem so focused on seizing control of things here."

"Not Astrachios and that propaganda devil," Melezheun said. "I have tasted their thoughts, and we heard them in the Arcanamirium. Their goals are different. They do not want control of territory—they want control of *knowledge*. Carn is right. We can hope for the best, but... be ready for the worst."

I nodded. They were both right. "Then maybe before we go, we should see about making a few modifications to the *Harrowdown*. We've got engineers in the community now, right?"

—

I don't know who's reading this (sometimes I don't even know why I'm writing it, except that all this stuff seems *very important*, and shouldn't somebody be taking notes?) but whoever you are, let me ask you this: Have you ever traveled for days through the void of space in a small vessel that smells increasingly of ysoki farts?

Androids aren't machines, or at least, not purely so. We're biomechanical, and yes, that means we have biological functions, in all their disgusting splendor. But nobody could be as biological as Carn, especially with a steady diet of the high-calorie, protein-dense rations we'd packed in order to save space. Let's just say that we ran the air filters at maximum, and as I mentioned, not for the first time in this document, I wished I had finer control over my olfactory sensors.

The trip was easy to start with, though, in the larger sense. Once we input our course, the ship pretty much piloted itself, and there wasn't a lot to see between us and Castrovel. Oh, we all enjoyed the view at first: actually seeing Absalom Station from the *outside*, especially once we got enough distance to take in the place as a whole? I'll never forget that. The station is a glorious feat of construction, truly, an irregular star with a spike on the underside and the immense dome of the Eye on top, like a great jeweled amulet floating in the void... or some kind of immense predatory insect, maybe.

There were a few other ships hovering around the outside, not docked but keeping close, but none of them gave us any trouble or even hailed us. We didn't see any Hellknight ships covered in spikes and fiery red sigils, so that was good. Soon the station and the other ships dwindled into distant specks, and there was nothing to see after that but the sun and stars... and the one point of light that wasn't a star at all but Castrovel. We couldn't see Elindrae on our sensors—it was behind Castrovel from our perspective.

At first, we kept our comms open so we could talk with our community (people had taken to calling it the Society, which I thought was a bit grandiose). But then again, the indigenous name for most species usually translates to something like "the people," and the native name for most worlds is something like "the world," so we were participating in a grand tradition.

Our communications equipment back home wasn't great, though, so after a while, we suffered from significant message lag, and then from interference, and eventually we were reduced to sending messages back and forth and communicating asynchronously. Finally, Carn didn't even let us do that much, for security reasons: Even with encrypted data, someone with the right equipment might be able to extrapolate our destination based on our signal traffic.

So it was just the three of us, alone together, in the void. We watched some of the media stored in the ship's data banks, but all the vids suffered from major data corruption, presumably to cover up the secrets hidden in the Gap; as a result, they were basically incomprehensible. We played games all the next day, but I tended to dominate games that involved bluffing, Melezheun usually won those that depended on logic and strategy, and Carn somehow always had an edge in the games that were mostly luck, probably because he was bold and took unpredictable actions that put us on the defensive. We all had fun... but we didn't necessarily all have fun at once.

Normally, long trips like that provide an opportunity for people to connect with one another, talk about deep and serious matters, share secrets and confidences, and generally bond. But we were all, in a sense, only a week or so old, and we'd spent most of that time together—so we didn't have a lot we *could* share, and we were already pretty bonded. We did have that one secret, Melezheun and me, but if we'd shared that with Carn, it would have made things awkward, and maybe even destroyed that bond. Or maybe not. Carn liked to present himself as blunt and straightforward, no more subtle than that massive hammer he liked to swing so much, but he demonstrated surprising depths and insights at times. Maybe we should have opened up to him about things. I'm not sure. I'm good at making decisions, but I'm not always sure, in retrospect, that I make the right ones.

On the third day, things got interesting, but in a bad way: Our sensors picked up a ship on our trail, one that popped up seemingly out of nowhere. "What are we looking at?" Melezheun asked, peering at the readouts in the cockpit.

Carn said, "Uh. Energy signatures are real strange. They aren't burning thasteron ore. I don't know what kind of ship that is. Might just be random, nothing to do with us, some kind of alien or something."

I groaned. "Are we that lucky, Carn? No. I bet it's a Helldrive."

The two of them looked at me blankly.

"I don't know why I know this," I said, "but the Hellknights have access to infernal starship technology. I couldn't tell you the technical details, but I think they basically... take little shortcuts through Hell, disappearing from our plane at one point and reappearing in another. It must be Astrachios and Rakhiel and their grenade-launching friends. Either they managed to track us, or they figured out how the statue worked and got the coordinates themselves."

"Can we outrun them?" Melezheun asked.

"I don't know exactly what their ship's capabilities are, but we've got a good head start, so... maybe?" I opened up an engineering screen and started to turn off safety features and activate emergency overrides. "I'll push the ship as fast as I can. In the meantime, we should get ready for a fight."

23

THE NEW ORDER

(Tyrcell)

"We should get ready for a fight," Astrachios said to Rakhiel as they tromped through their citadel, heading for their meeting with Mikiel. "Our illustrious leader isn't going to like the idea of giving up his authority over us. If we become our own order, we stop operating within his chain of command, and you can tell he loves being in charge of everything."

"As lictor of a new order, you would, in fact, be of higher rank than Mikiel." Rakhiel said. "As far as we can tell, he's a paralictor of the Order of the Pyre, which is high up, to be sure, but not the top of the top. There aren't any lictors or masters of blades on the station, according to the rosters, which admittedly have some data corruption. Nobody is eager to claim a higher rank, though—they all seem happy to let Mikiel run things. If it all falls apart, it falls on him, after all."

"I'm happy to let him run things too... mostly," Astrachios said. "But someone needs to control the chaos of information, misinformation, and disinformation on this station, and we're the obvious choice. For one thing, we're the only ones who understand how important it is."

"He strikes me as a reasonable man," Rakhiel said. "But he's also from the order that burns heretics alive, so... pluses and minuses. Still, it's worth trying this the easy way before we do it the hard way and just steal a bunch of supplies and a ship and rebel."

Two burly knights stood guarding the imposing doors to Mikiel's meeting chamber, which were carved with reliefs of victims writhing under the attentions of Hellknight torturers. The doors swung open, and the knights nodded Astrachios and Rakhiel in.

The chamber beyond had a high ceiling lit by glowing orbs of light that reflected on the polished floor, a large meeting table surrounded by chairs, and walls lined with shelves that held data cores and gleaming implements: pincers, branks, pears of anguish, thumbscrews, and the like. Mikiel was sitting at the table next to another knight whose back was to the door.

Astrachios strode through the doors boldly, while Rakhiel sort of slunk in sideways, but Astrachios stopped dead when the other knight turned in his chair and revealed himself to be Storg. He was holding a scroll in one hand, as delicately as one might hold a baby bird. (Well, Storg would probably crush a baby bird, but someone *else*.)

Betrayal! Astrachios thought instantly. *Treachery!* Storg had come to Mikiel to—what, inform on them? The mission to the Arcanamirium hadn't exactly gone smoothly, but Mikiel already knew that, and most of the more awful things had been done by Storg's hands personally, and Wilhum's. So... what was this?

Mikiel frowned at them. He was in full dress armor, gleaming and decorated with flame motifs. "Please, both of you, sit. I see you've *also* smeared your chests with blood and ashes. Some sort of exercise in unit cohesion, I assume?"

Astrachios looked down at his chest and the ashen circle with its corona of red, though it had dried to a reddish-brown. "Something like that, sir." He sat down, and Rakhiel took the chair between him and Storg.

"My intention in calling you here was to formally reprimand you," Mikiel said. He leaned back in his chair and looked at them from beneath lowered brows. "You were sent to the Arcanamirium to assert our authority and gather intelligence, but instead, you blew up their front door and then got into a firefight in one of their basements."

"Force was necessary to achieve our goals," Astrachios began, but Mikiel scowled at him so hard he went silent.

"I don't care that you killed a few wizards. But your siege of the library was partly *broadcast*, with commentary from Zo! impugning our good names and claiming we were asserting control over the station under false pretenses, murdering innocents, and doing *other* things that might cause the citizens of Absalom Station to waver in their obedience." He leaned forward, mailed hands flat on the table. "We had to do quite a lot of spinning to make those events fit our preferred narrative. Tyrcell and the others are now officially terrorists who were trying to *destroy* the Arcanamirium, in league with the evil necrovite Zo!, and you stepped in to stop them, because we take our mission to protect the denizens of this station seriously. Unfortunately, not everyone believes our account, and Zo! is pushing his own version faster than we can scramble his transmissions. The best we've managed to do so far is confuse the issue so much no one knows *what* to believe. But I don't want confusion. I want certainty."

Astrachios cleared his throat. This wasn't a promising start. "Sir, they *are* terrorists, and we *were* trying to—"

"I said I *planned* to reprimand you," Mikiel interrupted. "But then your man Storg here brought me an interesting document he says he found in the library." Mikiel raised one eyebrow, as if to say "Can you imagine *Storg* in a *library*?" Astrachios couldn't, and he didn't know what was going on, and he didn't like that. "As a result, the agenda has changed. Tell us what you've found, Storg."

The knight laboriously unrolled the scroll. "It says we can, ah, do that thing... that we were talking about," he said.

"May I?" Rakhiel asked as she plucked the scroll from Storg's hands. As she read, her trunk twitched, and when she finished, she gave Astrachios the scroll before turning her gaze to Mikiel. "Well, *this* is fortuitous. This is exactly the subject we hoped to talk to you about today, sir."

"It is fortuitous indeed that a known fabricator of documents should bring me a document that supports her current wishes," Mikiel said.

"I don't fabricate anything, I craft legislation," Rakhiel said crisply. "And I didn't bring you the document. You said Storg found it in the library."

"It's quite convincing; I'll give you that," Mikiel said. "The document is even missing information—it has dropped words and clauses, redacted sections, just like every other useless piece of data in the place."

"Those little gaps are wonderful for us, sir," Rakhiel said. "I think of them as holes in the law, just waiting for us to fill them in with whatever suits our cause the best."

Astrachios was struggling to make sense of the document, not because the language was so ornate—it was, a bit, but that was legalese for you—but because he was also trying to follow the rest of the conversation. A few relevant passages caught his eye, though, and he said, "This... this lays out the mechanism by which new orders can be founded in times of emergency!"

Mikiel cocked his head. "By the layers of Hell, you seem genuinely surprised, Astrachios. Are you seriously telling me you didn't have Rakhiel draft this and hide it in the library and send Storg to conveniently discover it?"

"I have never seen this document before, and I didn't know it existed until just now," Astrachios said. "I will swear it by anything you wish—"

"Swear by your honor as a knight." Mikiel gazed at him intently.

"I swear on my honor as a knight," Astrachios said promptly.

Mikiel grunted. "Hmm. I see. I'm not convinced this whole situation is... entirely *organic*, let's say... but an oath is an oath. All right, I'm prepared to listen to your pitch. Why should *you* get to lead your own new order, especially given your... overreach at the Arcanamirium?"

"May I?" Rakhiel said. Astrachios nodded; she seemed better prepared for this meeting than he was, which made him somewhat furious, but he was good at hiding his fury.

The propaganda devil said, "If I'm reading it correctly, this document states that in times of crisis, a new order may be enshrined if no existing order's strictures are suited to the nature of the current emergency. I'm sure this is how many of the smaller orders, outside the core seven, were founded—like the Order of the Coil, the Order of the Wall, and so on. They arose to meet the needs of a particular emergency, and some of them were quite small at the start, with only a few members."

"Your group has *four*," Mikiel pointed out.

"That just gives us room to grow," Astrachios said.

"And what's the particular emergency you would form to meet?" Mikiel asked. "The one the rest of us are so *unqualified* to address?"

Now Astrachios took over. "The crisis is information, sir. That has been my focus ever since I woke up with no memory of who I was. I immediately saw the dangers, and the opportunities, inherent in the situation. Seeing that fool Zo! spreading chaos with his broadcasts only brought home how urgent the control of information is. Our order would crack down on those who broadcast propaganda, incite unrest, or try to destabilize society. We would punish seditionists, rabble-rousers, journalists, teachers, and others who spread dangerous ideas. It's so easy to communicate here—the public address systems, the vidscreens, the infospheres! Someone has to control all those channels. It's the only way to ensure unity of voice and unity of purpose. If anything, the... trouble at the Arcanamirium... only shows how vital such a group is right now. Once my new order is at full strength, crushing heretical broadcasts like Zo!'s and ensuring our version of reality is the only one anyone ever hears will be easy."

"Hmm." Mikiel's face was blank. "And your first mission would be?"

"Tracking down the android Tyrcell, the ysoki Carn, and the lashunta Melezheun," Rakhiel said. "They aren't just a small group of terrorists. They're the leaders of a group that formed near the Lorespire Complex—they call themselves the Society, if you can believe it. So grandiose. They are a rogue state, and they're gaining power and influence on that side of the station. These three—originally four, but we neutralized one of them earlier—are fanatically devoted to finding out the cause of the Gap and revealing the truth to everyone. And, as you know, they found a message in the Arcanamirium that promises to lead them to that information, hidden away by Yaraesa."

"We have to reach this secret before they do," Astrachios said.

"I agree that would be best," Mikiel said. "Revealing a secret that powerful, whatever the details, would make things here even more chaotic. Not to mention the likelihood of attracting the ire of the other gods. At the very least, no one should have access to that information—except us, so *we* can decide what to do with it. Where are these rogues of yours right now?"

"We're in the process of tracking them down," Rakhiel said smoothly. "But they're certainly making preparations to head off-world. If you approve the founding of our new order, we'll have the resources necessary to intercept them."

Mikiel leaned back again and sighed. "As I see it, I have three choices. One, I can refuse your request, but I suspect you'll bury me in appeals if I do that, won't you, Rakhiel? Annoying me with trivialities when I have a whole station to tend to?"

"I believe in due process, sir," the devil said.

"Two, I can grant your request, and you'll all go off and do what you were going to do *anyway*, permission or not, with your newborn Order of Four. Or three… I can exercise my power as paralictor of the Order of the Pyre to have you all dragged off for heresy *and* exercise my power as leader of the combined orders of Hellknights to have you seized for insubordination and dereliction of duty, and in either case, you'd all immediately stop being a problem for me and become a problem for the janitors in the dungeon instead."

"We don't want to be a problem for anyone, sir." Astrachios asserted all the false humility he possessed. "We want to *solve* problems."

Mikiel swiveled back and forth in the chair, thinking, then stopped and jabbed his finger at each of them in turn. "All right. This helps me actually. Since I've branded this Tyrcell as a dangerous terrorist, it looks strong and decisive to send you lot after him. The announcement of a new Hellknight order is also likely to dominate the news cycle for a bit, pushing more troublesome stories down in the attention queue. And when the mages at the Arcanamirium complain to me about the assault, I'll explain that you're an autonomous order, acting on your own authority, and they should take their complaints to you directly, Astrachios. For those reasons, I'll allow this." He raised the jabbing finger in the air. "With one caveat. I am *still* in charge of *all* the orders of Hellknights on Absalom Station during this time of crisis, including yours, which means you will *not* outrank me here." He waved his hand. "You can run off after your troublemakers while I get this station under control. Rakhiel's documents have given us a legitimate pretext to seize control, and while we've met a certain amount of resistance, I think our chances of prevailing are good, as long as our opponents remain fragmented and don't present a unified opposition." He actually smiled then. "I am grateful to Rakhiel in particular for laying the groundwork of our new law. Her contributions have brought you this much leeway, Astrachios, and no more. Understand?"

Astrachios nodded. "Thank you, sir." He looked forward to never having to thank this man, or anyone else, ever again.

"All right, then," Mikiel said. "We'll get your founding paperwork started, and there's a suite of offices and living space we commandeered in the Freemarkets that you can use as a base of operations. What's the name of this new order, anyway? The Order of the Censor? The Order of the Blackout?"

"We'll just write down 'to be determined,' for now," Rakhiel said, rubbing her hands together. "Oh, now I get to write a press release. I love this part."

—

After a few hours of tedium, the proper articles of incorporation were all drawn up. As his first official act as head of the Order to Be Named Later, Astrachios formally commended Storg for his assistance, and then sent him off to give Wilhum the good news.

Mikiel shooed the other two out of the meeting chamber with a final, ominous "Don't make me regret this."

"I thought that went well," Rakhiel said as they walked past the guards. Once they turned a corner into a private stretch of corridor, Astrachios grabbed Rakhiel by the throat and slammed her up against the wall, pinning her in place. Then he grabbed the end of her trunk and wrapped it around his other fist, one turn after another, until it wrapped three times around his hand.

"I should pull this oozing thing right off your face." He stared into her eyes, reddened and rheumy and... amused? He squeezed harder. "You sent Storg to find that document and talk to Mikiel behind my back. You wrote that thing yourself, didn't you?"

"I told Storg he should look in the library for information about starting a new Hellknight order," she said. Her voice came out a little snuffly because her trunk was twisted, but she didn't sound particularly bothered. "And, lo and behold, he found something, just where anyone would have expected such a document to be. He was so excited he ran off and told Mikiel about it himself, with no prompting necessary. This is a *good* thing, Astrachios. Why are you trying to crush my throat?"

"I am the leader of this new order, and you shouldn't make moves like that without asking me first!" He eased up on the pressure. "I don't like people sneaking around behind my back and plotting—" He almost said "plotting against me," but she'd been plotting *for* him, hadn't she?

"If you'd known about it, you couldn't have truthfully sworn you *didn't* know about it, and that vow of yours went a long way with Mikiel."

Astrachios growled. "I am the one in *charge*." He slammed her against the wall, but not hard enough to hurt, just hard enough to emphasize his point.

She gasped, then said, "You *are* the leader, which means you set the policy and define our goals. I'm your lieutenant, and that means I implement your policies. You told me what you wanted to achieve—to create a new order of Hellknights—and I took steps to execute your vision. I didn't realize you wanted to be informed about every little thing, but we have our share of micromanagers in Hell, so I'll be sure to run everything past you first from now on."

Astrachios released her, then unwound her trunk slowly, flicking away some of the mildly acidic goo that had gotten onto his gauntlet in the process. His fury ebbed, replaced by... amusement? "If I tell you I want to be fully informed about your actions going forward, you're going to ask for my formal approval on everything, aren't you? Requisitions for armor polish, whether Wilhum should get a haircut, what the members of the order should have for breakfast—everything, right? Bury me in paperwork until I realize the error of my ways?"

"We call it 'malicious compliance,'" Rakhiel said. "None of that seems necessary to me, but I serve at the pleasure of the lictor of the Order to Be Named Later and will do as I'm told."

"Lictor," Astrachios said. "I do like the sound of that. It would be... impractical for me to oversee every little detail of the workings of our order. You're right." He put a hand on her shoulder and squeezed, hard, feeling her bony plates shift under the pressure. "But I would appreciate it if you exercised more judgment, in the future, when it comes to deciding which details I might be curious about. We're in this together, Rakhiel, and we should make the big moves as a team. Do you agree?"

"How could I disagree? You're the lictor."

"And you will be my mistress of blades, my field marshal... if you can remember to keep me in the loop about important things. *Actual* important things."

Rakhiel bowed her head. "You honor me, Lictor. I humbly accept the role and will lead our knights to glory." She paused. "Our knights are, currently, just Wilhum and Storg. Oh, Hell, are we going to have to make them paralictors? Or maralictors at least? To fill out our hierarchy?"

Astrachios chuckled at the idea. "They are knights, and I think they'll be most effective in that role. We don't need a very complicated organizational structure when there are only four of us. As you said, I'll set the vision, you'll execute it, and Wilhum and Storg will..."

"Execute anyone we point them toward," Rakhiel finished.

"But our ranks will grow," Astrachios said, gazing past the walls of the citadel corridor and off into an imagined future. "Information is power, and *we* will control that information, and recruits will flock to us, in time, once we've established our reputation."

"So what's your vision for the immediate future, Lictor? How do we get that reputation started?"

"We need a ship," Astrachios said. "So we can pursue that android and their horrible friends and stop them from finding Yaraesa's secret."

Rakhiel stroked her trunk thoughtfully. "I confess I expected this request, and I've already done some research. The Hellknights have a whole hangar of ships equipped with Helldrives, which probably makes them the fastest vessels on the station. Of course, access to those ships is tightly controlled, and they don't let just anyone stroll in and check one out."

"How do we get one, then?" Astrachios asked.

"There are loads of forms to fill out, in quadruplicate, including a form to request the form that lets you request a ship, and then there are various authorizations to secure, and you have to schedule the ship in advance according to the needs of the existing schedule," Rakhiel said. "But... there's an exception for knights requisitioning a ship for purpose of immediate pursuit of fugitives, which can be expedited immediately and would jump us right to the front of the line. Sadly, those provisions are just for the Order of the Chain, and you've left their ranks. There is another option, though."

"What's that?"

"An emergency authorization, signed by a *very* high-ranking member of a Hellknight order."

Astrachios grinned. "Like, say... a lictor?"

Rakhiel nodded. "Or even a lowly mistress of blades. I submitted the paperwork already, and our ship should be waiting for us now."

"You weren't mistress of blades until a few minutes ago!" Astrachios said, but he couldn't help but laugh.

"I knew I *would* be," Rakhiel said. "The authorization bears today's date, and I attained that rank today, so it's all legal and proper."

"I'm lucky I found you," Astrachios said, feeling a rare surge of appreciation.

"I'm lucky I found *you*," Rakhiel said. "I love taking shots, but I need someone to call them, and you're a natural leader."

(Tyrcell here: What does being a "natural leader" even mean? That you think you know what's best for everyone else and you like to shout a lot? I've had to do a fair bit of leading in my time, but I never thought I was a natural; I had to work at it, and the work was hard. But anyway.)

"We're going to do great things together," Astrachios said.

"Not only that, surely," Rakhiel said. "We're also going to do *awful* ones."

24

HELLDRIVEN
(Tyrcell)

Castrovel loomed in the viewscreen before us, while the Hellknight ship loomed on the radar off our rear starboard. The planet ahead was a swirling mass of green, white, and blue, all steaming jungles and massed clouds and glittering seas. The Hellknight ship was an ominous red dot.

"We might as well parlay," I said, and I sent a comms ping to the pursuing ship. I'd talked my way out of lots of things, after all. Maybe I could talk my way out of this.

A moment later, a channel opened, and Astrachios's blunt, scowling face filled my vidscreen.

"Hello," I said. "I wish I could say it was nice to see you again. Did you want something, or do we just happen to be traveling in the same direction by coincidence?"

"By the authority of the Order of"—he hesitated—"the order I represent, I order you to cease your unlawful pursuit of the truth."

"What is that, three orders? That's too many orders, even for someone as orderly as you."

"Surrender yourselves to us," Astrachios said, "and you will be placed in custody and confined to a cell in our citadel until the emergency has resolved."

"We're the ones trying to resolve the emergency, Astrachios," I pointed out, pointlessly. "How can the emergency possibly end unless we figure out what caused the Gap and whether it's possible to reverse it?"

"They don't want to resolve it anyway," Melezheun said. "They want the emergency to go on and on, because then they can claim emergency powers and try to take control of the station."

"That will never happen," I said (presciently, as it turned out). "You get that, don't you, Astrachios? Right now, Absalom Station is broken into scores of individual communities and gangs, all squabbling with one another for territory and resources. But there's one thing that could make them put those differences aside and prompt them to unify, and that's *a common enemy*. There's no enemy more common than the Hellknights. Please, keep blustering and threatening and trying to take over the station—I can't think of a better way to get everyone else to cooperate."

"Your opinion on these matters is irrelevant," Astrachios said. "My order is devoted to stopping the dissemination of destabilizing information. We're already *mired* in chaos, and you want to make things worse by spreading inconvenient truths and exciting the ire of the gods?"

"We're all the walking wounded, Astrachios," I said. "You can't heal from a stab wound while the knife is still jammed inside you. We need to find out what happened, and once we know, *then* we can decide how to proceed."

"I'll show you wounded," Astrachios said, flicking off his screen.

"Now's the part where they start shooting at us," I said. "Carn, are you ready?"

"Aye, aye." Carn was in the navigator's chair, since the *Harrowdown* didn't have dedicated battle stations. He was holding a tablet, though, hooked in to the weapons systems our engineers had set up on the ship.

I couldn't decide if I regretted the installation of all those armaments or not. If we *hadn't* taken the time to make the *Harrowdown* into a nasty little warship before departure, maybe we would have reached Elindrae in advance of the Hellknights. But they would have caught up to us eventually, and even if we'd avoided a fight before we landed, we would have gotten into one when we departed, and we would have been weaponless for that.

Well, this was the path we'd chosen, and we just had to follow it to the bloody end.

"Activating defensive measures," Carn said. Our mechanics and engineers had cobbled together a pretty robust suite of weapons and signal jammers back on Absalom Station; the junk shop in our community had a back room where the erstwhile owner had kept the good stuff, probably acquired through illegal salvage or criminal trade, and the best of his inventory had been welded and wired into the *Harrowdown*.

We had a bunch of modules hooked up in the cockpit that lit up with cheery green lights when Carn turned them on, indicating active countermeasures, which should make it hard for the Hellknight weapons to lock on to us. They could shoot all they wanted as long as none of their shots hit their target.

"Releasing drones," Carn said, jabbing at his tablet. We'd snagged a bunch of small surveillance drones too and jammed transponders on them that mimicked *Harrowdown*'s signature, so with luck, any targeting systems that *did* manage to lock on would kill the wrong things. And when it came to us *returning*—

"Their weapons are hot!" Melezheun said, hunched over a console, and I swiveled in my chair to look at the readouts. "They just fired some kind of energy weapon; there was a massive discharge!"

Starships can shoot at each other from great distances, and the waiting is the hardest part. Piloting was my job, and even though "evasive maneuvers" are of limited use when you're dealing with highly sophisticated weapons systems that can send a pinpoint bomb straight up your ship's most tender, unguarded nacelle from a distance of a thousand miles, I did what I could. Mainly, I tried to get far away from the drones we'd deployed, so if the shot hit them, we wouldn't be caught in the explosive backwash.

The increased acceleration pressed us all back into our seats uncomfortably until Carn did something to our gravity and made us more comfortable, which prompted me to push the *Harrowdown* even harder, past the point of safety for biological entities (even me), but I'd made a point of building in overrides for all the limits and guardrails while the other modifications were being made to the ship.

I was used to fighting in corridors and hangars, where you can *hear* the bombs going off next to you, but space, as you may know, is generally silent. Carn whistled, looking at his readouts. "Two of our drones are down, and... I think they fired a shadowbolt projector!"

"They're shooting mystical black lightning at us?" I shouted. "All we've got is a chain cannon, some plasma torpedoes, and a repurposed mining laser!" I'd felt good about our weapons load before that, but the Hellknights were pursuing us in an *actual* warship, not a pleasure craft with a bunch of guns grafted to it.

"If that weapon hits the *Harrowdown*..." Melezheun said.

"Oh, it will tear us open like a bag of snacks at a birthday party," Carn said. "Let's hope they have to charge it up between uses. How soon until we make landfall, Captain?"

Captain? Well, why not? It's always nice to accrue more titles, and "fearless leader" was no longer accurate, since I was absolutely terrified. Fortunately, androids are famed for our coldblooded calm, which is to say we're good at not *showing* when we're terrified. "Not much longer, but how are we going to stop them from following us wherever we're going once we get there?"

"I've got an idea about that," Carn said. "But first we have to live long enough to use it. I'm going to shoot back and give them something to worry about for a change—deploying plasma torpedoes." The *Harrowdown* rocked against the recoil of the improvised launch tubes, and I briefly lost control of our trajectory, not that it mattered; we weren't going to crash into anything out there, since the only thing nearby was a whole *planet*, and—there, the moon, Elindrae, just a rocky little speck against the backdrop of Castrovel, like a bit of dust in an eyeball. I shifted our course accordingly toward the satellite. "Carn, can you send some of drones down toward the planet so they'll think we landed there? Maybe they're just following us and don't have the actual coordinates from the shrine."

"Worth a try," he said. "Our torpedoes aren't doing too good; their shields are just soaking up the impacts, but they've *got* to be taking a toll. Maybe if we keep hammering them, we'll crack their hull." He whistled. "This Hellknight ship... it's close enough to get a visual now. Will you look at this ugly thing?"

One of our vidscreens lit up with the view from our rear... magnified by a *lot*, I hoped, because if that thing was actually anywhere near us, I didn't like our chances.

The Hellknight ship was sleek and black and *spiky*—it seemed like every square foot of the hull was festooned with horns and spines and wicked curving blades. Then you had the infernal insignia, eye-watering glowing red designs etched onto the hull, and the dark nodules and protrusions of their weapons systems. The vessel looked like the head of a morningstar created by the sort of weapons designer who wears a lot of black eye makeup and silver jewelry and listens to the kind of music that ruptures unprotected eardrums. "They're trying to intimidate us with that thing," I said.

"It's working," Melezheun said. "They're charging up their energy weapon again!"

I muttered various curses. If we could just get to the *moon*, to wherever we were *going*, maybe we'd have a chance. I hoped Yaraesa had some kind of secure bunker waiting for us, with big, heavy, locking, blastproof doors. Or maybe the goddess herself was there, ready to do some divine smiting against the Hellknights who were climbing up our collective ass.

It crossed my mind that we might reach the coordinates and find *nothing*, that the other gods might have stopped Yaraesa from doing whatever she meant to do, or that this whole thing was a sick joke from one of the pranksters in the pantheon. Wasn't that elf goddess Calistria famous for playing nasty, complicated little jokes? *Have some faith, Tyrcell,* I thought, but the problem was, the last person I'd had faith in was Melezheun, and she'd betrayed us, even if she'd meant well at the time.

Our countermeasures worked... mostly. The bolt of black lightning didn't hit us directly and blast us open, but it grazed our comms array, so we wouldn't be getting any more entertaining broadcasts from Zo! or updates from Starla and Valentine anytime soon. That hit was close enough to make the whole *Harrowdown* shake and set off flashing red and yellow lights and blaring alarms, which were *not* conducive to smooth piloting. Fortunately, Mel quieted the alarms down quickly enough, though the echoes reverberated in my head.

"They're close enough for us to hit them with the chain cannon," Carn said, relish in his voice. "Let's see how they like *this*." The ship jolted again, this time because we were launching a torrent of spinning, jagged metal, designed to chew through hulls (and anything softer the shrapnel encountered on the inside). A few moments later, Carn said, "A hit!" He grunted. "But not much of one. Their shields are faltering, but they're not gone. I think we damaged their shadowbolt projector, but otherwise—"

Yet another shrill alarm blared, until Melezheun slammed it silent. "Another set of contacts! They're firing missiles now!"

I could *see* the missiles launch on the vidscreen, little puffs of air from the Hellknight hull, followed by dark fishlike shapes schooling through the void. "Carn, will those hit us?"

"*Most* of them won't hit us," Carn said. "But, uh... they sent a lot of them."

The moon, Elindrae, was visible on *another* screen, alongside telemetry readouts and flight-path predictions. The moon was looming larger than Castrovel because it was so much closer, and it was a pockmarked, bare hunk of rock, airless and hideous. "I'm going to try something. Carn, can you ease the gravity situation in here again?"

"What are you—" Carn said, and I took that as a yes and slammed the *Harrowdown*'s thrust to maximum at the same time that I executed a wickedly sharp course change to slingshot us *around* the moon, to its far side, where our designated landing site was anyway. I wasn't smushed into jelly, which meant Carn was keeping the worst of the effects at bay.

Of course, at the speeds I was going, and with no atmosphere to provide friction to slow us down, there was *some* chance that I wasn't going to "land on the moon" so much as "crash into the moon like a runaway comet."

We whipped around the moon, and *all* the vidscreens filled with images of the approaching gray surface. Alarms screamed throughout the cabin as the ground loomed up, and up, and up, but we barely heard them because we were all also screaming ourselves.

—

"Where did they *go*?" Astrachios demanded, his face inches from the tactical panel. "I didn't see an explosion, but they're gone!"

"They executed a maneuver at a frankly suicidal rate of acceleration," Rakhiel said, "and put the moon between themselves and our missiles. In fact... there they go." She pointed at a vidscreen, where the barren hulk of Elindrae loomed, dotted by flashes of light and geysers of dust as their missiles added to the array of craters that already marred the moon's surface. "They probably turned themselves to suet and bone shards trying to get away," the devil added. "But we should make sure. They've proven clever and hard to kill so far. Wilhum, take us around the far side of the moon, and keep up active scanning for their ship."

"They'd better not have killed themselves," Astrachios said, looking at the dust plumes on the moon.

"Why not?" Rakhiel asked. "We have the coordinates from the statue of Yaraesa. We know where we're going. If Tyrcell and the others have been reduced to goo in a tin can now, or smashed themselves against the surface of the moon, then we can land and secure the secret, whatever it might be, without worrying about their meddling."

"Yes, but I want to be the one to question them and then execute them for their crimes. Even if dying at the hands of a lictor is too great an honor for them."

"You really hate those three, don't you?" Rakhiel said, sounding more curious than anything else. "Is it because they escaped us in the past? Does that wound your pride? I make no judgment, pride is a virtue in Hell, but I'm curious."

Astrachios almost slammed his fist onto the console, but the electronics were delicate, so he settled for punching his own thigh. "Pride has nothing to do with it. Those three and their Society are a threat to everything our new order holds sacred. They want to share galaxy-shattering secrets with *everyone*. If we don't stop them, they'll take whatever they learn straight to that walking corpse Zo!, and from there, the knowledge will propagate throughout the galaxy, destabilizing things even worse than they are now. It could take us generations to impose order again. But if we can stop them, if *we* control the truth, then we can control the narrative and remake the galaxy as it *should* be."

Rakhiel looked at him for a long moment, then smiled, her hideous teeth showing beneath her trunk. "I was right to sidle up next to you, Astrachios. I knew you had drive and focus, and you were trying to *do* something—that's why I stood beside you in the first place. I can't abide just sitting around and waiting for things to happen. But you're more than just energy looking for a direction. You've got a real vision, don't you?"

Astrachios tried not to preen. He said levelly, "In the future I intend to make, truth will be whatever our order says it is, and anyone who dares to disagree will suffer in our chambers of correction."

Rakhiel shivered in delight. "Are you sure you don't have a little devil in you, Astrachios?" She paused. "And if not... would you *like* to?"

The lictor of the Order to Be Named Later blinked at his second-in-command. "Ah. We should... focus on the mission, for now."

"Of course, my lictor," Rakhiel said with a wink.

Wilhum, who piloted the ship with competence but little deftness, brought them around to the far side of the moon. "No ship," Storg said from the sensor array, his massive hands manipulating the screens. "Just moon. No energy signatures either."

"Most of our sensors aren't much good in this situation," Rakhiel explained. "It's hard to pick up something as small as a ship against the background of a celestial body, and if they shut off their engines, they aren't emitting any other detectable signals. We might have some luck with thermals, though, let me recalibrate." She shouldered Storg aside, and the massive knight moved without complaint, despite being twice her mass; Wilhum and Storg weren't very imaginative, but they respected the chain of command. "The moon is cold, and whether they landed or crashed, they should still be hotter than anything else in the vicinity... Aha. There we go." She tapped at a console, and one of the screens zoomed in on a patch of the moon, where a pale orange smear glowed in the thermal view. "There they are."

"But did they land," Astrachios asked, "or did they *crash*?"

25

IN THE DRIFT

(Chk Chk and Dae)

The friends took Dae's ship, the *Light Fantastic*, a little two-person racer they'd purchased with their winnings from the *Pan Pact Worlds All-Talent Extravaganzanarium: Dance-Off Edition*, one of the few wildly popular system-wide programs that *wasn't* produced by Zo! Media; if it had been, it probably would have ended with the finalists engaging in a death match to determine the winner instead of a dance competition that Dae had won handily.

The ship was in a private dock near Chk Chk and Dae's quarters in Drifter's End, the neighborhood surrounding the Lorespire Complex. As they walked through the halls, Dae said, "So this is where Tyrcell built their community. Did they name it Drifter's End, I wonder, or did that part come later? Hey, what if our apartment was *Starla*'s apartment?"

"*I think our apartment is much larger,*" Chk Chk said. "*There's been a lot of remodeling in the hundreds of years since then. I suppose they had a lot of blaster damage to cover up, for one thing.*"

"But the Drifter's Inn, that's *got* to be Bric's "Blank" Bar, right? It sure looks like the place they described."

"*It's a dive bar, and those all have fundamental similarities,*" Chk Chk said. "*It could be the same location, though. It annoys me that it's called an 'inn,' even though they have no lodgings available. It should be the Drifter's Bar or the Drifter's Pub.*"

"But then there's no pun. You have to respect the wordplay, Chk Chk. You should know that, you're a poet. I—" Dae suddenly whirled and whipped a ribbon of solar light from the mote drifting beside them, lashing it through the air before crouching and showing their teeth. They pointed one clawed hand at a figure in a dark cloak who'd just rounded the corner of the corridor behind them. "You've been following us!"

The figure pushed back her hood, revealing a human face that wasn't much improved by several bulging cranial implants. "I have *not*! What are you talking about?"

"*The person following us wore a cloak of forest green,*" Chk Chk said. "*This cloak is more of a hunter green. Also, this person is shorter.*"

"Oh." Dae wound their solar ribbon into a loop and let it disappear back into the mote. "Sorry about that. I mistook you for someone else—"

The human widened her eyes. "Hey, wow, are you *Dae*? I saw you on *Dance the Light Away*, and it was just so... *whoa*, can I get a photo?"

"*We're in a bit of a hurry...*" Chk Chk began, but it was too late: Dae was already putting their arm around the stranger, grinning and winking, and one of the bulging implants detached from the fan's head and hovered in the air, revealed to be a small camera drone. Chk Chk bore the interruption patiently, continuing to read Tyrcell's memoir in the corner of his eye until the fan-personing was done.

"I love meeting my public," Dae said. "Aren't hunter green and forest green the same color, though?"

"*One is a bit brighter than the other. You know I can see finer gradations of color than you can. Than* most *people can, which is why so few of them are capable of truly appreciating my art.*"

Dae showed their pass to the automated guard at the dock, and they made their way to the tube that led to the *Light Fantastic*. The ship was a beauty, sleek and elegant, with a prismatic shimmer that resembled that of Chk Chk's robes, and the interior was lavishly appointed, though small. Dae took the pilot's seat, and Chk Chk eased down into the chair beside them, which Dae had specially commissioned to be comfortable for shirren anatomy. *They really are a good friend,* Chk Chk thought to himself, not for the first time.

"*How long will it take us to reach Elindrae?*" Chk Chk asked.

"Not as long as it took Tyrcell and Melezheun and Carn." They punched details into the ship's computer, and it planned a route. "Can you imagine trying to travel without Drift technology?" Drift propulsion tech was a gift from the god Triune—who'd manifested in its current form after the Gap, and thus wasn't directly involved in the conspiracy of gods described in Tyrcell's memoir—and allowed faster-than-light travel by transiting through a mysterious and mutable plane of reality. Using the Drift to travel long distances could be dangerous, but for a short intersystem jump like this, it was safe enough, especially since Castrovel and Elindrae had their own dedicated array of Drift beacons to aid navigation. "Looks like it'll take... just over a day to get there. We can entertain ourselves for a day, can't we?"

"*In the Drift, the sightseeing alone is always worthwhile,*" Chk Chk said.

Dae used conventional propulsion to move them away from Absalom Station first, and Chk Chk watched the glittering jewel of the Pact Worlds get smaller in their viewscreens. How much had it changed around the station since Tyrcell's time? There had to be new spires, at least, and new modules, and new hangars; construction was constant and never-ending on Absalom Station. What would the android think of the place if they could see what it had become—would they approve of the ways it had survived and adapted to the upheavals in the years since the Gap?

"Activating Drift engine," Dae said, and the deep machinery in the *Light Fantastic* hummed and whirred. Beyond the cockpit windows, the distant stars blurred and smeared, and the black void took on a prismatic cast... not unlike the colors of Chk Chk's robes, or the ship itself. Chk Chk had been on other ships that traveled via the Drift, and none of their entries into that plane looked the same: Sometimes the stars faded to blackness; sometimes a fissure of light opened in the dark; sometimes a crackling purple sphere of energy surrounded the ship. The Drift, as with so many gods-given things, was inherently a mystery.

The ship completed the transition, and then they were in the Drift—a void that shimmered with shifting patterns of pink-and-purple light, an aurora similar to those found on planets with strong magnetic fields. Clouds roiled in the distance, dust storms flickering with lightning that were composed of indeterminate blends of matter and energy. The space beyond the windows expanded and contracted like a creature taking deep breaths, and in an instant, a distant cloud formation was suddenly right beside them, strange illuminations washing through the interior of the *Light Fantastic*; a moment later, they were so far away from the cloud that Chk Chk couldn't even see it. Within the Drift, space was unpredictable, and only the connection between their engine and the beacon at Elindrae kept them from being lost forever or emerging in some unknown place. There was *some* correspondence between distance there and in the world they knew—trips to destinations farther away took more time in the Drift than trips to closer ones—but outside that basic relationship, the details were highly variable.

This wasn't *just* a plane of transit: The Drift had some permanent habitations, notably the asteroid city of Alluvion, populated mainly by androids, augmented verthani, and technomancers. Chk Chk had never been but hoped to visit someday. Maybe Dae could add the city as a stop on their next tour.

Dae turned on some of their favorite club music and took a tab of a mild hallucinogen, then settled back to watch the light show, pointing out occasional strange sights as they journeyed. Bits of other planes appeared and disappeared from the Drift, a side effect of the technology that allowed the travel, and there were occasionally floating islands or other interruptions in the void, bits of stone or globes of water or cascades of lava, winking into and out of view.

Chk Chk gazed at the landscape and thought of the transience of all existence and the nature of consciousness and the need for every individual to create their own meaning in life, to stand as a bulwark against the forces of decay and entropy. When he got tired of thinking about all that, he returned to Tyrcell's memoir.

"*Do you think the temple is still there?*" Chk Chk asked after a while. "*Or is it just a ruin by now?*"

"Even ruins are interesting," Dae said. "And it's better to know, either way, than to just spend forever being curious."

Eventually, they slept, and when they woke, it was to the beeping of the computer notifying them that their destination was near. Dae blinked sleep from their eyes, yawned, and punched the proper commands into the console. The pink-and-purple lights around them streaked and hazed, and in a moment they were back in conventional space, floating in the darkness beneath the great green, blue, and white orb of Castrovel.

"There's the moon." Dae zoomed in the feed from one of the exterior cameras, enlarging the little mote into a bigger blot. "Elindrae. Let's see if we can land near the coordinates."

Castrovel's unlovely satellite had changed a *lot*. In Tyrcell's day, Elindrae had been a barren rock with no atmosphere, but while it was still a barren rock with no atmosphere, it had also become crowded.

The lovely world of Castrovel wasn't cluttered up with chemical factories and starship yards and all the clanging, stinking machinery of heavy industry... because the inhabitants put all that ugly stuff on their moon instead. The lunar locals didn't worry about poisoning the air or water or soil, because Elindrae didn't *have* any of those things, just rock, and under that, more rock. And under that, if Tyrcell's account was to be believed... there were secrets.

They skimmed the *Light Fantastic* around the moon, passing over the vast overgrown structures of gantries, coolant towers, exhaust fans, and smokestacks belching impurities into the void. A shipbuilding and repair yard hailed them on the comms, thinking they were a customer, and when Dae replied that they were on their way to look at a potential investment property, which was the cover story they'd come up with ahead of time, the shipbuilders just cut the communication. "Rude," Dae said. "We're not worth talking to if they can't make a few creds off us?"

"*Capitalism,*" Chk Chk said simply, and Dae nodded. They were artists. They knew all about capitalism. It was the thing that made it harder to be an artist.

They left the tangle of factories behind and moved on to a relatively undeveloped portion of the moon. "*That's lucky,*" Chk Chk said. "*I was afraid Yaraesa's hidden temple would be underneath a drone factory or something.*"

"There's luck... and there's divine intervention. Hard to say which is which, huh? I think we can land there, by—Huh. That other ship."

There was a small explorer vessel, battered and dented, on a flat patch of ground near their coordinates. Dae eased the *Light Fantastic* down not far away from the other ship and flicked through their sensor array. "It doesn't have a transponder, there are no insignia or identifying marks, no life signs on board, and it's currently powered down… Maybe it's a derelict?"

"*Or maybe the person who's been following us somehow got* ahead *of us,*" Chk Chk said grimly.

"Again, *how*? We're the only ones who have this memoir!"

"*We went to the statue of Yaraesa and got the coordinates at the Arcanamirium,*" Chk Chk pointed out. "*You said you saw the stranger lurking around. They could have slipped in after we left and found the same information. Then they wouldn't need to follow us anymore—they could get ahead of us.*"

"Gods, is it the Order of the Eclipse?" Dae asked. "Still holding a grudge after all these years, trying to keep people from finding… whatever there is to find down there?"

"*Stealthily stalking us and piloting an unmarked vessel isn't really the Hellknight way,*" Chk Chk mused. "*They like intimidation and big shows of force. I don't know who it is.*"

"What should we do?" Dae asked.

"*I suppose… what we came to do,*" Chk Chk said. "*We'll follow in Tyrcell's footsteps and see if we can find their secret. But keep your weapons handy.*"

26

THE TEMPLE OR THE DUNGEON

(Tyrcell)

Did we crash, or did we land?

We landed, of course. There's more of this manuscript in front of you, after all, and you didn't find a pile of singed and bloodstained pages in a wreck on the surface of Elindrae. You found this... wherever I'll eventually put it, I guess.

But it wasn't a very *pleasant* landing. Once we got around the far side of the moon, I sent the thrusters screaming into reverse to slow our acceleration, and if it hadn't been for Carn adjusting local gravity, we would have broken a lot of bones and ruptured a few essential organs in the process. There was no atmosphere for us to burn up in, which also helped in the not-dying department. I did an excellent piece of piloting, if I do say so myself... but even with my myriad skills, we came in at a slightly steeper angle than I would have liked, and the ship actually *rolled* across the surface, spending the last of its momentum spinning us around like rocks in a polisher. We came to rest more or less upright, our cannons bent out of shape, our comms array not just damaged but completely snapped off, our hull dinged if not dented... but we were mere hundreds of yards away from our coordinates.

"That was some... impressive flying," Melezheun gasped, clinging to the edges of her chair with white knuckles.

"Only the flying?" I groaned. "You weren't impressed by the landing? I'm the *most* impressed by the landing."

"Thank you, Carn, for keeping us from being smeared across the inside of the ship," she continued, diplomatically choosing to ignore me.

"I do what I can." Carn rolled his head around on his neck, presumably working out some kinks from the tumbling we'd done.

"With luck, the Hellknights think we're dead already, so they won't come in too hot."

"We're here," I said, once I got myself unstrapped and standing. "But... where's *here*?" The vidscreens were flickering, but they still worked. In every direction, there was cratered gray ground and the occasional boulder. "There's no structure, no temple, there's nothing here!" *Calistria, you trickster jerk,* I thought.

"The ground-penetrating sonar says otherwise," Carn said. "There are chambers beneath the ground, right underneath the coordinates we got from the statue."

"Oh, thank the gods," I said.

"One of them, anyway," Melezheun replied.

"Let's hurry. If the Hellknights *do* have the coordinates, they'll be along soon, whether they think we're dead or not." We moved to the back of the ship and opened the lockers containing our environment suits.

We all double-checked each other's seals and air supplies, but the suits were high-quality metamaterials, adapting to fit our shapes perfectly. When you borrow a starship, always borrow it from rich people, is my motto. We opened the locker and got our weapons handy. I had my pistols, and Carn carried a sidearm too, and Melezheun had her neutriad pistol and a collapsible staff/stun weapon. We weren't expecting a big fight in a temple of Yaraesa, but I'd never regretted being prepared, and with the Hellknights nearby, I was vindicated.

We went to the airlock, opened the outer doors... and beheld the majesty of Elindrae.

I jest; it was not at all majestic. It was a rocky planetoid of no great distinction. But Castrovel filled the sky above it, and *that* is a beautiful planet (where I eventually spent a lot of time, after all this happened), all blue and green and swirling white, and we gazed up at it in awe for a bit until Carn cleared his throat and said, "Shall we?"

I had a navigational aid on my suit's gauntlet, and it displayed a little blinking dot a few hundred yards away, so we started walking—which was more like hopping, because the gravity was so low, and every step propelled us into the air. After a few minutes of skipping along, it became clear we were heading for a crater. Not one of the big sea-sized ones, but one just about large enough to nestle our ship inside, which is probably what we would have done if our landing hadn't been more of a "controlled impact" sort of deal.

We reached the edge of the crater and looked down. The bottom was about thirty feet away, but the inner slope was gentle enough for us to slide down safely, and getting out again would be easy since we were almost weightless on this surface.

"Is that some kind of hatch?" I asked, pointing to a glint of silver at the bottom of the hole.

"Seems likely," Carn said. "I hope it's not locked. Though I always have my hammer—"

"Oh, no." Melezheun pointed skyward.

We craned our heads around and saw the black, scabrous hull of the Hellknight ship as it began to descend. We all hunched, instinctively, and I was glad our suits were neutral gray instead of, say, bright red or yellow—their sensors would have trouble picking up individual people down there, and we should blend in with the environment well enough to make visual identification tricky. I was afraid they'd carpet bomb our landing site, but instead, they came in for a much more delicate landing than I had, settling down next to our ship like a carrion fly on a corpse.

"Oh, we're so screwed," I said. "They'll see our tracks in the dust and come right for us. Come on, we have to get into that hatch and hope it locks from the inside—"

"No need for all that," Carn said. "I told you I had something for this." He drew his tablet from a pouch on his chest and tapped at it with his gloved hands. "I was really hoping to find a stasis beam tucked away in the back of that junk shop, something we could use to lock up all their ship's machinery and pin them in place for a while if they got too close. I had no such luck. But I *did* find ten barrels of heavy-duty industrial expanding foam, the stuff they use on Absalom Station to plug up hull breaches. I rigged them up all around our hull, with shaped charges I can remotely detonate, which I will... do... now." Carn jabbed at the tablet, and we watched as three huge cylinders burst from the side of our ship facing the Hellknight vessel and smashed into its hull... and right onto its outer doors.

The result was immediate and dramatic. The barrels burst apart on impact, releasing a splash of bright orange goo—and then that goo just *foamed*, expanding across the hull and mushrooming outward, and within two seconds the side of the Hellknight ship looked like it had been colonized by immense fungal growths, all jammed up and gluing them to the surface. "It hardens up in about five seconds," Carn said. "They can cut through it, but it'll slow them down a lot. Let's get gone."

I grabbed him in a hug, and we rocked back and forth and almost tumbled down the slope but kept our feet. "Carn, you're a *genius*."

"I don't know about all that, but sometimes I have pretty OK ideas." He patted me and then nodded to Melezheun, and we all made our way down into the crater. There *was* a hatch at the bottom, set flush into the ground, a polished steel plate covered in complex symbols arrayed around a drawing of an atom with a brain for the nucleus. Good old Yaraesa.

Except what the hatch *lacked* was a handle.

"How are we supposed to get that open?" I asked.

"Hammer?" Carn gestured toward the mote of dark energy that hovered near him.

"No, no." Melezheun crouched and examined the markings. "This is a puzzle. Yaraesa values knowledge, study, and leaps of inspiration, you see? She can't give her secrets to just anyone. She has to make sure we're worthy to receive the truth. Which means solving this puzzle to gain entry... for a start."

"What happens if we can't solve the puzzle?" I asked.

"Oh, probably... traps?" Melezheun asked. "I don't know how else she would discourage unworthy interlopers from entering her temple."

"Temple?" Carn said. "Mel, when you've got a place and it's underground and it's full of puzzles and traps and there's treasure at the end of it, usually you'd call that a dungeon, not a temple."

"I suppose it can be both," Melezheun said. "Fortunately, I *can* solve this one. These symbols are in Lashunta. See how they're arrayed around the outer edge of the hatch? This one immovable mark indicates a full stop—a period. There are various words here, jumbled together, and see, if I touch them, I can move the words around. I need to make a sentence, but... hmm. I don't think I can construct a sentence that conveys any real meaning, but *I* can put them in an order that is syntactically correct, even if it's semantically meaningless. It's a linguistics puzzle. Do you see what I mean?"

"I do not," I admitted. "But I have faith in you." I was really trying to. The fact that Carn and I would have been stopped dead at the entrance to the temple-dungeon made me glad I'd brought her along instead of casting her out, anyway.

She knelt and touched the symbols, which glowed yellow under her fingertips, and dragged the glyphs around, changing their order. She murmured to herself: "Transparent... purple... concepts... slumber... angrily." She leaned back on her heels. "There. That's the best I can do. It doesn't *mean* anything, but it's grammatically sound—"

All the glyphs glowed, first yellow, and then green, and then the hatch dilated open like an eye, revealing a smooth tunnel that descended into darkness. "You did it!" I crowed. "So. Do we just jump in?"

"Seems like," Carn said, and then he did, disappearing into the dark. He gasped over our comms, and then laughed. "The orientation of the gravity *switches* in here! The vertical tunnel becomes a horizontal hallway once you get a few yards in! It's a good thing gravity is a friend of mine, or that could have been a rough landing."

I went in next, and Carn was right: The orientation switched, with one side of the shaft becoming "down" and the other side "up," and even knowing it was going to happen, I stumbled and tumbled in the dark. I just stayed crouched on the ground until Carn's suit lights came on, illuminating his shape—I didn't scream, even though at first I thought some kind of fire elemental or something was down there with me—and he gave me a hand up to my feet. Melezheun followed moments later and handled the transition rather more gracefully than I had. I looked along—up?—the shaft, and it was surreal, seeing Castrovel hanging in the sky beyond the open hatch. Like we weren't in a tunnel, but at the bottom of a well.

Then the hatch closed, and once it was sealed, soft lights filled the corridor. The hallway was round, except for the level floor, made of some polished white substance that looked like stone, with illuminated panels spaced every few feet in the ceiling. My suit informed me that there was breathable air in there, and I cautiously opened the faceplate of my helmet. "Seems safe," I said. The others followed suit.

There was a door about twenty feet ahead of us, covered in more glyphs. We walked up to it, and I said, "Another puzzle?"

"That's not Castrovelian writing," Melezheun said. "I don't recognize these symbols at all."

"Oh, I do." Carn pushed past us, surveyed the door, and chuckled. "That's a circuit diagram, and look, at the top, that indicates a particular voltage and resistance. I think I have to make the diagram match that output. The way it is, this wouldn't work at all. Let me see here..." He reached out and began to manipulate the glyphs, which slid around on the door and stayed where he put them. "Hmm, this will take me a few minutes. I know this stuff, but I don't think I used to use it every day; maybe I was just a part-time electrician. You think if I get it wrong, I'll get zapped?"

"How about... don't get it wrong?" I suggested.

"Aye, aye, boss person." He touched the wall a moment later, and there was a loud zap. Carn hissed, pulling his hand back and shaking it vigorously. "Did that happen because I mentioned it? I just *moved* the thing wrong. It was just a mistake; it wasn't an *error*!" He glared in outrage at the ceiling, I suppose on the theory that the gods are above us, somewhere. Melezheun and I asked if he was all right, and he nodded. "It was just a little buzz, not a whole electrocution, so I'm OK. Though I'm going to be a lot more careful now, in case the penalties for mistakes get stronger every time. Let me focus."

Melezheun and I took a step back and watched him work. "I think we're being led through challenges in assorted disciplines," she said. "We had to do astronomy to unlock the mystery of the sculpture—though really it only required knowing what *syzygy* meant. Opening the outer hatch required some basic understanding of linguistics, and of course being able to read Lashunta. This puzzle is harder, and it requires an understanding of electrical engineering. I wonder what awaits us. Mathematics, chemistry, physics? And what penalties will there be for mistakes?"

"Do you think the challenges are tailored for us?" I asked. "Were these puzzles generated because they're in disciplines where we have some knowledge? Like, if the Hellknights follow us, will they have to solve the same puzzles, in which case we might be OK because I think they're at least half fools, or will they get puzzles about... I don't know... the best torture implement to use on a given species or how to most efficiently stack bodies in a mass grave?"

"I'm not sure," Melezheun said. "I suppose if we hit a puzzle none of us have any clue how to answer, then we'll know they aren't tailored to us."

"But then we'd be stuck," I muttered, just as Carn said, "There!" and the door slid open.

The next room—the first room, really, since we'd been in an overgrown corridor—looked more like what I'd expected to find in the temple-dungeon of a god.

There was a circular white stone fountain in the center, topped by an immense statue of Yaraesa much like the one in the library at the Arcanamirium. She sat cross-legged, hovering unsupported in the air directly above an endless bubbling geyser of clear water that rose up from the waist-high basin. (My first thought was "divine bidet"—I guess I'm just a fundamentally blasphemous person.) Crystals studded at random intervals on the domed ceiling emitted bright white light.

"Is this it?" I asked as we walked inside. "Is this the inner sanctum? Is the secret here somewhere?"

"Nah." Carn pointed to the arch of a closed door in the far wall. "It looks like we have another puzzle to solve."

"There are no marks on the door," I complained, but then Melezheun called my attention to the far side of the fountain, where we found a series of nozzles and hoses and transparent tanks of various sizes, with drains and ramps and funnels connecting them all in obscure ways.

"It's some kind of fluid-dynamics puzzle," Melezheun said.

"Carn, are you a... plumbing engineer, by chance?" I asked.

He gazed at the tanks for a moment. "I have no idea what I'm even looking at."

Melezheun examined the glass tanks and pointed to a black line drawn on the side of one. "See this mark? I think it's a fill line... We probably have to fill the tank to this point without overflowing the others. See, there are faucets here and here to draw water from the fountain, hmm..."

"So you can figure it out?" I asked.

She laughed, sounding a little lost and scattered. "I think I see the *goal*," she said. "I have no idea how to achieve it, apart from trial and error and trying to think it through logically as we go."

I looked around. The walls seemed closer... and the ceiling too... and thin trickles of water began flowing from the bases of the walls, making little pools that crept across the floor. "Uh. I think we're also *in* a tank. If we don't solve this puzzle fast enough, we're going to get submerged."

"I can try to smash the door down with my hammer," Carn said. "Just saying."

"Let's save that for when we *really* get stuck," I said. I twisted the handle of the nearest faucet, which sprayed a torrent of water directly into my face.

—

The expanding foam the trio used to block their exit was too dense and hard to cut through in a reasonable amount of time, and Astrachios rejected Storg's suggestion to use explosives because they wanted the ship to actually remain operational, so he finally said, "Let's just cut a hole in the hull to climb through. We can patch it up later."

First they had to set up a portable airlock against the inner hull in the ship's small cargo hold, an inflatable blister, like a geometrically complex tent that would keep all the air on the ship from getting sucked out the hole. Astrachios went inside the inflated tent and handled the laser cutter himself, because if he had been left to pace around out there while the others did the work, he would have gone feral with impatience.

He neatly sliced a circle in the hull, then gave the thick metal a shove. The cut segment fell out, hitting the gray dirt of Elindrae and sending up a sad puff of dust that quickly settled in the lack of atmosphere. "All clear. Let's go." He clambered through the hull in his bulky suit; it was powered armor suitable for operation in a vacuum and high-heat and high-radiation environments, but it wasn't very nimble. Wilhum and Storg were in similar gear, but Rakhiel was just wearing an environment suit with some useful augmentations. Even so, once they caught up with Tyrcell and their friends, it wouldn't be any trouble to crush them into paste. Astrachios was increasingly uninterested in capturing and questioning them. He didn't really want answers. He just wanted things to *go* unanswered.

The order tromped around the side of the vessel, and Rakhiel paused to look at the orange slime that bulged all over their ship, ruining its sleek and menacing lines. "That was pretty clever, to repurpose industrial foam that way." Because they were using their suit comms to communicate, her voice seemed to be right in his ear.

"You sound like you *admire* them," Astrachios said.

"I respect them as adversaries, anyway," the devil replied. "For amateurs, they handle themselves well. When you go up against professionals, they're more predictable—you can anticipate what they're likely to do in a given situation, so you can plan appropriate countermeasures. But with people like this, it's impossible to tell *what* they'll do. Exciting, isn't it?"

"I'm glad you're enjoying yourself," Astrachios said sourly.

"Aren't you?" she asked. "You were Order of the Chain once—don't you experience the thrill of the chase, pursuing your quarry, closing in on the fugitives?"

"I think my favorite part is when the chase is over, and I've got my prey in my hands." He reached out his arms and made fists, imagining a vulnerable bare neck in each hand.

"That is a pretty good part," she agreed. "Look, they left a set of footprints for us to follow. We don't even need the navigation system."

They walked through the low gravity, adding their own widely-spaced tracks to those left by their enemies, until they reached the edge of a crater. They made their way down the slope and gathered in a circle around the metal hatch at the bottom. Rakhiel scanned it with the sensors in her gauntlet and grunted. "Looks like polished steel, but it's some exotic alloy, dense and strong. I'm not sure how we're supposed to get through it."

"How about grenades?" Wilhum said.

"Always grenades with you," Storg said. "Breaching charge is better."

"We have lots of grenades and only a little bit of plastic explosive," Wilhum said. "Grenades are good enough for making a hole in the ground into a *bigger* hole in the ground."

"But the shrapnel," Storg countered. "Omnidirectional. Risk of collateral injury."

They're practically eloquent when they're talking about blowing things up, Astrachios thought. "Tyrcell got through this thing, so it can't be *that* hard."

"They had divine inspiration," Storg said. "Message from their god. Cheating. Maybe."

"I hate divine inspiration," Wilhum said. "Infernal is better. Infernal is about *doing things*."

Meanwhile, Rakhiel was crouched by the hatch, head cocked, fingertips caressing the strange metal. "Oh, I see what we're meant to do," the devil said after a moment. "No bombs necessary, boys—sorry to disappoint you. It's just a word puzzle. Fortunately, I can read Castrovelian, and even more fortunately, I was perusing my old journals to learn about my past, and I learned quite a bit, despite all the smears and redactions. I wrote about the time I tortured a gnome linguist, and it seems while the irons were heating up, we had a fascinating chat about syntax versus semantics. Now, our discussion was in the context of the unreliability of coerced confessions, but the principles can still serve us here." She moved the glyphs around on the hatch, and then grinned when they all glowed green and the hatch spiraled opened.

Astrachios pumped his fist. "How did you *do* that?"

"Oh, I just had to help some transparent purple concepts slumber angrily." He frowned at her, and she chuckled. "Never mind the details. It worked, is the point. Storg, Wilhum, why don't you lead the way."

Storg jumped into the hole, which was a bit of a tight fit given his armor. He vanished from sight and then cursed over the comms. "Gravity's all wrong!" he cried out.

"This *is* going to be fun, Astrachios. You'll see," Rakhiel said. "You just have to open yourself up to the whole experience."

"I'd rather open up that android's chest cavity." He countered.

"Fun is where you find it," Rakhiel said.

27

TRUTH OR DOOM

(Tyrcell)

"They're in the corridor," Carn said dolefully. He'd used his black-box security device to hack into the Hellknight comms again so we could listen in, but given the limited range of the gizmo, that meant they were closer than we liked.

The three of us were soaking wet from our (successful, eventually) attempt to solve the fountain puzzle. By the time we completed it, we were waist deep in standing water ourselves, and the ceiling was nearly close enough to touch. We made it into the next room, though, where we were faced with three identical doors in a stone wall... and some floating words written in white fire that made me very happy.

I was unhappy about other things, though. "We should have smashed the water tanks so the Hellknights couldn't solve the puzzle after us." I sighed.

"I'm not sure Yaraesa would appreciate cheating," Melezheun said.

"You think she's watching us?" Carn wiggled his finger in his ear. "If she's really on the outs with the other gods, maybe she just set up this dungeon—sorry, temple—and then withdrew beyond the veil or wherever it is the gods go when they aren't meddling in mortal matters. If I was Yaraesa, I'd be lying low, so we could be on our own in here. I say if we get *really* stuck, we should cheat if it gets us to the next room."

"I suppose if the choice is turning back, then we must," Melezheun said, but I could tell she didn't like the idea.

"I don't really see how we can cheat in here, though." Carn gazed up at the words emblazoned above the doors. "In fact, this doesn't seem like a Yaraesa kind of puzzle at all. It just seems like a game of chance. Plain old gambling. I thought her whole thing was intellect?"

"It is very strange," Melezheun said. "I'm not sure I understand the point. It may be too subtle for me. There could be a trick we don't see."

It was gambling, and I *did* understand the puzzle, and there was a trick... sort of.

There were three black doors arrayed on the wall, side by side by side, without handles. The doors were identical except for a glyph at the center of each one: a triangle, a square, and a circle. Above the doors floated words of shimmering white fire that read:

"One door leads to the truth.

The other two lead to doom.

Speak your choice."

"There are no clues or anything?" Carn asked. "There's nothing in Yaraesa's lore about—I don't know—always picking the door on the left or something? Or a particular shape that she considers extra sacred?"

"Not that I recall," Mel said.

"Then we just guess, I guess." Carn looked at me. "Unless you have a better idea, Ty?"

I decided to put them out of their misery. "I have a more complicated idea," I admitted. "But it starts with guessing. So, what will it be: door number triangle, door number square, or door number circle?"

"Circles are nice," Carn said.

"Fine by me," I said.

Mel nodded and said, "We choose circle, Great Lady."

The letters shimmered and said:

"You have chosen the door of the circle."

And then:

"Behold a path unchosen."

We'd picked the door on the far right, and suddenly the door on the far left, marked with a triangle, slammed open, revealing a howling storm of black lightning and churning, poisonous purple clouds—the shrieking winds sounded like the cries of the damned, and for all we knew, they actually *were*. We all recoiled, though the effects of the storm didn't extend beyond the threshold.

The floating letters changed again:

"Do you wish to stay the course or change your choice?"

The deafening howls diminished, presumably so we could hear ourselves talk.

Melezheun and Carn frowned at each other. I, however, grinned, because that was exactly the response I was hoping for. I *knew* this one: We were experiencing an old brain-twisting probability puzzle that gamblers loved to drunkenly argue about. "We should switch our choice from the circle to the square," I said. "We had a one-in-three chance of choosing the correct door before, but if we switch, it becomes a one-in-two chance. Much better odds."

They stared at me like I'd lost my mind. "That doesn't make any sense," Carn said. "Nothing has changed. There are three doors, and we picked one, and just because we know what doom looks like now, it doesn't mean we picked the wrong door in the first place."

"I am afraid I agree with Carn," Melezheun said.

"I know it's counterintuitive," I said. "But you're mistaken when you say that nothing has changed, Carn. We have more information now."

"I am lost," Mel said.

I knew how to explain it; probably someone had explained it to *me* once, though I couldn't remember who or when. "It's easier to understand if you imagine we were presented with a hundred doors instead of three." I spread out my hands. "So, picture it: Yaraesa gives us a hundred doors to pick from. Ninety-nine of them lead to certain doom, and one leads to the truth. We have no rational basis for making a choice, so we just choose one at random, right?" I held up a finger. "Then the goddess opens *ninety-eight* of the hundred doors, every single one except our choice and one other, revealing howling-nightmare doom after doom after doom. So think about it. With two doors left, how likely is it that we just *happened* to choose the right one in the first place? The *other* door is almost certainly the right one. So what would you do then? Stay with your original choice or switch?"

"You'd obviously switch in that case," Carn said. "But with only three doors... huh. The principle is the same, though, isn't it?"

"I still do not really understand," Melezheun said. "Are you sure about this?"

"I am," I said. "We should switch."

"Still, even if you're right, we go from a one-in-three chance to one-in-two chance," Carn said. "A coin flip? That's not so great."

I shook my head. "My hope is that by switching doors, we'll prove to the goddess that we understood the puzzle and solved it correctly. That way, even if we did happen to choose the right door in the first place, she'll still let us move forward." I cleared my throat. "We'd like to switch, please. We choose the square."

"Then pass through, one by one, onward to truth."

At the burning words' final message, the center door swung open, revealing a hallway lit by dim red crystals.

"Yes." I pumped my fist. "Always trust a gambler when it comes to the odds."

"I think that might be terrible advice," Melezheun said. "But it worked out for us this time."

"Let's move on," I said, then stepped through the door and down the reddened corridor. I didn't hear them behind me, and when I looked back, the doorway was gone, with just a blank wall and no sign of my friends at all. I moaned. Crap. Had we messed the puzzle up after all?

When I turned back the other way, there was yet another door before me and more floating words:

"These next steps must be taken alone."

I moaned again and tried my comms. I couldn't reach either Carn or Melezheun, although, weirdly, I could still hear the aggrieved chatter of Astrachios and his grim band as they tried to solve the puzzles we'd already done. Yaraesa, it seemed, wanted to discourage group projects. I'd be reunited with my friends once we solved the next puzzles, though, right?

Right?

The door opened without any word or math games, and I stepped through. The small room I entered was dim, apart from a bright spotlight shining down on a black table, which was inscribed with white lines forming a grid of thirty-six squares arranged six by six. However, the square farthest from me on the right was open on one side. Words of fire appeared in the air and said simply "Escape," before shimmering away.

I frowned, unsure what I was supposed to do, but then figures appeared on the board, each small enough to fit easily on a single square. One game piece was a tiny version of *me*, complete with gray environment suit, standing on the square toward the bottom left, as far as possible from the "exit" square with the open side. The token looked around, shifted its weight, and fidgeted, seeming completely lifelike.

The other figure was a model of Astrachios, in intimidating power armor, wielding some kind of electrified mace. He was two spaces away from the exit and paced back and forth within the confines of his square, never taking his eyes from the little 'me.'

OK. So I had to get my figurine to the open square without crossing paths with mini Astrachios. That shouldn't be too hard, though I was sure there were limitations: Our pieces probably took turns moving, and I bet we could only move one square at a time. Could we move diagonally? An instruction manual would have been nice. I'd have to think this through. After a moment, I reached out toward the little version of me, and the figure flinched away and said, in a querulous, reedy voice, "Just say 'left,' 'right,' 'backward,' or 'forward,' all right?"

I didn't sound like *that*. Not even if I were tiny would I sound like that! "Left," I said, and my avatar obediently took a step to the left, watching miniature Astrachios all the while.

The tiny Hellknight promptly moved *two* squares closer to me. "That's not fair!" I shouted.

"It wouldn't be much of a challenge otherwise," my tiny avatar replied. "As long as he doesn't actually move onto my square, though, I'll be fine."

I paced around the table, running scenarios and thinking things through. I decided it was worth asking for clarification. "Is this little Astrachios clever or as straightforward and blunt-force traumatic as the real one?" I thought it was the latter—if he were clever, he'd just shift back and forth between the two squares closest to the exit, cutting me off from escape.

"He wants to kill me," my tiny self said plaintively. "More than anything else, that's what he wants. So he'll come straight at me, either two steps horizontally or two steps vertically, whichever gets him closer to me. If neither of those options allows him to gain ground, he'll just wait for me to move, and then take his turn again. I'm *also* allowed to wait, if you tell me to... but don't make me wait too often, or he'll get me for sure."

"Hmm." I thought about electric shocks and shrinking flooded rooms and howling voids of black lightning and said, "So what happens to *me* if tiny Astrachios captures *you*?"

My avatar chuckled and shook their head. "Have you ever heard the expression 'as above, so below?'"

That was vague but terrifying. Fortunately, I had the sense that I was *good* at games, and even though these were just little magical or technological representations of myself and my adversary, they did have an emotional impact: I wanted to save me, and defeat Astrachios. "Is there a time limit?"

"Not for turns in the game, no... but the *real* Astrachios is coming, you know. So in a sense..."

I grimaced. I'd tuned out the Hellknights to focus on the maze, but they were still talking, currently arguing about how to solve the three-doors puzzle. "Right." Since the tiny Hellknight would behave in predictable ways, I could plan out all my moves in advance if I could hold enough of them in my head. I should have gotten a computer implanted into my brain at some point, though maybe Yaraesa would have considered that cheating and shorted it out.

While I was pondering, I heard a distant boom, and the room briefly shook, making my tiny avatar flail their arms around to keep their balance. "What was that?"

"It sounded like a big boom," little me said. "But I'm just a game piece. Why are you asking me?"

I groaned and resumed my focus on the board. Nothing else mattered if I couldn't get out of this room and into whatever waited beyond. I ran through my moves and soon realized that I wasn't going to be able to solve this quickly; it would probably take me a hundred moves or so to lure Astrachios to a position where I could escape without being captured. I couldn't hold that many moves in my head, and I didn't have anything to take notes with, so I just gritted my teeth and began.

Way too much time later, I made it to the exit square one step ahead of the monster. The tiny, furious Astrachios slammed his mace down on the game board hard enough to crack the table. Tiny me pumped their fist, danced around on the table, and then jumped nimbly to the floor and ran toward the wall, disappearing through a two-inch-high arched opening that appeared in front of them, allowing them to exit.

Then an eight-foot-high arched opening appeared in the wall *above* their egress, revealing a vast glittering cavern of amethyst splendor that resembled the inside of a geode… and there was Melezheun, sitting with her eyes closed, as if deep in meditation.

"Mel!" I rushed to her, and she leaped to her feet and hugged me. I was suddenly painfully glad to see her, and while Sue's death kept me from fully embracing the idea of forgiving her, I knew forgiveness was inevitable… mostly because I knew she'd never stop trying to make up for what she'd done.

"Where's Carn?" I asked.

"He must still be trying to figure out his puzzle," she said. "What did you have to do?"

I described the maze puzzle to her, and she laughed. "I'm glad I didn't get *that* one. I was presented with a series of diagrams representing various unstable molecular structures, and I had to alter and combine them to create stable ones." She paused. "I was pretty sure I used to be a historian, but it turns out I'm also conversant in biochemistry, so I don't know *what* it was I used to do."

"Maybe you're a multidisciplinary genius, like Yaraesa," I suggested.

She rolled her eyes. "I wonder what Carn is doing. It's taking him a while."

(Before we get to how Carn was doing, let's see what the Hellknights have been up to, shall we?)

—

"I would have smashed the water tanks when I finished," Astrachios said as Rakhiel directed the flow from the fountain. "To make sure we couldn't get past this room."

"That's solid lateral thinking," the devil said. "But sometimes the gods get annoyed when you don't play by the rules they set up. I would have counseled against the move. Wilhum, please stop drinking from the fountain. You don't know where that water's been."

Astrachios paced around the tank, splashing in the ankle-deep water. "How much longer will this take? They have too much of a head start. What if they find Yaraesa's secret and the goddess opens up a door to the surface for them? Or creates a portal back to Absalom Station?"

"That would be unfortunate," Rakhiel said. "But making water flow faster is not one of my many skills." Eventually the complex arrangement of tanks was properly balanced, and the doors on the far side of the chamber unlocked and clockworked open.

Astrachios rushed ahead into the next room and confronted three doors, each marked with a different shape. Shimmering words of fire laid out the rules of this game, and he frowned, trying to figure out what the trick was.

"I think we do something like this in Hell," Rakhiel said. "Of course, we just *tell* the victims that there's freedom behind one of the doors—all three of them actually lead to pain and suffering. The poor souls know we're lying, of course, but they can't help hoping a little bit anyway."

"That's all well and good, but which one is the correct answer?"

"All we can do is take a guess... and then play the odds," Rakhiel said.

—

They proceeded to guess, experienced the horrible revelation of what waited behind one of the unchosen doors, and then had exactly the same discussion *I'd* had with Carn and Melezheun, with Rakhiel understanding the nature of the probabilities involved, Astrachios stubbornly arguing, and Wilhum and Storg suggesting they just use grenades and/or breaching charges on all three doors instead. Eventually they decided to defer to Rakhiel, and alas, the right door opened up for them.

They went through the door, one by one, and got separated from their fellows, and at that point I lost contact with their comms too. Why did I get cut off then? I have no idea. Yaraesa moves in mysterious ways. Just because I couldn't eavesdrop doesn't mean I don't know what happened next, though...

Astrachios ended up in the same room I had, with the same puzzle. Almost. He looked at the grid and growled. The miniature monster guarding the exit square was a knight of the Order of the Chain, and it looked suspiciously like one of the dead men from the other morning—the ones sent to apprehend him for his mysterious crimes. He looked around the room and shouted, “Are you taunting me, goddess? Or is this room psychic, drawing my opponent from the depths of my own mind? I grow tired of this! You’re no god of mine, and I won’t play your games!”

He reached down for the knight of the Chain with one of his armored gauntlets, picked the tiny wriggling figure up off the board, and crushed it in his augmented grasp with an audible crunch of abused metal. He flung the mangled game piece into a corner, then swept off his own avatar with a vicious backhand—it let out a keening scream that cut off abruptly when it hit the wall. He grasped the table, ripped the legs from their bolts on the floor, and flipped it upside down, then kicked one of the legs off. He was laughing the whole time, just a bit maniacally.

That’s when the roof of the room was torn away by some unseen force, and a bright, dazzling spotlight shone down on Astrachios. He shielded his vision and looked up, shouting, “Is that you, goddess? Come in person at last?”

Something moved in the space above the ceiling, eclipsing the shining light. It was a giant, *more* than a giant, an armored colossus with the face of one of the knights that Astrachios had killed the day the Gap began. “Caught you,” it rumbled, voice tectonic, and Astrachios whimpered and crouched, covering his head.

The immense knight reached down into the room with a hand so large that Astrachios might as well have been two inches high, its pillar-sized fingers curling to snatch him up.

28

THE FOOL ROOM
(Tyrcell)

(You've probably been wondering what became of Carn. After he passed through the room of three doors, his isolation chamber took the form of a classroom, complete with a whiteboard and several empty desks.) The board was filled with numbers and mathematical symbols—a dense forest of brackets and carets and parentheses and slashes and radicals and square roots and constants—arrayed in row after row after row... all leading to an equal sign followed by a simple question mark.

Carn looked the problem over for a while, hardly knowing where to begin—whatever he used to be, it wasn't a mathematician—until he heard a rustling behind him. He turned to see that one of the previously empty desks was occupied by a hulking figure made entirely of shadow idly twirling around a dark dagger of the same substance. While he watched, another seat filled, a second shadow fighter coalescing, this one with a gnarled club of shadow laid across the desktop.

"That's not nice," Carn said as he looked back at the board. He sighed heavily when the lines twitched and a new set of symbols (half of which he didn't even recognize) crowded themselves into the middle of the equation.

He stuck a finger in his ear and twiddled it. (OK, that part's a guess, but it's an *educated* guess.) Then he shook his head, said, "Nah," and reached into his solarian mote to draw out his gravity hammer. He cocked it back, chose his spot carefully, and then swung the hammer with all the inertial force he could muster right into the final "?" on the whiteboard.

Carn didn't really expect that to work—this was a dungeon designed by a goddess—but he smashed a person-sized hole through the wall behind easily, and on the other side, there was another chamber: a softly glowing white cube.

He told me later that he thought he'd actually solved the puzzle correctly: "I was thinking of that old story, the one about the imaginary warrior who wanted to be king, but in order to fulfill the prophecy or whatever, he had to untie this super complicated knot that nobody could ever untangle. Only, instead of picking at the ends and laboring over it for hours, he just chopped the knot in half with a sword. It's a—what do you call it—a metaphor, for using the direct approach, and I thought that's what Yaraesa *wanted* me to do."

So he stepped through the hole, feeling pretty good about himself, and then the wall sealed itself up behind him, and... nothing happened. He was just standing in a cube surrounded by waxy-looking white walls. "That's when I realized I was in the fool room. A holding cell for failures." He beat on the walls with his hammer, and he managed to smash holes, but they sealed themselves up before he could get through them, as if the walls were made of liquid, just flowing into any space he made. So then he settled down and waited for his friends to come rescue him.

They didn't. Instead, there was a titanic boom, and a hole appeared in one of the holding cell's other walls, smoke curling around its edges, and the Hellknight named Storg came through. He growled at Carn and drew his sword, and Carn readied his hammer, but then there was *another* explosion, and another wall opened, and Wilhum joined them, the pull ring of a grenade still in his teeth. He looked from Storg to Carn and grunted. "Did you get the math problem?" he asked.

"Yah," Carn said. "Couldn't solve it. I just hit the wall instead." He looked at Storg. "You?"

"No math," Storg said. "Little hexagons. Lines between them. Some connected, some not. Didn't understand. Used a breaching charge."

The broken walls sealed up again, but more slowly, maybe since the holes the knights had made were so much bigger.

"Now what?" Storg asked. "Kill the rat?"

"The lictor wants to kill them himself... or maybe take them in. He changes his mind," Wilhum said slowly. "So we'd better just hold him captive." Wilhum pointed an armored fist at Carn. "You're our prisoner now."

"Oh, I'm *your* prisoner?" Carn said. "Don't you mean all three of us are Yaraesa's prisoners? I don't think she likes it when we ignore her puzzles."

"We are her prisoners, yes, but you're *ours*, so you're... lower down," Wilhum said.

"Yeah," Storg said. "More prisoner."

Carn sighed and sat back down, the shaft of his hammer across his knees. Then he gestured, and the knights both rose ponderously from the ground, waving their arms and legs in panic as Carn shifted gravity to pin them flat against the ceiling. "And now you're the prisoner of your own prisoner, and it doesn't get much lower than *that*. Speaking of 'lower,' be nice, or I'll drop you. Well, I'll drop you anyway eventually, but I'll drop you *harder*. Now—"

A sizzling sound interrupted his triumphant speech, and sparks began to leap from one of the walls. Within moments, someone kicked a large oval section of wall into the room, opening a more precise hole than Carn or the Hellknights had.

The devil Rakhiel strolled through, her cutting laser in one hand, a pistol in the other. She looked at Storg and Wilhum on the ceiling and chuckled. "Put them down, ysoki. Gently." She pointed the pistol at Carn almost casually.

"You won't shoot me. Astrachios wants to deal with me himself."

"You aren't as confident about that as you sound." She stowed the cutting laser at her belt and tapped the side of her hideous oozing trunk. "This close, I can smell your fear, clear as the stink of a dung heap. My people are good at sensing emotions. That's how I found all three of you fools. I could have solved my puzzle and moved on, but there was all this passionate *roiling* on the other side of a wall, so I sliced my way through instead. When you have a laser torch, walls are just suggestions. As I was saying, though." She fired a blast from her pistol that went right past Carn's head, searing a hole in the wall that quickly sealed up.

Carn flung himself down. "You could have hit me!"

"I know. I missed on purpose. Wasn't that nice of me? You're right that Astrachios wants you, but he *mostly* wants Tyrcell, and I'm his mistress of blades, so I act with his authority. If I kill you, he might be annoyed, but not enough to matter. Now, please put my knights *down*."

Carn sighed and gestured, and the two knights landed in an ungainly but unharmed heap. They surged to their feet, drawing weapons, but Rakhiel mildly said, "Settle down, boys," and they stood to attention instead.

"Now we all get to be prisoners of the goddess," Carn said. "I can't say I love the company. It almost makes me wish I'd tried to do the math."

"I think we can get out of here," Rakhiel said. "We have a *lot* of combined firepower—" She jolted, cocked her head, and extended her trunk in Carn's direction. "Storg, Wilhum, open up that wall! Open it up *wide*! Something's wrong with Astrachios! I can *smell* him!"

Carn scrambled across the room and out of the way as Wilhum lifted his grenade launcher. "Remote detonation sticky bombs?" he rumbled at Storg, who stroked his chin in a reasonable imitation of deep thought and then nodded.

Wilhum grunted, and then unleashed Hell, or the nearest local equivalent. The room was only about twelve feet across, so the globular grenades he fired didn't have far to go, and he could aim them carefully. Within seconds, the far wall was almost entirely covered with dark red smears, like blobs of wax but with glowing green lights in the center of each one, indicating they were armed.

"We're going to get turned into *paint* if those things all go off!" Carn shouted.

Storg looked at him with withering disdain, which really hurt, coming from such a source. "Force field," Storg said, and released a small hovering drone from a compartment in the chest plate of his power armor. The whirring, spindly thing turned in the air before them, orienting its projectors properly, and then produced a shimmering blue shield between the four of them and the wall of grenades.

"Boom-boom," Wilhum said, and activated the grenades. They all went off simultaneously, a flash of white that was only slightly muted by the intervening force field, and then the far wall was *gone*, revealing a dark cavity beyond. But the wall immediately began to heal with the substance crawling from the adjoining walls, floor, and ceiling and flowing to meet in the middle.

"Go, go, go!" Rakhiel grabbed Carn by the back of the neck and propelled him ahead of her as Storg dropped the force field and Wilhum charged for the opening. Wilhum made it through first, hunching his shoulders and ducking his head to avoid the encroaching sides and top of the hole. By the time Carn and Rakhiel reached the opening, just two steps later, the aperture was down to about six feet across.

"Jump!" Rakhiel shouted, and she shoved Carn forward. He had no desire to be stuck in the room, by himself or with Storg, so he obliged, leaping through the opening and landing gracelessly on the bare floor beyond. It was dark in there; the only illumination was the light that came through the hole in the wall and Wilhum's suit lights.

Rakhiel came through next, immediately after Carn, landing in a somersault and then springing to her feet. She aimed her pistol at the ysoki, which he thought was a bit unnecessary at just that moment.

Then Storg tried to jump through the hole... and it closed around him halfway. His head, shoulders, and upper chest protruded almost horizontally, his arms pinned to his sides. He grunted and struggled, but he was thoroughly trapped.

"Storg!" Wilhum went to the wall—it was a dull gray from this side instead of a waxy white—and began punching the surface with his gauntleted fists, to no avail. "We'll get you out!"

"Is that wall going to kill him?" Carn asked, sitting up on the floor and looking with interest. "If it keeps closing up..."

"It doesn't look like it." Rakhiel strolled forward and considered the situation, several of the lights on her environment suit focusing on the thrashing Storg. "We'd hear the armor starting to crunch and crumple, and, of course, there'd be screaming. Does it hurt, knight?"

"Just *stuck*." Storg thrashed around.

"If we use more bombs, you'll get hurt, maybe killed. I could cut you out with my torch, maybe, but..." She winced, and her trunk writhed. "Astrachios is close, and he's in danger. He's *terrified*—"

"Save the lictor," Storg said. "I'll wait."

"We will come back for you, brother." Wilhum awkwardly patted Storg's pinned shoulder.

"Are they actual brothers or just cloned off the same chunk of dim-witted half-giant?" Carn asked.

"Who remembers?" Rakhiel said. The devil again grabbed Carn by the arm and yanked him upright. She was the smallest of the Hellknights, and clearly the one who brought something other than brute force to the group, but she was still plenty strong—that was devils for you. "Come, Wilhum, we need to hurry. We'll return for Storg after we help Astrachios." She shined her lights around the space they were in, defining its parameters. Narrow passageways led off in two directions, unilluminated and unlovely. They were in the back rooms—the maintenance areas and crawl spaces—of Yaraesa's dungeon.

"This way." She hauled Carn after her, down one of the corridors. Carn considered pinning her and Wilhum to the ground with gravity and making a run for it—he could probably hold the two of them for a while—but unlike Rakhiel, he didn't have any way to sense the location of his lost friends, and he worried he'd get lost, wandering in the darkness. Besides, once they found Astrachios, especially if the lictor was *hurt*, maybe Carn could get the drop on all three of them—

"The rat is feeling hopeful all of a sudden," Rakhiel said. "Knock him out for me, Wilhum."

"Hey—" Carn began, but then the butt of a weapon crunched into the back of his head, and he ceased to possess any insight regarding ongoing events.

—

Rakhiel wasn't thrilled by how things were going, honestly. She'd been enjoying the dungeon, since intellectual puzzles were relatively few and far between in the ranks of the Hellknights. She couldn't remember her personal history, of course, but she assumed she'd been born in one of the nine layers of Hell, and if so, she could hazard a guess regarding why she'd left—constructed planes of brutal, unchanging order were probably *boring*. She'd doubtless craved the excitement of life on the mortal plane. Oh, of course she loved law and order, but *imposing* that law on a mutable world was a lot more interesting than living in a place where it had been imposed all along.

The reason she'd joined up with Astrachios was because he had plans and ideas that were more interesting than just "seize control of a space station." He wanted to seize control of *information*, to own and govern the truth itself. Granted, he'd gotten a little obsessed with this android Tyrcell, but passion was no bad thing in a leader if it could be properly channeled, and tracking down Yaraesa's secret truth was a reasonable goal.

But the interesting-intellectual-challenges portion of the endeavor was over, and they were reduced to blowing holes in things, knocking hostages unconscious, and getting stuck in walls. Wilhum had the slumbering ysoki draped over one shoulder like the world's ugliest fur stole as he stomped through the corridors. The scent of her lictor's fear became more potent, filling her trunk pungently, and if it had been coming from anyone else, she would have savored the tang. Sigveir devils had the ability to incite and intensify emotions, and they fed on the resulting psychic energy, but making Astrachios *more* afraid wouldn't help. He was getting close to catatonic levels of terror. What kind of puzzle had he been confronted with, and how badly wrong had he gotten it?

They reached a dead end, a blank gray wall, and she could feel Astrachios on the other side, cowering, emitting fear like an unstable isotope emitted radiation. She didn't dare blow a hole in the wall, not with her lictor on the other side, but with luck, this wasn't like the self-healing holding room they'd escaped (Storg excepted). She unholstered her laser torch and began to cut an oval in the wall, hoping Astrachios would notice the sparks and at least be distracted from his fear, but no, whatever frightened him, he was lost to it.

How badly will it frighten me? Rakhiel wondered, but she pushed that away and completed her cut. She kicked the wall inward, and looked inside, expecting... what? Monsters, wraiths, demons (those chaotic scum), or maybe the goddess Yaraesa herself, emitting waves of horrifying awe?

All she saw was a small room lit by a spotlight, with an overturned table against one wall and Astrachios huddled in a corner, covering his head and sobbing.

Rakhiel darted through the opening to her lictor. "Astrachios!" She put her hands on him, embracing him, not so much because physical affection came naturally to her—ha, the very idea—but just to ground him in reality. "I'm here, you're all right! What's wrong?"

He blinked up at her, his eyes red and swollen, his cheeks wet, his nose dripping, his mouth slack and wet with drool. "Ra-Rakhiel? Is it really you?" He looked up at the ceiling. "Where did it *go*? It had me... in its hand... it was crushing me—"

"It must have been some kind of psychic attack," Rakhiel said. His fear was subsiding, replaced by the acrid stink of confusion, but that was preferable. "Whatever you saw, whatever you feared, it wasn't real."

He drew a deep, racking breath, then visibly pulled himself together. "Thank you. That cursed goddess did something to my mind."

Rakhiel released him and looked at the table. "I take it you chose not to play her game, and she disapproved?"

Astrachios laughed, harsh as always. "Something like that, yes." He struggled upright, wiping his face with the back of a gauntleted hand, which only served to move the snot around. Rakhiel fished in her suit's pockets until she found a square of cloth she used to clean her drone lenses and handed it over silently. He wiped at his face and muttered his thanks. "Where are Wilhum and Storg?"

"Storg is... stuck, but not hurt. Wilhum is on the other side of that hole in the wall—I didn't cut it big enough for him to get through. He's got a nice little hostage, though. We caught the ysoki. That could be the leverage we need to..." She trailed off, frowning.

"What is it?" Astrachios asked, his focus instantly sharpened.

"I can sense emotions, and for the last little while all I could sense was your, ah... discomfort... but now that you've calmed down, I'm getting something else nearby... it's *excitement*." She hissed. "I think Tyrcell and the lashunta must have found something."

"We have to get to them!" Astrachios said. "Come on!" He rushed to the door on the far side of the puzzle room and kicked it with one armored boot. The door dented but remained intact.

"I don't think—" Rakhiel began, but then Astrachios unholstered his electroflail and smashed it into the door, again and again, hitting the door so hard that it eventually squealed off its hinges and folded in the middle. The opening he made revealed the soft white glow of the room beyond, and—

"Why am I looking at Storg's ass right now?" Astrachios demanded. "Is he *stuck* in a *wall*?"

"There's some magic involved in these rooms," Rakhiel said. "Some sort of spatial strangeness—we all ended up in that same holding cell when we smashed through the walls of our respective puzzle rooms. Breaking *out* of a puzzle room by force just leads you there. Yaraesa's dunce corner. But we escaped that holding cell, barely, and found... I don't know what. Maintenance tunnels, the back rooms of the dungeon. And I've just proven it's possible to break *into* another room from out there. I guess the Lady of Wisdom wasn't wise enough to predict that possibility." *Or using our space that way counts as lateral thinking and problem-solving of a sort she admires, so she allows it,* Rakhiel mused. "Let's go to the back room, my lictor, and then"—she tapped the side of her trunk—"we'll just follow my nose."

29

THE INNER SANCTUM

(Tyrcell)

Melezheun and I didn't know *any* of that stuff was happening. We were in the heart of Yaraesa's dungeon, worrying about Carn, hearing occasional booms and explosions and *maybe* distant screams. Mel tried to do her detecting-thoughts trick, but there was no one in range except me, and I think she didn't want to know what I was thinking; too worried I was still angry about her betrayal. (I wasn't, really. I was mostly sad about it, and truthfully, too distracted by other matters to think much about being sad.)

(I told you the temple chamber was like the inside of a geode, but that doesn't convey the splendor of the place. Imagine a cathedral, but the curved walls are made of glowing yellow-white crystals, and the vaulted ceiling glitters like diamonds in the light of the sun.) The floor beneath our feet was black, flecked with white motes like stars, with a mirror polish, so it gleamed in the omnidirectional light. I have not often felt awe, but in that crystal cavern devoted to the one god who wanted the people to know what had befallen our universe, I knew I was in the presence of the sacred, and I was moved.

Not that I showed it, of course. Androids mostly don't. Melezheun was stoic too, though tears ran down her face. "I wish Carn were here to see this," she said.

"He'll be along," I answered with more confidence than I felt. "He probably just had a hard puzzle. What do you think is in *there*?" I pointed toward the only structure in the cavern, a crystal the size of a house, glowing white, with an arched doorway set into the front. "Another hovering statue of the Lady of Wisdom, with a bunch of mathematical symbols floating around her that we have to arrange to unlock *another* clue?"

"Mmm, no," Melezheun said. "I think this is the destination. We have proven ourselves worthy, and if we go in there... we'll find out what we're worthy *of*."

"Shall we? I think Carn will forgive us if we take a peek." I reached out a hand, and Melezheun took mine, giving me the first real smile I'd seen from her since Sue died. We walked together, hand in hand, beneath the archway, and into the final temple of Yaraesa.

There was a short corridor inside, bristling with glowing crystals. The passage twisted and turned and descended for some distance. "Why is it never a straightforward path?" I complained.

"The path to true knowledge and understanding is never straightforward," Melezheun replied. "You must learn to think your way around corners." We *walked* our way around corners instead, or at any rate around curves, and at last reached the final chamber *within* the final chamber.

This was no crystal cavern, but a cozy nook, the walls lined with shelves full of books (old ones, on paper), and there were comfortable chairs and small tables that held decanters of dark liquors and battery-powered teakettles. There were soft geometrically patterned carpets on the floors and glowing brass lamps on the walls. Melezheun went to the shelves and ran her finger along the spines. "Linguistics, electrical engineering, biochemistry, game theory, hydrodynamics—these are reference works for all the puzzles we had to solve to get here."

"A bit like a teacher locking away the answer key where the students can't find it. There's nothing up there about this mysterious Golarion, then? Some book titled *The Pre-Gap Atlas*?" She shook her head, and I sighed. "So what are we missing?"

"There's this." She bent over a small table, which held nothing but an unassuming ovoid of gray stone about twice the size of my head. She rapped the object gently with her knuckles. "This doesn't really fit in with all the polish and warmth of the rest of the room, does it?"

"I think it's a geode." I paused. "And I *wonder* if it's something else. A time capsule, maybe?"

"Let's crack it open and see if there are secrets inside," Mel said.

There was no hammer and chisel handy, of course; that would have been too easy. I drew a knife and placed the point against the top of the stone, then used the butt of one of my guns like a hammer to gently tap, tap, tap until I'd created a notch in the rock. I followed that up with divots on either side of the original notch, forming a dotted line across the center of the geode. Then I hit the knife harder, widening the seam, and continued to move my makeshift chisel along the line of demarcation until finally there was a loud crack, and the stone yawned open, split neatly in two.

The inside was filled with yellow-white crystals, like the cavern above us rendered in miniature, and at first, I thought that was all... but then I noticed *another* crystal, with a clearer coloration, nestled on the inside. I picked it up and held it to the light and saw tiny shapes floating within the crystal—letters, maybe, or glyphs? "Am I supposed to be able to read this?" I asked.

"I think I've seen those before," Melezheun said, "though I don't remember where, of course. It's a kind of data crystal, but very old-fashioned, and they don't hold much information. We used to have them in primary schools on Castrovel, I think? You slot the crystal into a special projector in order to access the information."

"I don't suppose we have one of those special projectors in here?"

"I don't see one. But I *did* notice one in the back room of the junk shop, back home in the Society, when we were looking for weapons."

I clutched the crystal in my hand and nodded. I was frustrated—of course!—but also hopeful and, honestly, quite excited. (So excited a devil could smell it.) "OK, then. We'll get out of here... and find Carn... and get to our ship... and disable the *Hellknight* ship... and get back home... and *then* we'll find out what this crystal has to say. Maybe we can even get in touch with Zo! and have him broadcast the whole thing live, so we can all find out the secret at the same time."

"What if it's something terrible? Shouldn't we look first and see what it says?"

"That's what I used to think. I wanted us to vet the information first, just in case. But I've been thinking... Whether it's good news or terrible news, is it really our secret to keep?"

"We'll do whatever you think is best," Melezheun said. "I've proven *my* judgment isn't to be trusted."

I took a step toward her and hooked my arm around her shoulders. "Mel. Don't say that. You made a mistake... a bad mistake. I won't pretend otherwise, and I know you'll never forget what happened, unless the gods wipe all our minds *again*, which we can't rule out. But you're a smart person, and a *good* person, and every day that you make better choices is a step toward redemption."

She pressed her face into the space between my shoulder and neck and snuffled, and then she lifted her eyes to mine. "Thank you, Tyrcell. I'll try. I'll never stop trying. I'll devote myself to helping our people and making our society thrive."

"There's no one I'd rather have by my side." I tucked the crystal into a pocket on my environment suit and zipped it shut. "Let's try to find Carn—"

The temple rocked as a resounding boom went off above us, shaking the inner sanctum hard enough to make books fall off the shelves and one of the liquor decanters fall off the table and shatter, filling the space with the sweet reek of alcohol. "What in the hells?" I said, looking up. "Is the temple collapsing? Is it one of *those* dungeons?"

We hurried along the winding corridors, back toward the surface—and then froze, one curve away from the exit, when an amplified voice boomed through the hall.

It was Astrachios. "Come out, android, and hand over whatever you found! If you don't, we'll kill the rat!"

—

Carn was awake by then, though groggy, and he thrashed around enough that Wilhum took him off his shoulder and set him down on his feet. He didn't let the ysoki free, though; the knight wrapped one of his tree-trunk arms around Carn's throat and pressed him back against his armored chest, pinning him in place.

"Try to mess with my gravity, and I'll crush your windpipe," Wilhum growled, and Carn believed him. Sure, they were using him as a bargaining chip, which meant they probably needed him alive... but Wilhum didn't strike Carn as the best at advance planning.

The big knight turned his attention to Astrachios, who was standing impatiently before the archway to the inner temple, arms crossed, one of Rakhiel's amplified-broadcast drones hovering beside him and waiting for his next shouted demand. "Lictor, why don't we just lob some grenades in there and bring the whole place down on top of them?"

"Because it might bring the larger whole place down on top of us," Rakhiel answered, kicking aside a shower of broken crystals that had rained down from the ceiling when they first breached the wall. "Not to mention destroying whatever secrets the goddess hid down there."

"I'd be fine with that," Astrachios said, but he winced as his voice boomed out through the drone. He slapped it away and continued, lowering his voice. "It's easiest to keep a secret if no one knows it in the first place, after all."

"You really aren't curious about what your life was like before the Gap?" Rakhiel asked.

"I was a Hellknight. That tells me all I need to know. And it's not like finding out the truth, or even restoring the old order, would fix anything. People would be outraged or terrified or whatever irrational response the truth prompted in them, and they might decide to go to war against the gods, and there's no way *that* ends well. No, the level of chaos we have now is controllable. It can be cultivated. It can be fixed." He paused. "So I did consider grenades, but your point about bringing the whole cavern down on us is well taken. I would, of course, sacrifice myself to achieve the goals of the order if I had no other choice, but... we aren't at that point yet. We have leverage instead."

He reached out and nudged the amplifying drone back into place before bellowing again. "Do you hear me, Tyrcell? We can all walk away from this situation unharmed if you just give up what you've found."

"But what if they know the secret already?" Rakhiel said. "If they know, they can tell."

Astrachios turned toward her, voice low. "They're unlikely to leave this place alive anyway, but even if they do, so what? Without actual evidence in the form of whatever Yaraesa hid away, they're just two more crackpots with theories. We can work to discredit them—that's your whole area of expertise, isn't it? Plus, we'll bomb this site into rubble on the way out so no one can follow up or find any shred of evidence to back up their story." He amplified his voice again. "Come out now or—"

"Gods, do you ever shut up?" The android's (that's me) voice crackled over the Hellknight's comm.

"How did you get on this channel?" Astrachios demanded.

"Oh, we hacked into that first thing," Carn said, with just a trace of pride.

"That also means I overheard everything you just said," Tyrcell said. "About planning to kill us all. Which makes it difficult for us to negotiate in good faith, don't you think?"

"Now, now," Rakhiel said. "My esteemed lictor merely said it was unlikely you'd leave this place alive. Given our dangerous location, and the fraught nature of our situation, that's a reasonable assessment, not a threat. If you make a deal with us, we'll stand by it, of course."

"Of course," Astrachios growled. "What did you find in there, android?"

"A data crystal," Tyrcell said (it's so weird writing about myself in third person). "But we can't read what it says."

"You're lying," Astrachios said.

"Mmm, I'm mostly smelling despair off them." Rakhiel's trunk snuffled in the direction of the inner sanctum. "I don't think they know Yaraesa's secret, or that they ever expect to. They know they're stuck. Isn't that right, my noble truth-seekers?"

"I won't hand the crystal over to you," Tyrcell said. "I can't let you have it. I can't even imagine the damage you'd do as the sole holder of the truth. But... I'll destroy it. I heard you say that's just as good, right?"

Astrachios grunted. "All right. It's a trade. You smash the crystal, where I can see it, and we melt the shards into glass, and then you can have your rat back, and we'll all go our separate ways."

"No attacking us, no backstabbing, no treachery," Tyrcell said.

"I guarantee a total cessation of hostilities," Astrachios said. "Until we get back to Absalom Station again, of course. Then I intend to lead a sortie of Hellknights to annex your precious little society as part of our protectorate."

"Good luck with that," Tyrcell said. "When I left, my lieutenants were in the midst of securing a mutual aid treaty with the conductors and the Arcanamirium." (That wasn't true—or rather, it was an optimistic interpretation of Starla's and Valentine's plans—but I didn't want Astrachios to feel too smug.)

"I look forward to the battle," Astrachios said. "But for now, we can have peace. Come out."

There was a long pause, and then Tyrcell said, "Mmm, no. I don't trust you. I've seen how you operate. You killed my friend Sue, and they were harmless. I just don't believe you'll honor the deal."

"I don't think I can flatten them out, Ty," Carn said. "I wish I could be a better man on the inside, but the big one has me by the throat." He gurgled as Wilhum tightened his grasp.

"We can solve this!" Rakhiel said. "We're *Hellknights*, Tyrcell! Your android brain may be riddled with holes and addled by paranoia, but surely you understand what that means? We're followers of the law and of order. When we make a deal, that deal sticks."

"Then swear," Tyrcell said. "You, Astrachios, swear by your order and your honor and whatever Hellish oaths you find most binding, that if we destroy this data crystal, you'll release Carn and let us return to Absalom Station without interference."

"I swear it," Astrachios said immediately. "By my order, and all the others; by the Chain, and the Gate, and the Nail, and the Pyre; by my obedience to law and my honor as a knight. Destroy the crystal, and the two of you and the ysoki will be allowed to leave unharmed and unhindered." He cleared his throat. "There. A vow is a law, and by my hands, all laws are upheld."

After a long moment, Tyrcell said, "Good enough."

—

I turned off the comms and looked at Melezheun, who was profoundly downcast. Most of the despair the sigveir demon had sensed must have been coming from her. "I'm sorry," I said. "I know we came all this way, but... it's Carn."

Does discovering the truth matter more than protecting your people? I'm sure mystics and philosophers could make arguments either way, but for me, it was never even a question. Given a choice between saving Carn and solving the secret of the Gap, I'd pick the former 100 percent of the time. (Which doesn't mean I'd stopped trying to figure out a way to do *both*.) Of *course* I chose to save my friend. Just as I would choose to help my fledgling Society if I were forced to choose between that and Yaraesa's secret. The world is strange and chaotic and unpredictable. All you can do is decide what's important to you, what truly matters, and stay true to that as best you can. The reality of my loved ones would always trump the abstraction of a great mystery.

"Of course," she said. "I understand. I even agree. It's just, to come so far, to lose so much, and to leave with nothing, it's... hard. Do you think the Hellknight will keep his vow?"

"I hope so. From what I know of their order, I even think so. If not, we still have our weapons, and if we can distract the big one, Wilhum, then Carn can help too. It would be nice to talk our way out, though."

I took Melezheun's hand, and we turned our back on the inner sanctum and its secrets and walked out into the temple.

30

VOWS AND PROMISES
(Tyrcell)

Astrachios drew a hand across his throat and then conspicuously shut off his comms. The other Hellknights followed suit so they couldn't be overheard by their foes in the inner sanctum and then moved into a huddle. Their lictor punched his palm with his fist and grinned into the struggling Carn's face. "You'll like this, rat. When your two idiot friends come out, we'll capture them, find out everything they know, and then get some *proper* revenge—"

"We will *not*," Wilhum said, shaking his head slowly back and forth.

Rakhiel took a step away from Astrachios, then narrowed her eyes and cocked her head, frowning. "I don't understand what you mean, Lictor. I was hoping you'd include some loophole we could exploit in the promise you made, but your vow... it was unfortunately straightforward."

Astrachios frowned. "What do you mean? These are just—they're scum, they're rabble, they're *criminals*. Did you think I'd actually let them go free?"

"You swore an oath to do just that," Rakhiel said, enunciating each word carefully. "You made a binding oral contract. You can't just... *break* that. You can exploit imprecise wording, and you can skirt the spirit of an agreement as long as you honor the letter, but this... your oath was too clear. As long as they destroy the crystal, as promised, we must give them back their comrade and let them go free. Rules are rules."

Astrachios felt the world shifting beneath him. "But... we *make* the rules. Isn't that the basis of everything we're doing on Absalom Station? We make the laws, we interpret the laws, and we enforce the laws?"

Rakhiel nodded. "Yes, and the law *you* just made is if they crush the data crystal, they go free. You made the agreement. It's done. I doubt they'd be willing to renegotiate." *Is her hand drifting, ever so slowly, to the butt of her pistol? Is* Wilhum *looking at him with a gleam of speculation in his dull eye?*

Astrachios shook his head quickly, like he was trying to shoo away a fly. "But, no, that's... We're allowed to lie to criminals, aren't we? We don't have to be honest with them. They're lawbreakers... and... and fugitives—"

"Lies are fine," Wilhum said. "But you swore. Swearing is different. If Storg was here, he'd say the same. That's what being a knight *is*. If we go around breaking our vows, what are we? We'd be oathbreakers. We'd be *criminals*."

"The big man is right," Rakhiel agreed. "We got what we wanted here anyway. There's no reason to kill them—unless they try to break the terms of our agreement. They'll leave, and we'll leave, and then we'll bomb the entrance on the way out, bury it in rubble, so no one else will stumble on this place—even empty, this temple raises too many questions." She shrugged. "We won. Be happy. It's not worth becoming an oathbreaker over." She lowered her voice. "Do you know what the Hellknights *do* to oathbreakers?"

Astrachios nodded. There was a roaring in his ears he couldn't identify; was it his own blood boiling? "Of course. I'm sorry, I was just... I wasn't thinking. Heat of the moment. Apologies." He understood then what he'd done—the reason he'd awakened into this new life in his quarters next to the corpses of his brethren.

He'd broken an oath. That was the flaw within him, the weakness, the fracture that ruined his devotion to the law: He couldn't accept, on a fundamental level, that the law also applied to *him*. In his mind, the law was meant to protect him and bind others, not to bind *him* and protect *them*. But his followers believed otherwise, and if he hoped to continue leading them, he had to accept that belief. At least where they could see it.

Astrachios didn't know the nature of the oath he'd broken before he lost his memory, of course. He just knew that breaking oaths was inherent in his nature. Or it had been. Could a person change? Or at least devote themselves to a cause so fully that they removed the temptation and opportunity to transgress? "We'll honor the agreement, of course."

Rakhiel took her hand off her sidearm. He pretended not to notice. "We all have moments of weakness," Rakhiel said. "That's why we have our fellow knights, to keep us on the straight and narrow path. Here they come."

Astrachios turned and watched Tyrcell and Melezheun emerge from the glittering arch. Tyrcell held up a data crystal, the light gleaming through it. "I'm going to crush this," Tyrcell said, "then toss the fragments on the ground." They proceeded to do so, grinding the crystal into shards, then scattering the pieces on the ground.

"Rakhiel?" Astrachios said, at which point the devil pointed a flame pistol at the shards and released a burst of searing energy, smoothing them into a smear of glass.

"Are we done?" Tyrcell's face was utterly blank.

"Now, now," Astrachios said. "*We're* honorable, but you're criminal scum, so Rakhiel is going to search you two, to make sure you don't have anything hidden on your persons, and then I'm going to duck into the temple there and make sure that crystal was the real thing. If you tried to switch it or hide anything away, I'll consider our arrangement void and your lives forfeit."

"Please yourself," Tyrcell said, holding out his arms to let Rakhiel pat him down. Melezheun sighed and extended her own arms for her turn.

Astrachios ducked into the tunnel and followed the crystal-studded curves, alert to the possibility of booby traps or tricks. He reached the inner sanctum and grunted with surprise to find a space so homey, then gave the place a quick but thorough toss: Searching for contraband was one of the skills he'd retained from his old life, it seemed. He didn't find any great secret or any more data crystals, just books and booze. He scattered the books all over the room, tearing out their pages for tinder, then soaked the paper and furniture with alcohol. Once the contents of the room were thoroughly wrecked and heaped into a pyre, he set it all alight and walked out of the tunnel with the burning of the inner temple at his back.

He emerged and glanced at Rakhiel.

"They didn't have anything hidden away," she said.

Astrachios closed his fists, opened them, closed them, and opened them again, and then said, "Wilhum, let the rat man loose. You're all free to go. For now. But next time I see you, you will answer for your crimes."

"I'd make a witty, cutting remark, but it would be wasted on you," Tyrcell said. They and Melezheun moved warily to join the ysoki, and then all three of them backed away, toward the open door the android had entered through. They vanished from sight as smoke began to billow out of the archway of the crystalline temple.

"That's that, then," Astrachios said. He felt curiously empty in his moment of triumph, because it wasn't the kind of triumph he'd wanted. "What now?"

"You're the lictor," Rakhiel said. "So it's up to you. But my counsel would be: Let's leave, collapse the entryway to this whole accursed complex, return to Absalom Station, and get on with the important work of establishing our power. First, we have to go and save Storg, though. We can hardly give up a quarter of the membership of our whole order."

Astrachios grunted. "Lead on, Mistress of Blades."

Rakhiel guided Astrachios and Wilhum through the shattered wall into the back rooms, heading for the wall where Storg was still pinned. "You seem doleful, Lictor."

"I wanted their blood in my teeth," Astrachios said. "That's all. Anything less feels like a disappointment."

"We can get them later," Wilhum said. "I still owe that ysoki for sticking me to the ceiling."

"I see I missed some things," Astrachios muttered.

"I'm sorry you're disappointed," Rakhiel said. "We'll try to avoid that in the future. Maybe I can help you craft your oath next time, to allow a little more wiggle room?"

Astrachios grunted sourly.

"On a happier note," the devil said, "when we were approaching this moon and watching the shadow of the planet fall across its surface, it made me think about the efforts and goals of our order, and I think I've got a name for us."

"The Order of the Moonshadow?" Astrachios said. "I thought of that myself, but it sounds a bit... elfish."

Rakhiel's trunk twitched. "I was actually thinking," she said, "the Order of the Eclipse."

A smile spread across Astrachios's dour face. "Oh. Yes, Rakhiel. That's good. That's really very good."

—

We're close to the end, now, as you've probably guessed. I've taken you on a reasonably epic quest that ended in a fairly unequivocal failure. Not what you were hoping for, I know; not what I or Mel or Carn were hoping for either. But maybe there's a glimmer of hope at the end, eh? There. That should keep you reading on.

So, yes, it was Rakhiel who named the Order of the Eclipse. Over the years to come, Astrachios would convince himself he was the one who came up with the name, and any records to the contrary slowly disappeared into the order's memory holes.

That run-in on the moon wasn't the last time I tangled with Astrachios, and a lot of the details in this document were things I discovered later, as he grew his nascent order into the annoying busybody scolds of the galaxy we've all come to hate.

A few years after the Gap, I even spent some time with Rakhiel in what *she* would have called an interrogation room and *we* called an interview room, and that's when she provided a lot of the information I've included in this document. Of course, she's a propaganda devil, so half of it might be lies, but by that time she was pretty disaffected with her lictor, and I think it's true enough, at least in the outlines.

She's the one who told me about the foundational crime of Astrachios's life—the murder of his brothers—a crime *he* confessed to her one drunken night after they did unspeakable things to one another. (I'm not going to speak about them, anyway; she did, because she could tell I hated hearing it.) "He carried that guilt inside him for years," she told me, "and it all just came pouring out in a noxious flood. Inevitable, really, but I was horrified. I know we've had our differences, but as disturbed as you look right now, I felt the same way when he told me. I pretended to understand, of course, and said it didn't matter, that he'd turned one mistake into something wonderful... but he regretted telling me almost immediately. I was going to report him, of course, but..." She sighed, her trunk ooze bubbling.

"He beat you to it?" I said.

"He must have been afraid I'd turn on him. He was always paranoid. So he planted evidence that I'd been stealing from the order's coffers for years. Such convincing evidence that he must have laid the groundwork for the frame-up long ago just in case he needed a reason to get rid of me. I got out ahead of the thieftakers, but now I'm on the run, and I don't even have all that supposedly stolen money to fund my escape. You're sure you can get me out of the system?"

"That's the deal," I said. "We get your story, and you get your freedom." The Society was already in the business of collecting lore then, and we had the resources to pay for the good stuff.

We did get Rakhiel out, because we honor our arrangements, but I hope she was subsequently eaten by a space monster. I'm happy we got her perspective, though. It means this is the most accurate story of the founding of the Order of the Eclipse ever documented. Gods, how Astrachios and his small-minded censors would hate this memoir. It's a shame they won't ever get to read it. Maybe nobody ever will.

Yeah, about that. It turns out, there are secrets in this account I've come to believe *should* be locked away. At least for a while. Until things settle down. Until society—not just *my* Society, but the whole organized-intelligent-species endeavor—has a chance to stabilize and begin to function smoothly again. As I write this, we're still in the midst of total chaos, recovering from a mass disabling event, a collective trauma that's probably unprecedented in history (not that we know for sure, since none of us *have* any sense of history, except maybe for Zo! and some other long-lived weirdos like him). The point is, though I don't regret our quest for the truth, I've come to believe that now *isn't* the time to challenge the gods and demand to know why they did this to us and what actually happened to Golarion. We're all too busy trying to keep our children safe and our bellies full and our morale up and our souls intact. If we suffer any more damage, we might all shatter irreparably.

Plus, we're just too damn busy to worry about the truth right now. I'm trying to run a community, and it's gotten *big*.

But in a few years—maybe decades, maybe centuries, depending on the challenges we confront—we'll be ready, and the gods will have to answer for their crimes. Maybe *that's* why I'm writing it all down, including the coordinates to Yaraesa's temple-dungeon. It's still there, hidden away, and now I'll tell you another secret the Order of the Eclipse would viciously censor if they knew about it:

We lied to Astrachios at the end. (You're allowed to lie to fanatical fascists.) We didn't hand over all Yaraesa's secrets.

The truth is we found three data crystals in that geode, and we only crushed one of them to powder. The other two I took with me when we left the inner sanctum, almost all the way down the passageway. When Astrachios started shouting at us, I hid them away. Where? Why, I just tucked them in with crystals that grew in such profusion from the walls and ceiling. They were hidden in plain sight. Astrachios walked right past them before he set the inner sanctum on fire, and on his way back out, he never noticed.

We never went back for the data, though. Melezheun and I *talked* about returning, but the Hellknights made good on their plan to bury the entrance to the temple-dungeon, and they kept a watch on the moon for years too, since they were suspicious sorts. And after a while, as I said, I came to believe knowing the truth would be too destabilizing, and we tabled the issue. Then... life got away from us.

We had to fight back the Hellknights, who at one point controlled nearly 25 percent of the station, which is horrifying even to recall. They had checkpoints, secret police, and roaming "peacekeepers" who doled out beatings for even the smallest infraction. They were starting to fall apart even then, though, with the individual orders asserting their independence and squabbling over duties and privileges. I think their little business of hegemony would have collapsed eventually on its own, but then outside circumstances intervened and forced all the issues at once.

The atmospheric support systems on Absalom Station almost failed, you see, either by accident or sabotage, and oddly, that was the key to getting all our fiefdoms to band together for mutual survival. That gave us the combined political will to finally break the Hellknight hold on their territory.

With all that going on… finding out what happened before the Gap seemed less important than making a good life *after* the Gap. Sure, we'd lost our memories, but on day one, we all started making new ones, and after a time, that felt like enough. It's amazing what wounds time can heal… or at least scar over.

There are still secrets hidden beneath the surface of Elindrae. I don't know what those other crystals have to say or whether they'll even make sense on their own. Do they contain actual revelations at all, or are they just more breadcrumbs on the trail to the truth, leading to a *worse* temple-dungeon somewhere farther away?

I don't think I'll be the one to find out. I'm going to hide this memoir away in the wall of my quarters in the Lorespire Complex (the hub of our thriving Society, by the way, headquarters of several communities that banded together to fight the Hellknight coup, and that are now devoted to exploring the mysteries of our system and the world beyond). Someday, after I'm long gone, someone will find my story… and then, I wonder what they'll do.

So, dear reader. What *will* you do?

31

IN THEIR FOOTSTEPS

(Chk Chk and Dae)

"Those crystals *can't* still be down there," Dae said after Chk Chk filled them in on the end of Tyrcell's memoir. "Can they?"

"*We will see,*" Chk Chk said. They followed a set of footprints toward the coordinates given in the manuscript. Just one set, though; the ones left by Tyrcell and Carn and Mel and the Hellknights must have been obscured when the latter bombed the site to cover the entrance.

Once they reached the appointed spot, they found automated digging machinery arrayed around a rock-filled crater. There was a rough hole dug into the ancient rubble, and at the bottom, a gleaming round hatch. "Our mysterious stalker cleared a path through the rubble the Hellknights piled up. That's... thoughtful."

Dae slid nimbly down the slope to the bottom and looked at the hatch. "It's just like the story says!" They gazed back up the slope to Chk Chk. "Can you read Castrovelian?"

"*Well enough.*" The shirren half slid and half clambered down the steep slope, then crouched to examine the glyphs. They were different words this time, but the point of the exercise was the same. "*Weightless-heavy-screams-tremble-silently,*" Chk Chk said softly, and then the hatch opened.

They dropped into the shaft, prepared for the gravity-orientation change, and landed gracefully enough. The hatch sealed and the lights came on, just as they once had for Tyrcell and the others. "How is this place still intact?" Dae said.

"Yaraesa built to last, it seems."

"You'd think some grave robber or dungeon delver would have found it over the past few centuries."

"Perhaps Yaraesa hid it from view? Or it could just be luck. Elindrae is not a promising site for archaeological expeditions, and the galaxy, after all, is vast."

They proceeded down the corridor to the first door, and Dae wrinkled their nose. "Unless there's a choreography question, I'm in trouble."

"*Once I read about these puzzles, I took the liberty of loading several relevant texts into my heads-up display,*" Chk Chk said. "*Allow me.*" He completed the circuit diagram on the first try and didn't even get zapped.

The fountain room was next, and Dae solved the tank puzzle before the room became too claustrophobically small. "*How did you know how to do all that?*" Chk Chk asked.

Dae rolled their eyes. "Chickie. It's just about flow. I am the *master* of flow!"

From there, they confronted the three doors, just as promised. When the wrong door opened and revealed the churning black lightning and poisonous clouds, they both flinched away, even though they'd been expecting it. Once they confirmed their desire to switch doors, and the next passageway opened, Dae said, "It feels like cheating, knowing the answer in advance, doesn't it?"

"*We learned how to solve these puzzles by studying an ancient text,*" Chk Chk pointed out. "*I think Yaraesa would approve of that, don't you?*"

"Let's hope so. Are you ready to get separated? I think I'll be OK if I end up in the maze puzzle room, but if it's the math room, ugh."

"*I have loaded the relevant texts into your system too, Dae,*" Chk Chk said. "*Fear not.*" The shirren stepped into the doorway and vanished.

Dae followed suit... and ended up in the room with the table and the spotlight. "Yesss," they said. "I love games." They went to the board, delighted by their tiny avatar. "Little Dae!" they shouted. "Oh my gods, you're so cute!"

"Big Dae!" the squeaking avatar said. "You're the best!"

"Who's our big bad enemy here?" Dae looked down at the board and grunted. There was a mysterious figure in a green cloak there, and the pahtra hissed. "Who are you, and what do you want? Ugh, you'd better not be with the Hellknights; I'll claw your stupid brains out if you are."

The guardian avatar merely crossed its arms and waited impassively.

Dae solved the puzzle in eighty-seven moves, faster than Tyrcell had. "All just *flow*," they said, as they offered a hand for their avatar to give a tiny high five. "Can I take you home with me forever in my pocket?" Dae asked.

"I have to go and live my tiny life!" tiny Dae squeaked, somersaulting off the table and doing cartwheels across the floor before disappearing into the opening at the base of the wall.

Dae looked at the miniature stalker, who gave them a salute. "Was that an *ironic* salute?" Dae demanded. The figure shrugged. The pahtra huffed and walked toward the door that opened in the wall... into the crystalline cavern, where Chk Chk already waited, sitting cross-legged, apparently meditating. The walls were undamaged, which meant the cavern had healed itself after the Hellknight incursion and fire.

"What room did you get?" Dae dropped down to sit beside their best friend.

"*The math problem. My computer solved it. That did feel a bit like cheating. All those equations ultimately reduced down to a simple two-digit integer, where the first digit was the same as the second digit multiplied by two—*"

"No math," Dae said sternly.

Chk Chk opened his eyes. "*There is someone waiting for us in the inner sanctum. See their footprints?*"

Dae nodded. "I did. How do you want to handle it?"

"*Perhaps—*"

"Oh, just come on in," a voice boomed from the passage; it sounded amused. "You're supposed to be Starfinder agents. Walking headlong into the unknown is part of the job. Hurry up. I want to show you something."

Dae and Chk Chk exchanged glances. The shirren shrugged. "*It is what we came for.*"

The solarian whipped their ribbon of burning light from the mote. "Walk into the unknown, sure," they said. "But don't walk into the unknown *unarmed*."

"*Is that one of the Starfinder Society's mottos?*" Chk Chk said. "*If not, it should be.*"

32

EXPLORE, REPORT, COOPERATE

(Tyrcell)

Hello, again. I really thought I was done writing. It's been a long time since I felt the need to add anything to my history of the Gap and its immediate aftermath, and you must admit, that was a really good ending I did before. It had a direct address to the reader, a call to action, and the promise of revelations to come. I was so proud of that ending.

But it wasn't really an ending. A good bit of time has passed since I wrote that, and a lot has changed on Absalom Station and in the solar system as a whole. I settled long ago into a hands-off, elder-statesman role in my Society, but I could tell that hanging around was just causing trouble—people kept looking to me to see if I approved of their decisions, and I didn't want the pressure or the responsibility anymore. I was making them just a little bit stagnant, and I always wanted my Society to be *vibrant*.

So I took off and traveled for a while, exploring new (to me) worlds, at first with Carn and Melezheun, and later, on my own. (Carn died old, and happy, and surrounded by a vast family; Melezheun died before her time, but she gave up her life to save others, in an act of valor so great it humbles me even to think of it. I did my best to stop her, of course, but I was just too slow. She was always faster than me.)

Even in the course of my solitary wanderings, I stopped back by Absalom Station occasionally, to see how the Society was doing. In truth, it surpassed all my greatest expectations, becoming something new that managed to hearken back to something old. I kept a few lines of communication open too and made sure I received news, even though the agents sending me the news didn't know who was receiving it after a while. It's a strange thing to see yourself fade first into legend and then into obscurity over the course of your lifetime.

I was mostly curious about whether anyone would find my memoir, but for the longest time, nobody did. And then I got word that someone *had*, and that a couple of junior agents were being assigned to—

Ah, hold on, my visitors are here. A pahtra solarian dancer, and a shirren mystic artist, good friends to one another; the best of friends, really.

I remember having friends like that.

I've been following the two of them for a while, making sure they put the pieces together properly, but once I knew they had the right destination in mind, I took steps to reach the temple first and clear a path. We should try to make things easier for the generations that come after us, shouldn't we?

Now it's time to welcome them and pass the torch.

33

THE TRUTH
(Chk Chk and Dae)

Chk Chk and Dae reached the end of the curving passageway and found a figure in a green hooded cloak standing in the ashes of the inner sanctum, with a small folding table beside them supporting a blocky, old-fashioned looking apparatus... and two small white obsolete data crystals.

They pushed back their hood, revealing the rather unremarkable face of an agender android. "Hello, Chk Chk. Dae. It's great to meet you both, officially."

"Are you *them*?" Dae said. "Tyrcell?"

The android nodded. "I go by another name these days—anything gets old eventually, even your name—but yes."

Chk Chk's mandibles clattered. "*You are not just the author of this memoir. You are the founder of the Starfinder Society. You were the first First Seeker!*"

"You picked up on that, huh?" The android grinned roguishly. "To be fair, it took a few decades before the Society became the Starfinder Society, but yes, that's where we ended up. The annals from way back then are fragmented and vague, so it's hard to find my name unless you know where to look, and, like I said, that name isn't attached to me anymore anyhow. So..." They rubbed their hands together. "Shall we see what's on these crystals? I managed to source one of those antique lashunta projectors so we can actually see what the Lady of Wisdom has to say. But I leave that up to you. We can just hide the crystals away again if you prefer."

"Why did you wait for *us*?" Dae cried. "You could have come here at any time and looked at those crystals!"

The android shook their head. "I haven't even been in this system for decades. I only came back when I got word my manuscript had been uncovered. But even if I'd lived right next door... no. This isn't my world anymore, kids. I am old, *very* old, and the very old should make way for the young. The present is yours, and you should be the ones to shape your future. The secrets held here, whatever they are, will mean something very different to people like you, who grew up thinking of the Gap as a curious quirk of history, not a grievous psychic wound. I'm... too close to all that trauma still. I shouldn't be the one to decide what to do with this information. This opportunity."

"*That makes sense,*" Chk Chk said. "*And it's... very thoughtful and honorable of you.*"

"I considered asking you to call up Zo!," Tyrcell admitted. "Just to see a familiar face and to get a little insight from someone like me, who *understands* what it was like back then, in the early days. But I know that old ghoul a little bit, and he'd want to broadcast whatever we found system-wide, and like I said... I don't think that should be something the old-timers get to decide. So it's up to you." Tyrcell gestured at the projector. "You just slot the crystal into the top there, and it should project the data for us." Tyrcell stepped back, leaned against the wall, and folded their arms across their chest. "I have to admit. I'm pretty curious. But if you don't want to—"

"Of *course* we're going to look!" Dae cried, snatching up the first crystal and turning it over in their hands. Then they looked at Chk Chk. "Right?"

"*A chance to find the answer to the most profound mystery in the galaxy?*" the shirren said. "*Yes. I think we should look.*"

Dae crouched, looked at the projector, and then carefully slotted the crystal into place. It nestled neatly in the aperture, just like it was meant to.

"Just flip the switch there on the side. The projector should be charged," Tyrcell said. "I tested it before I left Absalom Station. I wasn't about to come all this way and be stymied by equipment failure—I've actually got a spare projector on my ship, just in case."

The pahtra put their hand on the switch, looked at Chk Chk, looked at Tyrcell, took a breath, and turned on the projector.

A bright light shone from a lens, illuminating a large square on one fire-blackened wall.

Words of white fire shimmered into existence, and Tyrcell, Chk

Chk, and Dae all released long, awed exhalations of surprise.

The message began:

"So you'd like to visit lost Golarion..."

ACKNOWLEDGMENTS

First, let me thank author, editor, and game developer James Sutter for doing so much pioneering work on the Starfinder setting and for bringing me into the Paizo family many years ago when he first hired me to write a bunch of Pathfinder Tales novels. Thanks also to the current team, including Thurston Hillman, Jenny Jarzabski, Mark Moreland, Mike Kimmel, and all the game designers and artists who brought this world and these characters to life. My gratitude to my agent, Ginger Clark, who's the best advocate an author could hope for.

My appreciation goes to Emily Lane, MD, for answering all my medical questions (like "If I stuck my hand into a brain wound, would there be enough blood for me to finger-paint with? What if it was a really big brain?").

As always, I couldn't do any of this without my closest loved ones, especially Heather and River and Sarah and Katrina and Emily (again) and Amanda and Aislinn, who all support me in so many ways.

I'd also like to give credit for the inspirations for some of the puzzles in the temple-dungeon. There was, of course, the famous Monty Hall three-door probability problem, which you can still find sparking infernos of arguments all over the Internet. I also referenced linguist Noam Chomsky's "colorless green ideas sleep furiously" from his 1957 book *Syntactic Structures*; it's his example of a sentence that doesn't make any sense, despite being grammatically correct. The escape-the-grid puzzle Tyrcell plays in their last room (that Astrachios totally fails, and Dae nails) is a simplified variant of Robert Abbott's "Theseus and the Minotaur" logic maze from his 1990 book *Mad Mazes*.

ABOUT STARFINDER

Era of the Eclipse takes place in the universe of the popular Starfinder Roleplaying Game, a science-fantasy tabletop roleplaying game that puts players in the roles of intrepid intergalactic explorers, weird aliens, and more. Launched in 2017 as an offshoot of the tabletop fantasy RPG staple, Pathfinder, Starfinder has sold more than 2.5 million copies of rulebooks, adventures, setting guides, and gaming accessories. In August 2025, Starfinder Second Edition will debut, bringing the game into full compatibility with the bestselling Pathfinder Second Edition rules set. Starfinder has been adapted into board games, comics, and the Starfinder on Alexa interactive skill, starring Nathan Fillion and Laura Bailey. *Era of the Eclipse* is the first novel set in the Starfinder setting.

For more information about Starfinder or to subscribe to get future releases sent to you automatically, visit **http://paizo.com/starfinder**.